MW01127145

The
LAST GAMBLE of
DOC HOLLIDAY

The
LAST GAMBLE of
DOC HOLLIDAY

L. T. BROOKS

www.ivyhousebooks.com

PUBLISHED BY IVY HOUSE PUBLISHING GROUP
5122 Bur Oak Circle, Raleigh, NC 27612
United States of America
919-782-0281
www.ivyhousebooks.com

ISBN: 1-57197-400-8
Library of Congress Control Number: 2003095470

Printed in the United States of America

For Doc

➤ Acknowledgments ➤

To my husband, Steve, for his unending support. For Conn and Jeanne Withers, who have been my family and support for all of my life. For my friend Linda Bacchus, who gave up many sleepless hours while we brainstormed over ideas about the book. To my sister of the heart, Mary Billings-McVicar of Leadville, Colorado, for keeping the coffee pot hot while we swapped ideas. To David Sheen, for his interest in Doc and his ideas that kept the campfire alive. To my wonderful friend Suzanne Clauser, who kept me on the straight and narrow with her friendship and support. To the faculty of the Antioch Writers' Workshop— Sandra Love, Jimmy Cheshire, Ralph Keyes—for their guidance. To my wonderful friend Paula White, whose friendship has meant so much. To Michel Marriott of the *New York Times*. To writers Jeff Gundy, Cynthia Crane, and Mary Grimm, who helped me with my quest. I want to thank Christopher Stanwood of the College of Physicians of Philadelphia Historic Reference Library and F. Michael Angelo of the Thomas Jefferson Archives, formerly of the Independence Seaport Museum Library. Georgia Historical Society. Mrs. Frank Martin, and Lionel and Helen Turner and Karen McAulay.

⊰ *Chapter* ⊱
ONE

On August 14, 1851, to Mr. and Mrs. Henry Burroughs Holliday of Griffin, Georgia was born a son, John Henry. The times were hard and countless babies were lowered into the ground. The Hollidays knew that grief well when their own rosy-faced Martha Eleanora was put into the cold earth before she saw seven months.

"I know that it's only been a little more than a year since we lost Martha, but we have the boy now," Henry told his wife, "and he's going to be strong."

Alice knew that vocalizing her wishes would displease her husband, so in silence she bestowed them on John's feathery head: happiness, freedom to do as he wished, and a loving woman of his choice. These things were secondary to Henry, because he wished for his only son to be a soldier, as he had been, and his father before him.

The Hollidays had emigrated from Ireland in the late 1700s to Charleston, South Carolina. Two of the brothers went their separate ways, however, Robert Holliday, Henry's father, had taught him that a boy grew to manhood following in his father's footsteps. He also learned that to be of service to his country was as inherently Southern as religion and politics.

From an early age, Henry was the protector of his siblings. As he grew older, the habit of taking charge and making decisions was firmly entrenched. This personal resolve carried Henry Burroughs through several wars. In 1846, he enlisted for service in the Mexican War. Following the campaign, Henry, quite handsome in his uniform, was one of several suitors to come calling at the home of William Land and Jane Cloud McKey.

Born on April 21, 1829 in South Carolina, Alice Jane McKey was a tender respite for the war-weary Henry. And in the midst of the boisterous McKey brood, Henry felt a welcoming kinship. To Alice, everything about Henry was bigger than life. He had a commanding presence about him so that when he entered a room, everyone and everything seemed to pause as if in awe and wait for his pronouncement.

Henry was not as tall as some of her beaus, but by his very carriage he appeared much taller. Without standing on tiptoe, the top of her brown head brushed the bridge of his nose. His eyes were formidable until he smiled at her, then what a smile it was. And yet, just behind the smile, there remained a chill.

Alice's father admonished her. "Give the rest of these young men the mitten, but not Henry. That man knows his mind. And if you don't set your cap for him soon, he'll absquatulate to a warmer hearth. You'll end up a spinster for sure. You're already most twenty-one."

The reticence that Alice felt had nothing to do with Henry's resolute character, but rather gruffness in his manner of speaking like a barking dog. Henry, she was reminded many times by her father, had seen two military campaigns, so he had to sound authoritative.

"And he's ten years older," Alice whispered to her mother one evening when the candles had been lit.

"He knows his mind, child."

"But I don't think he knows my heart," she had replied.

However, on January 8, 1849, Alice Jane McKey became Mrs. Henry Holliday. If Alice had misgivings after the marriage, she kept them to herself.

The Holliday household was a busy one, but on the third Tuesday of the month the ladies' sewing circle would gather. In spite of the Georgia heat, which often reduced the stiffest crinoline and starched petticoat into wilted collard greens, teas were de rigueur in the parlor. The number of guests varied according to childbirth, illness, and sometimes death. Gathered at the slippered feet of the ladies would be colorful reticules bulging with gay bits of cloth, stitchery of all kinds, and correspondence which was often read to the whole group. Each lady would take a turn. Child rearing was an important subject spoken of and agonized over. Home remedies, health concerns, morals, and manners were also important topics. It was not a formal group, yet formalities were strictly observed. Chapped and blistered fingers artfully concealed by lace gloves were not idle. Tired backs never touched the upholstery on back of the settee or Alice's new circular sofa. Alice's back often ached and she longed to nestle her weary frame into the comforting rungs of her Boston rocker, but she did not. A lady must not nestle in a chair, however inviting.

Alice confided when it was her turn to speak, "There is something that gnaws at Henry. I've spoken of Henry's nightmares before. They are of such an intensity that he thrashes and calls out names and most acts as if he is dodging enemy fire."

"Do such things occur when he is awake?"

Alice plucked at the fine bit of linen that she was sewing. "Awake his eyes are open, but it is as if the nightmares continue beyond his eyes where I cannot see or venture."

"Henry's nightmares, do they trouble you?"

"Yes, for then he believes that I am the enemy."

One of the older ladies wagged her head. "When you are with child, then his nightmares will lessen."

"Perhaps."

A year later, Alice remembered those words. Henry's fears had not been allayed by the birth and swift death of his daughter. Instead he had turned into himself and away from the solace of family. Jane Cloud had ready advice for her daughter, but she chose her words carefully and took Alice's hand in hers before she spoke. Alice held her breath.

"I have lost babes. It is a mother's greatest sorrow. We cannot understand what God has in mind. Henry suffers the way that a soldier suffers. For him there are few choices. You can help him. Become in the family way quickly and give him a son. Henry will forget when he has his own son."

Henry could be so charming and full of life. He had booming laughter and a quick wit. When he accompanied her to church, Alice would feel her heart swell in pride at the sight of his broad shoulders looking even broader in his flowing, black frock coat. Alice made certain that Henry's high-topped boots were as polished as the hooves of Henry's favorite horse, that his gaiters were brushed and cleaned, and that his shirts were freshly boiled.

Henry was pleased with Alice's piety and her well-spoken words. He tried to be indulgent, although Victorian fashion and society flustered him. He noticed that while Alice wore solemn clothing, she preferred bright colors. For her twenty-first birthday, he gave her a cherry-colored burnoose and a gold net for her hair for when she put it up in a chignon. Because of her youth, he tried not to order her in the way that he ordered his men.

Henry's excitement about his newborn son, however, was fraught with uneasiness. Henry was certain that John would become a farmer after fulfilling his military duty. Then there must be marriage to a socially acceptable woman. John had to carry on the Holliday name. It was obvious, too, after the difficulty that Alice had in delivering young John that there would be no more Holliday children.

Henry prayed that what he yearned for as a parent would come to pass and in the proper order. It was obvious to Henry that the baby favored Alice with his light hair and sensitive features, his full mouth, broad forehead, and restless hands. It was the baby's hands that worried Henry. They were Alice's hands down to every nuance, including the little curling of John's baby fingers. Sensing his discomfiture with the child, relatives tried to minimize his distress.

"Oh come on, Henry, lots of babies have that light hair. And his eyes will undoubtedly darken. He'll be as hard-nosed as you are in a couple of years."

Henry smiled, but he was unable to take this to heart. Try as he might, the baby didn't take to him either. When Alice held him, he cooed and gurgled and snatched at her cap and laughed a laugh as wide as his pink gums would allow. As soon as Henry's hands closed around the wriggling frame, the baby would fall silent and no amount of rattles or heart-felt fatherly bounces elicited anything except a belch.

"If he stays with you too much," Henry grumbled, "he'll turn into a Nancy boy. Pass him over here."

"Gently, Henry." It was as close to chiding, as Alice would allow. "He can tell the difference. They can't see very well, so they know you by your touch."

"That's an all-fired notion, that my son knows me by my touch."

"Yes, he does," Alice replied, and she bent her head over her sewing once more.

Henry held the baby away from his body. The two regarded each other. "Here," Henry thrust the infant back to his wife. "He's wet or something."

As John grew, there came the matter of family history taught with pride by both his parents. Lessons were taught at Henry's great roll-top desk near the hallway. With his father at the helm, the dark, stolid desk took on human characteristics. The vast expanse of polished wood with the squiggle in the center appeared to be a large ear that swallowed John's childish words before they reached his father.

"Speak up, John Henry. I can't hear you when you squeak. Are those squeaks supposed to be words? Come on boy, speak up."

The many drawers gobbled papers drawn with a child's toil. It was not hard to imagine that the drawers looked at him. There were no windows nearby and the books that his father gave him had few pictures. John was quite glad when his mother taught him instead.

One day, Alice produced a wrinkled map of South Carolina to show how the Hollidays arrived in Georgia. The date meant nothing to John except that his father must be very old indeed.

"Was he in the Revollootinary?"

Alice chuckled. "Even the Revolutionary War was before your father's time. I don't expect you to understand any of this right now, but when you are older, your history will become an important part of your life. It's always so necessary to know from whence you sprung."

"Was father a soldier?"

"Oh yes, in the Cherokee Indian War and then in the Mexican War. He's very brave."

John's earliest memories of Griffin were a tangle of green. In the back of that green, there was the throb of insects. To his boyish ears, the sounds were like a heartbeat. Years later he would recall Griffin as a pastel sky, with the humid water running over the sluggish soil, and the sigh that it made before it was swallowed up by the sweeping green.

Mother was the healer and maker of music. To her he trotted all childhood complaints whether they were real or imagined. If the physical need was dire, she immediately consulted the Great Black Book, the one that came from the old country. Remedies abounded for every ill and complaint that the human body could make. To aid in her nursing, Alice grew herbs in her garden. Every morning before the sun had burned the chill away, Alice would don Henry's heavy black coat and slip outside. Fresh herbs were the most potent and had to be culled immediately. Each time her fingers dipped into the earth, small prayers like blessings fell from her lips.

As to the making of music, Alice's voice was merry and sweet as she played hymns on the small piano. Sometimes before the lamps were snuffed at night, the lament of "My Old Kentucky Home," or John's favorite, "Pop Goes the Weasel," would drift through the windows and be swallowed by the slumbering trees. Even Henry's fine baritone voice would join with gusto.

Katydids sounded on late summer afternoons. The insect noise was the first thing John heard in the morning and the last sound he heard at night. His mother's voice was a lot like the soothing katydids. John did try to find admirable qualities in his father. Father was the head of the household and John quickly learned that what Father said was law. His mother talked often about those qualities, as did all of John's relatives, but the clumping boots, the angry words, and the looks he intercepted between Mother and Father chilled him.

Though he was still quite young, John had learned how particular his father was of family possessions, especially the animals. One day, John trundled out to the barn where the horses were kept. He'd been trying little tricks all week to catch his father's approval such as helping out with the making of soap and butter, cleaning up after meals, and making sure that the eggs were well-preserved in lime water. The latter chore entailed going down the cellar stairs. For a longer legged person like his father, the task was not hard at all. But John's short legs struggled with the slanted steps and the lantern. Several times, he tumbled down the stairs, but refused to cry when questioned later by his mother.

His one wish now was that his father would hang the harness on a lower hook. Taking a deep breath, he hoisted himself up on the large barrel nearest the grooming tools and reached out to grasp the currycomb. With a crash, he fell into the barrel. Shorter than the barrel was tall, he determinedly tipped it over, crawled out, and righted the barrel once more. John lost track of how many times he fell into the barrel. His fingers were cut and his forehead was bruised. Though he feared his father's wrath, he yearned to do this one thing even more.

At last, his hand grasped the currycomb and he gave a convulsive pull. To his horror, the heavy leather harness came away from the wall. Scrambling from the floor, he looked at the mess at his feet.

Henry boomed behind him, "Boy, what in hell's name are you doing? Here, get away from that. Why can't I turn my back just one time? Give me that before you cut yourself again."

The unpleasant scene of Father against Mother was replayed that night after dinner. Henry's voice rose to its usual pitch. The words were the same. "You coddle him too much. He'll grow up a damn Nancy boy. He's already a damn Nancy. It's my household."

Alice's rejoinder was muffled. From his room, John clenched his fists and struggled to hear. He wanted to fight his father himself, if only to be able to yell back into that red face that was set in dislike.

Henry's voice came again. "He's not growing. He's weedy. He's too quiet. What's wrong with him? What are you feeding him?"

Alice was philosophical about Henry's rage. "That's just your father."

John was six years old when Henry slapped him for the first time. The cries that he had heard from his parent's room the night before had convinced him that his father was having one of those dreams again. As always after such a night, breakfast was tense. Henry chewed with short, hard chews and his eyes were bloodshot. Several times, he wiped his brow, muttered, and shook his head, as if that would somehow clear his mind. No one dared to speak. The dishes filled with eggs and beaten biscuits were passed without expression.

It had begun innocently enough with a trip to the garden to pick flowers for his mother. As soon as he'd come back into the kitchen, John realized that he had tracked his muddy feet through the parlor, which was the pride of his mother. There was a small spot on the treasured rug from his errant tracks. Before he could sit down, his father stood and delivered a hard slap. The slap stunned him so that, at first, he had no reaction. Shocked that his father had raised his hand, the little boy looked up, expecting a verbal explosion to match the blow.

No explanation came. Instead, Henry's face was twisted in the peculiar pattern between his eyebrows that often occurred after a bad dream. With an oath, Henry, now quite pale, flung his napkin to the table and stomped from the room. The door banged shut. John's head still thundered from the slap. It seemed that the air around him had been sucked from the room. His mouth quivered. Looking over at his mother, he saw that her hand was fluttering at her throat.

"Mother," his voice quavered. "I'm . . . I'm sorry. Father hates me. I know he hates me. He tells me so all the time."

After a moment, Alice cleared her throat. "No, your father doesn't hate you. We'll speak of this later. You get ready for school. Don't forget to wipe your feet when you come home."

John expected his mother to talk to him about the incident, but she never did. His father never mentioned the slap either. It was as if it had never happened. Troubled about his father's temper, John asked his mother. She pursed her lips before answering him and gently lay one of her hands on top of his head. "Your father is weighed down by many cares. You are young, so you don't understand such things. It is the reason for his troubled sleep. It is only because your father cares for you that he shouts."

Alice was silent, however, when John brought up the subject of hitting. His mother's patience was as enduring as the power of his father's anger. When Alice braved the wrath of her husband to take up her son's cause, John feared for her. It tormented him to think that his father hit his mother, but he believed that it happened. And after his father's first slap at breakfast, others came more frequently. Some came with explanations: "You forgot to feed the horses. We depend on those horses!" "You tracked into the house! What's wrong with you?"

John could almost live with those since there seemed to be a reason for his bruises and humiliation. But punishment that came with no explanation was the worst.

Relatives saw the relationship differently, although they were never present when Henry struck John. Uncle Robert told his nephew, "Your father is a good and decent man. He puts food on the table. He takes in family when they are in need. Who are you except an ungrateful whelp who doesn't recognize such a bountiful and beneficent father?"

To get away from the rage of his father, John escaped to his special place in the woods near his home. It was a quarter of a mile away within a thick bracket of trees. The sweeping fronds, witch's hair as he called it, were so long that they made the trees seem to sway in the breeze. Underneath the trees, John made a seat for himself out of leaves and the remainder of a log. The trees did not stand in judgment of him. It was all that he asked.

In the bosom of his family, there was judgment. Alice's quiet rejoinder was "John," spoken sometimes firmly but always in love. John hated the sound of his name when his father barked it, "John Henry," in three distinct syllables. When he was younger, the harsh calling of his name made him sick to his stomach. Older now, the sound filled him with self-loathing.

Like the castor oil that his mother made him take each night, it was hard to gulp the "yes sirs" and, "no sirs." It was difficult to listen to the litany of orders from his father and the complaints that came after he followed the orders. His father's disappointment was acute. Sometimes abruptly, Henry would quit the room, leaving John confused and sore at heart.

Later he would steal away to his special hideout. Time was suspended there and, except for the sound of nearby running water and a canopy of hissing insects, there was silence. John shared the secret of his hiding place with his mother, but dared not say anything to Henry, there being no sense of whimsy in his father's soul.

When his father spoke about the skirmishes in which he'd taken part, John could see that his father carried that pride like a badge. The uniform that Henry had worn in his Mexican Campaign was trotted out for John's dutiful homage.

"That's what it's all about, son. The marching, being part of something larger than yourself. There's nothing more noble than laying down your life for your country."

John noticed that his mother was sewing furiously in the corner. "Did you get wounded?"

"Some nicks and cuts," Henry rolled his sleeve back for John to see. "My badges of honor." Seeing his son's eyes shine, Henry expounded, "You hear the march of feet first. There's nothing like that sound. It comes up on the wind and you think at first it might be your imagination, but then it catches the rhythm of your heartbeat, so there's that pulse and the wind, and the feet tramping. You draw your bayonet. The blades flash in the sun, like silver fire. The canons roar with the smell of smoke and the sound of a thunderclap."

"And then what?"

"After you beat them and win, you go home. It's ended until the next time."

"I want to do that." John looked over in the corner at his mother, but Alice had left the room.

"Women are a squeamish lot," Henry told him. "War isn't for women. And I'm not sure your mother is all that well."

Coldness, like a finger, touched John in the middle of his chest. "I know. She just stops, stares into space, and makes this little sound in her throat and touches her lips."

"Well, you tell me if it gets bad, okay? I'm counting on you to be the man of the house. You know, in case something happens."

"Well, what if . . . I mean . . . do you think it will?"

"The times are pretty uncertain, boy."

He knew about the times well enough. Once or twice a week, his father and other men in town would get together. Alice would lay out cold sandwiches on her best linen and china. There were decanters of liquid that glowed in the light and looked like honey and dark molasses. The men would click their glasses and speak of the times. "The Democratic Convention has been a failure. There will have to be a new one convened, this time in Baltimore instead of Charleston. The Republicans have already picked their candidate. We in the South must be very clear."

The booming oratory that John heard shouted on the streets in town often sounded from the parlor at home when Henry's brother, Robert, came to visit.

"And by God, I tell you, Henry, there will be no Republican in Washington. If that happens, we'll have war, as assuredly as we're talking here now. We shouldn't even be part of the Union anymore. Georgia has her own business to tend to and so does the rest of the South. It's not Northern business. Do they really think we can be part of the Union? They don't till the land. We do. And they want to pass judgment on us? Want to tell us what to do with our property, want to impose their laws on us? We have to secede."

John wasn't sure what secession meant. In asking his father, he was told, "It means that when the time is ripe, Georgia won't be a member of the Northern machine. It will be a part of the South, it's own country. The Yankee Northerners sit on their lofty pedestals and hand down edicts to us. Are we like them? Hell, no. You're not too young to understand. You have to know what it means to be Southern."

John listened raptly.

"If we secede, there is nothing the powers in Washington can do. They must accept. We have a right to govern ourselves. If this Lincoln becomes president, it will be the ultimate disaster for us here in the South. We'll have to wait and see, boy, what happens."

Waiting, John learned, was the hardest. News was slow in filtering down and when it did come, it was unsatisfactory. Howell Cobb resigned as Secretary of the Treasury. John had heard a lot about Howell Cobb from his father. Cobb was a Georgian, one of her finest and most capable diplomats.

"What shall we do?" the townsfolk shouted.

"March," was the reply.

≁ *Chapter* ≁
TWO

Hurried though the day might be, the evening meal was for coming together and reflection. Henry made certain that he had periodicals or a current Griffin newspaper that offered articles on politics, religion, and sporting events. In his fine baritone voice, he denounced the difficulties with the North, but thoughtfully mentioned items of more general interest to his family, including the columns on manners and morals that Alice liked. He cleared his throat and the timber of his voice changed. "There will be a war, and it will be bigger than all of us," he told his family. "You will see things happen once Georgia secedes."

Georgia seceded on January 19, 1861, but not even the best politicians could foretell how the occurrence would affect the military and civilian populations. Henry continued to theorize on the state of the Confederacy, but Alice said little about her thoughts except to John. The flutter in her throat sounded more and more like a cough. On well-meant advice, Henry began to keep the house open, so that fresh air was abundant. Sometimes it was cold, but Alice attended to her sewing and wifely duties, cared for John, and made no complaints.

It was only when Henry saw a bright bead of red on her lace handkerchief that a physician was called. After a hurried consultation with Henry, the doctor went into the bedroom and shut the door. John watched his father pace the confines of the parlor. The swishing sound of his father's footsteps across the carpet kept time with the cherry mantle clock. Tick-tick, tick-tick, tick-tick. John wasn't sure what to make of it, but each moment spent with the door shut and with his father's pacing increased the cold pressure in his stomach.

John wished that he could say something to his father because, once in a while, Henry would look up as if really seeing him for the first time. Perspiration, blotted often from the older man's shaking hand, continued to stain his collar. Tick-tick, tick-tick, and the moment was lost.

The door creaked opened and John leaped to his feet.

"Well, suh?" Henry asked as he dabbed at his face once more.

"The wasting disease," the doctor replied. "I applied some leeches and induced Alice to empty the contents of her stomach. This will help clear the poisons from her body. She is resting now. I'll leave you with some calomel and jalap. Mind you that she rests and finishes the calomel. Beyond that, only Providence can tell." And he left the house.

The cold in John's stomach became hot and his mouth tasted of metal. "What does it mean?" he stammered.

"It means that your mother will die."

John couldn't remember how he spent the rest of the day. Henry, expressionless, listened to John's lessons without complaint. There was dinner and homework. Alice looked no different when John came in to kiss her goodnight. The lace cap that she was wearing had a faint lavender scent. She smelled of new soap. Her cheeks were rosy. Surely, the doctor was wrong.

"Goodnight, Mother."

Alice offered her cheek as she always did. "Remember to say your prayers."

It was just his imagination, John thought after the oil lamps had been extinguished, that the house had taken on the same cold feeling as what lay in the pit of his stomach. He said his prayers and leaned out the window of his bedroom to stare at the black strings of Spanish moss adorning the tree outside. He heard the crickets and the faint sound of what he thought must be marching feet.

John wanted to believe that his mother wasn't going to die. In the morning light, her cheeks were still rosy and her thimble flashed with unusual vigor. She made him breakfast, laughed at his jokes, and teased his father with girlish jocularity.

Henry smiled in spite of himself. "According to the newspapers, Mother, the Confederate machine should well nigh be in motion by April. Mark my words: That the South is able to do this at all is by the very grace of God and a tremendous achievement for us."

The Confederacy and Georgia were all that father and son could agree upon. Plagued with the uncertainty of his wife's health, Henry became more easily vexed. If he told John not to dawdle after school, the boy spent time playing mumblety-peg with his chums. If he told his son to tend to his studies, John left the house. Later Henry would learn from the neighbors that John was seen playing chuck-a-luck with older school chums or splashing around in the local swimming hole. Unable to reason with words for what Henry perceived as rebellion on the part of his son, he began beating him with whatever was handiest whether it was strap, whip, or fist.

John learned not to cry or to show weakness. For Henry, John reserved a blankness of expression that was colder than frozen diamond chips in an ice storm. For Alice, John's gaze was a warm wellspring from the heart. The difference rankled Henry.

There came a time when it was all Henry could do to keep from snapping John in half. Despite his diminutive height, John carried himself very erect, neither crying out when he was struck nor making piteous sounds that might have arrested Henry's fury. Alice wrung her hands at the demons that seemed to possess her husband and her son whenever they disagreed, which was often. Neither her words nor looks had any effect on the combatants. She trembled at Henry's words and quailed at the rage she could see in her son. John was quiet, but with feet braced, shoulders back, and eyes raging, he took what his father meted out and waited.

The winter had been a harsh one, but the Georgia spring of 1861 was poking its way from the fertile soil. Newly planted seedlings were sprouting and the trees were frothing with pink and white blossoms. The animals could feel it, too. The horses, playful in the warm spring sun, were allowed to caper before being harnessed. Alice was hopeful that this season would renew a spirit of forgiveness between father and son.

"Henry, it's April and one of the first beautiful spring days that we've had. Why not let John stay on a bit after school and play with his chums if he wants? He's worked so hard."

Henry hesitated as he looked at her. "Mother, I know you mean well. But the boy pays me no mind. He does what he chooses anyway. No, he comes home today, same as always. He's got chores to do. There is no time for play. Right after school, John Henry, I want you back here. I mean it."

John shot his father a look of dislike. "See you after school, Mom. Love you." And he was out the door.

Henry's fist hit the table. "Why must it always be a fight? Why can't he just—?"

"Bend?" Alice asked softly.

"I knew my father was right. I never questioned him. I expect nothing less from my son."

"That," Alice replied, "is something you'll never have."

Henry's head jerked in response and fury kindled in his eyes. Alice felt his anger without looking up and knew that John would be tardy in returning from school. On this soft spring day that was bright with blooming trees and promise, dread lay like a pall over the house.

Alice hoped that her cough would lessen with the advent of the warmth, but the slowly strangling hand in her chest had not lost its grip. Breathless after bending in the herb garden, she coughed, bringing up blood. Slow tears dropped from her eyes. What would happen when she could no longer be a referee between her husband and son?

Henry came home at noon, but Alice, busy in the kitchen with cooking and boiling mint tea to soothe her cough, didn't hear the door bang shut. So quiet were her husband's footsteps that she jumped when he placed his hand on her shoulder.

"You are home early," Alice said. Her husband's face was flushed and the large hands that suddenly clutched hers were trembling. "What is it? I thought I heard shouts and gunfire a while ago."

Henry took a sudden breath as if it was all that he could do to speak. "Ft. Johnson has fired on Ft. Sumter. Do you understand what that means? The war has begun. We are at war."

There were shouts off and on the remainder of the afternoon and heavy commotion on the road. When John didn't arrive from school, Henry nervously began to pace the house and look out the window. "Where is that damn boy? Where can he be? I promised I'd hide him for being late. Why must he do this?"

The air was beginning to cool when John shouted from the backyard. White-faced, Henry stamped through the house to greet his son. Taking a deep breath, Alice tremblingly hurried after her husband. Short of the door, Henry stopped. "Stay inside, Mother, I'll handle this."

Alice clutched her apron, her face white, "Henry, please."

"I know what I'm doing," he snapped. "You stay inside where it's warm. It's almost time for supper."

Stifling the sob in her throat, Alice stumbled back to the kitchen. Outside came Henry's roar, followed by John's higher pitched voice.

"You'll have to kill me," John shouted. "That's the only way you'll have satisfaction." Blood ran down from a split lip and the flesh around his right eye was purple.

"You're my son, damn you. You do as I say. You never question me," Henry retorted in rage.

"I'm not your property. You'll have to kill me."

The rise and fall of their shouts came for some time. Then, silence fell. Hands shaking, Alice scurried about the kitchen. The silence was the most terrifying of all. She had tried to put together a good dinner. Her chest ached from coughing and her fingers had twisted the crispness from her apron. Finally, two voices were heard at the door.

Henry stumped into the kitchen, trying to pretend nothing had happened. "The food's getting cold," he announced and sat down at his place at the head of the table. Silently, his family sat.

Alice coughed into her handkerchief and refused to meet his gaze when she passed him a plate of salted meat. Around the table, forks dropped from nervous fingers and silverware grated. Only John was defiant, wearing his purple eye and split lip like a badge of honor.

"Shame on you," Alice told him later as she put a compress on her son's eye, smoothed his forehead, and soothed him with her words.

"Shame on me?" John shouted. "Shame on me?" He started off the bed, but Alice pressed him back on it.

"Shush. Shame be on the both of you. You devil each other."

"Suppose you're right," he grinned the lopsided grin that he shared with only her.

"Your father is concerned as to what will happen."

"To us, Mother?"

"Well, to the South."

"Oh, yes, the South. Sure seems that he thinks of the South first, while we come in a distant second."

"That's not true. But the firing on Ft. Sumter is a specter of the things to come." Her voiced dropped lower, "At night, I fancy I can hear it. You know, right here in the dark."

"Hear what?" John asked faintly.

"You'll think me a silly old woman," she dabbed at her lips as her throat gave one of its convulsions. When it stopped, she patted the perspiration off her forehead. "I can hear way off in the distance, the march of feet. Not cannon fire, just the march of feet. Each night it seems one heartbeat closer."

Many periodicals editorialized the growing divisions in the new Confederacy. Kentucky was pointed to as a state that considered herself Southern in temperament and sympathy, but of a Northern political mind. Five days after Virginia's secession on April 17, 1861, West Virginia announced her split from Virginia and shockingly proclaimed herself a new Northern state. By late June, North Carolina, Tennessee, and Arkansas had severed their ties to the North.

The firing on Ft. Sumter had only been the beginning in that desperate spring. Orators shouted day and night. Young men drilled with fervor. There was in the air a vast unseen cloud that permeated daily living, bubbled out of the ground, constricted throats, and moistened the eye. There were no answers for John struggling to make sense of his father's rage, his mother's illness, and his own growing turmoil. There were no answers for the South.

Prayer halls were filled as never before. Inflamed by the war fervor, John waited for the timbers of the church to creak with God's commandments and to see if the angels would come from heaven like his father said they would.

South Carolina had seceded and neither South Carolina nor Lincoln would relinquish Ft. Sumter. Henry was certain that Jefferson Davis would stand up to Lincoln. In the face of this respected and genteel man, how could Lincoln not think him sane and sober and not want to give in? The South wanted to be seen as her own entity. Georgia had the right to stand up to Lincoln.

Henry said little of his plans, but he grew restive. Since the spring planting was complete, Alice knew that it was only a matter of time before her husband would go to war. She tried to steel her heart against it, all the while knowing that it would come as a shock. There had been good days since the time in early spring when she had begun to cough up blood. For some weeks, the cough had lessened and her breathing was easier. She wished that John and Henry could find a reason to be at ease, but they both seemed locked in a terrible struggle.

Not long after John's tenth birthday, Henry spoke what was in his heart. "I am going to war tomorrow," he said as he ladled red-eye gravy over the biscuits on his plate. "The planting's done. I can't stay any longer. I suspicion that the war is going to be short. President Davis has promised that we'll lick the Yankee devils and come home."

There was fierce pride in the look that he shared with all the members of his family. Alice stopped chewing and put her napkin to her lips. John, smarting from an earlier beating for failing to clean a harness properly, offered no comment.

"I'll help you get your things in order," Alice told her husband. "John, you can clear the table and do the dishes."

Sullen, John had stared at his father. After Henry had left the table, the boy did his mother's bidding and then slipped outside. It was too late in the evening to escape to his woodland retreat and dangerous now with strangers passing through town. He had expected for the last two months the inevitable news that his father would go to war. There had been a growing frenzy in Henry's eyes as he read editorials from the newspaper.

John was still bewildered by his father's rebuke about the harness. The leather oozed from earlier applications and the man from the tannery had told him that the new saddle soap was superior to the old and that it only required two coats.

"Your father will understand," He had said. His father hadn't.

John felt guilty on many accounts, the most important one being gladness that his father was going, taking the beatings and eternal prodding with him. There was also a part of him that felt guilty for having to stay behind and a smaller part that nagged in shame for feeling that way. He knew that it was possible that Henry Holliday might not come back. There was also the possibility that his mother would die before his father returned.

"John, wherever you are, it's not safe. Please come in," his mother called from the backyard. John could hear the sound of tears in her voice.

There was no real time to talk with his father. There were some things that John decided he should say and other things that he wanted to say very much, but his parents' bedroom door remained closed.

It was a short night with a lead-colored dawn. Breakfast was hurried as Henry wanted to get underway. John tried to talk to his father after breakfast, but Henry's eyes gazed far away.

"If we hurry," he told Alice, "we can get to town before the parade is over. There'll be a speech and you can see me off."

There was an impromptu parade, as many were at the time. A speaker's box had been hastily erected and decorated with red and blue crepe. There was jubilation, banners, and cannon fire. No sooner had the minister said a prayer for the men going into battle, than a thunderstorm doused the crowd. It failed to wash the haze and humidity from the air and hardly dampened the spirits of the spectators. For the group of family and friends who saw Henry Holliday off to war, it mattered not at all.

After the storm and commotion of the men leaving for war, the town was gripped in silence. The sodden blue and red crepe hung in tatters on the deserted podium. A small group of women, including Alice, thronged about the pastor, who appeared to be talking quite earnestly. At one point, Alice turned and motioned for John to join the group, but he waved and shook his head. Instead, he made his way to the podium and gently broke off a piece of the crepe. For a moment he stroked it, then pushed it into his pocket.

The ruined crepe was like the final words that passed between father and son. Seated on his horse, Henry looked down with an expression that John had never seen before and didn't know how to classify. "Look after your mother, boy." Then he rode away. John watched until the horse had rounded the bend and his father was lost from view.

Reluctantly, he kicked some of the small puddles of water made by the storm and ambled toward the general store.

"John, aren't you coming home?" Alice called.

"No, Mother, I'd just like to mosey around by myself. Is that okay?"

"Just be careful. Don't pick up any bungtown coppers."

John smiled. When he was small he had kept a glass bottle full of the coppers that he had collected from all over town. Some were bright. Others were bent, having been run over by buggies. His father had told him how important they were to save and he had taken that to heart. When the collection threatened to over-run several of his mother's glass canning jars, his father told him the truth: the coppers were worthless. John wasn't sure why he had remembered this particular incident or why his throat had constricted so suddenly at the same time.

Countless brothers, fathers, uncles, and sons were riding to war. He knew he wasn't the only one with an aching heart and that tight feeling in his throat. All across the South, there were families just like his saying the same things. "Make certain you eat. Keep your feet dry. Take good care of yourself."

He suddenly wished that he'd been able to say those things to his father.

His mother, too, seemed relieved that Henry had gone, although Alice McKey would have never voiced such a thing. In contrast was her son who let the words tumble from his mouth or, when riled, shouted and shook his fists in the face of heaven. Alice knew her son's depth of feeling. Henry had brutalized her boy and for that she would never forgive him. While she lived, she had to be the buffer between father and son. No one had told her that she was going to die, but Alice knew that it was inevitable just as Henry going to war had been inevitable. It was much easier for her to accept than either John or Henry. Henry had left. John had remained to be torn between duty and honor, hearth and home. She wished at his tender age that he would not have had to shoulder so large a burden, but there was no help for it. At all costs, she determined, John would never know how sick she really was.

Alice missed Henry's presence by her at night and sometimes, while she lay coughing, she would reach over and pat his absent pillow.

Over his protests, she had packed a wallet-sized housewife, cramming into it as many of her precious needles, buttons, and thread as she could spare and the slouch hat that she'd bought for him because it would help keep the rain off his face. After two previous military campaigns, Henry knew well the kinds of items that he would need in the field. Because there were some things that military issue did not provide, Henry had taken his own comb and his toothbrush with the bone handle and boar bristles as well as the writing box given to him by his wife.

Camp life was very lonely, he had told her, and staying in touch with family was considered necessary above all. Often in the quiet of the night could be heard the scratching of quills by the soldiers. The writing boxes contained ink bottles, pen, stamps, and personal stationery. Henry's own stationery was monogrammed, as was his cherry wood writing box with a place inside for a small candle and candleholder.

There were other things taken that could be easily packed such as woolen socks and gloves, a copper soap tin and, last but not least, Henry's favorite briar pipe. This one item, of all the things that she helped him pack, indeed signaled his going off to war. The curved stem was graceful while the bowl was intricately carved with Georgia's seal and the Holliday family crest. Henry was very proud of it as his own father had given it to him.

The nights were the hardest. Alice tried hard not to cough, but that was impossible. She tried to be brave, but her son knew better. Keeping anything from John was difficult. He watched over her like a hawk with one chick. Henry had lamented before he left for war that his son was not tough, but Alice knew that John had inherited the McKey toughness.

She could sense the desperation in her husband and the panic, too, at his realization that John could not be broken like a recalcitrant horse. In spite of her husband's many campaigns, in spite of his pride in being a professional soldier, the most fearsome adversary he had ever encountered was his son.

Alice knew that John was never meant to be a planter or a farmer. Not only was his constitution unsuited for the labor, but he had no inclination. As he had grown older, his hands had begun to give him away. Whether he was at the piano composing music for her or in his new pastime of whittling, his restless fingers betrayed him. John had whimsy, too, which Henry in his earthiness could not understand or abide.

Although Alice and John struggled to keep things the way they had been, life was radically different since Henry had ridden to war. The South was different. John wondered if his mother was as haunted as he was by the memory of the rainy morning his father had left. Though the scrap of crepe from the podium was almost unrecognizable, John kept it still. Never having been superstitious before, he feared that if he got rid of it his father would die.

The letter that arrived from Camp Pickens in Manassas, Virginia, around the first week in September, however, made him feel a little better. His father was in the quartermaster corps.

"Things are lively," Henry wrote. Noticeably absent was any mention of possible fighting that had gone on or would come about. It was a long letter written in Henry's flowing penmanship. "Don't forget to play my favorite songs at the piano. It's one of the things that I miss the most."

"He's always had such beautiful writing," Alice said as she wiped tears from her eyes.

In spite of the increasing uncertainty of the times, Alice and her son continued the tradition of gathering at the piano after supper. "Bonnie Blue Flag" was the first and last song played in the evening. Henry's favorite songs such as "Jimmy Crack Corn" and "Camp Town Races" were always played. Sometimes to tease John, Alice would slip "Pop Goes the Weasel" into the nightly repertoire.

"Oh, Mother, I'm not a child anymore. That's a baby song."

"No, it's not. I like 'Pop Goes the Weasel' and I'm not childish."

"I prefer 'Bonnie Blue Flag.'"

"Whether 'Bonnie Blue Flag' or 'Camp Town Races' makes no difference. And it matters not where you go in the future or what you do, but if you keep a melody alive inside, you'll always have the South."

John's lips curled in a half-smile. "Yeah, I understand."

Alice realized that her son had grown up fast. He was like a miniature adult at ten. John had a man's eyes: sharp, uncompromising, and very intelligent. Her John never missed a trick.

"Come over here and play for me."

"I'm kinda rusty."

"That's okay. Who do you think taught you to play in the first place?"

He sat down beside her and Alice put her arm around him.

"Oh, Mother."

"Come on."

And he played "Bonnie Blue Flag."

While Henry was away at war, John taught himself other skills. The secret hideaway in the woods became more than a refuge and more than a place to whittle. There, where no one could see or hear, John would hone his marksmanship. Henry had taught him the rudiments of using a gun when he was very young.

Carrying a gun and knowing how to use it were necessities. The papers spoke of it and John had seen with his own eyes how the craziness of war could turn human beings against one another. He was learning how rage and desperation affected individuals and how it made them carry off food, belongings, livestock, and cherished items. And how it made them kill. He wanted to know how to protect his family to the best of his ability.

John knew that he would never have the bear-like paws of his father or Henry's height, weight, and bulk. What John lacked in these qualities, he made up for with an extraordinary dexterity in both hands. He practiced every day and did exercises to strengthen his hands. Playing the piano, which he performed as a daily ritual, forced him to stretch his fingers.

"What can I do to strengthen my grip?" he asked his mother suddenly one evening.

Seeing that edge in her son's blue eyes, Alice patted his arm. "This is good exercise, but to really strengthen your grip, you need to work your hands against an object that doesn't give."

"Like?" John prompted.

"I'll roll up some small towels and you can squeeze those but not too hard at first. Unless there's some other reason for the request, John, fess up."

John ducked his head. "Caught, I guess," he mumbled. "I've only got my little shotgun. It just doesn't seem like enough."

"You've filched your father's old Patterson pistol out of its hiding place, haven't you?"

"More'n a couple a times. He told me never to touch it, but it looks like it could do the job."

"I don't opine that it's right for a boy of your age to know about that particular gun. It served your father well, but I know he'd be sour on you using it. If you promise not to take it out anymore, I'll help you with your grip."

It was the kindness in his mother, John thought, to not judge him harshly when she thought he erred and to help him attain his goal. The strength that she talked about was gradual. To hasten his progress, John whittled a ball out of wood and folded towels around it. Enthusiastically, he worked his hands until he couldn't bend his fingers. He tried suffering in silence, but Alice found him out.

"This is my two-fold remedy for gout," she told him, "so I don't see why it wouldn't work just as well for your swollen hands." John found the boiled comfrey leaves and poultice wrap soothing, but he balked after a whiff of the tea.

"Mother, what is this?"

"Brewed tea made from yarrow and stinging nettles. Drink it all and be done with it."

He wanted to be done with it, but drinking the bitter tea was like patiently waiting for the war news. The wires were silent on the war. When there was news, it came like an explosion, yet it seemed disconnected as if the battles were waged on some other country's shore.

"We can beat them just like we did at Manassas," the newspapers said. "Their troops are green. They have no stomach to fight. We shall win."

John felt the pride in that statement and that pride overshadowed the fear.

"They ran like rabbits," one of the circulars said, "ran into the brush and kept on going."

It had been more than a month after Manassas and still folks talked as if it were yesterday. The zeal was still evident in the faces of the young men remaining. Alice could see it in John's face.

"Mother, I promise, I'm not going to go."

"A lot of your friends are."

"I can't say that I haven't thought of it, but I'm taking care of you. And no, it's not because I promised my father. This is a promise that I made to me."

Alice worried knowing that scores of young Georgia men and boys were begging to be inducted but were turned away due to the government's inability to process the ever-swelling numbers. Instead of going home, they refused to leave and said that they would wait however long it took. She wondered how it was in the North.

Swept by this juggernaut of humanity clamoring for action, the leaders in the North as well as their Southern brethren could only watch as this tidal wave sent reason, welfare, and sanity over the abyss like lemmings. Soldiers went into battle without arms, training, discipline, or clothing, some having been sent in homespun or yarn or whatever else could be gathered and patched together for the occasion. For some coming out of the hills, there were no commissary supplies, no proper satchels, or even pockets in which to place ammunition. Some had no ammunition at all. All wanted to fight. Henry had taken the family's best horse because the South could ill-afford to equip her soldiers.

Of his father, John heard little except in the periodic letters that came further and further apart.

Northern industrial goods no longer appeared on Southern shelves such as necessary parts to repair cannons, revolvers, and other weapons. British and French imports vanished. Any goods produced went first to the Southern army. Spiraling inflation gripped the economy. Precious stamps doubled in price to more than ten cents. Coffee and tea became luxuries overnight. The cotton card utilized to make all the clothing was disappearing at an ever-faster rate.

On the homefront, in-fighting on the subject of secession battered states across middle America. Kentucky was in the war now, her careful plan for neutrality in the midst of the madness having failed miserably. In opening up Kentucky, Tennessee was caught in jeopardy. Missouri was sandwiched between abolitionist Kansas and a Northern-sympathizing Illinois that did not want a Confederate state on her border.

One dusky evening, a refugee came limping to the Hollidays' house. Since the war had started, the twilight had seemed even deeper, mingling purple and black shadows into the green thicket of trees. The moon was furtive in the branches as if it, too, feared becoming a casualty.

The refugee was a tomcat who demanded entrance, food, and protection. His arrival came well after the dishes had been cleared and Alice was sewing by candlelight. There was not much candlelight to be had, since candles and the tallow that made them were becoming precious in their scarcity.

The cat had one ear, missing patches of fur, and looked to be a thoroughly disreputable character. When Alice opened the door to see what the scratching was all about, the cat bolted inside and plopped himself on the settee.

"Well, sir, you certainly have taken over."

"Don't suppose we can keep it, can we?" John asked, for once sounding remarkably like a ten-year-old boy.

"I'll get something to feed it, but you'll have to take care of him," Alice wagged a finger at her son.

Tom proved his value soon after his arrival with rats becoming a particular specialty. The first few weeks, however, were spent in John's room resting up and going no further than he had to in order to eat and drink. Gradually, he worked his way outdoors, preferring to take up watch on his household from the shrubs. John brushed him daily and lavished much attention on him. The bare places on his hide grew back and his disposition improved.

Alice saw that John's studies weren't neglected. Everyone pulled more than his or her share of the workload. Everyone was tired. Alice's cough began in earnest and refused to let go. John dreaded what that meant.

"Mind you," his mother told him, "I'm not at death's door. So let me hear you play."

"After you drink this," he shoved one of her crystal glasses into her hand.

"Oh, Lord, John, this is whiskey."

"Well, the doctor said it would cut a cough, so you're going to drink it. Toss it back like I've seen Father do it." In the end, she did.

"I won't tell Father. Promise."

♣ ♥ ♠ ♦

In the fall of 1861, it was beginning to be understood that the war was not going to be over quickly. A longer war meant bloodshed. It meant fathers, sons, and brothers would not return. For the first time, the enormity of war was brought home. John didn't know with whom he agreed or what to believe. He was but a child in a very adult world. He still looked like a child and, at times, as his mother said, acted like a child. But how he felt was far from childish.

There were times when he caught his reflection that he expected to see wrinkles, taut features, and cold eyes. He thought he could see them now, blurred though they were by his youthful visage but present nevertheless. When John was alone in the dark, listening for the sound of invasion as his hand clasped the shotgun, he was as far removed from childish things as the sun was from setting in the North.

Helplessly, Alice watched him struggle. She could not shield him from the war anymore than he could shield her from her illness. They tried to protect each other as best as they could and tried to maintain a way of life that had been before hell broke loose.

Tom the cat was a savior in one respect, giving affection, asking for nothing in return, and allowing John to relate to him as a little boy toward a pet. Henry didn't believe in animals unless they served some purpose. If there was a dog, it was for hunting. Horses plowed or carried a soldier into battle. Goats gave milk. The people in Henry's life had to have a purpose as well.

It was useless to ignore the truth that life was more pleasant with Henry gone. Alice didn't have to watch her boy beaten into the ground. She didn't have to listen to Henry's carping, prodding, or grumbling that she'd only been able to produce one child, which thankfully had been a son. Sometimes it was easier to believe that God's taking little Martha Eleanora had been the best of plans. She had sorrowed greatly about her little girl. Now she felt only relief.

If Alice's ennui occurred in the daytime, for John, it was the nightfall. He had stopped many months before thinking that the night was his friend. Perhaps it had commenced with his father's heavy-handedness and lying awake afterwards, smarting in body and soul and plotting revenge. At night, he tried to put himself to sleep by thinking pleasant thoughts, such as the picnic that he'd taken with his parents a few years before. Several of his friends had been allowed to come and the affair had been a happy one with his mother smiling and Henry effusive.

Suddenly, Yankees poured over the hillside, in his dreams, bringing with them slaughter that reddened the green grass to gore. Smoke filled the air. John woke convulsively clutching the shotgun. Never far from his reach, he kept it fully loaded by his pillow. It was now the first thing that he grasped.

Sweat had drenched his forehead, but he made no effort to wipe it away. His foe—and he was sure that there was one—had to be lurking near the house or was inside already. For a long time he lay in bed while his heart thundered in his chest, then he padded to the door and slowly eased it open. Sweat pooled on his neck. He held his breath as the wood floor creaked. There was silence. Then the noise came again, softly and more regular as a cautious foot might tread across brittle seashells.

He saw the shadow glide through the sitting room until the moonlight coalesced into the figure of a man. Hunkered over, the man appeared to be more apparition than human. The moonlight gleamed on silver. It was his mother's candelabra, about the only thing she cherished that had belonged to her grandmother.

John cocked the trigger, "Put it down."

In the failed light, it looked as if the man was grinning at him in the way that adults grin at children when they don't take them seriously. John let him know that he was serious, although the explosion from the shotgun surprised John as well as the intruder. With a howl, the man dropped his prize and ran from the house. John could hear him as he crashed through the brush.

In the meantime, Alice tumbled panic-stricken into the room. When a candle was finally lit, she found John standing in the middle of the parlor, smoking gun in his hand and death in his eye.

"I don't think he'll be coming back, Mother."

It was a curious moment for mother and son when a day later they made their weekly purchase at the dry goods store. The son of the store's owner waited on them. John knew the young man's brother from school and the two were great chums. Five years older than John, Beau would have already been drafted if it were not for the severe malady afflicting his right leg.

"Is that all, Miz Holliday?" he asked, not meeting John's eyes or Alice's.

"I believe so."

John hadn't taken his eye off of Beau for one moment and Alice was wondering why her usually polite son was so rude.

"Tell me, Beau," John leaned against the counter, "where'd you hurt your arm?"

Beau flushed an ugly shade of red and beads of sweat popped out over his brow. "Funny, but I, uh, tripped and fell down, uh, some steps a couple of nights ago."

"Yeah, I know. Those steps outside the back of our house are really hard."

Outside, Alice was speechless, but not for long. "We don't have steps out the back of the house."

"I know, Mother," John's smile was wicked.

She tweaked his ear, her eyes quite sad. "Thank you for protecting us."

"You're my mother."

He knew that the incident was a sign of the times and that he had to be prepared for all eventualities, even if he had to kill to protect his mother and young aunts. One immediate ramification of the incident was the loss of his best friend.

"I guess I don't understand," he broke down in front of Alice one night several weeks later. She smoothed his hair, which had bleached to the color of corn silk.

"Frank won't talk to you anymore, will he?"

"No, and it wasn't Frank who tried to steal your silver; it was Beau."

"They're brothers. Perhaps Frank is ashamed of what Beau did."

"It doesn't make sense."

"Nothing about this war makes sense. And it will only get worse. We could be driven off the property."

"No," John shouted. "I won't let that happen."

Alice held up her hand. "It's contrary to all that you and I believe, but here we are just as much at war as Henry is on the lines of battle."

"Why can't it just be over? Why can't people just let each other be?"

He was so weary. Lines were etched on every inch of his small face and the wrinkle at the base of his neck seemed to be getting larger. "Why don't you put your head in my lap for a while. You don't have to go to sleep."

"I'm not a baby anymore," he said.

"No, you're not. Think of it this way. Tom curls up in your lap, doesn't he? And he's not a baby. So you can curl up in mine and you don't have to be a baby either."

"I'd like that." And he did so with a yawn. "What about the shotgun?" he mumbled sometime later, before falling asleep.

"I'll use it if I have to," Alice said, knowing she would not. She was afraid of guns. That her son knew how to use one so adeptly was a godsend and yet a curse. It had to be the same for all mothers, North or South.

Although Griffin remained blessedly safe, pestilence struck elsewhere with no regard for age, sex, or accomplishments. Influenza and typhoid outbreaks terrified anxious families who could not afford the luxury of a doctor, even if there had been one available. Many if not all of the doctors had gone to war, leaving families to depend on their own nursing. Luxury, also, were newspapers, which were now a skyrocketing commodity. Desperate news, any news was badgered from weather-beaten refugees streaming across the countryside in escalating numbers.

"Tell us," people pleaded of the Tennessee abolitionists who crossed their land and of the marauders on horseback who came from war-torn Missouri and the Kansas prairie. Fanatics to be sure, but all coming with their own story.

"The typhoid's in St. Louis," one of the marauders said as he stopped by the Hollidays' house. "Gimme a dipperful of water, ma'am? Right thirsty. Just the boy here with you, ma'am? Maybe a couple o' female relatives?"

By the time Alice had returned with the dipper of water, John was the only one in the yard. The man was nowhere to be found

John indicated his still smoking shotgun. "Mother, I helped that varmint move along."

— Chapter —
THREE

After Alice's bout of "feeling poorly" during the early fall of 1861, John consulted with physicians once more. He was learning that consumption was a terrifying disease. His mother might feel strong on Tuesday and be bedridden on Wednesday with a heavy cough. Although it distressed the boy to witness his mother's agony, he would hold her during the bloody paroxysms and afterwards pat the perspiration from her brow. Silently, he cursed the rosy glow that was staining her cheeks. The deep bloom was the most insidious of lies and a harbinger that his mother's body was consuming itself from the inside out.

John was now on intimate terms with the Great Black Book. Early on, the boy had discovered what Alice had always known: the Book had no cure for the cough. Powerless, Alice watched her son struggle with the reality of her plight. He had begun to frequent the local drugstore, usually stopping by on his way home from school. The kindly proprietor who had known the Hollidays for a long time had not the heart to turn the boy away.

The store had changed little since John had been a small boy at his mother's side. As a child, he'd been drawn to the many colorful jars of peppermint and butterscotch candy sticks. Now that he was older, the dark cavern of woodwork and shelves was a fount of knowledge, tonics, elixirs, nostrums, and testimonials.

Cephalic pills treated ague and bodily ills. Brande's Tussilago promised that it had no equal for coughs and colds. Constantine's Pine Tar Soap was heralded as a healing agent. Sulphur Soap eradicated poisonous wastes in the blood. Hostetter's Stomach Bitters and Beef Tonics filled decorative pill tins or graceful bottles that swirled with Latin script.

There were special diets for the consumptive. Cream Emulsion was touted as made from the purest of sweet creams and malt extract. Its testimonial declared that the nostrum was superior to cod-liver oil. As elixirs became available, John would beg for a sample and trot it home for his mother to try. Of particular interest to John was an advertisement for Baudelet's Pepsine that the flyer said had been used in Paris hospitals since 1854. One of the local prescription clerks sympathetically made up a sample for John.

There were periodicals such as *The Lancet*, which described itself as a Journal of British and Foreign Medicine, Physiology, Surgery, Chemistry, Public Health and Criticism, and News. When the clerk saw the boy coming, he would pull out a copy from underneath the counter. Because of the war, *The Lancet* was no longer as plentiful and sometimes eagerly awaited copies arrived not at all. Desperately, John would peruse the articles, vainly trying to understand the big words that could mean longer life for his mother.

"Have you heard anything?" he would ask. "My father spoke of doctors who sometimes trained in the East or in Europe. Have you heard of any traveling this way? If so, would you send them over to our farm? Mother is unwell. I don't know what to do. If I promise to bring it back, could I have *The Lancet* for a day or so?"

The leaves were turning orange and brown when the first of the traveling physicians arrived. In past years, John had delighted in the autumn with its smell of wood smoke, the taste of apple butter that his mother made from her beloved apple trees, and the sight of fiery bittersweet growing nearby. This year, however, his father was at war, his mother was ill, and the approaching winter filled him with bleak dread.

The doctor's cutter was an impressive one that had been outfitted for inclement weather with its large top. Peering hard at the buggy, John saw that there were large, patched holes in the fabric and clumps of missing fringe. The physician who alighted from the driver's seat did not inspire confidence. He was a smallish man with a pinched face and sallow complexion. The hand that he offered John was as gnarled as a knotty oak tree and trembled with palsy.

"I'm passing through the area, Mr. Holliday. Newly come from South Carolina." There was a strangled sound in the doctor's voice when he pronounced South Carolina. He paused for a moment and then continued to speak. "I would like to say that I have at my disposal an astonishing array of medical miracles, but the fact is most of my medicine has already been used by our boys at the front. So I am lacking. Mind you, for certain ills, there is no cure. I heard that your mother was poorly. May I have permission to take a look at her?"

"I suppose it wouldn't hurt. Come on inside the house. She's in the bedroom."

John led the way. "Mother," the boy called, "there's a doctor here to see you."

"Are you expecting trouble, Master Holliday?" The doctor indicated the small shotgun by John's side.

"We've had some trouble," John said. "You can't be too careful these days."

"That's a fact. Well, if Miz Holliday here don't mind, I'll take a listen to her chest. I used to think that there was nothing better than leeches." He brought out the tin box for John to see. In flowing script it read, "Hirudo Medicinalis."

"And now?" John asked.

"We were treating our gallant boys in the field with these same leeches. I suppose some still do. I stopped. I'm none too sure of the efficacy of calomel now either."

John's lips thinned. "I know that mercury is one of the ingredients of calomel, and I know that's poisonous."

"I'm impressed by your knowledge. I've seen mercury poisoning and it's a bad thing."

"But do you think it will help?" John asked.

The man's face became gray and his eyelids closed momentarily. When he spoke again, his eyes seemed focused far away. "Well, suh, we can but try."

John considered that for a moment. "You go on in."

With a small bow in John's direction, the physician carried his black bag into the bedroom. Once alone with Alice, he began removing the contents of his black bag: wooden stethoscope, leech boxes, and medicinal tins. The boy could hear soft murmurs but nothing beyond that. Finally, the door opened. John stood up still clutching the shotgun with his left hand. The doctor's face was haggard and there was a look on his face that John recognized as futility. He had seen the same look when his mother was first diagnosed.

"I, uh, didn't bleed her and I didn't give her calomel."

John raised his voice, "Why not?"

"Because," the doctor replied with an anguished expression, "because there isn't anything to be done. Because medical science just doesn't know anymore than that Black Book on your mother's nightstand. I can't do anything to help her. I couldn't do anything for the boys at the front except hack off their ravaged limbs that had been destroyed by mini-balls. I couldn't help them. I can't help you. And I can't, like some, tell lies, for how else could I live with myself? But mark my words, there will come those who whisper lies."

"How much do we owe you?" John asked with a heavy heart.

"I couldn't do anything. I won't charge you." The boy scurried after the doctor. "Mind what I said, Master Holliday. Mind the ones who charge heavily, who do nothing, and who offer cures that do not cure. They will sell you a pretty tale that will only reap a harvest of misery."

"How long?" John asked. "What are we going to do?"

"Providence, Master Holliday. Only Providence knows. Geeup." The doctor slapped the reins on the horse's rump. "Geeup."

It didn't seem possible, John thought, that there was nothing that could be done for his mother. He was only one physician after all. Surely medical science, with all of its marvels, had to have a cure or a treatment or something. Providence, the doctor had said. Providence was what his mother said. John was as bitterly disappointed in Providence as he was with the autumn leaves and bittersweet that he had picked for his mother. Outside was no better. Brown leaves crumbled on the ground, while the bittersweet slowly twisted on the vine.

In early November, John heard a halloo from the front yard. There was a faint quality of familiarity about it, but John could not place where he had first heard the voice.

"Halloo to the man of the house."

Another doctor's cutter stood in plain sight.

"Halloo," the doctor intoned as he jumped off the seat. He was younger and taller than the physician from South Carolina had been. John noticed that the horse was sleek, too, and that the buggy was unblemished. The hand that grasped his was firm and smooth as a babe's.

"Halloo there, Master Holliday. Be ye the man of the house?"

"I am."

"I understand from my sources in the area, specifically from the most excellent Griffin apothecary, there is illness or infirmity in the house."

"Illness."

"Your mother?"

"Yes."

"Might I come in and have a look at her? I have at my disposal all the best in medical science. You know we can do so much these days to relieve the ill wills and ague of the flesh. I most recently have come from the front lines. We will win the war. There is no doubt."

"You were not on the front lines," John said pointedly.

"No," the physician remarked. "No, I was not to my utter chagrin, having just come from Atlanta where I was summarily turned away due to an irregularity of my limbs, which in the slightest does not prevent me from curing our gallant women-folk. There is nothing more important to me than sparing our gentle Southern belles the exigencies of war. Does your mother cough?"

"Yes."

"Then I most have the cure. Let me attend to her and you will see the marvels. And if you do not believe me, I have glowing testimonials to my good works, written documents if you will, of the efficacy of those cures. Of especial importance to your mother's care are these Cephalic Pills."

"My mother doesn't have headaches. She has the wasting disease. Looks like you repackaged these for fifty cents? I can get them in town for twenty."

"Lookit boy, these here pills have been around a lot longer than you have been alive. And they're hard to come by."

John reached into the doctor's bag. "You're selling Hostetter's Stomach Bitters for eighty cents? My mother grows the bitters in her herb garden. What else are you trying to foist on us?"

"It is for certain that your mother has a buildup of poisonous effluviums. You know these poisons must be flushed from her frail constitution. The calomel that I have will relieve and destroy the evil sludge that traverses the great pathways of her body. I can assure you that I am of the most impeccable repute. I have nursed our gallant lads on the front lines."

"How many died? My mother's already right peaked. You're not going to put leeches on her."

"Dr. Benjamin Rush believes that a pint or so of blood daily removed from the patient will release the miasmas that afflict the body. And, your mother's a woman."

"What the hell does that mean?"

"Consumption is a tricky thing. It means, as you're probably finding out, that your mother can be cheerful and productive one day while possessed and swooning of the vapors the next. Tell me, has your mother received the blistering poultice."

"If you mean the one that causes proud flesh, how does that help?"

"Your father must indeed be disappointed in you, young critter, for your utter lack of consideration or faith in my healing powers."

"My father, indeed, suh, is quite disappointed in me and always has been. But he didn't raise no fool. No matter how many noxious nostrums and elixirs that you peddle, they're no account."

"In that case, young Master Holliday, I will take my leave of this inhospitable house. That will be two dollars and fifty cents."

"You'll not get any of our money." Firmly, he put the shotgun to his shoulder and sighted the doctor in the barrel. The man's eyes widened. Clutching his medical bag, he bolted from the house and sprang into the driver's seat of his buggy.

"Highway shecoonery," John said as he slammed the front door shut. "Mother," he called softly and tapped on her bedroom door. "Mother, I'm sorry."

Wanly, Alice rested her weight onto her right elbow so she could see her son. "That's alright. I don't think he would have been all that bad as far as doctoring went."

"I wasn't gonna find out. It just feels like there's gotta be something else. Something we're missing, that we're not doing." John lay a cool hand to her hot forehead.

"The coughing has eased a bit. Your father has some of those Cephalic Pills. They do work on headaches."

"Just not on coughs."

"No, not on coughs."

"Maybe later in the year. Maybe somebody will know more what to do about it."

"Yes," Alice replied, "most assuredly later in the year." Her voice trailed off and her eyes closed. Pulling the snowy coverlet to his mother's chin, John gently plumped the pillow, looked at her face for a moment, and then left the bedroom.

Two days later the deep cough ended and Alice began to speak of the future once more. "You know when your father comes back from the war, he'll think you a grown man indeed."

John's stomach tightened. The cough wouldn't be gone for long. The bright color in his mother's cheeks gave testament as well as the small tic that had taken up residence in the corners of her mouth. Alice would never admit that she was in distress for that would mean a diminishing of her motherhood. Of late, John had wondered if he would, in the same circumstance, be able to carry the impending knowledge of his death with such grace.

Something else had begun to bother him, too. At first he thought it was a figment of his imagination, but the dead mouse smell continued to grow stronger. Thinking that perhaps a rodent had moved into his mother's bedroom, John brought trusty Tom to the rescue. Tom, however, wasn't interested in the smell. Instead he jumped on Alice's bed and snuggled himself into the clean comforter. Soon John and his mother could hear his sonorous purr.

In agony, John asked, "Mother, do you know what that smell is?"

Alice patted her son's hand with her icy fingers. "It's the way of things."

♣ ♥ ♠ ♦

Since Henry had left, Alice had taken up residence in her husband's favorite chair. Its size dwarfed her, but she found it comforting. Light beige, it was invariably overlooked amidst the stolid mahogany and scrollwork of the rest of the furniture. Alice found if she sat in the well-depressed seat long enough, there would come the heady whiff of Henry's pipe tobacco.

It was easy to lounge in the depths of the chair while reading letters, sewing, and directing household projects. Late at night, when Alice could not sleep, she would creep from the bedroom, look around to see if John was watching, and then nestle in the chair. In its confines, with the tobacco smell wrapped soothingly around her like a warm blanket, she would sleep.

While she slept, John tiptoed around the house doing his customary chores and chopped wood for the pot-bellied stove. November was promising to be a cold one, and John had been hard at work chopping wood. Alice had been oblivious to the sounds of the ax and only awakened when a letter was gently placed in her lap.

A soft smile wreathed her thin face. "It's from your Aunt Mary. She wonders how we are doing. And, if she is able, she will travel here for a few days to visit. She's bringing your first cousin, Martha Anne."

"Oh," John's face beamed, "I hope she likes cats."

"I'm sure she does," Alice said, understanding her son's excitement. Much of John's life had been spent surrounded by adults. Many of them, including Henry, felt that children should be seen and not heard from at all. John had always been reticent and the continuous crush of relatives had only reinforced that trait in him. However, Martha Anne was nearer his age. Alice hoped that cousin Mattie would coax John from his shell.

It was going to be a wonderful homecoming. The Hollidays had always been a close-knit clan. With the war showing signs that it would continue for a much longer time, the family struggled for the closeness that was their wellspring of stability. Mary Holliday came bearing stories of desperate citizens set adrift on the countryside and of the pillaging that was going on in most cities. She refused to say how close it was coming to her family, but Alice could see the truth on her sister-in-law's face.

Mary's visit was a reminder of more pleasant days when the family gathered en masse at picnics and barbecues. Her visit was accorded all the ceremony that Alice and her sisters could muster.

"Robert was telling me that if the war gets really bad, he might send us down here for a while."

"Henry was cheerful in his letters to me so I wouldn't worry, but now I don't hear from him at all. I think the war's not going the way anyone planned."

Mary took a long sip of her tea. "I know you wrote that you'd been feeling poorly. Has that passed?"

Alice looked around to see if John was in earshot. "Unfortunately, no. It will only get worse as time goes by. I have good days and others that aren't so good."

"I wanted to see for myself. I guess I'm just a nosy sister-in-law."

"Nonsense, Mary. I've so missed you and our talks. I've wondered how you and the rest of the family were doing in Jonesboro."

"We're biding our time. You know Missouri is now in the hands of the Yankees. Kentucky has been in constant upheaval and who knows which way it will fall. People are being arrested right out of their homes in the dead of night. Prominent citizens, some of the leaders in the army, and families are just taken, never to be heard from again. That word, *sedition*. Robert speaks of it in a veiled whisper. I can read it between the lines of his letters. He's afraid for us."

"There aren't rights anymore," Alice said. Then, seeing that the window was open, she lowered her voice. "People watch each other here. I've seen it happening. John sleeps with a loaded shotgun by his side. He's had to grow up so fast."

"I'm glad I brought Martha Anne. The two have always had an easy kinship. And I'm here right now, Alice. Try not to fret."

Outside, John introduced Mattie to Tom and then rocked back on his heels to see her reaction. It was a cool day, but not cold with high scudding clouds and bits of blue sky. Lingering still were a few blades of green grass. Mattie had made herself comfortable at the foot of the old oak tree and Tom had made himself comfortable in Mattie's lap.

"Oh, pretty kitty. I had a kitty at home, but she ran away. He looks like orange marmalade."

"Yeah," John grinned. Mattie's esteem had risen greatly in his eyes. "Has anybody tried to break into your house?"

"Not yet, but I'm so scared that it might happen any day now. It's so hard to judge character these days." Mattie tried to sound worldly.

"Someone broke in the other night. I've been practicing my shooting to protect Mother."

Mattie leaned forward and gripped his arm. "Do you keep a gun?"

"I sleep with my shotgun right by my side."

"Night's the hardest of all. I feel so alone. So you slept with the gun and then had to use it?" She was clearly impressed.

"I didn't want to kill him. I just wanted him out of the house. He was the brother of one of my best friends."

"Was?"

"My friend doesn't talk to me anymore."

"Maybe," she squeezed his arm, "he was ashamed."

"That's what Mother told me."

"How is Aunt Alice, John?"

"She's dying, Mattie. She's got the wasting disease. I do the best I can, but it's not enough." Mattie sat down and put her arm around him. John could see the tears in her eyes. "I'm really scared, Mattie," he whispered. "It feels like when Father beats me, only worse and deeper down in my bones. There's this coldness that won't go away. Just this coldness."

"I'm here, always," she whispered, "always."

The visit lasted a week, but it was a welcome diversion in the middle of the heartache. By December's end in 1861, Henry received a furlough home.

"I won't be staying," Henry told Alice as he arrived on the doorstep without warning or preamble. "We have to reenlist for three more years or for the duration of the war. Can't say which will come first."

Stupefied, his family rallied around him with hugs and kisses. John hugged his father, but pulled away, unsure of his feelings or his father's. Henry was gaunt and his shoulders were drooping.

"I'm in my fighting trim," he patted his stomach and offered his son a wide grin that drew an equal response from John.

"We'll be at it," he told the family over dinner, "much longer than Jeff Davis promised." He glanced around, "The war is not at all what some cracked it up to be. Generals are replaced if they don't produce results. Or worse."

"How worse?" John wanted to know.

"They're arrested and charged with treason. It's just not what anybody thought."

After supper, John gave his own report to his father when the two were alone in the parlor. Alice, seeing the look between father and son, silently left the room.

"I noticed that my whiskey supply is down. You taken to drink, boy?"

"No," John shook his head. For once Henry didn't seem angry. "No, it's for Mother when the coughing gets bad. She's afraid of laudanum."

"No, that's okay. I wouldn't have thought of that myself. She tells me you're an expert with a gun."

"I startled an intruder."

"That's good. You're coming along. Looks like I put the right man in charge of things here. Your mother looks bad. I didn't want to hurt her feelings."

"That bright color in her cheeks is consuming her."

"We've had typhoid in our ranks. Dysentery, too. It all looked easy-like when it started what with the parades, hoopla, and singing. But a man can't win a war on cheers or confetti. The troops—" Henry noted John's rapt eyes and decided not to burst the fragile bubble. John would learn soon enough. "The troops," he finished, "are a wonder. They make do when things are unavailable. That's what I want you to do. When things get bad, make do and hang on. They'll either get better or worse, but you'll never know if you let go. Afraid next year is going to be some lean kind of year."

"I guess we won't know if we give in," John echoed him.

♣ ♥ ♠ ♦

Henry's return in December and his quick departure upset John more than the boy thought possible. He had been glad to lay his burden down with his father's arrival. But then, in a blink of an eye, Henry was gone and the burden of caring for his family seemed greater than ever. At school and at home he was told to do more with less. Henry had given him money to provide for the family.

"You have to help your mother out," he told John. "I don't know how long this money will last, but use it wisely."

At first, John had enjoyed the brightly colored money. The twenty-dollar bill that his father had given to him for supplies was fearfully tucked into his sock and was meant to buy his mother enough cloth to mend their winter clothes. The roads were a quagmire of manure and mud, but they were still passable. Terrified that someone would knock him down and steal his precious money, John hugged the main road, praying all the while that he would not come to a trampled end as some before him. He shivered in the long line at the emporium, but when it was his turn to buy the cloth, he was told that the cloth cost twice the amount it had before. Twenty dollars was not even enough to purchase a tiny can of coffee or tea. The humiliation was dire, but much worse was trudging home through the mud and cold to tell his mother that he had failed.

"You know what," Alice said as she bundled her shivering son in blankets and placed him in front of a roaring fire, "I don't know why I didn't think of it before. I've got my mother's loom. We can make do with homespun. We did it for years when I was growing up. There were eleven of us and we passed the clothing down to the next in line. You sit there near the fire and I'll make you a hot cup of tea. We'll manage, John."

The year turned over. With the fall of Ft. Donelson in February and capture of New Orleans in April, there was no doubt in John's mind that the Northern avengers were on the march. Stories circulated that common folk burned what they could to the ground before the Yankees arrived so that they'd find only cinders. Consumed with hatred, John vowed that if Griffin were threatened, he, too, would strike a match that would burn his beloved home to the ground.

The capture of New Orleans shook the boy's faith in the Southern cause as assuredly as the news of enforced conscription shook his mother. The leaders in Richmond had promised that the gateway city to the Mississippi River was unassailable. Obviously, they had been wrong. In his mind, John could see pieces of the South broken off until the South itself was gone.

John learned that promises were meant for times free of strife. Winning the war was not enough. If burning hatred could become a living wish, then he would take it and single-handedly kill all the Yankees. That was the real crux of the matter. He knew that all the other problems would go away if he could do that one thing. Instead, he was ten years old and helpless.

Before the deadly battles of the U.S.S. *Virginia* and the Union's own *Monitor*, John had never given war waged by sea more than a thought. As a child, he had loved stories about the wooden vessels that had carried the Norsemen conquerors to glory. Overnight they became black monsters with iron plating that oozed up the banks and rivers of his dreams, traversed the very forests, and settled below his window.

Alice tried to comfort her son. "John, they're so heavy that they can't come on land. They have to have water to float, lots of water. And the water has to be deep enough for them to do that. They're like all other ships in that respect. They can run aground."

"They can come up the rivers. The newspapers all say so."

"Perhaps they can, but we won't let that happen."

After John's heart-rending screams filled the house night after night, Alice allowed her son to sleep on a pallet that she made for him on the floor by her bed. This was the result, she thought, of thrusting his tender youth into a manhood that his years could not accommodate.

Henry's letters came so infrequently that their arrival was a celebration. Not long after his return from furlough, Alice received a short missive from him.

On December 25 of last year, I was made major. I wish that I could write more to you, my dearest, but paper is dear and unlikely to be replaced. My love to you and our family as always. Please pray for me, pray for all of us.

Alice sighed as she reread the letter, and then gently tucked it away in the family Bible. The extra money that the promotion promised was nice, but more than ever, she prayed for her husband's safe return. For her, the tick of the clock marked the hours. Of late, she had been wondering about her own mother and in the dead of night, while listening to John's soft whimpers while he slept and her own coarse breathing, had addressed that dearly departed soul for comfort. "Mother . . . what I shall I do?"

Belt-tightening was an everyday part of life. Each day brought another reminder that nothing was like it had been. For John, nothing was more unbearable than the daily business of school and chores, then to come home and receive his mother's fond kiss, all the while consumed with the aching knowledge that she was dying. The war, like his mother's health, deteriorated one tick of the clock at a time. He came to hate the clock, not just the one on the mantle, but all of them. Alice punished him severely for dismembering her cherished cherry wood clock.

"That was my mother's clock. Why in God's name would you do something like that?"

Defiant, yet crushed, he looked at her as tears ran down his face and said nothing. Alice kept a watchful eye out for what might upset her son, but she had no clue until she found his hoard of old newspapers. Apparently his nightmares were following the current headline or telegraphic news of the day. He was obviously taking to heart what he read and believing what his friends were talking about.

Vicious rumors were rampant. The telegraphs chattered that war visited horror and pestilence with dispassionate complexity, that England would wait for a victory before importing cotton, and that the war had changed from a mockery by land to a watery grave. The telegraphs chattered of the Yankee hordes descending on the unsuspecting, raping women and children, and throwing their battered carcasses on the scrap heap of their plunder.

Perhaps it was true, but Alice didn't know. Sifting the news for the truth was hard enough for an adult, much less an impressionable child. She couldn't keep the papers from John or forbid him from talking to his friends, but she might be able to mollify his fears. It didn't help that Henry's last letter to her was so full of discouragement that it frightened her.

The letter was badly smudged for which he apologized. He was writing to her from one of those rough trenches that the engineers had scrambled to build in a cold rain. He said it was small and woefully shallow. He begged her pardon for a lot of things. He'd been ill.

"I just can't seem to get better," he wrote. "My stomach's on fire worse than ever. I long for your rhubarb tea and blackberry root."

Alice hid Henry's letter from John. May and June of 1862 passed like the creeping vines that wound their humid tendrils around tree trunks and chimneys and replaced the oxygen with a sucking mixture of mildew and algae. Mold was everywhere. In mid-summer of that year, Henry Holliday came home for good. As usual, he refused to talk about the circumstances surrounding his resignation from the army.

Understanding her husband's reticence, Alice didn't prod, knowing that her husband would speak his heart to her in good time. She was so relieved for him to be home that, momentarily, her disease seemed but a trifle. On Henry's first night back, he slept as if intoxicated, though he had not touched a drop of liquor. But the second night, he turned suddenly in bed.

"Guess it's my age. I couldn't cut the muster. Been sick off and on most of the year. Spent more time in the infirmary than where I was needed. Not that it would have made a difference, the way my stomach was going. I failed you, Alice. I didn't want to come home a failure."

"You're not a failure. I've never been prouder. I've never been gladder than I am now for you to be home."

"John will think I'm a failure."

"Your son understands more than you give him credit," Alice whispered and then was quiet for a time. Henry's breathing had become softer and shallower. "Tell me what is happening. The newspapers are almost done for. The silence is the worst."

"Second Manassas was a success. We're holding our own, but, uh . . ."

"Well," Alice smoothed his cheek, "we can only do what we can do. Beyond that is Providence."

The next morning at breakfast, Henry looked at his son's downcast face. "Thought you might want to know about the war, boy."

John's eyes suddenly shined. "I was kinda hopin' that you got to meet some of the generals."

"I was most proud to be in the service of General Beauregard in the Army of the Potomac. He spoke to me on one occasion. Asked me if I was a family man. I said, yes sir, I did."

"Is this like the last time? Will you leave again?"

"No, I'm home for good. Perhaps just as well. I can't hide it from you, son, that neighbor has turned against neighbor. Families are divided, some striking the names of their loved ones from the family Bible never to mention them again. Or if spoken, as if that person is dead."

Try though he might, Henry was not the same man who had left for the war, or the one who had come home on furlough some months before. The heavy tan did little to disguise how gaunt he had become. Each bone in his face stood in sharp relief and his cheeks were sunken. Often after a meal, he would clutch his stomach and groan, then rush outside to be sick.

In the ensuing days, Henry lost his temper and turned it on everyone in the family. Contrite, he would beg Alice's pardon only to lose his temper moments later. Alice was frantic to soothe the rages in his mind and stomach. A word or a wrong look was enough to set him off. Most of this fell on John.

"Henry, he took care of us when you were gone. He had all the responsibility of an adult. He even saved our lives," Alice explained.

"I know the boy did the best that he could but, by damn, I'm home now. He doesn't have to creep around like a chicken." Henry's voice rose with each new statement.

"Henry, he's only eleven. The way you two are going at it, he won't see his twelfth birthday. I won't let you start beating him."

Henry began to shake. "He's my son. I've got some say here. Why do you have to keep arguing with me? I'm home. Doesn't anyone understand?" He raised his fist over the top of Alice's head.

An incredible silence fell over the house as suddenly as the click of the shotgun in the room. Battle-honed, Henry knew the sound and froze in his tracks, fist still suspended in the air. Over the top of the gun, he met the dead gaze of his son sighting him in the cross hairs.

"No, suh," John told him. "You can strike me until hell freezes over, and I figure you will, but don't you ever raise a hand to my mother again. Father or no, you have to know that I'll do it."

Henry's fist uncurled and slowly lowered. Alice clasped a hand to her throat and stepped back. Just as slowly, John lowered the shotgun and went to his room. No one spoke for the rest of the day. At three o'clock, Alice went to check on John. At the movement by the door, John leaped out of bed. He was fully clothed and a small valise rested on the floor by the bed. Alice recognized it as hers.

"I, uh, guess I was planning to take off."

"If I had happened to be your father at your door, don't you mean? Your father isn't a bad man, John. He's a very good one."

"We've had this conversation before, Mother."

"Not so long ago either, I think. It's been really hard on Henry. He's not been well. He blames himself for being weak and not seeing the war to its conclusion. He feels that he failed us."

"So he takes it out on us? He was going to hit you. And what about before the war? He hit me then. He hit you then. What was the excuse those times?"

"I don't think he would have struck me."

"Mother, don't cover up for him like everyone does. It never stops."

Alice reached over and massaged his temples. The pulse under his temple beat fiercely.

"If you run away, it will break his heart. He wants you so to be like him."

"I can never be like him," John growled. "I don't want to be his little soldier anymore."

"I didn't see your kitty around this evening."

"No," John said dully, "I can't find him anywhere. He's nowhere. I've looked and called. I've looked everywhere."

"Well, I think," Alice smoothed his hair, "that he moved on. You know how he came to us. I think he must have moved on in the same way."

"Father was complaining about him."

"Do you honestly think that your father would have done something to your cat?"

"Yes," he told her, "I do. I want my cat back."

Gently, she reached over and gathered him to her. He lay his head on her shoulder and she rocked him until he was quiet. She looked so old when she let him go. John couldn't believe that someone could age so quickly, or maybe he hadn't taken a good look at her recently. But she was his mother and the wrinkles on her face and the patient pain in her eyes all faded when he looked at her.

"Do you want to see about getting another kitty?"

"No," he yawned, "I want Tom back."

"Try not to fret. Somehow we'll work things out."

Early the next morning, Alice looked for the cat, too. She found his tracks in all of his favorite haunts and some looked to be fresh. She called him for a long time, but he never answered her. The tracks led into the forest. It was so still and dark with the tall swaying trees. Alice looked about and called Tom's name. There was a faint sound. Turning, she looked hard at what appeared to be an orange pile of leaves.

"Oh, Tom."

He was still alive. With a glad purr he began to make his way to her, but halfway there he suddenly sat down. Alice gently picked him up and put him in her lap. Her knowing eyes looked for any telltale signs that he had been in a fight or injured. There were no bloody marks on him and his coat still had the same sheen on it from John's last brushing. His golden eyes looked up at her, and Alice recognized the look.

"You'll be getting there before I do. You wait for me, pretty Tom." He snuggled into her apron as he had done so many times before. Several minutes passed and then he gave a small tremble.

"Oh, kitty. Oh, kitty." Alice's head bent and she wept through tears so painful that they clogged her throat. Her hand smoothed the orange body over and over. "You made our lives so bright."

The tall trees swished. With a sigh, Alice gathered up the limp body of Tom, wrapped him tenderly in her apron, and carried him to a place well off the beaten path. Above all she didn't want her son to find his cat. After searching a small clearing, she found a half-rotted branch. Digging deep into the soil, she gathered wet leaves and small wild flowers and then gently deposited Tom. On her walk back to the house, a west wind brushed her hair.

"Your kitty didn't meet with a bad end," she told John at breakfast. "I found his tracks. He circled the house many times. I think he was deciding if he should go or not."

"And father didn't kill him?"

"Oh, heavens no," Alice said. "His paw prints looked deep and regular."

John was beginning to tear. "What do you think happened?"

"I think the west wind called him away."

"What's that?"

"It's that soft voice inside that whispers, 'Come.'"

"I've heard that before. Sometimes it's really strong."

"Well, that's where Tom went."

"Mother, do you still hear the marching?"

"Oh, yes."

＊＝ *Chapter* ＝＊
FOUR

For Henry, the Christmas of 1862 was filled with sadness. A boy-hood friend had been killed in the Seven Days' Battle at Malvern Hill. Two more friends died at Second Manassas on August 30, and by December 15 still another boyhood chum was slain at Fredericksburg. Fredericksburg was hailed as a victory for the South, but it came with a tremendous loss of life.

Henry knew how critical men, munitions, and supplies were to the Confederacy. The Fredericksburg victory meant the capture of ammunition, foodstuffs, horses, and even clothing. The South was holding her own, but Henry saw trouble coming in the lack of resources.

Good women like his wife, who in spite of long hours laboring at home, still found time to sew for the boys in the army or to roll bandages for the hospital. Small factories hustled to make up for the shortfall of weapons and ammunition. But the thousands of pounds of goods, food, and wares selflessly collected were rotting in warehouses because there was no way to get them to the front lines. Lack of rolling stock and destroyed rail lines meant no supplies and none forthcoming. Blockades also strangled supply lines. With New Orleans in the hands of the North, access to the vital Mississippi River and other waterways was closed. From the command staff came the orders to make do with less. Soldiers marched and fought barefooted. As a result, food rations had shrunk to an alarming level. Some went for hours without food except a taste of hardtack and cornbread. Some had no food at all. For those whose limbs had to be amputated, there was no morphine.

Henry tried to shut the sights out of his mind, but at night the screams of the living and dying replayed in his brain. In the morning, he was faced with the eyes of his son, who seemed to ask why he had left the field of battle when there was so much to be done. Never had he chafed at his lot in life more. When he was younger, he looked forward to the next campaign. At his advanced age, there would be no more campaigns. Bitterly, he watched the young officers ride through town and knew that he had far more experience at planning and execution than they would ever hope to learn.

♣ ♥ ♠ ♦

In his father's absence, John had become an apt student of geography and had made a detailed map of the Southern states for a geography project. Not only were topographic features included, but capitols, area roads, points of interest, and for extra credit, battlefields. Henry had heard much about the project, but had not seen it until it was brought home from school. The detailing was meticulous.

"I've seen worse from skilled cartographers, boy. You've done a pretty fair approximation on General Jackson's campaigns, too. Could it be that you favor him over General Lee?"

John flushed. "Oh no, sir. No general is better than our General Lee."

"Except General Jackson?" Henry asked, as an unaccustomed smile creased his lips.

John looked down at his shoes for a moment and then furtively turned to his father. "I have to ask, but I didn't want to in front of mother."

Arrested by the worried pucker in the middle of his son's forehead, Henry bent over. "What is it, boy?"

"If the railroads fall into enemy hands, won't the Yankees get here quicker?"

"General Jackson won't let that happen."

As April of 1863 waned, John's map became more complex with the addition of Chancellorsville in Virginia. Because of the boy's war fervor, it was sometimes necessary to remind him that he was too young for General Jackson to accept him into the Army of Northern Virginia, that water from the cistern was needed before Saturday's ablutions, and that the mule was unable to harness himself.

Henry said, "I think at some point in time it might be best for Jefferson Davis to boost the morale of the boys." He lay the paper down. "The boys as well as the officers are starting to desert the Army. His visit to the front might be just the thing to stop the desertion."

No one complained that the dinner was meatless for a fourth night in a row, that the lettuce and apples had been picked well before they were ripened, and that the tea had been made from the coarsest bark of one of the nearby trees. Instead there was the familiar clang of silverware, the scrape of forks against the crockery, and the thankful murmurs to Alice for her wonderful food preparation.

"I've had to memorize all the generals and which army they lead for history class," John said slowly, trying to gauge his father's mood. Too often jocularity became sarcasm, especially after Henry's trips into town. "Do you suppose that any of the generals will be there with President Davis? I might get extra credit, especially if I get to say something to him."

Henry shared a tiny smile with Alice. It was obvious that John meant General Jackson, not President Davis. He cleared his throat. "It's much too dangerous to travel now. When the war is over, I will take all of you to Richmond and we shall pay our respects. It will be an informative excursion, although Mother will probably want me to take her shopping."

The smiles all around the table were buoyant.

"I have been thinking about buying land," Henry said. "I know that we had to stint this last year and nothing went as planned." He smiled reassuringly again in his wife's direction. "With land values the way they are now, an investment for later might not be a bad idea. It's been apparent that the South will have to extend her efforts if we are to win." *If we are to survive* hung in the air unsaid by Henry.

Since the day that John had threatened him with the shotgun, Henry had been reluctant to speak to his son. Privately, he admitted that he was much to blame for John's threatened attack. Alice had warned him about the beatings. And Henry, not wanting to believe her, had persisted in spite of the growing evidence that John was very much like him in temperament and character. His son was not a coward and not a child either.

As with any campaign, Henry realized his blunder, yet could do nothing to make amends. The longer he waited, the harder it became. Alice had told him about the cat and about how much Tom had meant to their son. Henry had even ridden to a nearby farmhouse where he was told there were new kittens. In the litter was an orange tom. It was a thing that he should have done but did not. He had his pride and John had severely damaged it.

For now, all he could do was gaze at his sullen-eyed son who would one day strike back at him. Of that, Henry was certain.

Henry had hoped that his coming home might make the difference for his family. As a quartermaster, he had excelled in finding ways around supply problems. If there were shortages, contingency plans created new sources. At home, experience told him that if the cost of cloth was too dear, then homespun was the answer. Since coffee and tea were too expensive, the family drank tea brewed from the bark of trees or herbs. But at last, Henry could no longer deny that the civilian population was stretched beyond measure and in some areas worse off than the army.

If he'd had any thought that Alice would recover while he was away, that fantasy had died like so many soldiers upon the battlefield. When she would pass on was a matter of Providence, but the signs were there in the fevers that recurred with increasing severity. Because liquor was now a costly luxury, Henry experimented with home-brew in his potting shed. The best brew, with blackstrap molasses added, was given to his wife to ease her cough.

He had always considered himself a God-fearing Presbyterian, but there were so many mouths to feed these days, so many cares, and so much sorrow. It was hard to go about daily activities when his family clamored for advice and attention. It was hard to ride away in the morning all the while knowing that at home Alice was slipping from him. In moments of despair, Henry imagined himself akin to Jefferson Davis, besieged on all sides by all people.

"John is not keen on becoming a farmer," Alice told her husband one evening after supper.

In keeping with the frugality of the times, the lanterns were only half-filled and the wicks were trimmed. Henry had been trying to read, but the semi-darkness that permeated the room made it difficult. To accommodate his wife's cough, he had moved Alice's chair closer to the pot-bellied stove. From his vantage point in his favorite chair, he watched the shadows flick across her face and marveled that she could sew in such poor circumstances.

"I didn't realize that John has been reading *The Lancet*. He leaves them lying around. I've heard him rip through those big medical words. Not only that, but he knows what they mean."

Alice's eyes widened and she missed a stitch. "Have you noticed that he has an uncanny talent for sizing up situations by the look in a person's eyes?"

After a long draw on his pipe, Henry said soberly, "You've taught him the piano and good penmanship. He's taught himself God knows what else. Perhaps he'd be good in a medical profession where he can use that quick mind and wit of his."

"It's good to think of the future," Alice said, but then she laid her sewing in her lap and reached out a hand to her husband. "There will be a future, won't there?"

Henry's eyes narrowed, making the wrinkles in his leathery-skinned face even deeper. "I didn't tell John that General Jackson died today . . . shot by one of his own troops."

In the days that followed Stonewall Jackson's death, John's war fervor lessened. He did, however, continue to make new entries on his map based on what he heard at school or from the information that his father brought from town. On May 21, eleven days after General Jackson's death, John lightly penciled a notation by Vicksburg, Mississippi. Yet another entry had to be made by mid-June: Gettysburg, Pennsylvania. Neither Alice nor Henry had answers for their son about the failure at Vicksburg or for the heartbreak at Gettysburg. Lee had intended the Gettysburg Campaign as a foray into Pennsylvania to catch Grant unawares in a frontal assault and to secure fresh supplies. With the Mississippi River now in the hands of the North after the defeat at Vicksburg, the South was effectively split in two.

As the war progressed through September, there were more devastating blows. John struggled to keep up with his map, but the continuing defeat of the South reduced him to despair.

Alice suffered a relapse late in 1863. Inflation continued to skyrocket. Henry grew more restive and sullen. And in the New Year of 1864, Jefferson Davis suspended the writ of habeas corpus, causing an uproar that resounded throughout the South. By suspending habeas corpus, many felt President Davis was insulting the integrity of the Confederate States.

Henry argued that Davis saw his edict as a means to spur valor once more in the South. "Absenteeism and desertion is so rampant that it is necessary to take aim on the thousands of men who no longer march or fight."

There were many causes given for the failure of the Confederacy to bring about a swift end to the war and no consensus of opinion. John blamed the failure of the army on the North's destruction of the rail system. Henry defended General Lee, but he blamed Confederate defeats on youthful subordinate commanders with little battle experience.

John could not believe what he saw going on around him. His father had promised him that things would be all right. But in his thirteenth year, his mother was spitting streams of blood into her lace handkerchiefs. On her cheeks was the rosy glow of sunset while the rest of her face was strained as tight as a milk bladder and just as white. Although Henry said that a move to a larger place in southern Lowndes County near Valdosta would make the difference, John knew that it wouldn't. His mother would continue to cough until she died, and the Yankees would still wreak their bloody onslaught.

"It's coming to our doorstep," Henry told his family. "Sherman is on the march to Atlanta. We can't stay here lest we be swept away in a flood of blue uniforms and their sabers. We'll have to ride out the storm further south."

In the days before the move, John tried once again to find his cat by retracing Tom's favorite haunts and calling his name. There was also a last pilgrimage made to his boyhood hiding place. The thicket had been stripped bare. Even the rotting logs on which he had once sat had been shorn of bark and were nothing more than shards. With a sigh, John took a last look backwards, then straightened his shoulders.

Although the trek to Valdosta, near the Georgia-Florida border, was difficult, Alice bore the move as uncomplainingly as ever. It was too early to plant a garden, but the fallow ground had to be readied, as did a new potting shed for Henry's saplings, many of which had been damaged en route. However careful the family had been with fragile crockery such as the dishes, there were plenty broken, including the china that had belonged to Alice's mother. There was so much to do that at times Alice operated on spirit alone, her body exhausted with its struggle to breathe. Kindly neighbors welcomed the new refugees.

Throughout the spring, the South kept a wary eye on William Tecumseh Sherman and the three armies in his command—the Cumberland, Ohio, and Tennessee—which were beginning a three-pronged incursion into Georgia.

In smoking ruins, Atlanta surrendered to Sherman on September 2, 1864. Six days later, Sherman issued a statement that all citizens, excepting for his army, should take immediate leave from Atlanta to points either north or south. They must take with them what they could. There must not remain any manufacturers, tradesmen, or Confederate sympathizers. Some days before Sherman's edict, the family of Robert Holliday fled cross-country making their way to Valdosta.

Sherman's claim of smashing his way to the sea was accurate. It was attributed by Sherman himself that to remain long in Atlanta was to invite disaster for his army. Fearing that enemies would learn vital information, Sherman held his own council and set out across the face of Georgia. At first his intention was to repair heavily damaged and destroyed Southern rail lines for Northern service, but the gargantuan task was daunting. At one point, ten thousand men struggled for a week to repair a seven-mile section of track. With railroad repairs unable to keep pace as supply lines, Sherman gave orders for his army to take what they needed from the countryside. The blue locust horde moved and struck at will. Everyone was a target. Possessions, foodstuffs, and property were liberated to feed and clothe Sherman and his soldiers. Night fires stained the black sky orange.

In Valdosta, Henry breathed deeply that his family and his brother's family had arrived safely. Though they were out of the line of fire for the present, all that could suddenly change. Alice tried to rally. When she was able, she taught piano or fancy stitching to several of the neighborhood girls. Theirs was desperation born of the times. Money had never been more plentiful or purchased so little.

On the political scene, Jefferson Davis paid a visit to Macon, Georgia. Henry reflected that it was a way for Davis to assess what was going on in the heartland of the Confederacy. He discounted the rumors of a new Yankee offensive heading towards Richmond as the reason for Davis' visit.

An electrifying speaker, Davis appealed to all Southerners to attend the effort and bring back the light of the Confederacy to the battlefield. For some reason, there were many brave men about and yet the army was unable to get them into uniform. Alice clung to John in that year more fiercely than ever. There was a look in her son's eyes that defied all sense of reason.

"Henry, I know he's going to join the army. He looks old for his size. They'll think him ripe to join the ranks."

"Short of hogtying him to a tree, I don't know how to stop him."

"October has a sullen moon," Alice said as she patted her lips with her handkerchief and prayed for the deliverance of family and country.

For Mattie and John, the mortal danger they faced forged in them a togetherness of spirit that was not meant for adults to comprehend. Family members did not realize that Martha Anne Holliday felt a wondrous blooming of the heart for her first cousin, John, a blooming that would only grow with time. That she was older and of the Catholic faith mattered not at all. Life was too short. She had the witness of a dying Alice.

As far as Mattie could see, John would grow up without his mother who was the loving buffer between him and his father. It was ironic that Henry should wear the face of a good man. Mattie wholeheartedly believed that Henry Holliday was a good man until, in the private bosom of his family, the anger of dreams lost would raise itself to wreak vengeance on John.

"Are you all right?" Mattie asked after she tiptoed into John's bedroom late one night. The adults had retired. The candles were extinguished, and Henry's wrath on John had ceased.

"Mattie?" John whispered.

"It's me. Is your arm bad?"

"Both of them are bruised pretty much."

She found him in the dark. "Damn him. How can he? I don't understand."

So shocked was John, he could utter not a word. Warmth from Mattie's imprecation rolled over his bruised body as a soothing balm.

"He's been that way for years. Especially since he got out of the army. To be truthful, I can tolerate the beatings more than the sarcasm. I think he'll call me 'boy' until the day he dies . . . or until I do."

"Do you want to talk about it? I'm here," she told him in a whisper. Her breath trembled on his cheek and she reached out to clasp his cold hand.

"It's so hard to listen to his voice day and night. He has this sound in his voice when he shouts my name. I never want to hear 'John Henry' again, or 'boy' either. Dunno what else I'd be called. Mother used to get after him, but then she got so sick. Mattie, I'm watching her die the same way the Yankees are coming. What was that?"

The two stopped talking. There was thunder in the distance and a rustling in the trees.

"Is it—is it them? The Yankees?" her hand trembled.

"I can't tell. Canon fire sounds like thunder when it's far off."

"Is your father mean to your mother?"

"He was. I had to . . ." he began.

"Come on, tell me."

"I did a terrible thing, Mattie. He was upset. He's been so angry since he got back. I think he just wanted to be a soldier until he died. Then Tom ran away. I was upset. Mother was coughing. Father had already hit me a couple of times that day. Then he and Mother got into a terrible fight over me. I could hear their voices and he raised his fist over the top of her head. I . . . " John held his breath as the muscles in his stomach quaked.

"It's okay."

"When I saw that, I didn't think. I just grabbed up the shotgun and told him if he struck her, I would fire."

"Oh my." Mattie kissed his cheek. "That was a brave thing to do. No matter what anybody says, it's the bravest thing I've ever heard."

John put his head on her shoulder. "Oh God, Mattie." The words rushed out. He couldn't see her face because of the darkness. He was tingling all over. Their lips met. Horrified, both jumped at the same time and collided. Mattie bounced off of him. John sprawled on the floor.

"Sssh. Sssh." They waited, their hearts thumping hard.

"I better go. I'll see you tomorrow morning."

The next day they pretended that nothing had happened between them, but their relationship had changed. Mattie was no longer a playfellow to John. And John was Mattie's gallant knight. Their pretense was an instinctive armor against the wrath, dismay, and disapproval of the adults.

♣ ♥ ♠ ♦

John didn't want to worry his mother with the constant question, "Are you okay?" But every time he looked at her, his stomach fluttered. The question stuck to the inside of his mouth. The feeling never left him. He heard it in the tunes that his mother played on the piano, in the way she combed her hair, and in the still sureness of her fingers while she sewed. It was a cold feeling. He knew it was death.

Having Mattie at his side for that short period of time meant the world to him. He was going to marry her, he decided. He would build her a fine house and make sure she had all the things that she wanted. He pictured himself a man of means, in his frock coat and hat, departing in the morning for his profession and coming home at night to Mattie waiting for him with a kiss.

"Dammit, John Henry, get your tail out here. Dammit, where are you, boy?"

"Coming," John shouted back. One day he promised he would no longer answer to his father at all.

Valdosta offered sanctuary to the many souls fleeing from Sherman's army and from the burning and looting that was making children orphans and the elderly homeless. There were many Georgians on the road after the army passed. Farms were gutted and animals were slaughtered. The forests, once rich with game and birds, were startlingly quiet.

The government in Richmond printed more money, but it bought nothing. Factories ceased production because there were no more parts for machinery. The Confederate Army did without and downsized all rations. In the North, Lincoln was nominated for a second term. Although the nomination was deemed official, Southerners held the faint hope that he would be defeated.

"Perhaps then," it was argued, "we would have a chance. Perhaps if someone else took the reins it would be better."

On November 7, that hope was dashed. Desertions in the Confederacy had become so commonplace that no one was able to stop them. Fathers, sons, and brothers wanted to get home to their families or to desperately search in the direction that their families had fled. Jefferson Davis did not condemn them. The troops had given everything, including their lives to this faltering dream and could give no more. They could give no more trust, because their trust was as worn out as the shoes on their feet. Fancy words could not replace spilled blood or limbs that had to be sawed off with dull saws and without a drop of anesthetic.

It was hard with the wartime misery to make a place for Christmas gaiety, but the Hollidays did what they could to bring the peace of the day to their household.

January 15, 1865 saw the fall of Fort Fisher in North Carolina. In mid-February, the communication trickled out that the burning of cotton, tobacco, and other goods in Richmond was the action to be carried out. This had to be accomplished before the enemy could seize the city's commodities. On April 3, 1865, the call was made to evacuate Richmond. Although parts of the city were already in flames, two battalions were sent to stop mob violence and the ransacking of the city.

The articles of surrender were enacted at Appomattox, Virginia on April 10, 1865. John, upon hearing that General Lee had surrendered, ran from the house. He felt a great trembling under his feet but then realized that it was he who was trembling. Surrender to the Union meant the end of the South.

Henry orated that Lincoln would wreak havoc on all Southern states. John, confused by the swiftness of events, was rendered speechless by Lincoln's assassination. In the days that followed, Robert Holliday arrived in Valdosta to reclaim his family. Shattered, John was left in a silent house in an even more silent countryside. The quiet was worse at night when he remembered how he and Mattie had held hands, stolen kisses, and made promises.

"You'll probably forget all about me," Mattie had told him before leaving. "Someone with red hair will steal your heart from me."

"That," John reassured her, "will never come about."

Alice worsened. There were no cures, the doctor told her, and still no hope for recovery. A new copy of *The Lancet* yielded little help by way of nostrums or soothing potions. When Alice could stand the pain no longer, she acquiesced to doses of laudanum.

John went through the motions of daily life and pretended gladness for his mother's sake. He bit his tongue when his father's words were cruel and tried to become immune to the physical punishment. It was easier each time to mentally extract to the long ago hiding place of his childhood. This irked Henry, but also bothered him. John's eyes would glaze over with a blue deadness, as if John wasn't in there at all.

Henry allowed himself little time to reflect on the sadness of his home. Acres had to be managed and, with the war ended, some semblance of order had to be maintained. But the past tugged at him. In his dreams, he marched and fought. When he awoke, he was staggered anew by what lay ahead and what had to be done.

Life in the household was a struggle as mother, father, and son tried to cope with war and illness.

"It soothes me to hear John play," Alice told Henry one evening, thus getting around her husband's insistence that John not play the piano at all. Grumbling, Henry acquiesced and found chores to do in his potting shed while John played for his mother. In this way, Alice had free rein to correct her son's technique or to speak on subjects not intended for Henry's ears.

John treasured those quiet evenings with her. In the candle glow, he remembered the younger woman of his childhood, the one who had dried his tears and sung him to sleep. Alice had white hair now and, though she kept most of it under a cap, small tendrils would slide out to curl becomingly against her cheek.

"Your father is out in the field. We are alone. I want to know about Mattie."

John's fingers crashed on the keys. "What?" he asked so faintly, Alice had to lean forward.

"Mattie and you."

He could only stammer, "How?"

"If it is so, tell me. I have seen the look between you," Alice prompted.

John turned on the piano bench. "Yes, very much."

"It will be difficult. Your uncle's family is Catholic. Mattie is two years older than you are. Her people will be after her to marry someone of their faith and someone of means."

"I know that."

"You are fourteen."

"I know that. I also know that my father thinks of me as a boy and he's liable to most of my life. I'm never going to please him, Mother. There will always be something that he hates in me or finds fault with."

"You have your father's chin. I know that once you set your mind on a course of action, nothing sways you."

"I know she's most sixteen. Some women her age are already married."

"This could be puppy love."

"I know what's in my heart. Are you going tell on me, Mother?"

He looked so very young and old at the same time. His eyes were beseeching.

The shadows from the lamp flickered across her face. For a brief moment, John saw a heavier shadow about his mother. In a puff of breeze that ruffled the air, the shadow was gone. "I won't give your secret away," Alice said. "Cross my heart."

Mattie wrote long letters in her spidery writing as fine as the cameo necklace that John sent her. Her letters were cherished, but he was careful to burn each one. He could ill afford to have his father stumble across them.

With a gasp, turbulent 1865 ended at last. Like a heavy weight, the portents of the New Year and his mother's health settled about John's shoulders. Henry looked to him as never before for chores that had to be done and decisions that had to be made. Henry wasn't sure what his son needed, so he took Alice's word. By April, Alice had little to say. Coughing had strangled her breath and captured her words. Her needle fell silent, as did the piano except for rare occasions when a burst of noise would flood the house with merry tunes only to cease as if the noise was too much to bear.

John watched her cough and writhed inwardly. He brought her fresh handkerchiefs and washed the soiled ones, fed her shots of whiskey and laudanum, and went to school. Coming home meant starting the process all over. He shared no confidences with her unless she asked, because her daily struggle for air was all she could muster. He would have gladly traded his healthy lungs to her if possible.

Time measured itself in heartbeats instead of seconds and in the ticks of the clock that echoed the gasping of her frantic lungs. The very air smelled of a cloying odor that permeated the fabric of the house like dry rot. For once, Henry's gruff and grumble was silent. He no longer bellowed when he came through the door at day's end, and found many reasons to stay in the house during the time he would have normally been in the fields.

Alice was serene.

"Raging never gets you anyplace," she hoarsely explained to John after a coughing fit. "It just wears you out."

She kept her Bible by the bed and a picture of her mother. Other items were placed just within reach. The room was nice, she said, because from it she could see John going off to school and Henry walking in the fields. John made certain that there were always fresh flowers in the room for her.

Alice coughed and the clock ticked. When she spoke harshly to him, in a way that she had never done before, John accepted it without a word. In time, there was anger. John struggled with the impulse to leave but feared if he left that she might hurt herself. He could see on her face that she loathed for him to see her this way, but he felt compelled to remain if only to plump the pillows. On her good days, he recited his lessons until she signaled that she could listen to them no more.

Visitors tired Alice, but she never sent any away. All of it came as a struggle to be normal. On John's fifteenth birthday, she made him a cake and sang one of his favorite songs. As the final notes died away, she coughed until her eyes filled with tears and then hid her mouth in a handkerchief. John helped her to bed and told her it was the best birthday he'd ever had and about the letter he'd received from Mattie. His mother's eyes were closed though, and he watched the tremulous rise and fall of her chest. Turning quietly, he headed towards the door.

"Come over here."

"Oh, Mother, I thought you were asleep."

Her chuckle came with a soft rasp.

"You and Mattie are in love."

"Yes, yes, we are."

"Then," her voice sank very low, "don't let your father or anyone come between you. You be happy with Mattie. Whatever happens, I'll know. I give my blessing."

"I promise," John whispered.

On September 16, 1866, Alice Jane Holliday passed away. With her death, John's spirit shattered. It seemed as if his mother should be in the next room. At night, the piano echoed through the house awakening him with familiar refrains. He smelled the light floral scent she had worn and heard the rustle of her skirt. But she wasn't there.

He thought if he could shout, then in that place where his mother was, she would hear him and return. This tenuous and terrible barrier, however, lay between them. For weeks, John went by in a daze, unseeing of the family and friends who offered solace that did not register.

Mechanically, John attended school, did his chores, and helped Henry around the house. Henry, grieving in his own way, gave John little in the way of comfort. For a while, a woman from the village nearby came to clean and fix meals, but by then the many Holliday female relations, sympathizing with Henry's plight, rallied to do the same. They all had suggestions for John. They all spoke of Alice's love for the church, thinking that would comfort him. None of it helped. John found it hard enough to get up in the morning, much less to get through the day. Inside him was a heaviness that squeezed his chest. He was frozen in time with no will to move. There was no urgency to get on with his life.

Whatever Henry thought or felt he kept to himself, as isolated as his son. Alice had been his only contact with John, whom he had never understood. Now that John was fifteen, Henry was at a loss. It was his strong opinion that teenage boys needed a mother. Life had presented him with few options. Without mentioning the possibility to John, Henry made up his mind. He would marry again and quickly. There was on the adjoining property a woman of marriageable age, only eight years John's senior, but she was sufficient. On December 18, 1866, Henry married Rachel Martin.

Chapter FIVE

Henry Burroughs Holliday was forty-seven years of age when he took red-haired twenty-three-year-old Rachel Martin as his bride. Rachel's father was glad for such a fine man as Henry in which to place his daughter's hand. For months, Rachel had been an acquaintance of the Hollidays as the two farms were adjoining. She found them to be sociable people who cherished the virtues of family and industry. She saw little of Alice. John Henry, more somber of face than was usual for a boy of fifteen years, sometimes waved to her on his way to school. After Alice's death in September, John waved no more.

Not long after Alice Holliday's death, Stephen approached his daughter on the subject of marriage. Rachel had been dreading the subject. Her grief over the death of her beloved William on the field of Gettysburg was still raw. She thought Henry was too old and she understood in a way that her father did not that young John would feel resentment toward another woman taking the place of his mother.

Although she had not been on intimate terms with Alice, Rachel felt sorrow at her passing. There were so many passings. Although her heart was filled with the anguish of losing William, Southern society and her father dictated her actions. Rachel tried to see in Henry the same qualities that her parents told her were of high import. Henry was a solicitous suitor, always presenting her with flowers or small knick-knacks that he picked up in Valdosta. He spoke of moving into the town so that she would be closer to all the things and people to which she was accustomed. He took her on buggy rides and was deferential to her father in all things.

If there was any awkwardness, it was Henry's silence on the subject of his son. Rachel longed to ask about John, but the hard set of Henry's lips at the mention of such a subject silenced her. The courtship was brief, as were many of that time.

Christmas was approaching and Henry decided that the wedding should occur one week before. The household was made festive with decorations of tinsel and green garlands trimmed with plaid bows. Rachel, dressed in her grandmother's spider-lace wedding dress, said a silent goodbye to her William and became Mrs. Henry Holliday.

"Really, it's for the best," her father whispered to her as he placed her hand in Henry's.

The subject of John was no longer taboo. Indeed, once married, Henry acted as if Rachel should know how to deal with his recalcitrant son. It was clear to Rachel that John wanted no part of her or his father. Henry's tactic was to deal swiftly and harshly. Rachel bided her time. John would either come to trust her or he would not.

At Henry's urging, the family soon moved within the town limits of Valdosta on East Savannah Street. Since her father had owned the house into which they moved, Rachel was already acquainted with the niceties of living in town. At the time of the move, expanding Valdosta had over 250 residents. As the county seat, Valdosta boasted a business district of note with a courthouse and a rail line that connected to Savannah.

Settling into her new home, Rachel took pleasure in planting flower beds and an herbal garden, while Henry began to work hard on developing a hardy species of pecan tree. In the unfamiliar household that had been decorated by his new stepmother, John was too outraged to feel anything. It was easy to bury himself in his studies. John continued to excel in the precise language of Latin and let the mental rigors of algebra absorb his energy.

Gradually, as his passion subsided, cold logic took its place. The boy was certain that Henry had committed a mortal sin, marrying from no rational decision but pure animal lust. All the while, the image of his dying mother played endlessly like old church hymns, beginning and then repeating the refrains. A letter that his mother had left him went unread for months. The pastor of his parents' church tried to reach out to him, but John would have none of it. A higher power would have had the compassion to intervene. There had been no celestial intervention on his mother's behalf.

Often John recalled his mother's face and how peaceful she looked at her death. Sometimes, however, a film of gossamer would sweep across his mind and blur the images. At those times, John would panic. He had begun to take long walks when the anger claimed him and would run to a quiet field where he thought no one could see or hear him. From there he would scream his frustration into the wind.

The boy understood that his aunts and uncles meant to offer solace when they clucked over him, but their attention failed to reach his pain. So detached was John that his relatives seemed mere dots on a landscape. His father, too, had gone to a distant land, to that red-haired woman that he had taken as a replacement for Alice Jane Holliday. Reckless in his grief, John baited his father.

"I suppose," he said one morning at breakfast, "that you had an affair with her while my mother was ill. You couldn't wait, could you?"

True to form, Henry hit his son with a doubled fist that sent John crashing to the floor. Rachel froze with a platter of eggs in her hand. Hurriedly, she put the platter down and started to kneel by John.

"Don't," John mouthed savagely to her, "just don't. You people make me sick. Especially you, Father. I hate you. For as long as I live, I'll hate you." John's words ground from between his clenched teeth. His cheek bore a bruise from which blood trickled.

White-faced, Henry stared down at him. John got up and dusted himself off. "I'm sorry you weren't killed in the war." He stalked from the room and out the front door.

It seemed that there was nowhere to turn for comfort. He knew that if he asked to spend time at his uncle's home in Jonesboro, Henry would question the request. Lost, John looked towards the blood-red horizon and wondered if that was the place his mother had gone. What would his mother do in such a situation? If his father hadn't remarried, would it have made any difference? He almost pitied Rachel for having stepped into the middle of their battlefield.

Although Rachel's twenty-three years made her old by Southern standards, she was barely older than her stepson. Now in his teens, John understood how the dictates of a rigid society and the Martin family would view a recently widowed war veteran such as Henry. Moreover, Henry was a landowner. Though the acreage might be small, it meant that Henry Holliday was self-sufficient enough to support a family and heirs such as Rachel could now produce. John knew how badly his father hungered for male heirs to whom to pass the precious lineage of the Hollidays onto the next generation. This excluded him, the puny weakling called John Henry who took after the deceased Alice McKey.

All he could do, John concluded, was study hard enough to enter a profession and make a life as far from his father as possible. He was irrevocably alone. He trudged back to the house. With each step, the red Georgia clay sucked at his soul.

Henry said to John after he came inside, "You need a little different scenery. You pretty much took care of your mother when she was failing. Rachel thinks that you need to get away for awhile. Your grades are a cut above excellent, and your Uncle Robert and Aunt Mary can hear you recite them just as good as anybody. We can leave straightaway."

"Just like that," John snapped his fingers, "as if I have no say in the matter?"

"You hurry up now and pack. The horses are fresh. It's about 218 miles from here to Jonesboro, so it'll take a couple of days to get there. I'd put you on the train, but aside from the line to Savannah, there's too much danger for a boy alone."

"And you can't wait?"

The two regarded each other. John knew that he would never be able to look his father in the eye. His father's height had diminished. Of late there was a constant tic above the older man's right eye while the florid muscles below had softened. Before the war, Henry's brown hair had been thick and wavy, always well kept. As he stood before his son, there was a stoop to his shoulders and his gray locks were thinning.

"Go ahead and hit me. Maybe you'll be lucky this time and it'll kill me."

"John," Rachel's voice cut the air between them, "come eat your breakfast. Come back and eat." She tentatively patted his arm and, when he didn't fling her hand away, she pressed it kindly. "There's coffee, too. I drank coffee when I was your age. I made you a fresh batch."

John crept to his place at the table and sank into the chair. Rachel fixed him a plate and he devoured everything that was placed in front of him.

"I understand your aunt and uncle live in Jonesboro. I've never been there, but I understand it's a nice place."

John didn't hate her for trying. He packed in silence, barely hearing his father stumping around the house. Henry was hurriedly packing his saddlebag with canned peaches and strawberry preserves for his brother's family, but looked up when his son joined him outside.

"I didn't want Rachel to get a chill on the road. It's much too dangerous for her to travel. Most likely her father will stay with her. I confess that I'm not anxious to see the sights north of here. You need to brace yourself, too, boy."

Rage towards his father lasted for half a day. By then, a much greater anger took hold of him. Once great houses that had risen sublime and steadfast from the Georgia clay were bleak and fire-gutted caverns. John tried to hunker down on the back of his horse to shut out the sights, but the smell of smoldering decay was too livid. For the cities in the direct path of Sherman's army, the destruction had been worse. From his father's agonized expression, John realized that he was not alone in his outrage.

The two had ridden for almost a day and a half before the realization struck John that this was the first time in years that he had ever really been alone with his father. After his mother had died, Henry had been reticent and quick to anger. John had fumed in silence. The anger had kept him from noticing that his father was an excellent rider and horseman. When the horses were tired, Henry would ask John to dismount and loosen the girth on his saddle. If there was a bit of sweet grass to be had, the animals got a fair taste.

Although the Georgia countryside showed battle scarring in daylight, at dusk a creeping somnolence obliterated the visage of destruction. Henry had warned his son that wild game would be scarce, however this evening had seen the snaring of a rabbit. The animal was lean, but it meant a hardier meal than the hardtack and coffee that Henry had packed for the trip. While Henry made ready the fire, he watched his son's technique at skinning the rabbit. While John nervously skinned the rabbit, he struggled to think of something he could talk to his father about that would command Henry's attention without arousing his temper.

"Not bad at all," Henry said.

John nicked himself with the knife blade. "Oh," he replied, gripping the handle with a tighter grasp. "I, uh heard something in town the other day about that racehorse, Lexington; thought you might like to hear it."

"Tell on, boy," a small smile had warmed his father's lips.

"Well," John's face glowed, "well, sir, I heard about that stallion Lexington. His two colts, Asteroid and Norfolk, are supposed to be a real treat."

"I suppose for some," Henry drawled as he took out his pipe and filled it, "that there is some merit. But I still favor their pappy, the bay. Damn, I love a blood bay horse. They prance with black manes and tails a-flyin'. A man would look right good sitting on such a mount. Poor ol' Lexington's goin' blind though. Boston, his sire, was stone blind, too."

The glow remained with John long after the rabbit had been eaten. It was painfully hard, but he marveled that he could still talk to his father. If only Henry would remember that in the morning light.

By daylight, Henry stood ramrod straight and curtly issued orders. John obeyed. Breakfast was a cup of hot coffee and more hardtack.

"I know it seems meager, but I'm trying to save the other victuals for your uncle's family. I know we can make do with this.

When we were on the front, we dunked the hard tack in the coffee, you know, to soften it."

John tried and then made a wry face. "Oh ugh. It doesn't help."

Henry let out a bark of laughter. "Nope, but it does flavor the coffee a peck."

By the time they reached Jonesboro, silence had fallen between the two again.

"Oh my, you've grown," Mary Holliday replied as she scooped John towards her in a wiry grasp. "I've made lemonade. Go get yourself some. I put it on the sideboard in the parlor." Before John could respond, Aunt Mary put her arm through his and walked him out of the room. "There are vanilla cookies to go with that lemonade. You have yourself a goodly handful."

"Those were always my favorite," John gulped. He thought his aunt would leave him to return to the parlor, but he was wrong. Mary made no move to rejoin her husband or Henry and set about playing hostess. John looked at the neat rows of books placed along the shelves. In the light, the old wood gleamed.

"We've got Greek and Latin books here. I'll be glad to hear you recite your lessons."

John longed to stay, munch the cookies, and look at the books. Henry, however, would be wrathful as a meat axe if he were to dawdle. Discreetly pocketing a handful of the vanilla cookies, he followed his aunt back to the parlor.

The boy poked about the daguerreotypes of relatives that adorned the mantle. He found one of his mother. John's fingers quivered as he lightly touched the frame. Currier and Ives prints were hung on the wall while starched and yellowed lace doilies hid the threadbare furniture. On the floor was a remnant of a store-bought carpet kept scrupulously clean. But it was the smell of camphor from the carpet, the warm, just-baked vanilla scent from the cookies, and the whiff of lavender on his aunt's cheek that made John suddenly long for his mother.

Aunt Mary had stopped talking. "John?"

"I'm sorry, ma'am. I, uh, guess I wasn't paying attention."

The wrinkles around her eyes deepened. "Well, I do run on sometimes. Bring your cookies and get some of that lemonade. I'll show you where you'll be staying. Mattie should be home shortly. She can take you around."

It was a welcoming room. Hazy sunshine poured through the old lace curtains, and the tall bushes outside bloomed with frothy pink and white flowers. A blue and white coverlet on the bed provided cheerful color. The armoire already contained clothes, but there was adequate space for him to unpack.

As he put his clothes away, the vivid images of his ride northward blurred his vision. Christians would not have destroyed the very roofs over the heads of women and children or driven sick people into the rain. He sat on the comfortable bed and finished the lemonade and cookies.

"John?" Mattie's voice sounded at the door.

"Oh, Mattie." He said it like a benediction.

Mattie's face beamed. "Hi!"

"Hi, yourself."

"I'm so glad you're here." Her eyes took note of the livid bruise on his cheek, but she made no mention of it.

Her dress was a simple one, brown and trimmed with lace on the collar and sleeves. Mattie's hair matched her dress. John's throat caught for an instant as he imagined holding a jar of honey against the sun. Mattie's hair was the same finely spun color. Awkwardly, he held out his rough-knuckled hand.

"Don't be so formal, silly." She launched a kiss at his cheek, which fell lightly on the bruise. "Let me show you around."

"You're going to graduate this year."

"Oh, yes, finally. I thought that it would take forever. And you, John Holliday, I hear you have learned Greek."

"Alas," he told her striking a pose. "I have, forsooth, learned some of that fair speech. Would that I could converse with you a while."

Mattie's laugh was infectious. In the parlor, the adults smiled to one another.

"See Henry, he just needs time," Mary told him. "You'll stay for dinner and the night? We've hardly seen you since the funeral."

"No, I can't stay. I think it will be better if I depart soon. I don't want to leave Rachel alone too long. With the muddy roads, I don't know how long it will take me to get back. Thanks for the offer, though."

John watched his father leave and breathed a sigh of relief. "Mattie, are you sure it's going to be okay for me to stay?"

"Why not? We love family. Which is obvious since there are so many of us."

"I know. I know what happened in the war, too. I know Uncle Robert has been ill. I know your place was burned. Did you know that my father never asked me if I wanted to come here, even though I did want to and—"

Mattie put her fingertips to his lips. "I understand. It's been hard. The church helped us when we lost everything. Father didn't want any part of it at first, but he relented. There are so many mouths to feed and there are so many cares."

"But I'm here and—"

"Shhh, John, it's okay. You're family. And," she looked around, "we're going to have our own family one day."

"You haven't forgotten?"

"No. I keep it close to me when the times get very hard."

"And the times have been hard. Who knows what will happen or what President Johnson will do."

"They've been trying to rebuild the railroad. They are rebuilding everywhere I guess. But how can peoples' lives be rebuilt? The men that were killed can never be brought back. Those thousands of men and boys are gone forever. Father's business was wrecked. He worries about paying the taxes. He worries about us. And you have no mother now."

"I have a stepmother." John didn't realize the harsh lines that creased his face until Mattie reached over and smoothed them away.

"He was wrong to do that."

"You know what I miss the most? Holding hands in the dark." He leaned towards her.

"I miss that so very much."

"You've grown up."

Mattie blushed. "As you."

"Aunt Mary is going to listen to my lessons."

"She knows that your mother did that."

"I'm tired."

"I'll tuck you in."

"I want to lie down for just a little while," he told her. "Just for a moment."

"I'll make sure that you eat."

John kicked off his shoes and Mattie covered him with the coverlet. "Your mother made this for mine one Christmas," she told him and kissed his forehead. He was asleep as soon as his head touched the pillow.

He knew Mattie so well. He loved her so well. She was the part of him that was missing. If anyone found out, Mattie would be sent away. No one must ever find out.

John and Mattie made their pact. She would finish school. He would go to college.

"Do you know what you want, John?" she asked.

For a moment he looked into the distance and then his eyes focused on her lips. "I'm going to become a dentist. That way, no matter where we are, my profession can go with us. Even if the Yankees return to burn the South, we will have a life."

"You'll make a fine dentist," she said and then she kissed him.

Their time together passed quickly. Soon John returned to Valdosta. The glow from the trip disappeared with his first footfall into the house. The small piano that had been Alice's pride was gone. John remembered how the small instrument had been the first thing he would see upon coming home from school. His heavy heart compelled him to stop, but his legs kept on walking out the back door of the house to his waiting chores. He must never question his father or offer words of recrimination. Henry would not tolerate either.

That evening after the candles were lit, Rachel tapped on his door. She kept her voice very low and shielded the candle with her hand. "Henry's eyes are everywhere. I kept him from removing some things. I know it's not much."

"If he could get rid of me as easily as he got rid of my mother's things, he would."

Rachel pressed his mother's hymnal and locket into his hand and then blew out the candle.

"Rachel," Henry's garrulous voice sounded from the kitchen, "are you coming?"

"I'm coming," she called back.

"Have you thought, boy, about what you're going to do for a career?" Henry asked after breakfast the next morning. Since Henry so seldom asked him anything, the question took him by surprise.

"I had thought to go to dental school."

"Really? And when, pray tell, had you this miraculous thought?"

"Since the Yankees, Father, took everyone's land and burned their homes. The Yankees want nothing more than to come back and destroy us all over again. Possessions and property can be seized or burned. A dental profession I can take with me."

"Quite sensible. Yes, sensible indeed. I'll do some looking into that."

As John grew out of his middle teen years, Henry began in earnest to stress the kind of woman that he wanted his son to marry. Henry's words were soon a litany. "She must be socially and religiously acceptable, with a Presbyterian or traditional Christian education."

Henry's definition of the word traditional meant Southern tradition and following in his footsteps as he had followed his father. The older man believed that marriage to traditional Southern women not only insured a stable family and home, but propagated the very foundation of what it meant to be Southern.

"Just as I want you to marry a good Presbyterian woman, so your Uncle Robert wants his girls to marry good Catholic men. Robert has his heart set on Martha Anne marrying into one of the prominent families near Jonesboro." The blood slowly drained from John's face at his father's words, but he held his gaze. The thought of Mattie being married to someone else spurred John into a deeper application of his studies, lest that become a stumbling block against entering dental school. Henry's strict eyes missed nothing. John knew that his father didn't trust him and, if truth were known, while professing a stern love towards his only son, he liked and respected him not at all.

John had known this from an early age when he had begun to emulate his mother. Henry had found communication difficult with both son and wife. Indeed, there were times when Henry had grown so frustrated that he had quit the house for long rides or walks into the fields. John, for his part, and only in letters to Mattie, confessed that he was afraid of his father.

"With good reason. He's used his fists on you often enough," she had written.

Each letter that John received from Mattie, he memorized then burned. The two longed to be together, but they realized their feelings were a wildfire that would scorch their families. John could think of nothing worse than Mattie pregnant, himself unemployed, and of the consequences that would surely follow. By the same token, he yearned to share his life with her.

Henry raged when John failed to show any interest in women. Secretly John laughed that the biggest joke of all was the ultimate insult to his father. Rachel realized what was going on, but she refused to let on. John's admiration increased with her silence.

Stolen moments with Mattie were cherished because of their rarity, as were the precious letters. Mattie was his only living relative to understand how lonely and out of place he felt.

"I have all these people," he wrote to her, "and I'm not a part of any of them."

When Mattie graduated from school, John sent her a cameo pendant, one of the few remaining pieces of jewelry that had belonged to Alice. "It would please her," he wrote, "to know that you have this. Keep it as a token of my love."

She did so.

≍ Chapter ≍
SIX

As Valdosta grew, educational institutes strained to keep pace. By 1865, it became evident that the town needed a new school. A fine schoolmaster was chosen to head the new institution. As a further enticement, a building was refurbished for classrooms and renamed Varnedoe Institute. The new headmaster found his duties exhausting, but he was up to the challenge.

John had been one of schoolmaster's first pupils when the Institute opened in 1865. The older man had developed an affection for the towheaded youth who was serious to a fault. Over time, he grew used to seeing John's face in the third row on the left. The wooden desk was kept in immaculate condition. The ink well was always full, and his books were ordered into tidy piles with neither a page bent nor a spine broken.

The man could see how Alice Holliday's death had changed young John. Everyone dismissed the boy's reticence or, like Henry, overlooked it altogether. The schoolmaster knew well that the wound needed to be addressed, but speaking to Henry about such a subject called for finesse.

At last, he could see no other way for it and sent a note home to Henry. "I must speak to you of John's future. Please meet me at four o'clock tomorrow afternoon at the institute. Sincerely."

It had been some time since the two men had seen each other, except at church functions. He was distressed to see the iron set to Henry's jaw and the harsh furrows that had knitted the swarthy skin of the man's forehead like moldy, dried out leather.

The older man cleared his throat. "Henry, I'm so glad that you were able to come by."

"What's the scamp done? If I find out that he's caused any trouble, I'll hide him until he can't sit down."

The headmaster gave pause. He had known from the start that Henry beat John many times for no good reason. "Oh heavens, Henry, the boy's no trouble. Never has been. He's mindful of his lessons and is one of my most scholarly pupils."

Henry's balled fists slowly relaxed. "Well then, what is it?"

"I've been a bit worried about John since his mother died."

"Oh, that. The boy'll get over it. I see that he stays busy. He doesn't dawdle at home."

"Henry, aren't you worried about him?"

Henry threw his head back and let out a short bark that sounded like laughter, but wasn't. "I think that my son is fine, and I think that you're too concerned about the matter." With a nod towards the headmaster, Henry walked away. The matter was never spoken of again. John never spoke of it either, although, sometimes the schoolmaster could see the dismay on the boy's face.

Advanced subjects such as oratory and rhetoric, which Henry grumbled that his son learned too well, took the place of penmanship and English. John, knowing that dental school was on the horizon, approached his teacher about the necessity of studying higher math.

"I'm not sure what I will need."

"Algebra most assuredly. Perhaps calculus and, of course, anatomy courses. I do have some calculus books that I will let you borrow. You will need a preceptor. If you like, I will inquire to see if one of the local dentists might be willing to assist you."

A local dentist by the name of Dr. Lucian Frederick Frink had a competent practice and, upon hearing of young John Holliday's desire to attend dental school, agreed to help him.

There was a frightening amount to learn in the way of chemistry, but John doggedly persevered. As he grew more familiar with the dentist's routine, John was allowed to watch while Dr. Frink prepared the alloys and mixed the chemicals used in the making of dentures.

If Henry held any reservations about his boy's choice of profession, he did not say. Henry's dream of having John follow in his footsteps took a long time to die. Worse, the boy continued to show no interest in the young Presbyterian women that Henry aimed in his direction. John dutifully attended the teas, cotillions, and parties. He spoke charmingly to the young ladies as well as squiring them about with their chaperones. However, there was no spark in his eye. John's half-hearted courting left the older man totally demoralized.

At last he muttered to John, "I can't see how dental school will be such a bad thing. Maybe it'll be the making of you yet, boy."

John ground his teeth and shook his father's hand. He stayed in Georgia for a while longer, because in some respects, John felt that if he did leave for Philadelphia, he would never again be welcomed to that green place known as Georgia. In the end, his father made it easy. He said, "Get out. You're not being useful."

♣ ♥ ♠ ♦

By 1870, the fee structure for the Pennsylvania College of Dental Surgery in Philadelphia, while expensive, was not unduly so. Because Henry's practicality about finance could have made him balk at the cost of funding a full course of study, Dr. Frink earnestly spoke on John's behalf.

"Really, sir, the one hundred dollars will be a well met investment. Young John needs to have the option to study several courses. The five-dollar matriculation fee is paid but once, and the diploma will be thirty dollars. Used books are as sound as new ones, and the college does furnish the extraction tools. He'll have some other fees for the purchase of suitable dental tools and a nearby boardinghouse for meals and sleeping. You'll not have any cause for worry. I assure you." Because the words came from Dr. Frink, Henry acquiesced.

Although November 1, 1870 marked the official beginning of the fifteenth session of the school, the laboratory and dispensary were opened two months earlier. By the first week of October, John, along with sixty-five others, was already well ensconced in his studies.

At first glance, with the rigors of an academic life surrounding him, it seemed that there would be scant time to look around Philadelphia. Although the whitewashed boardinghouse where he slept was not far from the dental school, everything else, if one was willing to walk, was within a tolerable distance.

Free hours on Sunday meant time to walk about the beautiful parks that surrounded the Schuylkill River. The smells were different from Georgia. From the river's bend came the scent of pine tar, of manufacture, of leather, and bustling civilization. He was puzzled by the earthy way that the city called to him, so unlike the somnolence of Georgia.

From November until the following March, eighteen weekly lectures on a variety of subjects were delivered to the toiling students. Chemistry was taught by T.L. Buckingham, MD, DDS, and the department chairman. The course considered all aspects of chemical elements, the physical laws and properties of compounds, and technical nomenclature. Experiments demonstrating the physical properties of elements were included.

G.T. Barker, M.D, DDS, was the chair for dental pathology, materia medica, and therapeutics. His instruction emphasized that dental and general pathology together had far reaching consequences on other organs and parts of the body. Instruction was also given on the application of therapeutic agents to erase tooth disease.

Dental histology and operative dentistry taught the comparative anatomy of the teeth, as well as the functions and microscopical peculiarities of dental organs. Through his lectures and experiments, James Truman, DDS, fully demonstrated the materials and instruments used in operative dentistry, including a detailed description of the microscope, its use, and the proper preparation of specimens.

As the chair for physiology and microscopic anatomy, Professor James Tyson instructed the students on human physiology, histology, and physiological chemistry. There were ample illustrations, vivisections, and chemical and physiological experiments.

E. Wildman, MD, DDS, was the department head for mechanical dentistry and metallurgy. Students in his class learned the correct use of dental tools, how to work with precious metals, and how to combine base alloys for the making of porcelain teeth.

J. Ewing Mears, the chairman for anatomy and surgery, placed emphasis on oral surgery and the anatomy of the neck and head. Models, drawings, diagrams, and the dissection of cadavers were utilized. Under his guidance, a special surgical clinic pertaining to diseases of the mouth was made available every Wednesday from ten o'clock to noon.

Of all the professors, Dr. Mears' dedication towards science and its application had the most impact on John. It took several months before John felt safe to inhale around the cadavers. No prior warning was issued that vivisection was going to be part of the day's demonstration or that the students upon entering the lab would come face to face with trays of cadavers. Most of the class, including John, abruptly quit the lab. Dr. Mears' directive of "all queasiness will soon pass" was drowned out by the sound of retching outside in the gleaming hallway. By the time the students had taken their proper places in the lecture hall, they found Dr. Mears with his unruffled demeanor still standing behind his desk. He gave a meticulous lecture on surgery and then assigned two students to each cadaver.

Louis Lyon grinned crookedly over the corpse to which he and John had been assigned. "What striking figures we cut, hey? If only the girls could see us now."

"Only you, Louis, could find humor in this," John retorted.

"The grotesque and science, John, they go together," Louis said.

After a while the smells became less important, even the rank smell of death that accompanied the cadavers. John had to reconcile himself to the odor. That same smell had hovered about the wisp of his mother's body, and in the later days of her illness, she was never without a scented handkerchief. As the disease progressed, the odor became more marked. John remembered that sometimes he had had to fight with himself not to recoil when he hugged her. A mouth riddled with disease and tooth decay had the same cloying odor.

In the quest for learning, there were casualties. Sometimes a student could not grasp the necessary skill of vivisection or of the physiological nature of chemistry or physics. There were sometimes abrupt departures in the middle of the night from young men too humiliated to say goodbye to fellow classmates and admit their failure. The next day, a brief mention would be made as to the emptiness of the assigned chair: "Mr. Warner will not be continuing."

John never ceased to get a flutter in his stomach over such announcements. He became adept at seeing which students were at risk. It was all in the eyes, the desperate glint in the dilated pupil that soon became forgetfulness in class, despair in appearance, and then the empty chair. There was little time to feel regret. John determined that he must continue no matter what.

The school day was divided into sections, four hours being devoted to the applied skills in the operative and mechanical departments.

Edwin T. Darby, DDS, was the competent and patient demonstrator in the operative department. On him fell the responsibility of making sure that adequate lighting and special tools were available to all students. It was expected for the student to have his own set of instruments, except for forceps. These instruments had to be kept in the exact order stipulated by the demonstrator and returned to an assigned locked drawer after use. In this manner, all students gained a practical surgical experience, as well as good clinical skills.

J.M. Barstow, DDS, was the demonstrator for the mechanical department. Under his tutelage, students learned all the applications that were necessary in the preparation of artificial teeth. This included taking impressions of the mouth, constructing artificial appliances, and then the fitting of the appliances to the patient's mouth. Again, the students had to furnish their own tools and were given a locked drawer in which to keep them.

Knowledge of how to wield the tools required practice and tenacity. With the clear memories of his mother's instruction on learning the piano, John again began to undertake the exercises that would stretch the muscles in his hands and fingers. Wielding the instruments required finesse and a strong grip.

Medicinal materials and compounds were carefully stored in locked cabinets. John was already familiar with some of the compounds such as tinctura opii also known as laudanum. He had hated the reddish-brown liquid that he had given his mother. But now, he was forced to admit that there were some clinical uses for it. Calomel had also been an old enemy of his dying mother. The light-buff colored powder's purgative had succeeded in purging everything in Alice except the disease in her lungs.

John would trundle about with *Grey's Anatomy*, *Kirke's Physiology*, and *Heath on the Injuries and Diseases of the Jaw* under his arm. At night, the paragraphs swam in his brain. The models and diagrams crowded his dreams. His thesis, "Diseases of the Teeth," would have to be defended in front of the faculty. And a patient had to be obtained upon whom John could perform all necessary dental operations. Afterwards, the patient had to be brought before the quite formidable Dr. Mears. In addition, John had to choose a patient needing artificial work. Upon this patient must be performed all the steps of mouth restoration from taking the impressions of the mouth to the fitting of dentures. This patient had to be brought before Professor Wildman, the department head of mechanical dentistry. To further clarify the rules, only the operations performed within the college building were recognized as legitimate.

In addition to the college curriculum, there was a two-year study course with a private preceptor. Dr. Frink, John thought, had certainly fulfilled his part of the bargain.

John panicked when he thought about the degree yet to be earned before he could support Mattie, the things he would have to explain to his father, and the matters that he would have to explain to Mattie's parents. All other things being equal, becoming a graduate was the least of his worries.

≈ Chapter ≈
SEVEN

The never-ending whirl of classes, study, and lectures blended into the Pennsylvania autumn. Red leaves fell and the air was crisp with the pungent aroma of wood smoke. Money arrived from home for the purchase of a long, wool coat. John chose a black one, thinking that it made him look all the more scholarly and distinguished, like his idol Dr. Mears.

John's travails with academia and exercise had made him almost skeletal, despite Mrs. Weede making certain that he "had vittles to keep his bones warm." She would heap John's plate with an alarming amount of good New England fare. Overwhelmed by the portions, John begged her to stop.

By the time Christmas of 1870 arrived, John had almost forgotten that holidays existed. He was soon faced with the nagging problem of transportation. Although he had discussed travelling to see Mattie through his letters to her and had made discreet inquiries about rail transportation, logistical problems needed to be ironed out. Having seen *The Travelers' Official Guide* at one of the railroad offices near the college, John bought one for a dollar and then walked back to the boardinghouse to peruse it at his leisure. Connections from Philadelphia to Savannah were many, but they all involved transfer from one train to another or from one station to another. This, John decided, would consume most of his precious leave.

John inquired into the reliability of steamship travel, which elicited favorable reviews, especially of the two screw steamships the *Charles W. Lord* and *Wyoming*.

Mattie, enjoying the sea as much as John, had shared her love of Savannah and the city's seafaring industry. Although Mattie had not been to Savannah since 1864, there were enough Holliday relatives in the port city to mask the true intent of her visit: seeing John.

Each week like clockwork, there would be a long letter waiting for him at the boardinghouse. Mrs. Weede took especial pride in giving him the letters. Because the doughty widow reminded him so much of his mother, John readily shared all of his precious letters with her as well as the tintype that Mattie sent him.

"She's comely to the eye and such pretty hair she has. Is a date set for the marriage?"

"Not a firm date and we've had to keep it secret. My father would kill me. Mattie's parents would send her away. So there's naught much we can do until I get my degree."

Mrs. Weede pushed her gray locks back with a flour-covered hand. Her tongue clicked behind her teeth. At the flash of John's eyes to her mouth, Mrs. Weede blushed and put her hands on her amply padded hips. "Now listen, young master, I've seen that look in your eye before. There's nothing wrong with my dentures. Yes, they're a bit loose, but they suit me just fine. Besides," she gave a little sniff as her unneeded eyeglasses slid to the tip of her nose, "have you learned how to make dentures yet?"

"Uh, no," John said as a stain of red crept up his gaunt cheeks.

"Well, when you do be sure to let me know. Supper's at seven. Don't be late."

John waited until Mrs. Weede's lumbering steps sounded on the stairs, then he took Mattie's letter from his pocket once more. As always, she appeared to him as she stood in the shade of the sprawling oak tree near her family's home. Oddly, John had to squint to see her. Serene yet sad, her large eyes blinked at him. He gently refolded her letter. In spite of John's best efforts, the future before them continued to look shrouded in blackness.

He knew that he was working hard, but his doubts remained. What if they couldn't afford to get married? What if her parents sent her away? The old fears rose to choke his mouth with bile. What if after all his travail there was not money enough for a honeymoon trip? Mattie, of course, would keep the upset to herself. He took a deep breath and his levelheaded reason prevailed. Unaccustomedly, a small cough fluttered in his throat.

Excitement got him through his Wednesday classes. Thursday saw him awaken at four o'clock to make an early trek to the steamship ticket office where the agent informed him that his ticket for a single through passage to Savannah would be ten dollars.

On Friday, John fumbled and dropped his dental extractors all through Dr. Wildman's class, prompting Louis and Dr. Wildman to quirk eyebrows at him. It did not bode well for John that Louis' expression was one of unholy glee.

"So who is she? Anyone I know?"

"Louis, does it always have to be a she?"

"Yes, always. And it can't be Mattie; it has to be someone else." Louis' voice dropped to a hiss because Dr. Wildman's roving gaze had fastened on the two.

"Louis, just one time. Just one punch, Louis, I swear I can fell you with one punch."

"Can I meet her? Quick, here comes Wildman."

John patted the pocket of his lab coat and offered Dr. Wildman a seraphic smile, hissing to Louis at the same time, "No."

By the time, John labored through a demonstration that Dr. Wildman had bade him perform in front of the class, his nerves were jangled. Of balm to his weary heart was a new letter from Mattie waiting for him at the boardinghouse. Mrs. Weede dispensed the letters with the same kindness as she dispensed food to her charges. Wanting to be alone with the cherished letter, John pounded up the stairs to his room and shut the door. The dainty script was filled with stains, blotches, and lined through words, indicating that Mattie must have been in a hurry to get the letter off to him. It detailed her plans to meet him in Savannah.

My Dearest John,

I am so glad that you mean to travel to Savannah. I will be waiting on the pier with my chaperone. I've had to become more circumspect as Father has been questioning my decision to travel to Savannah. He has said nothing harsh, yet I fear that we must gird ourselves for the time to come. In my heart of hearts I know that it is essential for us to be together. In time, my parents and yours must reconcile themselves to this truth. We must abide in diligence, faith, and love.

The last sentence of Mattie's letter reminded John of the summons that he had received the week before from Dr. Mears. It had been with some trepidation that he had gone to his professor's office and tapped on the door. Once there, Dr. Mears politely discussed John's study and talked to him about his thesis. A bit bewildered John went along with Dr. Mears until he saw the letter from Henry resting on the professor's desk.

Seeing that the young man had correctly guessed the nature of the summons to his office, Dr. Mears offered a small smile.

"Before your vacation to Georgia, my colleagues and I have put together a letter that we want you to deliver to your father. Penned on official college stationery, it has been signed by myself, Dean Wildman, and several of your other professors."

"Is this something I need to worry about? Am I being instructed to leave the school?"

"Good heavens, no. You are one of our most capable students. You'll make a fine dentist. Rather think of this as a letter to calm parental concerns."

A spot of color touched John's thin face. "Oh."

"We do not write letters such as this all the time or for just anyone. I think in this case that your father will be well pleased to hear accolades from us concerning you."

John's fist slowly uncurled. Carefully, Dr. Mears folded the letter, placed it in an envelope, and struck the college's seal to the outside. "There, academically taken care of. In the meantime," his deep voice boomed, "abide in diligence and faith."

John had left the building and slowly made his way to the boardinghouse, the distance between Philadelphia and Valdosta having fallen away. Once more he had felt his father's presence like a surly ghost that would not stay banished and one who whispered the damning words: "You'll never be any good. You're no son of mine."

The young man shook himself, Mattie's letter still clutched in his hand. In the climate of academia, he had forgotten what it meant to be Henry Holliday's son. He had forgotten, however briefly, that he would be traveling to Valdosta from Savannah and that the purpose of the trip was Christmas to be spent with his father and stepmother.

Saturday arrived at last. He had packed the night before and was ready to leave by the time Mrs. Weede tapped on his door.

"You didn't have to do this," he told her as she thrust a small satchel at him.

Her teeth clicked. "I made breakfast for you and some snacks. You never know how you'll be fed on the voyage, so it won't hurt to carry what I know you'll eat."

"Bless you, dear Mrs. Weede."

The air was bracing when John left the boardinghouse two hours early. Dressed in his long black coat and clutching the carpetbag, he pretended that he was already a dentist and was hurrying to meet an emergency. As he neared the river, the tangy salt air assailed his nostrils. The sea had a smell that was as deep as blood. John took a breath. In the water before him, *Wyoming* was a low-slung and powerful looking vessel. His breath quickened again.

After securing his passage, he watched curiously while the cargo was being loaded. With nothing further to do except wait for the eight o'clock departure, he watched while horse-drawn omnibuses and hacks from the neighboring hotels began to arrive. The passengers made an interesting sight as they filed solemnly onto the steamer. Some of the women were dressed in the highest of fashion with bustled walking dresses and paletot jackets. Dresses of wool tattersall checks, green moiré, and silk mingled haughtily with the utilitarian gingham and printed muslin. Many gentlemen of the day were attired in the popular three-piece sack suit, while a few sported a more military style with frog-trimmed capes.

The children were an engaging lot. Little girls wearing starched, striped dresses and miniature button shoes tripped after their mothers. One child with heavy red curls paused and looked up at John as she followed her parents on board. She gave John an engaging smile and a tiny wave from her lace-mittened hand.

The *Wyoming* was a three-mast, screw steamship. Her hull had been tooled from live oak and fitted with a composite of iron and copper fastenings. Although she had but one engine, together with her mighty masts, she would undoubtedly skim across the water.

It was eight o'clock. John held his breath, not quite understanding what would happen. Under his feet and the tested grain of the wood, there came a mighty tremble of commotion. With a snap, the heavy surge of the sails caught the wind. *Wyoming* had begun her voyage.

Mattie's words returned in the throb of his blood, "You'll either love it or hate it. But you'll never be indifferent. And later when you hold a shell to your ear, you will hear that same blood-coursing thrill. It will whisper, 'I am the West Wind.'"

"I hear," he had whispered, only to have the wind fling the words back at him. By the time John went below deck, the *Wyoming* was already three hours at sea.

There were deluxe accommodations for a price. John's allowance furnished him with a utilitarian but clean eight by eight room. There was a bunk, a slop pot, a place to put his shaving kit, and a hook inside the door for his clothes. At least he had the room to himself. Steerage class in the bottom of the ship meant four or five people bunked together like oysters on a half shell.

The smell of the sea was everywhere. Once the shock of the blood-rich odor had passed, John found that he was quite buoyed by the experience. He spent little time below in his room except to sleep. Most days he spent on the deck staring out at the other schooners, fascinated by the variety of steamships.

There were lively games of poker and monte on board. Several times John was invited to join. He found it interesting to watch society at work. The women wearing their tattersall silks tossed their heads and herded their children away from their sisters of the linsey-woolsey crowd. The men were not so choosy, finding companions with others of a more common nature if the latter had a bit of tobacco, a deck of cards, or a wild story to tell.

Each day brought something new. At night, millions of stars blazed light that illuminated nothing, not even the ocean on which the *Wyoming* sailed. There were other ships in the night, but *Wyoming* sliced through the waves and left them behind only to be swallowed in the fog that rose phantom-like from the gray foam below. Soon the trip was over and the sparkling water of Savannah's harbor surrounded the steamship and pulled her safely to its bosom. With new sea legs, John touched dry land for the first time in a week and promptly lost his balance.

"Goodness," he found himself saying into Mattie's lacy bonnet. She had enveloped him in an embrace, much as the harbor had embraced the *Wyoming*.

"Cousin," she said with a proper smile fixed to her lips, "this is my chaperone, Mrs. Elizabeth Elkins."

"Ma'am," he took the gloved hand and pressed it to his lips.

He offered an arm to each woman and strolled towards one of the horse-drawn taxis that would take him to the train station and the last step of his journey. He was relieved that Mattie was traveling with him to Valdosta and disappointed that Mrs. Elkins was making the same journey.

Now used to the open sea, John found the atmosphere inside the rail car stifling. Rivulets of sweat popped from his brow and onto the freshness of his boiled shirt.

"I am mourning my deceased brother," Mrs. Elkins announced as she made a show of smoothing the wrinkles from her stiff black dress.

John dipped his head politely and offered her his hand that she gave the briefest of touches with her lace-clad fingers. Glancing at Mattie, John could see that she was struggling to keep her face in the proper mien. He could almost hear her whisper to him about limiting conversation to the weather, crops, and family activities.

"Mrs. Elkins, I believe I told you that Cousin John is attending dental school in Philadelphia."

The older woman gave a sniff from her dainty nostrils and tapped her foot against the floor of the hack. "I suppose that Philadelphia is fine, and I suppose that one cannot be choosy when it comes to dental schools. The Yankees, do they give you much trouble?"

"Oh no, ma'am, we are all so immersed in academia that it leaves little time for the intricacies of politics."

There was another sniff, this time louder. "Politics have nothing to do with the Yankees, young man. One is either a Yankee or he is not."

"Yes, ma'am."

There was more mundane talk. The weather was fine. The corn and cotton crops were bumper. The Holliday family was doing well. John realized that he had been starved for the green sights of Georgia and devoured the smell of the countryside in the crackling winter air. He committed Mattie's face to his memory once more. She was more beautiful than ever, from the sweep of her lashes over her gray eyes to the way that she wore the blue ribbons on her bonnet. Clear and even, her gaze told him what he had longed to know. It answered his question, "Do you still love me?"

A town coach picked them up at the train station. John, seated across from Mattie, could feel the warmth of her knees in the occasional brush that occurred when the wheels of the town coach hit a rut in the road.

"Are you certain that you ladies won't come in for a bit of Christmas cheer?" he asked as he alighted from the coach.

"Oh, no," Mrs. Elkins said, interrupting Mattie. "We are fine and will continue on to Jonesboro. It was an experience meeting you, young man."

Then the coach rolled away and John was alone once more to face his father.

During the visit, Henry and John were polite and made pleasantries. On Christmas morning, John had given him the letter from Dr. Mears. With his father looking hearty and warmed by the festivities, John had thought that the letter would bring a smile if nothing else.

Henry's response, "Well, now," was the end of the matter.

The crushing devastation that swept through John was swallowed. His father had never been one to bestow accolades. Why had it taken so long for him to realize that there was no pleasing his father?

Christmas vacation was over before John knew it. "I'll not dawdle here," Henry told his son at the train station. "Take care, boy." And that was the end of Christmas.

The *Wyoming* was a welcome sight. John boarded to the sound of leaping water, the smell of fresh, salt spray, and a keen wind. A new letter from Mattie, Mrs. Weede's famous chicken, and a summons from Dr. Mears greeted his arrival in Philadelphia.

"I hope that your Christmas was a prosperous one," Dr. Mears said over the tops of his glasses. For once, the older man's desk was remarkably clean of clutter. He regarded John solemnly and steepled his fingers. "This year is your second year here. It's time for you to seriously consider your plans after graduation."

"I have been giving some thought to this."

"Excellent. You have a practicality about you that is most refreshing. Although you probably yearn to return to Georgia and set up a practice, I have an alternate proposal that I would like you to contemplate. Would you consider remaining here in Philadelphia?"

John very carefully closed his jaw. "Well, it would be a lie to say that the idea never crossed my mind. I like Philadelphia and, plainly speaking, it is a fine city. But Georgia, on the other hand, has always been my home."

"Just think about my proposal. You don't have to give me your answer yet."

"I will. I will indeed."

Since declaring his thesis, "Diseases of the Teeth," John had applied himself with renewed vigor. This year, 1871, was going to be his make or break year.

♣ ♥ ♠ ♦

From his podium, Dr. Barker taught that the pathology of the teeth had a direct bearing on the pathologies of the body. A clear and concise knowledge of comparative anatomy was required for a student to grasp the whole concept of disease. For John, the concept of fighting disease had seemed an easy one. He had believed that nursing his mother until her death had given him a rare insight.

Comparative anatomy was John's Armageddon from the time he entered the classroom until he left for the boardinghouse at night. No longer was he an onlooker at the rows of desperate faces that marked a student in the throes of failing. He found himself going to class in wrinkled lab coats and wearing the same dogged, desperate expression as the ones who fled the college in the middle of the night, leaving behind silence and an empty chair.

Passing became imperative. If he failed at this, he would be finished. No longer was there free time on the weekends. Instead there were stops at several of the area's hospitals. He attended lectures and took notes until his fingers painfully cramped. He read until his eyes could not focus. He pored over volumes of books, remained at the lab, and skipped meals. To his great relief, he passed the course.

♣ ♥ ♠ ♦

The cough began in the autumn of 1871. New England autumns were not the autumns of the Deep South. Georgia's leaves turned brilliant in their fire and fell softly to mother earth. Philadelphia leaves were at first brown and then gold. Days later they were brittle skeletons that blew across the ground only to rattle underfoot. There were scarlet maples aplenty in Philadelphia. John, having enjoyed them the year before, was shaken by his ennui and a sense that something had gone wrong. An early snow fell that year, dropping a few white flecks that mixed with the red leaves and was soon gone. But the wind developed a life of its own, a cold that stung its way to the bone. It was unlike anything John had experienced. Many of his friends had become ill, including Louis. He was sure it was a cold. But as time passed, the tickle in his chest refused to go away.

"Just a cold," the doctor in Philadelphia reassured him. "Stay out of drafts. Stay warm."

John did all those things, but the autumn had taken up permanent residence in his chest. Autumn was followed by a hard winter.

Henry sent him a note with money enclosed for a good pair of gloves. "To keep you warm among the Yankees," the accompanying note had read.

John bought a furry, black pair of gloves to complement his black coat. Warmed on the outside, but not within, he coughed his way through the winter. Spring would come, he thought, to take the cold from his chest. And there were days in the approaching part of the new spring that he shed the gloves, when the cough was intermittent. The days of no cough he forgot altogether. Days and nights soon followed, when he couldn't.

The defense of his thesis came at last. He knew he had to be mentally sharp. First came the submittal of the specimen case that he knew would be placed in the college's repository. He took deep regular breaths, willed the cough to be silent, and pressed his fingers together in an unconscious imitation of Dr. Mears. He glanced at his patient, a man younger than he who had been procured from one of the area's hospitals.

"Anything to fix my teeth," the young man told him.

"It might not be pleasant," John said. "Are you ready for this?"

"Why not? I'm sparkin' a really nice girl. It'd be nice to have a pair of choppers that I wouldn't be ashamed of."

A proctor opened the door. "Mr. Holliday, it is your turn."

John nodded to his patient. He took a deep breath, gestured for the young man to follow him, then stepped inside the cavern that was the operative dentistry room.

He bade the young man sit in the chair and made sure that the chair was turned so that it would receive the maximum light available. Carefully, he laid out his instruments. Once the young man's mouth was open, John forgot about the professors so carefully monitoring his technique. He probed the cavities and looked at the lining of the mouth and tongue for disease. He readied the anesthetics. He took the hand drill and began cleaning the teeth. Gold foil was prepared for each tooth, five in all that had deep cavities.

His young patient held the sides of the chair in a white-knuckled grip, but said nothing while John tugged, drilled, and bent over him. Finally, John straightened and looked closely at his patient. The boy was gray-faced, but his trembling hands gave evidence that he lived.

John had little trouble in finding a patient for the artificial work. With some trepidation, Mrs. Weede with her loose dentures agreed to be his subject. After he was finished, John presented the good matron with great pride to Dr. Wildman.

A traumatic examination by the entire faculty soon followed. There was more waiting, but finally the ordeal ended. John Holliday would graduate. Of the sixty-six matriculants who had first entered the fifteenth session, only twenty-eight remained to graduate. At eight o'clock Friday evening on March 1, 1872, at Musical Fund Hall, Mattie and several of his relatives waited in the audience to congratulate him.

He should have felt elated, but a return of the vicious cough had sapped his enthusiasm. From the dawn of his graduation until his walk upon the stage, his lungs labored like a set of punctured bellows. Each time he strained for a breath, it took longer for the air to seep in. As he accepted his diploma, a deep flutter of fear singed his tortured chest. The hard winter had pared him to a state of leanness, but he had no idea how emaciated he'd become until Mattie embraced him.

"Oh, John," leaked out before she could catch it. She held her warm cheek against his icy one and brushed the beads of sweat off his forehead.

"I haven't been well," he told her finally.

"Maybe you'll feel better at the hotel. You can get warmed up and have dinner. We'll go there straightaway." Mattie lay a firm hand on her mother's shoulder. "Mother, Cousin John is exhausted after such a rigorous ordeal. I propose that we go to the hotel."

Before her mother could react, Mattie tucked John under her arm and helped him outside. The wind was a chill one. John gasped as the frigid air stung his nostrils and put a shaking hand to his thin chest. Mattie continued to hold him up and looked anxiously about for a passing horse taxi. After an interminable ten minutes, a cabriolet finally rolled into view. She helped her cousin inside and then wrapped the lap robe about him, keeping it snug until they arrived at the hotel.

John staggered from the cab and all but fell to his knees. Mattie led him up to the room and said in a steady tone, "It will be all right. Hot water will be brought for a nice bath and I'll make sure that you have some hot food."

Mattie kissed his cold face and left the room. In due course, hot water and food were discreetly dispatched, but amenities made no difference. Not long after the bath, a bloody paroxysm erupted like a geyser from John's mouth. By this time, the realization could not be denied. This malady was not a cold.

⇒ Chapter ⇒
EIGHT

Some things in life escaped Mary Holliday's eye, but a distressed daughter was not one of them. "Child, you have missed that same embroidery stitch for twenty rows. The thread is broken, and you're as white as a sheet. Come here and have a nice cup of tea with me."

The embroidery dropped to the floor as Mattie put a trembling hand to her mouth.

"What is this? You have to tell me. A daughter does not hold back these things from her mother. You must tell me."

Mattie looked at her mother's face from the beetling eyebrows to the indignation of the widow's peak under the laced cap.

"What is it?" Mary Anne asked.

"You must swear that you will not divulge what I will tell you to anyone."

Mary Anne took a breath. "I will swear on the graves of my parents."

"Our beloved cousin, John Holliday, has the wasting disease."

Mary Anne's knees buckled as she sank to the floor. "Is it not enough that the finest of our men were plucked from the bosoms of their family in the war?"

"Mother, I must go to him."

"Yes," Mary Anne said hoarsely. "I have to think of what we can do. I have to think."

Mattie quickened her pace as she closed the door to her mother's room. Would John turn her away or let her come in to comfort him? The stays of her dress felt like they were squeezing her heart into her backbone. She could neither inhale nor exhale.

She paused at the door and took a painful gulp of air. "John, let me in. Please John, please let me in."

The door swung open. John leaned drunkenly against the wall, but Mattie knew that he was not drunk.

She touched his icy face. He took a step back and she followed him.

"Oh, Mattie. Oh God, Mattie," his voice broke.

The young woman caught him as he sank to the floor. For a moment she was too stunned to realize that he was crying, then she gathered him close. John made no sound as Mattie rocked him back and forth. All his tears burst forward for his mother, for the misery of the war, and for the life that he and Mattie would not share. When his sobs had lessened, she raised his face from her breast and kissed him. Without warning, the kiss turned into a terrible need. Although John's feverish fingers plucked at her clothing he was unable to unbutton even the largest of the buttons.

"Hush, now," Mattie said as she removed the cameo at her throat.

A blush colored her ivory skin from forehead to waist, but she did not stop to cover herself or cease the unbuttoning of her dress. Like a spider's web, her delicate chemise was the exact shade of her rosy skin. Propriety said that he should look away, but he could not. He wanted desperately to feel some kind of shame. But there was no shame, only the pounding of his heart that roared through his ears and made his chest hurt.

Her hands were cool where his were hot. She took his palm and lay it on her breast. The heat of him made her cry out. John tried to pull his hand away, but Mattie pressed it more tightly to her.

"We can't do this," he said. "We can't, Mattie."

She kissed his lips and his brow and stroked his thick hair. His "we can't, Mattie" was lost in the uproar of their bodies. John's ears rang at the feel of her beneath him.

He lost himself in their lovemaking. The room whirled with scarlet and blue, with heat and cold, with her flesh against his. A cool brush of air flew into his chest. John used the cool draft to stagger to his feet, but his body flopped to the floor like a dying fish. Mattie tried to catch and hold him to her, but the young man would have none of it. He was silent as he stared up into her eyes. He gathered his legs and made a convulsive movement to stand beside her. Mattie's graceful fingers reached for his cheek, but he stepped back.

In his visage there was not a trace of her beloved John. As if already dead, he gazed into her eyes. He took in the rosy glow of her cheeks and smelled deeply of the lavender fragrance of her throat. Slowly, she reached out and touched his fingers with her warm ones. At the touch of her, his breath quickened. Mattie's eyes widened at the tortuous sound from his lungs. Carefully, John uncurled her fingers from his.

"Not in this lifetime," he whispered.

"What?" she asked.

"We can't be together, Mattie. I won't risk you. If you take care of me, it will become your fate and your deathbed. That's the way of this thing."

"I'm not going to leave you."

"I will give you no choice. I will not allow you to watch me die."

Her fingers scrambled to hold onto him. Again, he uncurled her fingers from his arm. Her eyes darted around the room as she seized her clothes that lay on the floor and automatically began to dress herself.

"Maybe it's only a cold. You don't know. You said the doctor told you it was a cold." The sound of her sobs wounded his soul.

"I watched my mother die one speck at a time. There was no end to it. Every day I watched her. There was a good day and then a bad day. I plumped the pillows, patted her brow while she coughed, and wiped the blood from her lips when her dear hands had no strength. Part of my heart died with her. You shall not, Mattie, be the one to brush the blood from my lips or watch as I struggle for air. You being with me now . . . the way we were . . . I may have already given it to you."

"No, you didn't." Mattie dashed the tears from her eyes. "If you go away, as I know you will, then I will go with you." At the vehement shake of his head, she continued, "Then I have also a request to make, one which you must grant me. I will not go back to my room this night. I will not be turned out. You may throw me out, but I will come back again and again. I will have tonight. So will you."

He backed away from her. "No, Mattie. We shall not. I will not accept this from you. I will not shame you further. No, my dearest, for once and all time, you must walk away. You will walk away and not look back."

Mattie's fingers violently twisted the fabric of her skirt. Some of the thread gave way. She looked down at the small tear and back up at John. "Why can't this be like the times when we held hands in the dark and waited for the Yankees to come? Why can't it be like that?"

John grimaced. "The Yankees have already come and gone, Mattie. They have laid waste."

"No," she screamed, "you don't know what you ask."

"Yes, I do. You will leave me now. I'll escort you to the door."

Mattie's hand flew to her throat. "You are killing me."

"I am already dead."

She shook herself and tried to smooth her cameo, but it lay askew in spite of the attempt.

"What will you do?"

"Tomorrow I will go again to the doctor. No, you may not come with me. I have to do this alone."

"Will you say goodbye? Will you walk away from me?" Her voice was incredulous.

"I will walk away," he whispered as he turned his back to her. A small sob escaped her, then the door opened and closed and he was alone in the room.

He shut his eyes and pictured her bowed shoulders as she left his room. A hard cough brought his handkerchief to his mouth smearing two new scarlet streams on the already soiled linen. Mixed with the salty odor of blood was the whisper of lavender from Mattie's clothes.

He spent the rest of the night staring out the window and listening to the distant sound of a railroad whistle. Never had it sounded more forlorn. He laid out fresh clothes. The plan had been to take the train with his Aunt Mary and Mattie. Irrevocably, those plans were changed. He thought about the gleaming promise of marriage to Mattie and an Atlanta practice, but those dreams were withered.

The hotel was quiet. There was time for a small breakfast, but he couldn't eat. The consummate Southern gentleman that was Dr. John Holliday smiled and escorted his aunt and Mattie to the train station. He refused to meet Mattie's agonized eyes with anything other than detached courtesy.

"I will see you soon," he told his Aunt Mary and divided a nod and a handshake between the two women.

For a moment, he feared that the stress would be too much for Mattie. Indeed, her face was quite pale. Just as it seemed that she might faint, her back suddenly straightened. She gave a small toss of her head and flashed a smile in the direction of her worried mother.

"We shall see you soon, cousin. Please don't be a stranger. Come, Mother, we must go."

John hesitated by the tracks and watched the train disappear into the distance. An unrelenting fury rose in his chest. Red spots danced in front of his eyes and with them his rage directed skyward at the Almighty for allowing this to happen. He wheezed for air and gripped his fingers around the carpetbag until his knuckles were white. With bent shoulders, he walked to the local doctor's office.

The exam confirmed John's fears.

"This is chronic pulmonary consumption," the physician told him. "Georgia will bring you to a sorry end very quickly. You need a dry climate, the drier the better. If you go to Georgia, you'll wither like a hothouse flower. Do you have family? Anyone you could go to?"

"No."

The physician spoke other words, but John's ears were deafened by the pronouncement. He had known, but to hear the diagnosis from another was the ultimate destruction of self. Numb once more, he walked to the train station and waited.

On the train, John dismissed the gaiety of the travelers around him and the antics of the children. Outside the window, a spring thaw was beginning to show itself. Sitting made his cough much more quiet and easier to hide in a discreet handkerchief. By the time he reached Valdosta, five days had elapsed since his diagnosis. Upon arrival at the station, he hired a horse taxi to take him to the house. Henry was not home, but Rachel welcomed him.

"Dr. Holliday." She curtsied and gave him a kiss on the cheek. John's smile was wan. "Your father wasn't sure when you were coming home. I know he wishes that he'd been at the station to meet you. I've readied your room and cooked some special things."

John stared around the house. It looked almost the way he had left it. Rachel left him alone to his devices. She did not see him pace his room, fling his clothes to the floor, or tear at his hair. Later, she discreetly tapped on his door for dinner, but John failed to appear, not even when he heard Henry's boots clump across the floor. Tomorrow at breakfast, he would look his father in the eye. Sleep would never be the same for him. After a restless night, he got up and tried to shave. Unable to look at himself in the mirror, he nicked his cheeks and chin.

Henry was effusive at the table, but that was his way. He looked at his son from heavy-lidded eyes. Henry's coffee cup stopped just short of his mouth. "You're looking a little peaked. Your studies must have been hard. Stick around here and Rachel will fatten you up in no time."

John sat on his anger as best as he could, but it itched for freedom under his burning skin and sizzled behind his eyes. Anger at his father came easily, but he didn't want to unleash it.

Georgia's beauty blunted John's anger somewhat. The soft rains had opened the blue tops of the wild chicory and white daisies. Spanish moss dripped into the long grass. On the damp road, his mare's hooves made a pleasant clip-clop sound. John had always loved the sluggish river, from the sound of the plump frogs as they splashed into the water to the bubbling sound that arose from the small whirlpools near the river's shore.

Too many things had changed for John to take them all in, most of all the disease that was eating him from within, a disease that, sooner or later, Henry would discover. And then there was Mattie whose love burned inside his soul. John knew he should leave Valdosta and quickly, but didn't he owe her a chance to see if he could open a successful dental practice in Georgia? If he tried, at least he'd know.

Burning indecision and his disease consumed his thoughts, but by early May he began to prepare for his trip to Atlanta.

Henry gave his son the usual encouragement. "Are you certain you can pull this off, boy? Mind you, if things don't work out you can't come running back here. You're a man. You'll have to take failure like a man."

"Are you so certain I'll fail, Father?"

John's first interviews in Atlanta were met with refusal for employment. Nevertheless, he received high marks for his knowledge and expertise. Finally, Dr. Arthur Ford hired him.

If Henry had any doubts about his son's practice, Dr. Ford did not. Pleasant and professional, the older dentist made certain that John knew what a valuable service he was contributing to the community. John was equally pleased when Dr. Ford received a missive sent from Dr. Wildman.

"You come with strong recommendations, young man. You will go far."

John ate well, slept as he should, and afforded himself ample exercise. He kept up his outward appearance with a starched shirt and coat, neat shoes, and combed hair. After a trial period of two weeks, he was given more work, but he coughed intermittently as he had in Philadelphia.

Mattie sent voluminous letters. Every day there was a thick envelope waiting for him. After a hard day of being on his feet, it was nice to relax in the magnolia perfume of them. Mattie's light script was as soothing as the hot peach tea that was served to him by his landlady. While his life was not the one that had been planned, he found comfort in those letters. But then a dark note began creeping into them. John was tormented that their brief contact could have already led to her being infected. It was too frightening a thing to ask outright as a gentleman did not take that liberty of a lady that he respected.

But it was not consumption that bothered Mattie. By the end of June, Mattie could no longer hide her pregnancy. She had been careful to raise the sashes of her favorite dresses to hide her slowly blooming stomach and, for a while, none of her relations caught on. However, Mary Holliday had borne too many children to be fooled. The evening that Mattie came to the dinner wearing a frilly apron evoked a raised eyebrow.

The next morning Mattie was awakened by her mother, who firmly shut the door behind her and sat down on her bed.

"If you will tell no one else, at least have the courtesy to tell me."

"What?" Mattie sat up and rubbed the sleep from her eyes.

"You've been vomiting. Your stomach is swelling. Don't lie to me."

Mattie faced her mother steadily. "I won't lie to you, but I won't tell you either."

"This will break your father's heart."

"Mine is already broken."

"Did a young man play fast and loose with your affections and then leave you?"

"No, Mother. That's not it. I was a willing participant."

For the first time in her life, Mary Ann Holliday slapped her daughter. "This will break your father's heart. How could you do this to us? How can you, the child of my heart, sit calmly and say these things to me?"

Mattie's lower lip trembled and her hands twisted in the quilt.

"You will tell us who this boy is. Your father will kill him. He has to. Do you know what you've done? Do you know that you'll have to be sent away? You can't stay here. We'll be ruined. Did you give a thought to what people will say?"

"If I had thought to tell you willingly, what you have said just now has sealed my lips. I will not betray him. You won't touch him. And neither will my father. If you want to hit me again, Mother, go ahead, but it won't make me tell you."

"You've taken everything we've given you and flung it in our faces. Bastard babes are insane. You know this."

"I'm going to have this baby, Mother, and I'm going to keep it."

Mary Ann's eyes flashed. "That you shall not do. There will be no bastard babe in our family. It won't be born. It won't exist. It will never exist. It will never be acknowledged."

Later, her father called her into his office and fixed his sorrowful gaze upon her. "Child, why can't you tell us who this boy is?"

"He's no boy, Father. And I will not tell you because mother has told me that you will kill him. I can't allow that to happen."

"Then the discussion is ended. I have my duty as a father to perform. It will be arranged so that there will be no further shame to the family."

"There is a place for young women who are in the family way," Mary Ann explained. "There will be others there in your situation. You will be recorded as a resident, but not under your Christian name. There will be no record of this, neither written nor spoken. This is not, did not, and will not happen."

Mattie accepted the pronouncement. They would take the baby from her, but she would not betray John. As the day approached for her banishment, her heart closed tighter. At night, she would awake remembering that first and last night in Philadelphia and the feel of John. In the darkness, she held the child more tightly inside of her and prayed.

♣ ♥ ♠ ♦

The uneasiness that John read in Mattie's letters began almost exactly to the day in late June when John first began to smell a puzzling odor. He dismissed the odor at first as being the chemical smell from his lab coat. He came to realize, however, that the odor was not on his coat.

As the days passed, the dead mouse smell grew stronger. John tried airing his room, once in the morning and several times in the evening, especially upon retiring. He scrubbed his skin raw and had his jackets laundered in lye soap. The routine continued until he woke one morning and coughed up a prodigious amount of blood. Trembling, he collapsed in the nearest chair. His heart pounded hard and his hands shook. He put his head in his hands and wept, but not for long because a killing fury welled behind the tears. Dashing them from his eyes, he hastily got up. He would have to leave Georgia.

"I'm sorry," he told his office partners, "but it appears that I will be unable to fulfill my commitment here. My health is not good. Thanks for all your help."

In silence, John haphazardly threw all of his gear, including his precious dental instruments, into the small carpetbag. So dark was his rage and disappointment, he didn't remember the train ride back to Valdosta.

The house was eerily silent when John came through the door. Rachel and Henry were nowhere in sight. John waited for the familiar sound of his father's clumping boots. When they finally did sound, the worn carpet absorbed much of the noise. Henry gave John a curt hello and looked him over so clinically that John felt insulted. The tic in Henry's right eye fluttered, while the cords in his neck pulsed like termite-riddled wood. Contempt showed in every line of Henry Holliday's craggy face.

"Your cousin . . ." he began, but his voice cracked so badly he had to stop. "Your cousin, Martha Anne Holliday, is retiring for a few months of rest. Do you know anything of it?"

Pure agony shot through John. Mattie had consumption. "No," he said, "no, I don't know anything." His knees trembled, but he stiffened them.

Henry's fist clenched then relaxed. "Nothing?"

"No, how could I? I came straight from Atlanta. I've even brought letters from Dr. Ford."

"Yes," Henry replied, "boy, you told me, and yes, you are correct in your facts." Sarcasm dripped from each word. "But relatives wrote me that they saw you and Mattie in Savannah."

John's stomach lurched, but he gave nothing away. "She met me once or twice when she was staying with her Holliday relatives. We were properly chaperoned by a Mrs. Elkins. I treated both ladies to lunch. As for Martha Anne, she is my cousin. You would have done the same."

"Yes, I would have treated her to lunch, but I wouldn't have kissed her as it is said that you have done."

"Is that an insinuation?"

John had no time to brace himself for the blow that knocked him from his feet as the full fury of Henry's fist caught him squarely in the jaw. With the wind knocked out of him, John rolled across the floor. Stars danced in his throbbing brain and nausea gripped his stomach. Moaning, he clawed his way across the floor to the nearest piece of furniture and heaved himself up. Blood ran down his face.

"Now I ask you again," Henry said, "what do you know of Mattie?"

"Is she ill?" John queried. His whole body was bruised and shaken.

Henry hit him again with a blow that deposited him on the wooden floor several feet from the fireplace. John coughed blood and wretched with dry heaves before attempting to rise once more. Henry followed his movements with all the intent of a raptor out for the kill.

"In the name of God," John moaned, "why are you doing this? What have I done?"

Henry waited for him to get up, fists clenched. John rolled over on his back and stared up at his father. The intent was clear, but John was not going to lie on the floor with his father standing over him like a victor.

"You'll have to kill me," he panted as he dragged himself up.

Once standing, John saw his father's fist covered now with blood. For the third time his body was hurled to the floor with a sickening thud. John lay sobbing face down. Henry rolled him over.

"I've got consumption," John said. His face was tattered and bloody. "I've got consumption."

Devoid of emotion, Henry hauled his son off the floor and tossed him onto the settee.

"Mattie is pregnant."

A paroxysm began at the bottom of John's chest and worked its raw way into his handkerchief. The coughing continued until it hurt too much to cry. For that, John was grateful. At the end of the fit, John thrust the handkerchief towards his father.

Seeing the bits of scarlet and black tissue, Henry blanched, but continued his diatribe. "You do know what this means, don't you? Not only did you ruin any chance for Martha Anne to marry a respectable man, but that the waste of your issue will be a bastard that the family must bear in eternal shame forever—not only a bastard, but insane as well." Henry cleared his throat. "How could you give so little thought to what you were doing or be so reckless in your actions? I wish you'd never been born to me."

There was a singular dignity in which John looked at his father. Beaten but not broken, he gazed at Henry. Slowly his father lowered his head.

Henry took a breath and in the next instant his voice sounded with assurance. "Where will you go?"

John knew his home was closed forever. "I was told that to remain in Georgia will be the death of me."

"Yes," Henry said, "it will."

"I thought," John replied, digesting his father's intent, "to head West. What of Martha Anne?"

"That," Henry said in his most singular baritone, "is a matter taken care of by the family."

He would never see Mattie again. Most assuredly, John knew, he would never see the baby.

♣ ♥ ♠ ♦

Winter came early that year. The cold was everywhere. Inside her, the baby was lusty with life. Mattie concluded that it was a little girl. She had always pictured a girl-child in her family. Her cruel fantasy was of herself and John living in Atlanta. They had a house, a small blue one with white gingerbread trim and flowers. She taught children, as was her wish. John had been supportive of that. He shared his practice with an older dentist and, though he worked very hard, they were able to have good times together with lots of laughter.

Those dreams wouldn't last, but she would have the baby. Mattie smiled. The little girl would have the soft, silvery hair and blue eyes of John, with a personality both willful and courageous. She would be named Alice and be as bright as a copper penny.

All the girls here were in the same predicament. Because of this, they clung together. Their stories were the same.

The routine was structured so that each minute and hour were filled with what the Sisters referred to as piety. Idleness had no piety. It was hard in these circumstances to get away and be alone, but it was aloneness that Mattie craved.

Her parents came to visit. Her name on the record was listed as Harris, Sandra. Officially, to the Sisters, she was S. Harris or simply, Harris.

Sandra Harris did all that was required of her as a model inmate. The girls took great pride in calling themselves inmates. That title was no more ignominious than any other. Sandra cooked, cleaned, studied, and was talked to about the exigency of repenting her folly. That S. Harris repented none of her folly was evident and related to her distressed parents.

"Hello, dear," her mother told her, squeezing her gently. Mattie was fairly large by now.

"Hello, parents."

They waited as though they thought she'd tell them who and why. "How are you?"

Mary Ann looked at her husband. "Fine, dear."

"I enjoy your letters."

"We enjoy yours."

Pleasant inanities they were, all of them. "Are you going to stay for the weekend?"

"Yes, we had thought to do that."

They waited. Mattie smiled brightly and said nothing.

Before they left two days later, they told her of their elaborate cover up with many things being said and written to relatives and friends, all of which Mattie knew were falsehoods. If push came to shove, she was visiting relatives.

In December of 1872, Henry came to visit. She was quite shocked at his arrival, since he had not written her of his intent to visit. From his face, she could tell that he had known for a long time, although he had not told his brother out of concern over the shock and pain such knowledge would cause.

"Are you well?" he asked.

Protectively, Mattie put her arms around her stomach. "Well enough."

"I came to see you," Henry said, following her movement with his gaze.

A slow rage began to build in Mattie. "You tried to kill him," she stated and stood up.

Henry took a step back, "What?"

"Yes," Mattie stepped forward. "Yes, you did. That's your method of communication. It always has been. You most beat him to death, and then you sent him away. You've always sent him away."

Ineffectually, Henry stood in front of her and then jammed his worn hat on his head and rapidly walked out the door. So brisk was his movement that he skidded across the landing. The meeting left Mattie shaken and crying.

One morning, Mattie woke violently with cramps that made her scream. The screaming went on forever and in the middle of the screaming and the hands holding her down, she thought she could hear a baby's cry. Desperately, she fought to lift her arms towards the sound, but there was a roaring darkness, pain, and the pressure from more hands.

Two weeks later, she was home once more in Jonesboro. Her mother was talking about the garden, her father was planning an advertisement for the paper. Outside, her brothers played. There was the smell of baking bread.

Mary Anne patted her daughter's cheek. "Really, dear, it was for the best."

Mattie looked through her. "Best for whom?"

Of John, she heard nothing. Since no one would tell her of his whereabouts, she was afraid to ask fearing that her father would learn that John was the father of the child. The laborious days with her family spent themselves much in the same way as at the home for unwed mothers. Mattie smiled when it was appropriate and painted on her face the emotions that indicated she was healing. Nothing, however, was further than the truth. Her heart burned. And nightly, she thrashed in the dark to excise the demons plucking at her, the sound of that wistful cry of the baby that she would never hold.

⇥ *Chapter* ⇤
NINE

The Selma, Rome, and Dalton pulled out of the Atlanta Station at six o'clock in the morning. There was a later train leaving at half past ten that evening, but for the first time, John wanted to escape the green confines of Georgia. He'd had some time to figure out where he wanted to go. New Orleans beckoned. While the title of Doctor of Dental Surgery had given him an honorable skill and had released him from the hated bondage of "John Henry," little else in his life was secure. Doc, as he now introduced himself, was for the dentist that he was. "John" was left for his Mattie in Georgia and his mother in her grave.

"Mind you, this is very safe," Doc heard one of the porter's tell an anxious woman holding her baby. "This train can travel at forty miles an hour without injury to wind or limb. So you settle back with your young one and have a pleasant trip."

The woman frowned and clutched at her tiny daughter's hand. "Oh surely not. That's much too fast. It's too fast for a machine to stop in time. We'll surely all be killed," she murmured, echoing the dark flames in Doc's mind that flickered at the loss of Mattie and his child. He looked sadly at the woman holding her infant. It should have been Mattie on the train with him. It should have been Mattie holding a bright little girl who liked to tangle her fingers in ribbons and lace. But it wasn't and never would be. Doc had to accept the facts. He even had accepted his father's beating because he had known that Henry had been keeping his rage banked for so many years. It was about a rage towards a son who would never be like his father, neither a soldier nor a farmer. In the end there was nothing left except silence. For Doc, fear had been swept away on that terrible night. That John had survived was testament to the strength of his being.

The physician he sought in New Orleans told him the same thing as the doctors in Philadelphia and Atlanta: "It's not going to get better. It will kill you. How, when, or why is anyone's guess. You were fortunate to leave when you did."

"As if," John drawled, "one is fortunate with consumption."

Sitting on a cold chair and nude except for a towel knotted around his waist, Doc had made good his decision for a complete physical in New Orleans. The mirror told no lies. If his chest was any thinner it would cave in and, indeed, there were places where it appeared to have done that. His ribs almost poked through the skin.

He held his arms out before him. "Think my hair is the only thing supporting my skin. Hell, I've seen better legs on a horse."

"You're not in the final stages," the physician told him. "Right now the disease is confined to your lungs. How long it will remain confined, I cannot say. Each case is different. Do you cough up blood? Even tissue?"

Doc nodded. "A bit."

"I'll prescribe laudanum for the pain."

Doc held up his hand. "No laudanum. I'm a dentist. I can't work drugged out. I'll not end my days as an addict."

"Young man, there isn't much else I can do for you. Molasses has some benefit and perhaps seltzer water, but you'll soon be in pain if you aren't already."

"There is a pressure," Doc indicated a spot high on his sternum, "right here. When I cough the pressure becomes this burning that most goes down to my navel. Sometimes further."

The man gave him a somber nod. "I wish I had something else to give you. They're working on some things in Europe, but it will be years before any of it reaches the States."

"What about whiskey?"

"There are some pain alleviating elements in alcohol. It can cut a cough and help you to sleep."

"I guess the cough makes the choice for me."

"You might give thought to what you'll do when you don't have the strength to practice dentistry. The day will come when your legs will refuse to hold you, when the instruments get too heavy, and when bending over someone leaves you gasping for air. And however fastidious you might be, your patients may dislike you coughing on them."

Doc frowned. "I had not given much thought to that."

"That's for down the road, though it may come sooner than you think."

"I thank you for your professional candor. I do not undress myself for just anyone."

"And one more thing. You might find that this climate is still too wet for your condition."

"I can only try. Being cursed as it were, it's the only thing I can do."

The experiment lasted a month. New Orleans had much to offer in the way of entertainment and music. Doc still felt the buzzing of life in his bones, not yet the wracking despair that would come from the countless hours of lost sleep and spitting blood. Before the week was out, he had procured an office amongst the ramshackle buildings near the wharf. It was a seedy dive in a back alley, but it could be had for two dollars. After a feverish four days of cleaning, he felt that he was ready to open for business.

For a dollar a week, Doc bedded down in an equally squalid boardinghouse. The proprietress, Abigail the Axe, was an aging behemoth from Texas who kept order with an axe that swung from a heavy leather belt at her waist. When she found out Doc was a dentist, she waited until dinner. Just as he was ready to bite into the greasy shrimp gumbo that was the usual fare, she hurled the axe into the table in front of him.

"Service or collops it be for ye?"

Familiarity with seamen had widened his vocabulary to know that "collops" was not another word for scallops. Odd stories circulated about Abby and her axe, and the other boarders were only too glad to share their information with Doc.

Doc dabbed at his lips as he put the napkin down. Rudeness to any woman was unthinkable, even to such a forcefully large one. "Service, ma'am."

"I ain't been a ma'am in a long time. I gots a hurtin' in my jaw. You claim to be a dentist. You kin help me out."

"That I will do. Shall we commence straight away?" Doc started to rise from the chair.

She gestured to her permanently grease-stained apron. "I been cookin' all day. You be obliged to finish what I set out."

Doc obliged.

In New Orleans, a glass of cheap whiskey could be had for two bits; a plate of gumbo, for a couple of centimes. Here, both were in abundance. John marveled at the resiliency of his body to subsist on this fare. He also found it easier to go to bed a bit hungry than to arrive at work in a slovenly jacket. The boardinghouse advertised a bathtub and Doc amazed Abigail by bathing in it.

"I had to come see," she said as she burst in on him one evening. "The boys told me. And damned sure enough it's true. Ye have to be quick," she cackled and pointed at the large crack in the porcelain finish, "the water's a leakin' right out."

The days were filled with work. For the first time, Doc's back began to hurt.

One of his special patients was a prostitute in her sixties named Babes. She trooped into the dingy office every Tuesday morning at ten. She would arrive reeking of cheap perfume and perspiration. When she opened her mouth, the bilious odor that arose was enough to make him faint. In spite of her dishabille, however, she would arrive with a face that was clean of paint and artifice. Doc spent several hours on each of those Tuesdays meticulously scraping and cleaning her rotting teeth. He removed the teeth that could not be saved. Others he filled. He even fashioned an upper set of dentures for her and showed her the results in a mirror.

Babes turned this way and that, admiring her new teeth. "Ain't had no upstairs choppers since ol' Mikey knocked 'em out fifteen year ago. Maybe now, with ma gums not hurtin', maybes I kin better ma station." She spoke with an old dignity born of desperation and tried to press a badly cracked cameo into his hand.

"No, dear, I don't want your cameo," Doc told her as he pressed it back into hers.

"I wants you to have it. Not many gent'men would work on the likes o' me. Where are you from, honey?"

"Georgia, ma'am."

"Well, I guess there still be gent'men in Georgia." She gave him an odd little bow and left.

Later in the week, a local paper published a story about a sixty-year-old prostitute killed in a fight down by the wharves. Doc prayed it wasn't Babes, but she never returned to the office.

Many of his patients appreciated the care that he gave them, but some were abusive, and one threatened to shoot him. To keep himself from being a target of muggers or worse, Doc purchased another sidearm and wore it under his jacket. He was content to stay in New Orleans, working until his feet gave out by day and losing himself in the wild music at night. But one morning, as he bent over to work on a patient, he sprawled to the floor.

That his patient had to summons a doctor for the doctor struck him as ironic. However, he could not arise, no matter how hard he tried. Despite how much he wanted to stay in New Orleans, the cough was ejecting him as firmly as his father had. When Doc felt well enough, he packed once more. By the time he departed for Galveston, the consumption was much worse.

Memories of Mattie made his dreams turbulent. He tried to guess how old the baby might be. He had yearned to call her Alice after his own mother. Fantasies were fine when he slept, but the consumption persecuted him with swollen feet and trembling hands when he awakened.

Having saved a little money in New Orleans, Doc was able to enjoy gracious dining at the Exchange Hotel in Galveston. Unused to such wonderful cuisine, he was sick to his stomach the entire night. Still nauseated from the night before, he barely arrived in time for the Galveston, Houston, and Henderson Railroad that would carry him fifty-one miles to the city of Houston.

Houston had great promise, but in 1873, the Houston and Texas Central ran to Kosse, Texas. In Kosse there was a stage connection to Dallas. Slammed about violently by the coach, whose chassis had no leather springs, John began to drink heavily to ease the strain.

Unlike a train, the most a stage could offer was about six miles an hour. It was oppressively hot. Sometimes the smell of unwashed bodies in the close atmosphere caused him to feel faint.

The 153 miles from Kosse to Dallas was one of the longest treks that he had ever undertaken. From the start, Doc knew that Dallas was not a city to be taken lightly. It was a hodgepodge of bitter youth from the North who hid themselves behind cheap bottles of whiskey. The sharp-eyed Southerners were easier to pick out. They sought out death and revenge with their swagger and fast guns. Then there were the ones from the West who were never going back to their homes as long as they lived. Doc found no solace in their company.

In the arid climate, the consumption became tolerable. When there was too much inner pain, the whiskey took it away. At first, he drank the liquor with molasses, then neat, but it was not his habit to toss back drink after drink until he was insensible. He realized how nervy he was by the quickness with which his fingers jumped to the trigger. Not that he ever used his guns. Because of his father's beatings, Doc had a phobia of physical violence, yet no one was going to mistreat him or impugn his honor. For those who treated him gently, there were smiles, sharp wit, and crackling blue eyes. Those who used him roughly received an unrelenting stare or the barrel of his gun.

Life was won or lost on the toss of a card in Dallas. Doc already understood that fools were not tolerated. The gambling tells he learned and practiced at the gaming table. Each man had his own tells. Dallas' gaming tables taught him to give away nothing unless it was needed to gain advantage. These were skills that could not be learned in mere hours or days. Doc had to wait and listen and watch, always watch. The first lessons learned were the last to be forgotten.

In the meantime, the consumption dictated how much physical labor he could withstand before collapsing, and it dictated how much sleep he would get. It ran his life in a way he had not thought possible since leaving home. He tried not to let it work on his mind. Although he knew he drank a great deal, he tried to keep the liquor from ruling him. The time came when two drinks were needed in place of one and later three instead of two. Several Dallas physicians advised him about the benefits of laudanum. To all, he thanked, tipped his hat, and continued to drink the whiskey.

Dallas had a glittering edge. Doc was a patron of the many saloons but not considered a fixture. He came and went with silence. Having always been a loner, he did not seek answers to life's questions among the many at the tables. In the matter of dress, gray suits with impeccable red brocade or oyster-colored vests accented Doc's ash-blond looks, as did his gracious manners.

Faro was the current game of choice, having heralded from Europe from the time of Louis XIV. In Dallas, it was the railroad men, buffalo hunters, and cattlemen who had the money to "buck the tiger." Not all saloons or gaming halls maintained a faro bank. The ones that did offer faro discreetly advertised by placing the picture of a tiger in their window.

Doc had a working knowledge of faro as well as Spanish monte, the latter having been played on those Friday and Saturday nights after dental classes. The games had not been sanctioned by the school, which made them all the more exciting. He had also been privy to a bit of snooping in his youth, of seeing his staunchly Presbyterian father playing faro, something Henry would have vehemently denied.

There were women of all kinds in Dallas: the educated daughters of council members, prostitutes looking for a good time and a fast buck, and the frontier-types who lived hand-to-mouth in town and moved on. All kinds of tinny piano music issued from the saloons, from sweet Southern melodies to raucous Northern tunes. While not classical in nature, it was enthusiastic.

He wasn't sure if it was the earthiness of Dallas that struck such a vital chord within him, but it seemed to reaffirm that he wasn't going to die right away. Sometimes he could go for several days without the consumption getting the better of him. Then the shakes would lay him out until his bones rattled, the blood boiled in his veins, and the tears blinded him. When a high fever followed, he prayed for death. When it didn't take him, he cursed the day he was born.

In 1874, Doc set up trade with another dentist. Office space was expensive and he had not the funds to set up an exclusive arrangement. Doc's partner worried about his young colleague's pallor, but not overly much until the day Doc failed to come to work.

"Good God, son," had been the older dentist's response after finding Doc prostrate and face down on the floor of his room.

When Doc awakened, he felt cold cloths pressing against his brow. "Not the whiskey," he managed to say before passing out once more. When he awoke for the second time, the pain had left his chest and the pounding in his head had subsided.

"You can fight me later on this, son, but I had a doctor come by. He gave you some laudanum."

"Oh God, no," Doc moaned as he tried to bat the hands away from his face.

"Quit fussing and lie there."

"You sound like my father."

"And what would your father have said?"

"'Get the hell out of my life, boy.' Then he'd hit me."

"Sounds like he made a habit of that."

"It's nobody's business," Doc tried to level his most intimidating stare at the older man, but his heart wasn't in it.

"Nope, it isn't. Sounds like you're carrying an awful lot of baggage though."

"Just my dental tools," Doc said.

"You have some mail."

Doc knew it couldn't be, but a wild surge of hope shot through him.

"You lie quietly and I'll bring it to you."

There were three letters from Mattie and one from Rachel.

Dear John,

This letter will have to be brief, but don't worry. Mattie is fine. She told me that she said something to Henry. I'm not certain what it pertained to, but he's acted like a wounded bear ever since. I'll make certain that she's okay. Both of us will write.

Love Always,
Rachel

Mattie was okay. Doc reread that part, and then his trembling fingers broke the seal on Mattie's letters. It was almost his undoing. He'd become so used to being no one's dearest anything that the tender words unmanned him.

My Dearest John,

I have vowed that I shall never marry, because he would never be you . . .

He could see her writing by the candlelight at night, away from the sorrowful derision of her parents that might suddenly question her letters sent to a first cousin who left Georgia for the West. She would sometimes purse her lips when she was being deliberate. She had a way of saying no in so gentle and yet firm a tone that no man could mistake her meaning.

The other two letters were of the same sentiment, though written at a later time, compelling him to reply.

My Dearest Mattie,

I can't bind you with the cord of loneliness or wrest from your heart the promise that you remain single. It is not meant for you to go through life alone . . .

Doc reflected on her words. His choice had been determined by the consumption. For him there would be no going back, not even for Mattie. But the letters that reached him in Dallas steeled him against the long nights.

My Dearest John,

You're out West. You are far from my arms and my care. I know there are those who don't care, because they are lawless scavengers. They will see you as a man alone, and they will descend upon you as their prey. You must defend yourself and your honor. If you must do so, then act expeditiously and take care of the matter to its fullest.

It was fortunate that the bulk of her letters arrived on Fridays for it was then that Doc needed them the most. Cattle herds and the drovers arrived on Friday and spent the weekend unwinding. He unwound with them. It was towards the end of the week that his temper flared the most. His office partner warned him that he would come to no good end. Doc agreed with him.

"Your death is not going to be here in the office, son. It will be over cards."

Since the latest "episode," as Doc referred to his worst bouts with consumption, had kept him from his patients for a week, he had been depressed and edgy. Perhaps no more than usual, but enough to want to do something about it. There were plenty of opportunities to pique his ire, but Doc let them go by.

He felt unwell and, in spite of constant practice, was not comfortable with his weapon of choice. Neither had he come to terms with the importance of the sporting life as a profession since the profession of dentistry was still his heart's desire. The logic was inescapable, and logic was beginning to temper his choices in a way that his fondest wishes did not.

The logic was that he could not stand for long periods of time without his knees buckling. Try as he might, he was not able to pull an abscessed tooth and breathe in the middle of a hard cough as the strain exacerbated the cough even more. Doc realized that the physician in New Orleans had been painfully right. Patients did not want him to work on them. In spite of his training and expertise, his dental career was slowly leaching away.

♣ ♥ ♠ ♦

Many people came through Dallas. All shapes and manner of men and women noticed Doc. One of them was Dave Rudabaugh. Although Rudabaugh played cards, he spent more of his time robbing stages and trains and rustling cattle. Dave had first sat down at Doc's table out of curiosity. But one late night he burst out his summation of Doc, "Hell, Doc, the first thing I see is this guy who looks like an easy mark. It's got a good package, all slick and dudefied up, but there's this devil just covered up inside all neat like."

Part of the gambling game was listening to the stories and watching for the tells and weaknesses of his opponents. In Doc's eyes and face was a story about Georgia that no man cared to disturb. The saloons were smoky and raucous with the sound of out of tune and tinny pianos. Doc trained himself to a fine degree of concentration to block out that music, not because of the din it made, but because it set off such a wave of nostalgia in him for Georgia. His eyes would flick around the table as he measured and watched and waited for the mistakes.

Dave Rudabaugh liked gambling. Because of that, Doc offered him a pleasant demeanor. Pleasant, however, carried only so far at the gaming table. Rudabaugh's beady eyes would always flick towards Doc's sidearms.

"They don't look very well balanced to me. Maybe too big for your hand." Rudabaugh's fingers were twitching at his side.

"They're just fine," he told Rudabaugh with a half smile tugging at his lips as he tapped the butt end of his guns.

While the consumption consumed his body, Doc consumed his time with gambling, bringing to the games a professional flair that set him apart from even the most ardent of professional gamblers. The saloon became Doc's office and proving ground as he slowly excelled in the mastery of all aspects of this new profession. "One that I can take on the road with me."

He wrote Mattie about this, aching for her approval as he did no other human being. He spared nothing in his letters, putting each raw emotion on paper for her view. Her reply, "My Dearest John, you worry too much." This brought a peal of laughter from him. He often wondered what Alice McKey Holliday thought of her boy. Perhaps she would have written, "My Dearest John, what choices do you have?"

Doc found it singularly interesting and odd that alcohol, while bringing him comfort from the distresses of consumption, brought him none for his memories. If he didn't have the physical comfort of a relationship with Mattie, at least he still had her in the voluminous letters and words that she poured out to him. He told her about the alcohol and how much he had to drink. He told her of the saloons and how each had its own personality. He told how they all had a long bar on the left, usually with a fine mirror to showcase the glasses and bottles. He recounted how the more respectable gambling houses sported heavily polished cherry and oak wood and of the elaborate paintings imported from Europe. He told her that some had wood plank floors covered with straw or sawdust to absorb the tobacco spit. To which she replied, "It sounds exciting. I'm glad you didn't take up spitting, although I do consider a fine cigar acceptable."

Doc's preference in cigars was for the thin ones called cheroots. They were hard on his lungs but a sartorial necessity. He carried his two sidearms under his long fashionable coats, as did many men of the day. The rule was "no sidearm in sight." This was easy to obey as guns could be pulled out whenever they were needed. Plenty were needed due to the proximity of liquor, gaming, and short tempers.

The winter settled around him in a way that Doc had never before experienced. Around him, others also felt the strain. Tempers were hot before and after New Year's, 1875, and if ever there was going to be a fight, Doc was certain this would be the time. The whisky and money flowed. Everyone—and he couldn't let himself off the hook either—was highly "likkered up."

It had all started shortly after Christmas when a saloonkeeper made the mistake of thinking that frail Dr. Holliday was a pushover and unlikely to offer much in the way of resistance to a personal affront.

As Dave Rudabaugh had put it, "There's a devil under Doc's elegance."

There was no devil in Doc, but there was a temper. Play had been going on for some time and, as Doc was aware, the saloonkeeper seemed insulted by Doc's winning streak. Doc could see the sidearm that the man was packing and folded his coat back so his own weapon could be seen. The saloonkeeper's demeanor was irritating. Doc said nothing, but his gaze unnerved the man as he stared at the latter's stained shirt, greasy trousers, and pomaded hair.

Doc was wearing a dark charcoal suit with a fashionably longer coat, a fine linen shirt that matched his eyes, and an oyster-colored vest with tiny flecks of aquamarine blue. To anyone who could read the tells like Doc, the fight would be no contest.

"Cheat," was the only word the bartender got out of his mouth before going for his gun.

Doc pulled his own and the rest of the customers dived under the tables or hit the floor. While uninterested in killing the man, Doc made it clear what he thought about being shot at.

There was a lot of smoke and screaming, mostly from the bartender who thought himself mortally wounded. The police arrested the two men, but the incident was explained away to the amount of libation and time of year. Whatever happened with the bartender Doc never found out. He did know that the man was too embarrassed to go to a doctor for the flesh wound in his hand.

After the New Year, Dallas lost its luster for Doc. Mattie wasn't there, winter was firmly ensconced, and his spirits had hit an all-time low. People bustled hither and yon with their families. The sight of happy-faced children added to his depression. His own child would be celebrating her second birthday.

Even though it was winter, Doc decided to travel once more. Fort Worth loomed on his horizon. From what the fur trappers and buffalo hunters said, Fort Worth was only a few short steps before the most rugged and violent part of the West: Fort Griffin. With a last look at Dallas, Doc got on Texas and Pacific's seven o'clock morning stage to Fort Worth.

❧ *Chapter* ❧
TEN

It was the time of the buffalo. From the Mississippi River to the Missouri, from the Arkansas River to the two Plattes, the millions of lumbering behemoths foraged and migrated. They were as much a part of the West as the golden waving prairie grasses.

But the railroad changed all of that. Eager for land, homesteaders poured onto the prairie. The land meant hope for a better future and a place to raise a family. Dazzled by the sweeping territory, they left the civilization of the East for dusty trails and the hazardous territory of rattlesnakes and scorpions. The waving grasses afforded no safety from the things that bit and stung, just as there was no safety on the trail from marauding whites or Indians.

To protect the flood of settlers, the army established a string of forts that stretched from central Texas to Oklahoma. Ft. Richardson in Jacksboro and Ft. Griffin by the Clear Fork of the Brazos River were established as barriers between the white man and the Indian. Sub-posts in between were designed to protect mail, stage lines, and passengers in transit to other forts.

Not long after Ft. Griffin's inception in 1867, a town sharing the same name sprang up. The flat burgeoned with promise at being the center of commerce and buffalo hunting. Dallas might cast a cool eye in the direction of the upstart, but to the prostitutes, ranchers, buffalo hunters, and Indians, Ft. Griffin was the new Mecca.

By 1875, the wholesale slaughter of the buffalo was reaching a fevered pitch. Wantonly, the rapacious hunters slaughtered the buffalo herds that at one point numbered some forty million. Then, with their groaning cargoes, the hunters would trundle into town and exchange the skins for guns, ammunition, and supplies. After which they would return to the prairie to kill more buffalo. All over America, there were hundreds of thousands of bone yards.

There were fur traders as well. Each of them had a story to tell and appropriate body odors that went along with the telling. But the odors, too, could be forgiven. There were no amenities on the prairie. A man used what he had: buffalo chips for a fire, buffalo tongue for a meal, and a buffalo robe to keep him warm. Bathing and hygiene were inconsequential.

Doc taught his nose to disregard prairie manners and smells. For Doc, the hides meant large quantities of cash money on the poker table. And the hunter who could get his hides to market fastest fared the best. The railroad now reached deep into the Choctaw Nation of Oklahoma Territory. With the railroad and the buffalo, there were thousands of dollars changing hands in the saloons and considerable money to be made. Along Main Street, the Busy Bee, Bee Hive, and Shannessy's Saloons catered to the cattleman, buffalo hunter, and railroad man. Enticed by the enormous wealth to be made, the professional gambler found the high stakes games the best in town. A good game could generate thousands of dollars just on the turn of one card.

Like a foaming waterfall, bawds and outlaws, sheriffs and gamblers arrived daily. It was a din of noise—neighing horses, mounted cavalry, and raucous laughter—from the saloons. Doc wrote Mattie and told her of his plans. With the mail service, he wasn't certain when she would receive his letters or who besides Mattie would read them. She had sent him a crucifix on a heavy gold chain that year for Christmas. He'd been too afraid to carry it on his person for fear someone would mug him for it. Now in Ft. Griffin, he wore it around his neck. That way, Mattie would be close to his heart. "I'll put down here for a while," he had written her.

On North Griffin, the prostitutes plied their trade from ramshackle tents or squalid shanties. Some had been good-hearted girls down on their luck that had turned to prostitution as a means of support. Unfortunately, those young girls became crones in only a matter of weeks. Garish red lipstick hid split lips given by a previous night's coupling. Heavy kohl covered black eyes. Skin-tight bodices uplifted bosoms long since hanging, bustles added shape to flaccid derrieres, and long-sleeved dresses hid emaciated bodies riddled with gonorrhea or syphilis.

For a buffalo hunter coming off the prairie, a woman, even with foul body odor and rancid perfume, smelled like heaven. The names they chose for themselves were far removed from their Christian names. Sweet Sal had pendulous breasts like overblown balloons and armpit hair that was not the same color as the frizzled bleached hair on her head. She boasted that she was twenty years old, but was closer to thirty-five and looked like she was eighty. Portia Patty had an ample bosom and even more ample derriere and was known to lift her skirts to show her backside whenever she got drunk, which was quite often.

Every man was a potential customer, and no one was ever turned away. On Saturday night, the cowboys or buffalo hunters rolled into town. Replete with money after a hard trail drive, the men wanted to have a good time and the whores were available to make sure that they had one. There was liquor, ribald sex, and cards until the money was spent and the cowboys went back out on the prairie.

For Doc, there was no woman like Mattie. He had seen all types, such as the ones who attached themselves to his arm without his invitation and with a greedy light in their eyes. If they really wanted to hang on his arm, he let them, but he made it clear from the beginning that they would not be permanent. They came, of course, in various sizes, shapes, and colors wearing tight, shiny dresses with as much gilt and glitter as could be crowded onto them. They offered themselves to him for whatever he was willing to spend. Being a gentleman, Doc did at times feel a certain obligation but, unfailingly polite, he refused their advances. In some respects, he was in the same boat, peddling his wares, cast adrift, and making it through life as best as he could. The prostitutes tried hard to make themselves willing if that's what he wanted. But that wasn't what he wanted. Instead, his gaze would focus on something far away, and the whores would fall silent recognizing that look.

Rough and ready Ft. Griffin was not a carefully planned town, but there were oases such as the gentility of the Planters' Hotel. The rooms well kept with gracious appointments, and the proprietors reminded Doc of Southern gentility and his mother. Many times he was invited to Sunday supper to enjoy the type of feast not available to him since Atlanta.

There were many properties such as a dining hall, bar, Occidental Hotel, and a livery stable. The Boarding House, while not on the order of the Planters' Hotel, was still an admirable retreat. The general store offered many items that other stores lacked. There were eggs, fresh fruit, and some canned goods that the buffalo hunters returning to town were starving to consume. Nearby were two Indian camps. One lay north of town by the Clear Fork of the Brazos River, and the other south of town by Collins Creek. Since the Tonkawa had fallen prey to vicious attacks by the Comanche, they now rallied behind the army for protection.

By word of mouth, Doc passed it around that while he was not taking a permanent job as dentist, he would be glad to take care of teeth, in particular the children of Indians, enlisted families, and homesteaders. Shyly, the frontiersmen came forward.

"I wish I could be of more help," Doc told Susie Dennis.

Her husband, Will, was one of the enlisted at the fort. Susie, no more than a girl herself, was fresh from the hills of South Carolina and clutched a red-faced baby.

"You was so kind ta see me and the young'un here. Will, he cain't hardly even git in ta town ta see us."

"I know the military run a tight ship," Doc told her.

"All the enlisted fellers like Will are stuffed six to a tent. If somebody complains, they sticks him with latrine duty. Then they git sick. I been washing clothes for some of the officers' wives, so I gets a little money." She was quiet for a moment, then cried out, "It's the wind, Doc. Such a howlin' I never heerd anyplace and the young'un cries so much."

"Well," Doc said slowly as he looked inside the baby's mouth, "this young man is teething. Put a little whisky on a dried buffalo hide, something he can grip with his little gums. Just a little, just a drop or two. The hide will help push the teeth through."

He wished he could do more. The room was scarcely big enough for Susie to turn around in. There was a small bed on sagging springs, dirt floor, and only the barest bit of dirty glass for Susie to look out of. It struck him as poignant that the baby had shoes while Susie went barefooted and was wearing a well-worn dress.

That weekend, as Doc was beginning a poker game at the Busy Bee, Will Dennis approached him. Doc excused himself with a bow, "Kindly do not start the game without me, gentlemen. I won't be long."

"Look, Doc, I don't got much money. They treat them officer fellas nice, but us enlisted get short shrift. Is there somethin' I kin do for you?"

Taken aback, Doc looked down for a moment. The young man's earnest demeanor had touched a place in him he thought was dried up. Clearing his throat, Doc gazed at him but not with his usual dead-eyed stare. "Look, this is embarrassing for me because I used to go hunting as a lad. Hell, this is downright ridiculous. My aim's off."

"Aw hell, Doc. I been shootin' the eyes outta quail since I was a tadpole. Maybe we can go shootin' together."

Doc's face lighted up. "Damn, that sounds fine. You come find me when you got more time. We'll plan on it."

For a soldier, there was little free time, but Trooper Dennis was able to come into town a few times.

"I was told that you was here. Hope I don't come at a bad time," he told Doc as he wiped a grimy hand on his pants leg and stuck it out for Doc to shake.

"Not at all. There is a decided lack of cards here to interest me, and I would certainly enjoy the time to see the countryside. It's a nice bit of a walk towards First or Second Street."

"I was wonderin' could I—ya think I could hold yer gun?"

Intrigued by the young man's lack of guile, Doc tossed over his pistol. The trooper hefted it about, tossed it in the air, and twirled it.

"Do ya like this here gun, Doc? I don't. Guns and women are kinda the same. You allus know when you got the right one. The wrong one, well, you allus know that somethin's wrong with that, too."

Doc began to laugh. "You remind me of a friend that I used to know."

"Used to?"

"He fell at Gettysburg."

"Sorry. Two of my brothers fell and Pa. Ma never got over that. She'd sit and rock for hours out on the porch just expectin' to hear their hallooin' over the hill. I wisht that I had never brought Susie here. Her folks was real aginst it. I didn't knowed it would be this way. Us Dennis' are prideful, though. We pull our own weight."

Occasionally, Doc would visit their home as well. Susie tried hard to look nice, but her dresses—and Doc was certain that she only had two—kept getting shabbier. Her one pair of shoes was kept for going shopping at the dry goods store. It would be nice to buy a new dress and shoes for Susie, but he knew that it would insult Will's fierce pride. And he would never do that.

"It's so hard to be away from home," she told Doc. "Let me fix you some tea. Sorry 'bout the mess."

"I don't want to be in the way, Susie."

"No bother. I don't git vis'ters. One of them Tonkawa Indian women showed me where to plant a garden. I knowed some things about that from Granny. She sure did throw a fit when we packed up and left. After I crossed on the train, I thought maybe I was never gonna be skeered again."

"How so?" Doc asked.

"Kind o' like it was the worst that could happen. Don't know why I'm carryin' on so. You got kids? Yer so sweet. You must have babes of yer own."

Doc's smile wavered. "Well, I, uh, have a little girl." Then quietly he added, "Maybe it's just a desperate dream."

"I bet she most favors you."

"Bright as a copper penny," he whispered.

As Susan Dennis said, the wind did howl. Goaded on by consumptive dreams, the wind kept Doc awake at night with its eerie pitch like the cry of a banshee. In this godforsaken land, it wouldn't have surprised him to see such spectral images.

When Doc wasn't occupied with dentistry or cards, he continued to hone his shooting skills. As well as he thought he knew the area, he miscalculated during a sudden snow squall. One blast of the frigid wind sucked the air from his battered lungs and easily flung him to the ground. When he came to, he found himself slung over the shoulder of a Tonkawa woman. He passed out again and when he opened his eyes, he was inside a teepee.

"I think all the rest of me is frozen, too," Doc gasped to her, "including my lungs."

The next thing he knew, he was wrapped from head to foot in a suffocating buffalo robe. It mattered not that the hide was old, moth-eaten, and riddled with worms. The woman gestured for him to sit by the fire. When he didn't move, she hefted him once more and plunked him down. Solemnly, she stared at him from under her black eyes and stoked the fire with fresh buffalo chips. When the task was completed, she drew a battered tin cup from a leather pouch and filled it.

"You drink," she told him.

Vile liquid that had the color of piss and the taste of gunpowder poured down his throat. When Doc tried to spit it out, the woman pressed the cup tighter to his lips.

"No, you drink."

A moment later, fire roared through his veins and the ice was no more than a bad memory.

Under her scrutiny, he drank from the cup until there was no more. She went outside the teepee. Soon, she returned leading a little girl. From the swollen jaw presented to him, it was easy to see that the child was in a great deal of stress. Small beads of sweat shined on her forehead, and she cast pleading looks at her mother to do something.

Doc stood up and patted the child's head. "Let me go get my instruments." Carefully, he folded the buffalo robe and placed it safely away from the fire. "I will be back as soon as I can."

From the sadness that he saw in the woman's eyes, he realized that many had failed her, many with his skin color.

Outside, the sudden snow had ended. It was cold, but clear. Doc mounted his horse that the Tonkawa woman had secured outside the teepee and headed toward his room at the Planters'. From the prostitutes' cribs, several of the bawds eagerly hailed him for some companionship, but he only lifted his hat in response.

He promptly returned to the Tonkawa camp thirty minutes later.

"It will be best if I examine her outside. I will need a lot of light," he told the Tonkawa woman. Carefully, Doc unrolled his dental instruments and motioned for the little girl to come to him. She fearlessly walked up.

"I'll be very gentle. I know this hurts. Okay?"

She nodded and opened her mouth. It was easy for Doc to see the inflamed gum tissue and bicuspid. As he gently probed the tissue, a thin stream of pus leaked out. Big tears rose in the child's eyes, but she didn't cry. Doc continued to probe and release the infection. With the inflammation finally reduced he could see the tooth more clearly. It would have to come out.

Cleaning, removal, and packing of the tooth took a long time and, when he did finish, it was another moment before he could stand properly. Upon straightening, he found many Indians gathered in a circle around him. They solemnly nodded at him, and he nodded in return. After that initial meeting, many of the Indians came into town, sometimes bringing their children. Doc always treated them with deference and care. It was sad that while the soldiers had accepted the Tonkawa, many of the towns-people were prejudiced.

His dental services applied to the prostitutes as well. "Don't worry about the money, dear. I do this for people to feel better. I know that tooth has vexed you for a long time."

"It's been so sore, but nobody else would look at me."

"Well, it's fixed now."

"I don't have any money ta pay."

"Your smile is payment enough."

From then on, Doc was afforded every courtesy and hospitality that the prostitutes could muster. He never swore at them. He never slept with them. When he rode by, it was always, "Hello, ladies," as he lifted his hat. "How are you all today? Do you need anything?"

"They're none finer than young Mr. Holliday," a newly arrived prostitute waved as she draped her bosom over the top rail of the shanty. She was very pleased that her bosom was about to fall out of her dress. The older woman next to her pinched her hard. "Ouch! What'd ya go do that for?" she asked.

"That, missy, is Dr. Holliday to you. He is a dentist and a man of fine character, and too much of a gentleman for the likes of you."

"I didn't know," the younger prostitute said with a blush. "I apologize."

Doc raised his hat. "No harm done, ladies."

♣ ♥ ♠ ♦

Spring arrived in full swing, and the town was popping at the seams like an overstuffed corset. When it seemed that it could pop no further, a fresh batch of prostitutes arrived from Dallas by stage. Accompanying the wave of gamblers and buffalo hunters was Kate Elder or as she was called, "Big Nose Kate."

It was easy to see what Kate was about. To one and all she claimed she was of Hungarian royalty. She fooled many, but not Doc.

"I know who you are," she purred.

"Dahling, your accent is as clear as the briny part of the Brazos River."

"What?" she spluttered in a guttural accent that was closer to her real voice.

Her mannerisms made the spangles on her many gowns glitter. Without asking for approval, she attached herself to Doc's arm with a smile that was lascivious and impulsive. For the first time, Doc felt like a specimen on the auction block.

Sometimes, to amuse himself, Doc would peel her fingers off his arm. Her grin would broaden as she reattached herself. She fetched him drinks, bent low over him as she poured those drinks, and laughed at his jokes. He stopped her, though, when she referred to him as her man. Her pout, as a result of his soft rebuke, didn't last long. In fact, Doc said and did quite a lot of things just to see how far he could go.

Kate was someone to talk to. She did not understand his love of books or, for that matter, most of what he talked about. Given what she knew of Georgia, she asked if he was a rich man's son. She demanded total loyalty without giving the same in return. It was an ensnaring relationship and one that he longed to shed without knowing how to go about that. Each day, she became more of a cancerous growth on his arm. Each day, he longed to scrape her off.

Sometimes, Doc would step back to watch Kate operate. She ran quite an operation with her roving eye and a come-hither attitude. She knew what she wanted and how to get it. But for all of her savvy, she never understood that Doc was nobody's fool, least of all her own.

"Dahling, if there is one thing I learned at my daddy's knee, it was how to tell the original from the false. You are no more of a Hungarian aristocrat, than my horse."

The small, serpent-toothed knife that she carried in one of her dainty boots flashed into her hand. Armed thus, she made a play for his face, hoping to lay open his cheek or his throat.

The insults wouldn't have been so bad if it hadn't been for the precious letters that Doc received practically every other day from Mattie. Mattie, Kate knew, was a true lady in the fullest sense of the word. If Kate could have, she would have torn Martha Anne Holliday from Doc's soul. Sometimes, when jealousy became too much for her, she would broach the subject, but the fiery blue explosion from Doc's eyes terrified her into silence.

Spellbinding and infuriating, Kate had become as much a part of the Ft. Griffin landscape as the rotgut whiskey, buffalo hunters. And then to top it all off, Dave Rudabaugh arrived from Dallas.

Eventually, Dave with tobacco spittle hanging on the side of his mouth and his spurs jingling sauntered up to Doc for an introduction to Kate. At first, there were only polite questions, but Doc could see that Dave was angling for something else.

Dave was nonchalant concerning Doc, but not long after, rumors began to float around town about Doc and Susie Dennis. Doc was certain that Kate and Dave Rudabaugh had something to do with the innuendoes.

"Hey Doc, word on the street is you're sparkin' some doxie up at Ft. Richardson."

Doc bore the insinuation like he would a pesky fly. His smile would thin and with a small signal from his hand he would indicate that the game needed attention. Kate's pretense grated as well, more so because she considered herself his partner.

There were some nights when the want of Mattie, Georgia, and the life he could never have became so terrible that he thought he would go mad before morning light. The words from her letters undid him and he would deliberately climb into a whisky bottle to forget. He knew that the whisky wouldn't help. Enraged by the finality of his condition, he smashed everything in the room and screamed at Kate to leave him alone. By five o'clock, as the watery light of morning crept across the prairie, sleep finally overcame him. By three that afternoon Doc rousted himself out of bed, spat into his handkerchief, and washed his face for another day.

While Kate was amazed by the amount of alcohol that he drank, she was even more dazzled by his ability to concentrate and his total control of the game, which never wavered no matter how many hours had passed. And he was not above showing her a few winning tips to make her own poker game better.

"Remember, dahling, you'll never make money at faro. Poker, now that's the sport. Is that your fifth glass of vodka?"

"Well, yes," she said in an alcohol coarsened voice, "but you always have a glass in your hand."

"Dahling, men drink. Ladies do not drink and remain ladies."

"Liquor helps me."

"And you seriously dabble in laudanum," he said. "If you start, I'll kick you out. Don't think that I won't." Of all Kate's habits, the laudanum disturbed him the most. He knew she took laudanum on the side, because he found the poorly hidden bottles.

Kate's nature dictated that she must needle him to the brink of madness before she backed away. He supposed that fighting with her took the edge off his anger. He knew he carried that anger like a badge, but it had been a part of him for so long that, like Kate, he didn't understand how to let it go. Every day of his life, he thought of that little girl that he had fathered or, perhaps worst of all, that Mattie had lost the child at birth. Every day she grew and laughed and grew some more.

"Do you have children, Doc?" Kate asked him.

When his look told her that subject was closed, Kate shrugged. "I got children." In those rare moments, her speech would slip from the coarse dialect that she fostered and her eyes would soften. Later when the liquor had fired her up, her loose tongue would harangue him across the entire Choctaw Nation and all the way to Georgia.

Longing for a change of scenery, Doc rode out of Griffin towards Ft. Concho. Not far down the road, Doc ran into a fellow sportsman from Ft. Griffin.

"You headed to Ft. Concho? Heard about some pretty good games," Doc said.

"Me, too. Needed a break. I'll ride with you a spell, if you don't mind."

"Much obliged."

By the time they arrived in town it was late afternoon.

"Oh, God. It's an election day. They'll be likkered from dawn until dusk. Politics mistaken for religion make terrible bedfellows." Doc looked at the wooden stage being decorated and set up for the obligatory oration.

"Do you think they'll arrest us before or after?"

Doc's lips widened in a grin. "They'll arrest us before the election and hang us afterwards."

"Damn, Doc, I wanted to see my old lady again before I died."

"Come on, I was kidding."

"Here comes the sheriff."

"Afternoon, gents. Are you here to imbibe in the waters and take in some victuals before you leave? I know who the both of you are, and I'm not gonna put up with no confidence games in this town. I run a clean town."

"I assure you, sir," Doc told him, "that a confidence game is far from the modest poker game that we were going to engage in."

Doc didn't know his riding companion very well, but the man had always treated him with civility and was a conscientious card player. He also didn't spit tobacco on the bartender and was polite to the barroom girls. But the sheriff was unrelenting and both men were arrested for running an illegal confidence game.

The evidence was flimsy and neither of the men had trouble posting bail, but Doc found it galling. Upset by the treatment, he rode back to Ft. Griffin on the fastest horse available. By the time Doc arrived back at the Bee Hive, there was already a sizzling poker game in progress.

"I was as surprised as you was, Doc. Kind of odd, don't you think? Almost like somebody tipped the sheriff off that we was coming. I didn't tell nobody my plans. And I know you didn't."

"Damned odd," Doc agreed.

"There's somethin' else, Doc, I've been meanin' to say. I swear to God, Doc, I wouldn't make up stories, but that there Kate was hangin' about and whisperin' with Dave Rudabaugh."

Doc's frown reached all the way up into his hairline, and his light blue eyes flashed with fire. "Really?"

The excitement of the game soon put him in a better frame of mind, but his mood quickly soured with Kate's arrival.

"I bet you came back just for me," she said and began to shower his face with kisses.

"I don't want to tell you," he explained with his teeth on edge, "what will happen to you if I discover what your part in that mess was?"

"My part?" she asked.

"Kate, you're not that good of an actress," Doc said as he deliberately pried each of her grasping fingers from his arm. "Is that a new dress?"

"Yes." She swirled the red and black spangled confection before him and raised her skirt just a trifle so he could see what fine ankles she had.

"A gift from Rudabaugh?" It was a shot in the dark, but Kate whirled again this time in a huff and left the saloon.

By the time Doc got to the room that Kate shared with him, she was compliant, generous, and soothing.

"It was so pretty."

"It's odd, Kate, that you showed up when you did. And damned odd that Rudabaugh always hangs around. Would you care to elaborate?"

"Elaborate?" she stumbled through the word. "I don't understand."

"Tell me why you let Rudabaugh buy you that dress?"

"I don't know nobody with that name."

"That's what I thought."

"Does your chest hurt? Do you want me to rub it?"

"Kate, where I hurt, you can't reach."

He went outside for a long walk. He was no one's fool. He had never trusted Kate, and he trusted Rudabaugh even less. Rudabaugh continued to smile and bide his time. At first, there was little except arrogance. Then, while Doc was officiating a faro game at Shannessy's Saloon, the enmity exploded.

"I hear tell you was sparkin' the wife of that Ft. Richardson soldier, cheated him at cards, and murdered him to shut him up. You cut him with that big machete knife you allus carry."

It took all of Doc's nerve to keep from drilling Rudabaugh and his foul mouth in front of thirty witnesses, but he knew that's what Rudabaugh wanted.

"Tell me," he asked, "how, suh, do you believe that I, as a man of five feet and eight inches could carry a machete at my belt without vivisecting my privates? This is a preposterous bald-faced lie that I don't have to deny."

"Whatever you say, Doc. Guess you oughta know, but there's been some marshals hangin' about askin' questions. Don't be surprised if they asks you some." Rudabaugh picked up a gold coin near Doc, tossed it in the air, and pocketed it.

Doc's fingertips twitched in the direction of his gun, but he could see Dave's band of followers loitering nearby. He knew all of them were armed, and he knew all of the guns were trained on him.

"Fer services rendered, Doc," Rudabaugh said and left, taking his band of men with him.

About an hour after Rudabaugh's departure, two men approached Doc. He knew that they were marshals. Shannessy escorted them to the table. The older of the two marshals had the lived-in look of the outdoors, sun-leathered skin, and eyes that had been sunk deep in their sockets by the sun. The younger man was a carbon copy. From their rolling gait, Doc knew that they spent long hours in the saddle. Outwardly, he stayed relaxed. Inwardly, he waited.

⇥ Chapter ⇤
ELEVEN

"My shift is over for a while, gentlemen," Doc indicated the chairs across from him. Under the table, his fingers tapped ever so slightly on the butt of his gun.

Shannessy cleared his throat. "This here's Virgil Earp and his brother, Wyatt."

"Name is Doc Holliday," he told the brothers. "My given name is John, but no one calls me that except in emergencies."

The brothers exchanged glances. "We're investigating for a private company that has a great deal of interest in the welfare of its rail and stage lines."

"You mean Wells Fargo?" Doc said as he poured himself a drink.

Virgil looked at him steadily. "We're interested in getting the goods on a gang that has been stripping decent people of their funds."

"Are you speaking of Dave Rudabaugh? And are you accusing me of being a member of such a gang, suh?"

"No, no, no," Wyatt added hastily. "But you know this man, Dave Rudabaugh. We heard you were friends."

"That I can assure you," Doc coughed into his handkerchief, "is a falsehood. It seems, for some fiendish purpose, I have been misrepresented."

"The Rudabaugh gang makes a good living up and down the way," Virgil remarked.

"Yes, and he brings the money here from its place of liberation."

"Do you think Rudabaugh has ever liberated it honestly?"

"Honestly, suh?" Doc drained his glass. "No, he is not a fellow to liberate honestly if it is something he can procure quickly. It is curious that he, who is so careless of personal attire, can come and go with such great punctuality."

"Like for the arrival of a stage or train?"

Doc shrugged. "As I have indicated, I care a great deal when Dave Rudabaugh surfaces."

Virgil leaned forward and his voice took on a harder timber. "Have any of your business transactions ever included the Ft. Richardson area?"

Doc's eyes narrowed slightly. "The road between Ft. Griffin and Ft. Richardson is well traveled. However, I have neither the time nor the inclination to take up permanent residence in Ft. Richardson."

"There is a rumor that you killed a soldier in an argument over a woman. Do you wish to comment on that?" Virgil asked.

Doc stared so steadily at Virgil that the older man dropped his gaze. "The last few years have been unkind to me, suh, consequently I have not been in the best of moods, but I have killed no one. Let my accusers come forward if they will and I shall gently speak to them of their lies."

"About the Rudabaugh matter," Wyatt broke in, "we have the authority to offer a stipend in return for information."

"Jaded though I am, I am not sanguine about money for information. And, as a faro dealer, I hear tales from many and all. But I have no knowledge as to the whereabouts of Dave Rudabaugh." Doc took a drink of whiskey. "If I can help you, I will. He has plagued me too often to escape my notice."

Wyatt interrupted, "Would you consider being deputized and riding with us to catch him?"

"Your offer sounds like a most fantastic opportunity, and one that I would normally relish. However, at this time, my tuberculosis respectfully declines." Doc drained his shot glass yet again.

Wanting to be friends above all else, Wyatt tried to steer the conversation back in a different direction. "Abilene, Dodge, Denver, and believe it or not Old Granada, Colorado have a lot of ripe saloons. You might find the companions boon and the tables flush."

Doc's eyes twinkled. "You sound as if you speak with authority on the subject."

"I know Colorado and Missouri well," Wyatt said.

Doc said, "We must pool our resources at a more propitious time."

"Think over being deputized," Virgil said and rose from the chair.

"We'll know where to find you," Wyatt finished and held out his hand. He was not at all certain that Doc would take it. When Doc did, Wyatt blinked.

"In all probability, gentlemen, our paths will cross one day."

By the time Doc walked out of the saloon, the Earp brothers were gone. It was July and the prairie grasses were burning with heat, while irritating swarms of flies landed on man and beast alike. There was a little tingle in the wind that hadn't been there when Doc first came to town. To be sure, the excitement of the games was enough of a draw to make him stay. So far, he had acquired a roll of $15,000 that he had neatly tucked inside a money belt at his waist. But now his sense of self-preservation was bidding that he move on.

Before he left, he said goodbye to Susie and her baby. Rudabaugh had already set tongues wagging by strongly hinting that Susie was Doc's mistress when all Doc had done was treat the baby.

"I cain't thank you enough about takin care of my baby. I don't got nuthin' to give to you in return," Susie told him as she looked at the floor.

"You and Will did give me something, Susie. You gave me your friendship. You've got nothing to be ashamed of. Say goodbye to Will for me. I don't know when I'll be back. And you take good care of that youngster."

"Wish that Will was here. He sets quite a store by you, Doc. Fact is, he's out on patrol. I don't know when he'll be back."

"One more thing, Susie, if you'll mail this letter for me, I'd be much obliged."

"Pleased to. Oh, thought I'd tell ya, if anybody asks, I ain't seen you."

"Don't lie for me, Susie."

"No, Doc, it ain't nobody's business."

Doc smiled, kissed her cheek, and stepped back to touch the brim of his hat. Susie Dennis, clutching the letter to her bosom, scurried down the street towards the post office.

My Dearest Mattie,

I'm off to Denver. It may take a while.

Banking that his lungs would be well enough for travel, Doc boarded the Texas and Pacific Railway stage connection. The route would carry him through Palo Pinto, Weatherford, and on to Dallas. From there, the Houston and Texas Central would carry him to Denison, Texas. Never had he experienced more agony than in each bone-jarring, dusty, and cough-laden mile. He was wheezing long before Palo Pinto. By the time the stage arrived in Denison, Doc felt dead. He had pushed his body beyond all physical limits. Whether he wanted to or not, Denison would have to be his refuge for a while. As he staggered off the platform, he was the object of immediate interest fostered by his neat suit and shoes and blood-soaked handkerchief.

There were strict regulations in Denison. Along Main Street, for instance, there could only be legitimate businesses. Although the Crystal Palace was a saloon, it was maintained in the finest fashion. One block south of Main Street lurked the dark side of Denison. A ravine split the town into seedy dives of tents and prostitutes' cribs. There, excesses of drunkenness, cockfighting, and whoring occurred at all hours of the day or night.

The Alamo Hotel gave Doc respite for almost three weeks. The food was good, and the accommodations were comfortable. In the evenings, he gambled and afterwards retired to his room and let his head sink down on the plump white pillows. While resting his body, the Crystal Palace Saloon busily swelled his bankroll. After recuperating, Doc once more packed his valise.

Doc paused to look at his rail schedule. "I need to purchase a ticket through to Colorado," Doc told the stationmaster.

"Shall I set you up with a ticket to Denver?"

"That will be fine." He took his ticket and boarded the train.

Doc was thankful that he'd been able to get away without fanfare. Kate had been an annoyance at the very least, but Dave Rudabaugh was the type to gun him from behind in a back alley. Sooner or later, Doc knew he would come face-to-face with Rudabaugh and his band of cutthroats. Rudabaugh was extraordinarily deadly with his skills. Not long after Doc's conversation with the Earps, Doc had caught a glimpse of Dave carrying a satchel marked "U.S. Government." The bills Dave flaunted everywhere were quite large. Some had even gently landed in Kate's grasping hands.

After the trumped up charge in Ft. Concho and the rising swell of voices against him, Doc knew that he had been set up to take the fall for the Ft. Richardson murder. It was a well-established fact that Rudabaugh and his gang worked the trains. Doc guessed that Rudabaugh realized his mistake and wanted to get to Doc before Doc could do anything about him. The spreading of the rumor about the Ft. Richardson murder was a way to do that. In all likelihood Rudabaugh was the murderer himself.

Doc knew Rudabaugh and his gang watched the trains coming in and out of Denison and they would be sure to ask questions about a man fitting Doc's description. He knew his present journey would take him all the way to Prowers County and Old Granada, Colorado. The Denver ticket could be used for a more convenient time. Wyatt Earp had spoken favorably about Old Granada. Perhaps the distance involved would cool the military's ardor in wanting to find him.

Doc settled back in his seat and waited for Oklahoma to show him something interesting. The scenery was new for a while, but soon the view of stark lands, chalky washes, and burned out colors was depressing. Even the long grasses were bleached to a curious hue of pale gray. As the miles passed, Doc began to feel better. Because he had obtained a seat several cars away from the main boiler, his cough had lessened and the bleeding in his lungs subsided. After a layover and a good meal in Emporia, Doc felt much better.

The good humor remained with him for the rest of the trip. As Doc stepped off the train onto Old Granada's platform, his eyes widened. For the first time in his life, cool dry air rushed into his lungs. Tipping his head back, he closed his eyes and let the sensation of the dry wind cleanse his lungs like they never had been cleansed before. He took another breath and another.

He wanted to shout at the top of his lungs that he finally knew what it was to breathe. It was tempting to give in to the impulse, but a gentleman did not do that. Instead he cleared his throat, straightened his coat, and tucked his euphoria away.

Hard-pressed to contain his dignity, Doc walked down the street and took in the myriad of people and businesses. At first glance, it was a colorful town from the reddish-hued buildings and walkways to the hitching posts. So busy was he at peering in the windows that he was almost run over by a group of prostitutes dressed in all manner of finery from gold and silver cloth to black sequined gowns. They stopped, unfurled their parasols, and gave their shoulders a little jerk of disapproval.

"Ladies, it was my fault for being so rude."

"Ooohh, ladies is it now? We haven't been ladies in a long time," one woman guffawed.

One of her companions dug her in the ribs. "You're not nice. Oh, there's that old stick from the across the street. She's always gawkin' at us."

One of the younger whores muttered, "She thinks she's better'n us, just cause her husband has that fancy store. Anyway, now that she's married, she knows all those fancy airs, including that hifallutin French and wears fancy city-bought clothes. Well, let me tell you, she was a whore out of Miss Winny's incubator. You have ta remember Miss Winny. She was one of St. Louis' finest madames. Miss Winny has a real fine stone mansion. There are servants to wipe yer butt and a butler to serve you dinner. And the entertainment . . . Oooah."

"Was they French and Spanish? I hear tell these fancy madames import the girls when they're really young. Only the prettiest, mind you. Teachenum French and ferrin languages and all kinds of ways to please a man. Then they marries them off. The men feel so indebted to Miss Winny they give her a lot of money."

"Sssh, you cain't say stuff like that. If'n you don't make a fuss, they don't arrest ya."

"That's so stupid. Ain't you being the fine one, honey."

Doc lifted his hat, "Ladies."

They blushed and giggled. "You're new here, aren't you?"

"Well, I am. Just stepping off the train to take a bit of fresh air in your fair city."

There were more giggles. "Are you going to be staying long?"

"I might be."

"Well, if there's anything we can do to make your stay more enjoyable, just let us know."

"I will do that. In the meantime, where might I find a restaurant."

"The best place is the John Beasley Hotel. They'll take you cause you're a gentleman."

One of her friends hissed at her, "What are you talking about, Paula? Old John took you the other night."

"Shhh. I don't want his wife to find out."

Doc smothered a chuckle and doffed his hat. Never had he seen a more deliciously low-down and dirty town and one that was proud of it. No one asked where he came from since, as it was put to him, "We all comes from somewhere." Doc could see why Wyatt Earp had said that Old Granada was ripe. As the terminus for several railroads such as the Santa Fe, hundreds of thousands of dollars jingled like a waterfall through the streets, dance halls, and saloons.

He took up a short residence at the John Beasley Hotel, which boasted a restaurant. The best buckwheat cakes and steak were served there and Doc took his fill of them every chance he got. A battered sign outside read, "Best in the County." Old Granada was almost the only town in Prowers County, but no one mentioned that. There was also the Windran Hotel, and Wright & Rouths, a company that dealt in hides. Since the terminus for the Santa Fe Railroad was Old Granada, there were the commission houses of Otero, Sellar, and Co., as well as the Chick Brown, Co. The town was proud that it had neither a newspaper nor a mayor and hoped that it would remain uncivilized for a long time to come.

If life was dull during the week, it got incredibly lively on the weekend when the cowboys, professional gamblers, and buffalo hunters rolled into town. It was during Doc's first weekend that he became acquainted with Jane Canary. Female gamblers were not new to Doc. He soon learned, however, that Jane came in two different forms. There was the polite, bejeweled Jane who dressed in her finest clothes and asked if she might join the play. Then there was buckskin-clad Jane who pulled out her six-shooter and blasted the overhead chandelier all to hell.

Flirting up a storm, she bumped his boot with her foot. "You know, Doc, I really like men with blonde hair."

Doc cleared his throat. "Well, ma'am, I certainly thought that was a fine brace of horses that you were driving today."

"I've always loved a fine horse. And I've always loved men who love a fine horse."

Jane's rejoinders were always difficult to answer. She smiled wickedly and tapped his boot once more. Doc cleared his throat and looked around the saloon for someone else to carry the brunt of Jane's charms. No one was about. Sighing, he went back to the game.

"I don't suppose—" she said.

"Well, dahling, the only love I've ever been true to is Lady Poker. She has my heart."

"Yeah, she's hard to compete with."

Over the next few weeks, Doc got to know Old Granada very well. It was one of the few places where he could gamble unmolested, unconcerned, and unhurried. Other professional gamblers such as Clay Allison, Ben Thompson, and Mysterious Dave

Mather gambled, but did not stay during the week. Luke Short's appearance was always a delight to Doc. Luke and Doc had nurtured a friendship over the years, Luke being one of the very few who had staunchly stood by Doc during the Dallas trouble. Smaller than Doc, he was the epitome of elegant splendor and, for all outward appearances, might have stepped off a train from New York. Though Luke didn't stay in Old Granada long, Doc knew that he would run into him again.

Professional gambling was a fraternity. Even if one gambler had never met the other, the reputation always preceded. But the advent of the railroad and the opening of the rich gold and silver fields now combined to bring the fraternity together many times to the same place. It was an easy case of economics. The ores flowed from the mountains. The money flowed from the trains. The gamblers flowed after both. Towns with no railroads or gold were destined to become ghost towns on a forgotten patch of prairie.

Ham Bell, who ran one of the dance halls, was friendly and an occasional poker player. Except for Bat Masterson, Doc had a reasonable acquaintance with most of the members of his fraternity. Ben Thompson, best known for his surly attitude and sometimes blazing guns, gave Doc a rare compliment. "Holliday, I don't say this to many men, but you're always polite and you don't bother me."

"Much obliged, Thompson, much obliged."

And that was that. During a high stakes game, there were few words. After the games, when the liquor kicked in and the tongues were loose, boasts came frequently and hard. Doc ignored them, just as he ignored pointed questions from Bat Masterson concerning the killing of the soldier at Jacksboro.

"You can trust me. Come on and tell me the truth."

"Masterson, I killed no one at Jacksboro. If you want the culprit, I suggest you look in the direction of Rudabaugh and his gang."

After winning a $5,000 poker stake that evening, Doc realized Old Granada was losing its gloss. According to railroad sources, the Santa Fe would soon be moving on. When that happened, all that had made Old Granada pop and squeal would be lost. From then on, the saloons would do less business during the week. With fewer cowboys and railroad men, the prostitutes would be looking for other towns. By the next year, Old Granada might well be a ghost town. The best thing to do was to head West.

At nine o'clock the next morning, Prowers County and Old Granada were disappearing behind Doc. It had been a nice town in which to rest. His secret money belt was lined with two separate wads of bills totaling almost $20,000. Physically, he felt better. If he'd been someone else, he might have stayed to enjoy the lush meadows, wild game, and berries that grew around Old Granada and the nearby country.

He had found that poker was easier to master than sentimentality. When he was gambling, the questions about his family were tucked away in the recesses of his mind. But right before he fell asleep, they rose up like pieces of wood in a logjammed stream. In spite of himself, he remembered with fondness the evenings when his father read the newspapers. Did his stepmother, Rachel, like the columns on manners and morals to be read to her? Did Henry still have his love for horses? Did the family still get together on Sunday for picnics and barbecues? And the question that was the most fearful to ask: Was Mattie being courted by someone else?

Inner reflections remained unspoken. Doc knew that anyone displaying vulnerability would earn himself a bullet in the back. The self-preservation that had always helped Doc in the past told him what to do now. Deception had never been part of his makeup, but he felt compelled to move in a way that was contrary to his nature. By the time Doc arrived in Kit Carson to change trains on the Kansas Pacific, he was glad of his decision. Flyers with a poor likeness of him were now being distributed in the railroad stations: "Wanted for questioning in the murder of Jacksboro soldier."

Until he could figure who was behind this latest lie, he was forced into taking an alias. But maybe that wouldn't be such a bad thing. Kate wouldn't know. Masterson might guess but not right away. Of all the people in his life, Mattie would be the only person to whom this might strike as a terrible blow.

By the time the train reached Denver, Doc had finished writing a letter to Mattie: "Dearest Mattie, please forgive me . . . Love Always, Tom McKey."

Her answer arrived three weeks after he'd been hired to work as a faro dealer in a prominent saloon. "My Dearest Tom," at this point Doc stopped reading, because he could hear so very plainly Mattie's peal of laughter from Georgia. Doc began to smile and then reread, "My Dearest Tom, All is forgiven. Please let me know if J.H. is well."

If there was one person left on Earth who could make him laugh at himself, it was Mattie.

Denver's air was thinner than that of Old Granada and Doc was glad that he had waited for summer before traveling. He had held his breath when a new group of prostitutes arrived from Chicago, but Kate wasn't found skulking near his hotel room or in the gaming halls. Denver was a lot like Dallas, a town where beef on the hoof was varnished in gold and silver. Hundreds of thousands of cattle came up from Dallas to Dodge City and Kansas City, but at some point they were loaded through to Denver. The cattle meant money. And where there was money, there were gamblers.

Doc welcomed his new situation as faro dealer. The arrangement suited him as he had a certain number of hours to oversee the games and his off-duty times that he used to play poker in and around the city. The rumor mills had spread the word throughout the southwest about the Ft. Richardson soldier that J.H. Holliday had killed with his sword. Doc had noticed that as time went on, the murder weapon grew from a knife to a machete and then to a sword.

"Reliable" sources reported that Kate, fearful for John Holliday, set a fire outside the jail to lure everyone away so she could spring him. Then the two lovingly rode some eight hundred miles across Indian Territory to Kansas. Consumption not withstanding, the thought of riding eight hundred miles through Indian Territory with a crazy woman hanging on his arm was more than ludicrous. He was an intelligent, educated man who took the train, but the gossip of the day was hell-bent on making him travel through desolate and dangerous territory with Kate. The dime novels made it sound so good that it had to be true. The readership, starved for lurid and exciting tales, ate this up as if it were the truth. It added spice to their boring lives. Doc had no illusions. If people wanted to believe what they read, then they were beyond all help.

Doc enjoyed working in anonymity, although the owner knew who he was and respected him for the clean gambling house that he ran. Already an exemplary poker player, Doc was able to lift the game to a new height. All was well on poker's green cloth, but the trouble at Jacksboro continued to be a pair of Spanish spurs digging into Doc's sides. So focused was the attention on the whereabouts of J. H. Holliday that no one from Jacksboro cared if Tom McKey was the new faro dealer in a Denver saloon.

Doc had told his boss, because he didn't want the proprietor to have the idea that he was dishonest.

"Women trouble, huh?" he was asked.

"Some," Doc agreed. His shift had ended and, as was customary, he and the saloon owner shared a drink and went over the day's proceeds.

"Well, Tom McKey, makes little difference to me, as long as you do your job. Do you plan on being Tom McKey long?"

"Not long," Doc replied, "but enough time to know that she's not on my tail, or anyone from Ft. Richardson for that matter."

"I had an acquaintance who had that happen to him. Of course, the woman was his wife," He gave Doc a wry wink.

"This acquaintance, real close personal friend, was he?"

Denver gave Doc the opportunity to play poker with the best in the business. Buckskin Frank Leslie was one of the best and he stayed in Denver for a while. Frank knew who Doc was. Luke Short came to ply his trade in Denver, also. Natty, with a black top hat, a fashionable black suit coat, and diamond studs, Luke looked around the saloon.

"Hiya, Frank. Me and Frank aren't going to raise the roof on this one. Thought I'd let you know that it's probably Masterson going on with this Jacksboro shit or Rudabaugh. Damn, he's worse than a vulture on a carcass. Think the alias is a good idea. I haven't seen Kate. By the way, you look pretty spry after riding eight hundred miles through Indian Territory. Tell me, did Kate burn the whole jail or just part of it?"

As word of Doc's expertise at fair gaming spread through town, another saloon owner approached him. The proprietor of the Palace Saloon was generous to the people who worked for him. Of course, the Palace was classy and offered many games of chance that included Spanish monte. At any one time, several hundred gamblers might be crowded together. The bar was an artwork of carved wood, sparkling mirrors, and glasses. Behind the bar could be found domestic beers, wines, and imported liquors. There was also a theater for the enjoyment of orchestras and light opera. Doc, a lover of fine music, would often attend and listen to stringed orchestras or other musical groups. Sometimes Luke Short would join him, if he weren't busy gambling.

Many times after Saturday's rush, the only things left were empty bottles of imported champagne, a mountain of dirty glasses, and piles of crumbs. On those nights, Doc would stay longer to help clean up. It felt good not to have Kate on his arm. Even better was the absence of worry that he had offended her by some slight and how she would inflict the payment on his frail physique. Unfortunately, she was quite buxom and physically strapping. He'd known from the start that he was no match for her.

Luke Short loved teasing Doc. "I am shorter than you are, suh," Luke told him one night. His affectation of a Southern accent rather pleased Doc. "And I rather believe that the sweet dove from which you fled has the constitution of a bald eagle and the fortitude of a vulture." He poured Doc a drink. "Would that you be very careful not to hook up with such a woman again."

"Forget about that. Tell me about Deadwood."

"You might, when your tour is up here," Luke suggested, "take a whirl to Cheyenne or Deadwood. More and more gold fields are opening. You have to partake in these new territories while they are still lucrative. Abilene's a farmer's market now since the railroad pulled out."

"How far do you think the Santa Fe will push?"

"Mountains maybe. Depends on how much they want it. Those granite trails are mighty narrow. Can you imagine hurtling off the rails at thirty miles an hour?" Luke shuddered.

Doc had already thought about Deadwood, so Short's mention of it stiffened his resolve. Deadwood was Bill Hickock's territory, and Doc longed to pit his skills against him. Since Miss Jane Canary had a particular fondness for Hickock, Doc supposed that he would see her, too. One afternoon, however, she popped in from the street. She was wearing her most disreputable buckskin apparel and her hair stuck out from under the brim of her hat.

Bellying up to the bar, she slammed her fist down on the smooth wood. "Rack up somethin' to wet my whistle. Been ridin' fer hours. Ooo, you got nice company," she said as she turned to view the occupants.

Doc made a small noise in his throat that was echoed by Luke.

Knocking back what was in her shot glass, she grabbed both the glass and the bottle and headed to Luke and Doc's table.

"I ain't had me a good game since Old Granada. And I know you boys know how to play."

The bartender looked on from behind the bar. The threesome made quite an impression: two gentlemen, impeccably dressed in every way, opposed to Jane's dirty buckskin, frizzy hair under a porkpie hat, and dirty fingernails.

By midnight, Jane's eyes had glazed over like a wildfire over the Rockies, and her buckskin fringe floated in her vodka. She was on her second bottle and, although she kept slumping further down the table, when it came to play she would rouse herself and put the cards down.

"Hit me."

Always a gentleman, Doc finally asked, "Miss Canary, are you feeling well?"

Before he could say anything else, Jane jumped up and tackled him, sending him sprawling to the floor.

Shocked, Doc caught the dumbfounded look on Luke Short's face. The little man had jumped up as well.

Jane peered down at Doc and puckered her lips. "I'm likkered up pert near, honey. And I like 'em blonde."

In the struggle that ensued, it took the bartender, Luke Short, and two of the other dealers to peel her off of Doc. Before she could be escorted out, she balked long enough to tweak Doc's sweeping mustache. "See you later, sugar."

Doc brushed his fingertips across his forehead. He was pale. "Damn, I saw my life flash before my eyes."

"Gotta tell ya, Doc," Luke said, "thought I was gonna have to shoot her and put her out of her misery. Damn, I feel sorry for Hickock."

There were light-hearted moments, but gambling was a serious business. As he'd passed through the ranks from player to dealer, Doc had learned about the tells of the game. Included in that knowledge was learning the ways that a man could cheat. Body language, such as fidgeting, was an obvious giveaway. Subtle signals such as refusing to meet the dealer's eyes or tugging on an earlobe might suggest a communication to someone across the room. Cheating at faro was possible if the faro box had a widened slit for the cards. The cards could then be sanded, making them stick much easier. A seasoned gambler, no matter how good his credentials, was always a suspect.

Doc didn't worry so much about the regulars, but the hot-heads fresh off the trail were a source of continual trouble. All it took was one gun to ruin the game for someone else. Knowing this, extra security was hired to keep the games on an even keel. With the constant flood of high rollers, each saloon tried to outdo other rivals by attracting the best gamblers, featuring special menus, and by entertaining with loud piano music.

If there was trouble at the table, Doc was swift to correct it. He didn't want to draw attention to himself at this time, but the fluid manner in which he drew his .45 dissuaded many of the arguments. The other players didn't know who this slight stranger was, but they quickly understood that Tom McKey was capable of making good his threats.

To Doc, his card handling was just as good as ever, but he was beginning to notice the change in his face. Every morning in the mirror he could see how his eye sockets were deepening. His cheekbones became sharp as never before, and there was a loss of pigment in his blue eyes. It was odd that the things he missed the most were the simple things like the blue in his eyes. All the blue had fled until only a crystal color remained. He realized that it made him look frightening.

Restlessness tugged at him once more. While he yearned to use his dental skills, his poker skills were the top of the line. He knew which of these professions would see him through life to the bitter end. Like his mother, all he could do was wait. Two months passed and then one late summer afternoon, Wyatt Earp arrived.

"Glad to make your acquaintance," Wyatt said sticking out his hand. There was a decided twinkle in his eye.

"That's a fact."

Doc's voice lowered as he leaned forward. "I hear rumors that you're still undercover."

"That could be a fact," Wyatt replied.

Doc poured himself a drink and offered one to Wyatt, but the man refused politely pointing to his coffee cup.

"Are you checking up on me?

"Nope, on my way to Dodge, although thought I might try Cheyenne."

"A lot of gold there I hear."

"Everybody's headin' out. You headin' out, too?"

"Maybe," Doc said. Both men were in earnest now, all pretense aside, but Doc didn't want to tip his hand.

"Thought maybe I could get some information."

"Such as?" Doc took a long drink of whiskey. Standing in the smoke-filled room had irritated his already irritable lungs.

"I have it from an impeccable source that Rudabaugh killed that Jacksboro soldier."

"Rudabaugh or Masterson?"

Wyatt's voice dropped lower, "I don't want to believe it of Masterson, but he bragged so much in Old Granada."

"In the name of God, why won't that man let it go?"

Wyatt held up his hand. "I talked to him, and he got evasive. I didn't pursue it. The railroad still has wanted posters out on you. Fortunately, the likeness is poor. I don't know what to say. I know you didn't do it."

Doc sighed. "What kind of place is Kansas? I took a long look while I was coming out on the train, but how is it really?"

"Lots of money in buffalo hides, but they're fast disappearing." Wyatt smiled and stood up. "Listen McKey, you get tired of Denver here, come give Dodge a try."

"I'll take that under advisement."

Doc thought Earp did have a point. The Black Hills were pouring waterfalls of gold ore all over the territory. Boom or bust, the hurry was to dig it up before it was gone. Cheyenne was the new boomtown, and a mass of gamblers, miners, and businessmen were heading there quickly.

Masterson's tenacity in the Jacksboro murder did not endear him to Doc. The incident at Jacksboro was now too firmly planted in everyone's mind to wrest it out, including Bat's. Depressed, Doc imagined himself placing full-page ads stating that he, J.H. Holliday, had not killed the soldier at Ft. Richardson. Afterwards, in spite of his proclamation and the good offices from his friends, he would be arrested and thrown into jail for his audacity, inveterate temper, and alcoholic ways.

Doc's correspondence with Mattie mirrored his depression. Mattie had remained a devout Catholic in spite of everything, while Doc had trouble praying. It seemed that he'd stopped having faith in God after his mother died and never got back into the habit. He believed in a vengeful God and that the illness was a punishment sent from Him. If that was so, how much punishment was deemed enough? Or was there an end?

Of all the people in his life, Mattie's opinion was the one that mattered the most. Struggling to find the words, he finally put the question to Mattie, who sent him her reply.

My Dearest Tom,

God didn't do these things to you. I know you don't believe that, and I have a very real trouble in believing it myself. Losing you was never part of the bargain for me. It never will be. No one is ever going to be good enough for me. I can do what I do each day as long as I know you're safe. So, for my sake, do what you have to do to stay alive. Even if it means drinking more than you believe to be proper. I understand how ill you are. So does God. He is looking out for you.

About a week later, Doc decided. "Think I'm heading out for Cheyenne myself, Ed."

"Everybody's a leavin'. You need a reference? Let me know. I'll give you one."

TWELVE

The miners said that the Cheyenne hills ran with blood and gold. In the wake of promised wealth, hordes of prospectors and greenhorns arrived daily to stake their claim. It was a life not meant for the faint of heart. Old men with sunken eyes peered out to the hills without revealing their secrets. They left it for the young ones to learn that gold was heavier than water and lighter than blood.

Green prospectors learned their lessons the hard way. Many died when the earth collapsed around them. The old men knew how to pan for nuggets and that some of the best nuggets could be found at the bottom of a gulch. There it was sifted out of rocks and debris, thus coming free at the end. The prospector's best kept secret was to discover the pure ore chimney that was the mother lode. Following the mountain up through its washes, the miners tested for the mineral by digging into the side of the mountain. They would dig as their faces turned black from the sun and split into furrows. Nothing would relieve the itch until they could smell it and taste it and touch it.

While the miners toiled, the railroads furrowed through the dirt. The frenzy for gold and silver overran the rail lines of the Kansas and Pacific. The lines hummed a sonorous tune of civilization to Omaha and echoed it westward to Deadwood, South Dakota. Gambling on a rail car was a novelty for a while. Some gamblers thought that a stationary saloon was the best, while others became partial to the rambling games of chance that a smoky rail car offered. At that time the rail lines could easily accommodate that form of gambling.

Along the way, railroads supplied the temporary housing for the workers needed to expand the rails westward. At the terminus of these points, gamblers congregated and new towns sprang up. When the money was gone, the gamblers were too. Some of the towns folded. Some of them didn't.

Doc's enchantment of gambling by rail lasted a day. A smoky rail car had no outside view. The amenities were nonexistent. The lighting was poor and the air was fouled blue with tobacco stink. By the time Doc reached Cheyenne, however, this practice had almost been completely shut down. Although it was Doc's intention to winter in Cheyenne, breathing remained difficult and the alcohol failed to mask the problem as it once had masked the pain. Doc felt neither like Tom McKey nor J.H. Holliday, but perhaps a combination of the two.

Besides the allure of gold, there was the happy absence of Kate Elder. He hoped that she was anchored to someone else's arm and not available to torment him. The Jacksboro problem continued to plague him so a return to Ft. Griffin was out of the question. Still smarting about his treatment in Ft. Griffin, Doc did not care to experience the ravages of frontier life in Cheyenne.

Prairie saloons kept the rumor mills churning with fodder to spew for anyone willing to listen. Rumor, quoted as fact by those who claimed they were there, had the Texas fire set by Kate Elder firmly entrenched in the minds of all. Doc gave up hope of the real truth ever being written or said.

Cheyenne, in that year, was the melting pot of everyone who lusted for the gold and silver of boomtowns. The pattern of arrival, exploitation, and departure never varied. Doc knew that he would test the waters of Cheyenne's gaming tables before making up his mind to stay. In the wake of Bill Hickock's arrival came Luke Short, Wyatt and Morgan Earp, and Bill Cody. Doc stayed away from some and was friendly with others. Buffalo Bill Cody lobbied hard for Doc to become a member of his show.

"You would be my main gun talent extraordinary. Why, we could pack in the crowds in no time at all," Cody had told him after Doc had bought him his favorite drink. Doc waited for Cody to finish his fourth one before he graciously declined.

"My health, suh, might not be up to such a grandiose endeavor."

Cody didn't remember his offer the day afterwards and Doc failed to jog whatever memory Cody may have had. It was during this time that Doc, Wyatt Earp, and Luke Short became reacquainted. The three men had a lot in common and liked the telling of lively tales. Wyatt entertained Doc and Luke with stories of Wichita and Abilene. Dapper Luke Short had changed little since Texas.

Wyatt Earp looked at the men seated around him. "There's always trouble in Delano, Kansas. My brother, James, is a barkeeper in Pryor's Saloon, right next door to a keno hall. Get this, all the brothels are within sight and sound of the sheriff's office. And it floats across the river to Wichita. The sheriff looks the other way and, uh, sometimes partakes."

There was a commonality in the affairs of the heart between Doc and Wyatt. As Wyatt said to him late one night after coffee, "I lost my wife to a scurrilous illness."

"And I," Doc replied, "had to go West so I wouldn't inflict mine on the woman I love. I hated leaving Georgia."

It was probably close to three in the morning when poker had been more than profitable and the manager of the saloon was counting the proceeds in the back room. Wyatt and Doc were seated at one of the back tables, not in sight of the swinging doors and well aware of anyone coming behind them.

"You ever watch someone you love die the slow way?" Doc asked as he gulped back a whiskey and poured another. "No matter where I stroll here in the West, I can't get away from those last hours of hearing my mother trying to breathe. I can be here amongst the camaraderie of my good friends," he indicated the surroundings with a sweep of his hand, "and yet see exactly what I was doing and what I felt like in that one instant when she stopped."

Wyatt nodded. "Yeah," and he poured himself a drink, the first and only one Doc ever saw him take. They touched glasses, tossed the whiskey back, and went their separate ways, but Doc never forgot that moment.

Having adopted from his father a keen enjoyment in being well informed, Doc kept an eye on the news from Kansas while he remained in Cheyenne and thought about it when he traveled to Deadwood. By 1876 the two towns were practically in shouting distance of each other. Gambling parties traveled from Cheyenne to Deadwood and back. There were around-the-clock saloons, brothels of all sorts, piano music, and every vice known to the common world. There was no such thing as silence. Piano playing, ribald singing, even troupes of players offering a selection of theater traveled from New York and kept the town jumping.

The golden cornucopia spilled its molten contents in a never-ending supply through the saloons. It was in one of these saloons that Doc got a chance to play against Wild Bill Hickock. Rumors painted Wild Bill as moody and quick to kill a man for any kind of imagined slight. Doc didn't know if that was true and was quick to point out that he had never seen the murderous side of him.

Hickock was, if anything, a paranoid player, wearing within easy reach an entire arsenal of guns and knives draped about his person. His bulky shoulders had long since ruptured his tanned leather jacket. His salt and pepper hair was as craggy as wolves' hair and just as long as the fringe on the bottom of his jacket. He had a way of speaking as if each syllable was a knife being honed on a grinding stone. Not surprisingly, his teeth bore heavy tobacco stains, while his eyes looked stained by hardship, pain, and death. Beefy hands held two pair. He looked at Doc.

"Come on. You either got it or you don't."

Across from him sat Doc alone, as all of the other players had retired due to lack of money and sheer terror. Doc, attired in his favorite suit of gray with splashes of red and charcoal, clean hands, fingernails trimmed just so, and his strong dentist's wrists, was holding a full house of queens and tens. In the light, his clear blue eyes peered through the smoke at Hickock.

Bill's hand lacked and he knew it. There was a prodigious amount of money between the two and a solid gold watch belonging to Hickock and a ring with a diamond belonging to Doc. There were also expensive watches and diamond tie tacks that had belonged to the other gamblers who had lost their nerve and quit the game.

No one moved, neither card nor muscle. There was no clink of glass, and the piano had stopped its tinny whine. Blue smoke filled the room, but no one was smoking. The bartender filled drinks, but no one drank. There was a bottle next to Doc on his right, and Bill had one on his left.

Because of the smoke, Doc coughed, but even that was hushed. If Bill's gaze was hard, so was Doc's, who had in the course of the game developed a dead stare. It was this same expression that had cleaned out all other players except for Bill Hickock. And it was this same expression from both men that caused the proprietor's hand to tremble.

"Call," Doc told Bill with a deceptively soft voice.

Hickock's eye flicked over Doc's hand, the one holding the cards. Doc was right-handed, so anyone else might think that Doc would have to throw down his cards to draw his gun. Bill knew that J.H. Holliday possessed an equal dexterity in his left hand. He could not see Doc's left hand, which was out of sight beneath the card table. Their gazes locked. The saloon itself seemed to inhale.

Hickock deliberately pulled his coat back. Doc did the same from that waist-level stance. His cards hadn't dipped. His jaw didn't tremble. The two continued to stare for quite a while.

"Well," Hickock began and deliberately turned to look at the thunderstruck people in the saloon. Horrified eyes met his. He turned to look at Doc who had also turned in his chair and raked the denizens with those unnerving blue eyes. "I've been called," Hickock said with a sigh. He might have been announcing a weather change. "What do you think?" he asked Doc.

"You're right," Doc told him and both men threw down their cards. Hickock caught a glimpse of Doc's hand and gave another shrug of his massive shoulders, as he pushed the money and the gold watch towards Doc.

"I'll buy you a drink," Doc replied and got up from the table.

No one knew what to do. The piano player tried to play a lively tune, but his hands nervously crashed on the keyboard. Many glasses were clinked and many more bottles of whiskey were purchased, but no one congratulated either Bill or Doc. The two lounged against the bar in solitary splendor.

"Another day's work," Bill commented.

Doc, a half-smile on his face, agreed. He took a long thirsty drink and looked up at Bill. "Temptin' fate though."

Bill looked around and everyone within earshot scurried away. "They're hopin' to hear what we're talkin' about. But you're right. Temptin' fate. What about that fire down in Texas?" Bill asked sotto voce.

Doc laughed. "How's Calamity Jane these days?"

Bill tossed his drink back and reached for the bottle. "About like Kate Elder's fire."

The two men never played each other again.

♣ ♥ ♠ ♦

On May 10, 1876, Wyatt Earp's sheriff job in Wichita, Kansas came to an end. But before it did, Doc received a letter describing Wichita life and Kansas in general. For his part, Doc had spent such a miserable winter in the Dakotas that he vowed never to repeat the mistake. Kansas sounded good and warm. His chest had a permanent cold and if there were passable nights, they were all but forgotten in the raging cough that racked him from dawn until dusk. Daytime was easier to handle because he was awake. For the first time, he seriously considered taking laudanum.

Another letter from Wyatt followed on the heels of the first one. Wyatt had taken up a new residence in Dodge City, Kansas. He wrote:

You know how the Army feels about liquor regulations? The city itself is located five miles from the fort. The prairie is black with buffalo. Some of the newspapers say millions. There's a lot of money to be made in Dodge, Doc.

Doc wanted to see Dodge in person. He kept hearing about it secondhand, but that didn't satisfy him. He wanted to experience the excitement for himself. He also had the itch to see Ft. Griffin without the cloud hanging over his head. He had made a lot of money playing poker, but money wasn't the only thing.

Doc sorely missed a family and the easy comradeship of blood ties. However, relatives were not a guarantee that a family would stand by one of their own.

Doc wasn't ready to give up the gold at the poker tables even though Dodge City and Wichita sounded exciting. There were other reasons to stay, but the Indian issue had become a troubling matter for everyone in that early summer. Doc read about it in the comfort of his hotel.

Being a scout like Wild Bill or Custer required the physique of a giant and a personality larger than life. It required a man who could stand in the fiercest of winds, kick it in the shins, lasso it, and haul it to town.

Dust and silence rolled through town on July 8, 1876. It gathered in back alleys and it swept the landscape. News of Custer's death hit Bill hard. He had scouted for Custer back in '67. His tales to Doc had been all about the adventures with the Seventh Cavalry.

"They were my blood brothers. God bless them," Bill said with tears in his eyes.

In the days that followed, Bill's demeanor became increasingly morose and perceived slights were dealt with swiftly. On August 2, Bill scuffed his way across the floor of the No. 10 Saloon around mid-afternoon and began a game with some cronies. Doc, seated two tables over, exchanged pleasantries and continued to play Spanish Monte with some out-of-towners recent to Deadwood. By four o'clock that afternoon, Bill was still losing and having to borrow money. He was not sitting in his customary place, which would have put his back to the wall, and he didn't seem to be aware of what was going on around him.

Always on the lookout, Doc was keeping an eye on his own game, but from where he sat, he could also see the doors. From the number of tables in play and the crush outside, it was impossible to get a clear look at the street. Suddenly Doc's head snapped up. The sizable jackpot in the middle of the table was momentarily ignored.

Half rising from his chair, Doc saw a man by the name of McCall step directly up to Bill Hickock's back, draw a .45, and fire. The gunfire in close quarters reverberated like an explosion. Doc whipped both of his guns from their holsters and leaped to his feet. Bill lay slumped on the table, still clutching his cards, a queen, a pair of aces, and a pair of eights. There was smoke, the acrid smell of burned blood and burned hair.

Still holding his guns, Doc butted McCall on the back of his head. Completely calm, he waited on the street for the sheriff and the undertaker to arrive.

"I'll give you a deposition whenever you want it. There is no doubt that McCall shot Hickock in the back in cold blood."

The sound of gunshot brought most of the town. By the time Doc was making his way back to the hotel, gawkers were still crowding outside. Once in his room, he poured himself a drink, tossed it back, and waited for the shakes to subside.

My Dearest Mattie

I was witness to a sight today, the likes of which I hope never to see again. It was an act committed by the most heinous and cowardly of characters. It has, despite everything I've seen and been privy to, unnerved me completely. For the rest of my life, may I never have or plan on having a seat that does not back to a wall.

Your Most Loving,
John

After Hickock's death, Doc felt the tug to leave Deadwood stronger than ever before. He wrestled with the pros and cons for several weeks before deciding to stick it out. The money was good. His hotel was comfortable, and there were boon companions to while away the hours. His health was bad, so he might as well make the best of it. He vowed that 1877 would be different.

It was his habit to stash more of his winnings in the fall to guard against the leaner times in the winter. He always tried to make sure that he was settled someplace before winter began. Above all, he feared being caught with a shortage of funds and unable to leave. If he left a place, it must be through his own choosing, not from sickness or a lack of funds.

He thought about his father in that autumn of 1876 and green Georgia. He looked at the contrast between the two. Deadwood was a savage beauty of dust with a canopy of wind-blown blue sky and unbroken prairie grass. Pastel soft Georgia was the beauty of green growth and the sound of water bubbling over rocks. Cheyenne was a shout at the top of the lungs. Georgia was a whisper of fireflies over the cotton fields.

Doc carried all those images in his heart. Nobody understood why things happened the way they did. He thought about his father and wrote to him. It was not a son asking for forgiveness, but rather an acknowledgement of his being alive. He steeled himself, because he knew that his father wouldn't write. Henry didn't disappoint him in that respect.

Doc was pleased that Rachel wrote him a long letter. She filled in the gaps about family and friends. Doc mused on those letters when he received them and most of all how odd it was for Rachel to write to him. She was not a blood relation and yet she treated him more like family than his own did. It occurred to him that families didn't have to be made up of blood relations. Heart ties could be stronger than blood.

Autumn blew into Deadwood like Sherman's fury. As the trees lost their leaves, the word came from Denver about the amount of gold flowing through its saloons. Immediately, most of the professional gamblers left. Doc traveled with them. He had forgotten what the frigid air of Denver could do to his cough. What weight he had acquired during the summer melted before the onslaught of Denver's temperature, wind, and altitude. With a wad of $15,000 in his pocket, he bought a heavy black winter coat to warm his 121 pounds. As brutal as the Denver winter was, Doc remained convinced that he would die by a bullet. It was the one thing that comforted him.

Hoping for a bullet had nothing to do with the fear of death. Rather it was his revulsion of seeing the ruin of his mother's body until there was no shred of flesh for bone to cling to and the knowledge that it would be his own fate. His moral code was Spartan, that of dying on the battlefield. No matter how often he placed himself in the pathway of a bullet, there was the hard-wired human part of him that compelled him to draw his gun first.

People often thought Doc was taller than his five feet, eight inches. His erect carriage had something to do with that. He was ramrod straight. Standing or sitting, he might have had an iron bar sewn into his spine to keep him so taut. Then there was that flash of blue fire from his eyes that made folks so uncomfortable. He never slouched. He looked life in the eye head on, and if life fired at him, his was the faster draw.

Doc's return to Denver surprised no one. Upon hearing that Doc was back in town, he was good-naturedly badgered about running one of the faro tables. "You know all the angles. You run a tight ship. They wouldn't steal me blind with you on board. You think about it."

Politely, Doc turned the offer down. Someone else had asked him first. Bat Masterson was as disapproving as he'd been when Doc met him during his stay in Old Granada. Bat never let on, but there was a speculative gleam in his eye that Doc found hard to swallow. He had seen the look quite often while growing up that indicated he wasn't good enough to run in the some circles.

"Bat is back here with me in Dodge City now," Wyatt wrote.

"Guess I'm J.H. Holliday once more," he wrote back to Wyatt. "Thought I'd let you know. Guess you've heard that it's been pretty interesting here, too."

Scams had always proliferated in mining towns or wherever there was a heavy exchange of dollars, goods, hides, and ore. The scams slowly stripped the railroads of their funds. Anything that could be filched, stolen, bartered for, or obtained through illegal means was fair game. There were many bunco artists, but Jefferson Randolph "Soapy" Smith, Jr. was considered the best.

Soapy Smith learned each game and twisted it to suit his own purpose. Poker and faro provided many opportunities for the quick hustle such as sticky cards and the false shuffle. There were elegant games of deception such as using the crooked faro box. So widespread was his reputation that he was often asked to leave before he could clear the saloon's door. If Soapy Smith didn't know a con, he would set about learning with zeal. His cohort, Mysterious Dave Mather, was cut from the same cloth and thoroughly enjoyed the notoriety. Dave was a gambling acquaintance of Doc's, but not a friend.

There were stories about the origin of Dave Mather, but no one really believed them since he lied so much. He loved working both sides of the law and had little compunction about switching his affections

Standing next to each other, there was disparity in height. But sitting, Dave was as thin-boned as Doc and his silhouette could easily pass for the young dentist. A gifted mimic, Dave wore the same kind of hat with impunity. With his fine-boned hands, wrists, and nimble fingers, all that was required of Dave to complete the illusion was a natty suit favoring the kind Doc wore.

"You want to get in on some easy money?" he asked Doc in that Denver spring of 1877.

"Such as?" Doc returned, not looking up from his faro bank. "Gentlemen, place your bets."

"Well, me and Soapy have come up with a gold brick scam. You take a brick and wrap it in layers of gold foil. Then you sit down beside someone on the train who looks like any easy mark. You sell it to them for a great deal of money. All happy and dumb, they take the bait. We'll have a bogus sheriff come on board and threaten to arrest the greenhorn for running a scam. When he begs to keep his good name quiet, we'll have him pay us a hefty sum twice what he paid for it. We'll make off with the money and gold brick until the next time."

"Mm, interesting, but not for me."

"We'd like to have you join us, or at least your alias of 'Tom McKey.'"

"Well, Dave, I will be doing something else."

"Such as?" Dave prodded.

"Such as doing something else," Doc told him.

"Damn, but you're close, Holliday."

"My sympathies and luck to you."

"What a pity," Dave said as he left the table.

Doc watched him go. There was a very thin smile on his face.

"Gotta tell ya, Doc," one of the players said, "you give me the creeps, smilin' like that."

"Well, Mikey, that's good. You'll remember not to cross me."

There were other matters to occupy him in that Denver spring, especially a letter from a tearful, distraught Mattie that put Doc's whole life in turmoil. He still carried the blotched letter, written in a trembling hand so foreign to her.

My Dearest John

I was alone in the house when I found it. You know it's not my way to look at others' possessions. It was an envelope with an address I did not recognize at Mother's great desk. I went ahead and opened it. Some people from Eastern Kansas were writing to her about a little girl they had adopted. She was a baby in 1873. Oh, John, I know this is our child. You know I have always felt we had a little girl. I memorized the address. I know you're in Colorado. Can you, would you, see clearly and let me know, please. Please . . .

He heard Mattie's sobs from Georgia and knew what he had to do.

♣ ♥ ♠ ♦

Doc got off the train in Dodge City only long enough to see if Wyatt was available. Bat, however, met him first.

"You stayin' long, Holliday?"

"No," Doc replied, keeping his voice softly modulated.

Bat chewed on the stogie that he had in his mouth. "For the night?"

"No," Doc said.

There was silence as Masterson digested that. "Guess there's nothing for me to worry about then, is there?"

"Don't suppose there is."

"What brings you through these parts?" Wyatt appeared suddenly over Doc's left shoulder. Doc spun quickly, but Wyatt was smiling and his hand was thrust out to shake.

"What's eating him?" Doc asked after the retreating figure of Masterson.

"Train robberies. They're using Dodge as an entry point by robbing the rails up and down the line. Agents are on all the trains these days. Railroad's losing a lot of money. Some of it going to Kansas City."

"That a fact?" Doc asked. "I, myself, am on my way to Kansas City."

"Sounds reasonable. Lots of money in old K.C."

"That, Wyatt, is what I want to find out."

"You traveling solo?"

"As we speak," Doc glanced over at the window of the sheriff's office. Bat was watching him from inside.

"I'm on my way there, too," Wyatt told him. "Doesn't look like grass is gonna grow under your feet."

"Nor yours."

And it didn't. The Santa Fe to all points East was headed for Kansas City, Missouri with Wyatt and Doc onboard. At night, Kansas was a black cloth against mile after mile of flat plain. Wyatt had been contemplative since dinner.

"So, you expect us to get robbed?" Doc asked.

"Why would I expect that?" Wyatt queried, taking a sip of coffee.

"Cause you're one of the agents on the train."

"You don't miss much, John."

"I think I told you when we met, I'm called John only in an emergency."

Wyatt snorted. "This might qualify. Funny thing about the truth, Doc."

"I take it we are waxing philosophical."

"No. Just thinkin' out loud. You haven't told me why you're making this trip."

"Soapy made me an offer to sell a gold brick," Doc replied.

Wyatt's smile grew wide. "Do tell. Has to be Mysterious Dave and Soapy."

"I was going to be cut in for a hefty percentage."

"Did they tell you how they were going to do it?"

"They did, but I've got other concerns. I have to take care of business in Kansas City."

"Ahh, how is your alias, Tom McKey?"

"Well, some say still practicin' in Denver, some say Deadwood."

"So Dave as Tom McKey is there, and you're in Kansas City."

"It was an equitable trade," Doc coughed hard as a spasm shook him. Clawing for his handkerchief, he covered his mouth. Wyatt could see that there was blood on the cloth.

"It's getting worse, isn't it?" He waited as Doc swallowed a drink from the handsome flask he carried.

"I don't winter like I used to."

Wyatt paused. "I'm here, too, but technically I could be someplace else."

"Makes it easy to get around, Wyatt, I'll grant you that. I've never been much for folks knowin' what I'm doing every minute of every day. Sometimes stretchin' the truth isn't a lie. For instance, we could be in Ft. Griffin having this very same conversation. So if folks ask, sure, Wyatt Earp and Doc Holliday met in Ft. Griffin, we discussed politics, and everyone saw us."

"Let's make it something exciting. The truth is always dull. How about Wyatt Earp and Doc Holliday met in Ft. Griffin and talked about that scourge of the plains, Dave Rudabaugh."

"I'll drink to that," Doc emptied his glass and refilled it and emptied it again.

"Who's bein' Tom?" Wyatt's voice dropped.

"Dave."

"Mysterious Dave?"

Doc nodded.

"Oh, hell, with the right hat, clothes, lighter hair, as long as he doesn't stand up."

"Or even if he does," Doc chuckled. Doc's laugh sounded rusty. He tugged at his collar and swallowed another cough.

"Well," Wyatt replied, as he refilled Doc's glass, "best of luck to the gold brick and its road West."

"Here, here."

The train ride was uneventful. Several shady characters boarded at Newton, Kansas when a stop was made to take on water. Several more boarded at Lawrence. Wyatt's show of a weapon dispersed what might have been an ugly situation, and the remainder of the ride transpired without mishap.

Wyatt pushed Doc once again to tell him the real reason for his trip. Doc eventually confided, "I'm here to find my child."

"Do you have the address?" Wyatt asked as the train pulled into Kansas City.

"Wyatt, you don't have to do this."

"It's late, but we can rent horses tomorrow. Just so you know," Wyatt said, as he slipped into a fair rendition of Doc's accent, "the good houses are between Fourth Street and Missouri Avenue, around the west side of Main. Faro number three is quite nicely laid out."

Doc's downcast face began to brighten at the prospect.

"The food is superb. Beats Denver and Dallas. They have shrimp and champagne that's always chilled. It's not that cheap stuff either."

"Sounds like we can't miss," Doc told him. "And I am hungry."

When Doc saw the opulent surroundings of the gaming hall, his jaw dropped. "And I thought Kansas City was only a cow town. My hat is off to you, Wyatt, for a stroke of sheer genius."

There was linen on the tables and chandeliers pouring streams of rainbows upon all the occupants.

The proprietor welcomed the two men as he did all his customers. He recognized in Doc a kindred spirit and showed deference by the way of amenities and play at the gaming tables. By three in the morning, Doc had amassed a goodly amount of money at one of the poker tables. At half past three he walked away with over $5,000 in his pocket. Wyatt was just finishing a game of poker.

"Gentlemen, I'm out," Wyatt replied as he got up. "Doc, I hope you have enough to buy us breakfast."

Doc remained jocular, although Wyatt could see that he was deep in thought.

"You want to start out around nine o'clock or so? We could meet here for breakfast?"

"That will be nice. Nine it is then."

Doc was punctual, but uncharacteristically quiet. Wyatt let him be. Although he was Doc's friend, he knew this was a matter that only Doc could sort out. The street address was in a nearby section of town.

"That's farm land. Got lots of fertile soil. Hope you boys come back tonight, even though you, sir," he said to Doc, "relieved me of much of my hard earned money."

Doc touched his hat. "A true gentleman, suh. It's nice to make such an acquaintance."

"I have a dreadful hangover this morning. Your friend here introduced us, but I'm terribly sorry, I can't remember your name."

Doc made a small bow. "I'm Tom McKey and my friend here is—" A cough rumbled in his throat.

Wyatt jumped in. "I'm Barry Stapp. Everyone calls me Barry."

Once outside, Doc turned to Wyatt. "Tom and Barry?"

"Well, Tom gets around. I mean he's always in more than two places at the same time, and Barry happens to be one of my middle names."

He'd been told where the livery stable was located, but Wyatt felt awkward. Doc was still uncommunicative and at one point he snapped, "I don't need you to wipe my nose."

"Surely not," Wyatt replied, "but you gotta admit if someone gets you in the back, nobody's gonna know."

The road was fairly straight for three or four miles, but then it began to wind. It had been deeply rutted by wagons and buggies and cattle and sheep. Wild honeysuckle, boysenberries, and Queen Anne's Lace tangled together along the roadside and across the pathway. The vegetation grew thicker until the road was nothing more than a one-lane path. Abruptly, the lane ended on the edge of a large meadow. In the distance, the two men could see a small white house.

"I think there's something wrong with this girth. You go on ahead. I'll catch up in a while," Wyatt told Doc as he dismounted and began to fiddle with the saddle.

Doc nodded curtly and kicked his horse into a canter. He rode about one hundred yards before he checked his horse's speed. What if she wasn't there? What if the people were mean to her? What if she didn't like him? What if she didn't look like him? How would he tell? He was writhing on the inside. For the first time since he'd left Georgia, he found himself immobilized with fear.

He and Mattie believed the child to have been born in December of 1872. She would be four and a half, maybe a little older. A cramp in his stomach reminded him of how little he'd eaten for breakfast. Closer to the house, Doc could see a winding lane and a small girl romping with a dog. He rode forward slowly. When he drew even with the house, he halted his horse and dismounted. The child stopped playing and stared at him with big eyes. Doc still couldn't tell from the distance what color they were. Fumbling with the reins, he took out the piece of paper that Mattie had written the address on and tried to be nonchalant.

His chest hurt from his heart beating so hard. He could face men down but not this little girl.

"Hi," she piped behind him. "Are ya lost?"

Doc turned slowly so he wouldn't frighten her. "I think I am."

She had Mattie's nose and his chin and two exquisite little ears that curled to her head like a pair of rosy teacups. Curls bounced over her head, Mattie's curls. Staring at him were the most beautiful china-blue eyes. A deep lump formed in Doc's throat that wouldn't allow him to swallow. The crickets across the lane stopped chirping. The day around him grew still.

"Don't you know if you're lost?"

"That I do," he whispered. "I've been lost for a long time."

"Will you get found again?"

"I'm not sure," Doc whispered softer than before.

She was barefooted and wore a homemade red and green calico dress. Her hair was combed and her eyes were bright.

"You got nice eyes."

Doc glanced up to see a woman coming across the road towards him. She was wearing an apron over her dress, and her hands were pressed worriedly together.

"Mama, he says he's lost." The little girl tugged on her mother's apron to make her look down.

"We don't get many people out here, Mister . . . "

"Mr. McKey, ma'am." Doc touched the brim of his hat.

"Mama, he talks funny."

"Ssh, let's not be rude. Well, Mr. McKey, as I said, we don't get many visitors." While she spoke, she looked from the child to Doc to the child once more.

Doc read the look in her eyes. "The child favors you, ma'am."

"Thank you," the woman blushed and smoothed the little girl's hair. "We only purchased the farm about six months ago. It's peaceful. We thought Mary would like it. She's taken to it like a duck to water." There was now a perceptible pucker on her forehead as she gazed at Doc.

"I'm thoroughly lost. I was to supposed to be several lanes over, and I ended up here."

Mary reached up and tugged on the bottom of Doc's coat. "Your horsey is pretty. Could I ride him?"

"Oh honey," the woman said, "I don't think that would be such a good idea."

"It's fine," Doc replied, but not evenly. His lips were trembling hard. "Here let me help you up."

Mary was a featherweight. She smelled of newly made soap and gingham. Clinging to him, Doc hoisted her into the air and gently set her down on the horse's back. She laughed. Doc walked the horse slowly and the little girl fiercely held the horn.

"When you get bigger and have your own pony, you can ride all the time. Of course, being a lady, you'll have to ride side-saddle."

Mary wrinkled her nose at him. "I'll ride just like this. Can we go around another time?"

"One more time," her mother told her. Her eyes widened at the glimpse of the two guns under Doc's coat.

At last, Doc halted the horse and picked Mary out of the saddle. She stared at him while he held her, from his forehead, to his mustache, to his chin. Then gently she kissed his cheek. It felt like butterfly wings.

"Honey, why don't you go run and play. I want to talk to Mr. McKey for a moment."

"Okay, Mama. Thank you for the ride. You got nice eyes." She scampered away.

"You do have her eyes, or rather she has yours," the woman said to Doc. "I'm Mrs. Kelly, but you already knew that, didn't you?"

Doc looked at the ground. "I only wanted to see her. I don't want to take her from you."

"Where are you from?"

"Georgia. My people are from Valdosta."

"Is your name really McKey?"

"No, ma'am. I'm John Holliday," Doc's voice had become so hushed, that Mrs. Kelly had to lean forward.

"She's always known us. We've thought about telling her for some time, but we haven't." She looked at Doc's guns once more.

"I guess it's pretty obvious what I am," he told her. He looked old and sad.

"You're a nice man who gave my little girl a horse ride."

Doc pulled his watch fob out of his pocket and very gently undid the clasp that held the crucifix to the watch. "When she's old enough, you give her this." He pressed the chain and crucifix into Mrs. Kelly's hand.

"This is a fine thing. Are you really sure you want to do this?"

"I'm sure," Doc's voice broke. He gathered the reins and mounted.

"You won't be back, will you?"

"No."

"She'll have that pony. She's actually quite fearless. She's stubborn, energetic. She has a temper. She's very loving."

"Just so," Doc nodded and touched the brim of his hat once more.

"I'll tell her of you, John Holliday."

Doc turned in the saddle. "Be kind, won't you?" He put his spurs to his horse.

By the time Wyatt was back in the saddle, Doc had already passed him, riding hard and fast towards the main road. Wyatt let him go and headed for the livery stable.

"You've already missed your friend. He turned his horse in already," the blacksmith told him. "I can rent these two out to ya tomorrow, if yer stayin' in town."

"I don't think so," Wyatt said, "but we'll let you know."

Upon reaching the hotel, Wyatt found Doc nowhere in sight. Knowing that Doc had to work out his grief, Wyatt got dinner and strolled over to a lively saloon down the street. There he fell into a game of keno that didn't break up until four in the morning. As he was leaving the saloon, Doc stepped up alongside of him.

"Looked to me like you were doing okay," Doc said.

"Some," Wyatt replied.

One of the restaurants was still open. As they waited for an early breakfast, Wyatt toyed with a cup of coffee, and Doc sloshed some whiskey into his glass.

"You know," Doc leaned forward against the table, "funny thing about the truth. If a thing happens and no one acknowledges it, it's not a lie, is it?"

"No," Wyatt said. "It makes it a sin for the people denying it. That's worse than a lie."

"Just so," Doc told him.

‍‍

⇥ *Chapter* ⇤

THIRTEEN

Joining Soapy Smith in his 1877 gold brick scheme were other equally light-fingered compatriots. Everyone knew of Smith and another young man by the name of Dutch Henry Born. With Mysterious Dave Mather to round out the trio, the three men felt they had a plan that would work. Like Mather, Born worked both sides of the law and made many enemies, not only lawmen, but also anyone else with whom he came in contact.

The scheme was simplistic. Smith being such a smooth operator and the instigator of the con was unanimously chosen to play the part of the sheriff. Dave Mather, looking much like J.H. Holliday from a sitting aspect, posed a striking figure. He had a courtly demeanor and bearing, an impeccable Southern dialect, and dressed in charcoal gray suits. Such was Dave's "Tom McKey." Dave Mather as "Tom" would belly up to an unsuspecting businessman with a heartfelt cry. Ailing children, wives, and mothers were a favorite theme.

"I don't want to do this, but a serious exigency is forced upon me by the times."

It was then that the gold brick, which was foil wrapped, would be sold for a substantial sum. After receiving his money, Dave was apologetic and effusive in his thanks, leaving the buyer to smile and ponder his new investment.

Because Soapy and his company did not want the buyer to examine the brick too closely, the second step taken after the purchase was the most critical. Quickly, bogus railroad agents would arrest the hapless businessman, who was certain that he was going to jail.

"My God, my wife can't find out about this. Here . . . here's more cash to restore my good name. Will that be enough? Promise this won't get out to the papers. You've got to promise."

"Certainly," Smith told him. "No one will ever find out about your troubles."

"Bless you. Bless you, sir."

Since Doc had used the alias of Tom McKey previously in Denver, everyone assumed that Doc had fallen back on his old alias of using the gold brick scheme. Mysterious Dave made himself up to look like Doc, enjoying the discomfiture that it placed on Doc Holliday. It became one more piece of rumor that Doc had to bear—that of a lie.

"I tell you, Doc Holliday played that scheme from one end of the railroad to the other. I seen him with my own eyes."

"Yeah, so did I. He came into town and bragged about it. Somebody ought to do somethin' about that. Just a disgrace it is."

♣ ♥ ♠ ♦

That same summer, Wyatt worked as an agent for the KATY. Never was the time more dangerous. Crooked company officials hired armed "agents" to steal from the company they had been hired to protect. It was Wyatt's duty to work the rail line from its origin to terminus, seeking those individuals who used their weapons for profit. Sworn to secrecy, Wyatt could not inform family or friends of his activities, as word might leak to the wrong source. This entailed a high profile of misinformation fed to newspapers, close friends, and even family. Wyatt disliked lying to his family, but he felt a great responsibility. At stake were the lives of the passengers and the existence of the railroad on which many depended for their livelihood.

Late in that summer, Wyatt headed back to Hayes, Kansas for much needed rest. At one in the morning, the poker game at Wyatt's table was winding down. Doc, playing poker two tables over from Wyatt could see that he was exhausted. In fact, he'd never seen him look worse. What took him aback was that Wyatt had looked at him several times and ignored him as if not recognizing him. Puzzled, Doc had to take a second look to make certain that it was Wyatt. After deciding that it was he, Doc glanced around the table at the other gamblers. Not only were Wyatt's reflexes off, but he had allowed himself to be seated with his back to the door. With growing consternation, Doc noticed that the gambler on Wyatt's left drummed his heel on the floor every time Wyatt spoke and fiddled constantly with his left coat pocket where there was a prominent bulge. After the game folded, the man followed Wyatt outside.

It was an early Saturday morning and the table had been rich with money. The players themselves were rich with the fruit of the vine, especially the gambler who now shadowed Wyatt, who left with a great deal of the gambler's money in his pocket.

Doc quickly folded himself from his game and walked out to the street. At first he missed seeing Wyatt. He heard rustling sounds from the shadows, but the street had an empty, eerie look. Pulling his gun, Doc headed towards the alley. Halfway down, he paused, hearing voices.

"I lost seven months worth o' money to you. I think you got enough."

In the hush, Doc heard the click of the hammer and lengthened his stride. He felt rather than saw the gun being shoved into Wyatt's back. The gunman was weaving. In his drunken state, he could easily misfire, sending the slug into Wyatt's spinal cord.

Before the bullet could be discharged, Doc's gun ever so softly and firmly pressed against the man's temple. "Don't," was all he said.

The would-be gunman's arm dropped as if his muscles had atrophied "He cheated me outta my money," the man whined.

"What a squealer," Wyatt said turning around to look at Doc. "What the hell are you doing here?"

"I could say the same to you."

"Don't I count?" the drunk asked.

Doc looked him in the eye. "No. I'd love to drill your sorry ass right here, but it's late and I feel generous."

"You better believe him, son. Tom here don't feel generous all the time."

♣ ♥ ♠ ♦

After Hayes, Kansas Doc traveled back to Ft. Griffin, Texas to winter inside a whiskey bottle. The winters were hard in Texas. He spent a lot of time in the Bee Hive Saloon and for the most part went unnoticed.

At one time, he broke some of the poker tables, then turned around and promptly lost all of it. His heart felt as stone-cold dead as the wind and snow blowing to Mexico. Mattie wrote often, but everyone else in town stayed clear of him, except for Shannessy. Doc heard an earful of the doings of Tom McKey. According to rumor, J.H. Holliday was in Kansas City. No, he wasn't, he was in Colorado. He ceased to care that he was coughing up blood and losing weight, and if Shannessy hadn't nagged him, he wouldn't have eaten.

Shame had gravity all its own and it pulled him further and further into a downward spiral. The memory of his little girl haunted him from dawn to dusk. If he hadn't contracted the consumption, he'd be living in Georgia with Mattie and Mary. He'd have a life instead of being a drunkard coughing up his lungs in some forgotten hellhole. It was the first time he'd ever drunk himself into a stupor. When he awoke, he was vomiting. After he finished being sick, Shannessy poured coffee in him until he vomited some more. Once Doc opened his eyes, the room was whirling so hard he thought his head would explode.

"Dammit, Doc, what're you doin'?"

"Tryin' to die," he croaked.

Mary had been so pretty. How could he, of all people, have produced such a little blonde doll like that? She'd been his all right, his and Mattie's. Her clear, blue eyes offered a picture of heaven that he would never have. She would grow up and he would never see that. He saw that only death would release him from his misery, but it was not yet his time.

Quite an assortment of vultures had collected waiting for him to cash in. "Sorry to disappoint you gentlemen, but I'm still alive, as you can see. Care to play a few hands?" They wanted to play for blood. Doc was happy to oblige. After a thirty-six-hour card game, Doc made his way back to his hotel. He was several thousand dollars richer and in a much better frame of mind.

Trinka Godell was one of the most overblown whores ever seen. Because she weighed three hundred pounds there wasn't a dress in the dry goods store that could or would fit her. Instead, she managed through the machinations of a huge whalebone corset to stuff her body into several sewed-together and colorful feed sacks. She brayed when she laughed, and the odor that came from her had on occasion cleaned out many a saloon. In Griffin's heat, her clown-like makeup melted and made garish rivers down either side of her splayed nostrils.

In spite of all her shortcomings, she was an able poker player who could hold firm until the end. She was also an astute judge of character. "I ain't givin' up on you, Doc," she'd whispered. "The way you're carryin' on has ta be about some woman."

"Lady Trinka, it's about a lady."

All the money that he won did give him an idea.

Dear Mrs. Kelly,

I want you to take this and use it for Mary, for whatever you deem best. Please don't return the money. It's for a pony and school- ing and things.

Doc left the note unsigned. The money didn't come back to him.

Christmas passed and by spring of the following year, Doc had gotten his fill of Ft. Griffin, which had begun to dry up. The once plentiful buffalo were skittish and harder to find. Hunters no longer frequented the bars. On roads once busy, weeds were beginning to reclaim the buildings. As the money slowed to a trickle, the gamblers left. Doc knew that he wouldn't be back. Mysterious Dave had exhausted his stint as Tom McKey. In fact, the authorities had gotten wind of the game and were actively seeking to put the scheme out of business. As quickly as they had banded together, Mysterious Dave, Dutch Henry, and Randolph Smith, Jr. went their separate ways.

Upon Doc's arrival in Dodge City, he sought out Ham Bell from Old Granada days. Bell, in his chatty way, told him all he needed to know about the changes in Dodge, whom to avoid and all about the personalities gathered there. Doc plied him with coffee, liquor, and lunch.

"Damn, Doc, thanks. Call on me if you need anything. And stay in the Dodge House, you get a view of the whole town."

Dodge City was a sight to behold. There were any number of saloons, restaurants, and gambling halls. Front Street was booming, and the booming began a bare step or two from the Santa Fe Railroad. The money got off the train, and the gamblers followed behind it.

The Dodge House was located two blocks or so on the east side of Second Avenue. Familiar sights such as the Long Branch Saloon, with friend Luke Short officiating, welcomed him. Doc recognized Wright and Beverly's Store, and saw that there was a new opera house. Just as he began to feel that he'd come to stay, he spied Kate hanging on the arm of a cowboy, her favorite perch.

Better him than me, Doc thought and tried to make a quick escape to the other side of the street. He lost the gamble.

"Oh my," she voiced in her best gin-soaked voice. "Oh my. My man."

Doc's reply was printable for neither polite nor rude society.

"Oh my," Kate kept squalling in his ear. "Oh my."

"Kate, darlin', I warn you," Doc said through clenched teeth, "not one more 'oh my.' Got it?"

"Of course. I'm just oh so happy to see you again. Why you know, I should be angry for your precipitous departure, but I'm not."

Having become accustomed to less strident voices, Doc found hers to have the tonal qualities of a calliope gone flat. He removed her hand from his arm and Kate happily put it back. If he got into a gunfight now, he might with luck be able to shove Kate in front of the bullets.

"Where are you staying? Don't you want to freshen up?"

"I'm staying with you. Oh, it'll be so much fun. Just like old times."

"Having rabies is fun."

"Oh, you're just grumpy. Come on. We'll go eat. You can take me to Delmonico's."

"I've eaten."

She displayed her prettiest pout. "I haven't."

"Won't your cowboy be jealous?"

"No, I told him we were married."

"Kate, the only way, and I mean the only way we would ever be married is that I would have to be rabid, drunk, addlepated, suffering from amnesia, and someone else. Hello Ed, glad to . . . goddamit, what are you lookin' at?"

Kate began to cry. Doc uttered another obscenity and, cupping a hand under her arm, jerked her in the direction of Delmonico's. Miraculously, her face cleared of tears. She smiled at him.

"You're just tetchy cause you haven't had any in a long time."

"Shut up," Doc roared.

While Kate ate practically everything on the menu, Doc contented himself with soup and a sandwich. Between bites, Kate chattered. Between bites, Doc tuned her out.

The town was growing by leaps and bounds. One hundred thousand head of cattle or more were pouring into Dodge from the Western Trail. He envisioned new businesses giving birth while he ate. He could practice dentistry once more. He felt that he wouldn't lack for patients. And as for Kate calling herself Mrs. Holliday, maybe he would allow her to do so if she wanted. Perhaps she was sincere. He owed her a second chance at respectability at any rate. Besides, if he tried to stop her, she would make his life more unbearable than it already was.

It didn't take long to decide that the Dodge House was the best place to set up a dental practice. And the much drier climate of Kansas might help his consumption. Perhaps that's all it would take to make a difference. He could still fall back on gambling if the dental practice proved to be too rigorous. If the newspapers could be trusted, new cures and treatments were being discovered all the time.

"Consumption will be a thing of the past next year," a physician in Deadwood had told him. "Mark my words."

Doc wished he could be as enthusiastic, but he couldn't. His disease had progressed, and he was feeling from firsthand experience what his mother had been subject to. Small rituals must be attended to every day, from the fat pillows that pushed him into an upright position to the morning clearing of his chest, which revolted him as he literally coughed up his lungs.

The whiskey that cut his cough was second nature now. Miraculously, the fluid in his feet had not spread to his hands and he was able to keep a clear brain in spite of the alcohol. He never thought about the cough. He just coughed. It would be like forgetting to breathe.

Kate offered shreds of comfort. He wasn't alone, though she taunted, tormented, and teased him until he wished that he were dead. She kept him in a state of constant agitation and thorough anger. He sent heavenward to a God that he was unsure of this prayer: "Lord, never let me feel like Kate is keeping me alive."

Doc penned a letter to Mattie on fine linen stationery that he purchased at Wright and Beverly's Store. Mattie had helped him through the winter in Ft. Griffin and Denver. In Denver, he'd stayed incognito because of an Austin, Texas incident, though that had occurred some three years earlier. Three years seemed like a century. He thought he looked a century older, too, with his sunken cheeks and eyes that were dead except for the spark that made men look away. He figured that the consumption would take his soul eventually, as it was taking everything else.

The plan was to reline his pockets with money and settle in Dodge where he could finally practice dentistry on a permanent basis. Wyatt and his friends were there. Kate calling herself Mrs.

Holliday was a pipe dream of hers, but she would be as respectable as her nature would allow. Kate preferred being her own boss to accepting the constraining bonds of polite society.

Under Dodge City's bustling exterior there was still the bitter pall of the murder of Ed Masterson, Bat's brother. Bat had become more dour since then, and though Doc didn't blame Bat, he didn't relish the way Masterson looked at him. If it hadn't been for Wyatt's presence, Doc was fairly certain that Masterson would have asked him to leave town or put him in jail. Case in point was Doc's quiet announcement that his new dental practice would be located at No. 34 Dodge House. Wyatt rejoiced, but Bat bought himself a double shot of vodka.

The Dodge Times ran Doc's advertisement on June 8, 1878. Full of pride, Doc sent a copy to Mattie. Mattie had been quiet since Doc had written her of Mary. He knew that she was grieving as much he was and that neither could comfort the other except in words. So it was that she rejoiced over his decision.

My Dearest John,

It pleases me so very much to learn of your plan. You are talented and can succeed in any endeavor that you set your hand to. I do not want you to be unprotected. So please accept this ring, wear it, and know I am with you.

The ring was gold with a cross heavily etched inside the band. Such a gift made his hands tremble. Somehow Mattie knew that the ring was a perfect fit for his finger. He had no choice but to wear it on his right hand since Kate would have apoplexy to see it on his left.

Kate took it badly anyway, and the walls of Deacon Cox's excellent boardinghouse were filled from floor to ceiling with her vituperation.

"Miserable, miserable slut, " she screeched before realizing that she had never seen Doc so white of face or that he'd actually clawed his gun out of its holster.

What he called her, she never forgot.

"I'm never coming back."

"If hell freezes over, it'll be too soon, you bitch."

Kate flew at him, nails extended towards his eyes. Doc hit her. She scratched back. Blood was running on the both of them when she ran out screaming. It left him sick and coughing in bloody spasms until he cried. Unable to leave the room, he eventually collapsed on the bed. He felt mortally ashamed and so great was his hatred of himself that if he'd been a different caliber of man, he would have killed himself. Around ten o'clock that evening, there was a rap on the door.

"Ain't in," he snarled.

"Doc, it's me, Wyatt."

Doc scuffed over to the door and unlocked it. "What do you want?"

"I got some whiskey."

"Well, the doctor likes the sound of that."

Wyatt had brought food, too, and Doc, not having eaten since noon, was hungry. He polished off three of the five sandwiches and two pieces of cake.

"So I guess everyone in town heard our, uh, altercation."

"A body would have to be blind, deaf, and dumb not to get some sense of it." Wyatt had already noticed the pile of bloody handkerchiefs that Doc had tried to kick under the bed. He took a breath. "Are you okay?"

The air oozed out of Doc. "Damn, I don't know."

"Did the bleeding stop?"

"Yeah, finally. My head's pounding."

"Why don't you come over to my place for a while and get away from here?"

"I'm pretty unsteady. Been drinkin' more than usual. I'd rather not yet."

"Well, I'll leave the rest of the cake," Wyatt told him.

"I keep hearing these rumblings about Santa Fe," Doc said.

"Yeah," Wyatt said. "You and I both know the Royal Gorge has room for only one railroad."

"How did the winter go in Griffin?"

"In a whiskey bottle. I sent Mrs. Kelly a sum of money for Christmas. Nobody sent it back or threw it in my face."

"That's nice."

"Nice, Wyatt? That's one thing I'm not."

"Doc, if you really were the hard-assed son-of-a-bitch prick you tell everybody you are, we wouldn't be friends."

Doc's lips twisted in a smile. "You're sadly deluded, Wyatt."

The other man shrugged. "You ain't lookin' from my side of the mirror."

"You're a stubborn bastard," Doc grasped the whiskey and took a swallow.

"I need you to take a look at Leadville for me n' Bat. See if there are any Rio Grande agents up there. We think they're trying to cut the Santa Fe off. And I want to know about the silver lodes."

"You want me to go to Leadville? Bat's not keen on me, you know."

"I know, but he will be if I tell him. Santa Fe will pay for your time. Pay really good, too."

"My dentistry business has been slow. Yeah, I'll go up there and nose around."

By this time, Doc's color had returned and his shakes had stopped, but Wyatt didn't care to push his luck. "We'll have the funds ready for you by the end of the week."

"That sounds good," Doc said and waited until he heard the door close. "Thanks, Wyatt."

♣ ♥ ♠ ♦

From Buena Vista, the approach up to Leadville's 10,152-foot altitude didn't seem so bad. There was an incredible view of the mountains with a clean, blue skyline. Battered by the stage ride, Doc disembarked in Buena Vista, had a stiff drink, good supper, and a soft bed to soothe his bruises.

Leadville was ore capitol of the world. Gold mining had passed its peak, but there was plenty of silver to be had.

Horace Tabor, owner of almost the entire town and most of the silver mines, paid $2.50 to the miners who worked for him. *Slave wages,* Doc thought but kept quiet. There were a lot of takers for Tabor's money, which included bankers, lawyers, and those who had married into old money. Aside from Tabor, Doc liked Leadville for her unpretentious air. Most all of the action occurred on Harrison Street. Looking towards the west was Mt. Elbert and its larger twin, majestic Mt. Massive. Although it was summer, Doc was certain that the winters must be fearsome, as there was still snow on Mt. Massive.

It was heartening to see that not all the miners had given up. To be sure, mining was for the hardy of soul and body. Most of the miners were poor, and the saloons catered to that fact. Saloons, such as John Larsh's Pioneer Bar, succeeded in making the miners forget themselves and their money. There was a city government, of which Horace Tabor was prominent as mayor. Aware of how sticky politics in a boomtown could be, Doc moved with care. He had already come to the attention of Tabor, although the man had not made any monetary overtures. Not only did Doc find him unsavory, but there was too much of a land shark in Horace Tbor. He watched everyone coming into town and how he could use them.

The silver and gold seekers weren't the only entrepreneurs in Leadville. Denver and Rio Grande agents had quietly entered the town and were poking about. They passed themselves off as land speculators, but they asked too many questions about silver and the Santa Fe Railroad. Doc was familiar with the railroad and collected as many names of Rio Grande agents as he could for his report. Tabor, of course, knew everyone and asked as many questions about Doc as Doc asked about the agents.

"I have a fine a saloon. I could set you up as a partner and let you have the run of the place for a percentage. You'd do a good job for me, don't you know." He squinted hard at Doc. "You look really familiar. Do I know you?"

"Much obliged, Mr. Tabor, but I'm just passing through the area."

"Well, I can tell what you brought in your suitcase just by the way you dress."

"You could call me an entrepreneur," Doc replied.

"We all are here. Are you cashing in on Leadville's silver lode? There are thousands of pounds of it leaving here everyday for sale in Colorado Springs. I think sixteen or even eighteen dollars to the ton."

The questions exhausted Doc. Tabor, the baron of Leadville's silver and everything else in Leadville was certain that Doc had come for the silver. Why else would he be here?

Gratified to leave, Doc headed back to Dodge City and his report to Bat Materson. "The Rio Granders are fast losing a lot of their money. I don't think they will build across the gorge anytime soon either."

The fight got Doc's blood rolling again, and he began to feel his despair lift. Kate's appearance didn't even set him back. "To hell with Kate."

She was all smiles and somewhat piqued that he kept running off to Colorado. "Here I am honey," was not music to his ears.

Kate remained glued to Doc's arm no matter where he went. Encouraged by the railroad's proximity, Doc heartily wished that he could fling Kate into the path of an oncoming train.

"She'd probably gull the engineer," he told Wyatt, "and then abscond with the train."

"It would be better for all of us if she'd tone down a bit."

Doc coughed and laughed. Kate had no intention of toning down. It infuriated her that she could not lower Doc to her level. Doc admitted that Kate fed on his weaknesses. For the most part, except when she was calling herself Mrs. Holliday, she went about her business much as she pleased. When a fresh batch of cowboys or drifters came to town, Mrs. Holliday faded away. Kate took delight in flaunting them at Doc. It hurt all the more because he felt that he had fallen from God's good graces and was an outcast from polite society. Wyatt sensed the wound and tried to mend it. He considered Doc part of the Earp family, if no one else did. There was Thanksgiving and Christmas and parties. Kate loathed Wyatt Earp and hated every minute with the Earp clan. But as soon as Doc was out of earshot and in the confines of their bungalow, the fur would fly and it was usually Doc's. If she got to him enough, he hit her.

Even Masterson, never a Holliday admirer, said, "Dammit, Doc, unload that bitch."

Fighting was the only life Doc knew now. All the forces about him had conspired to drive away or destroy what softness he had known in the form of his mother, and Mattie, and most recently his precious little girl, Mary. Mary had just celebrated her sixth birthday. In Doc's dream, Mary had a pinto pony. Mattie was in the sitting room doing needlework after supper, which Doc knew her still to do. He and the gentlemen in town were gathered over cigars and brandy, while the air was lively with talk of politics and religion. It was a foolish dream, but it was all he had. He continued to pray, although the words felt like chaff in his throat. As spring brought the herds up the Western Trail, he prepared himself for another year under the sun.

In the spring of 1879, the court handed down the decision that the Denver and Rio Grande and the Santa Fe railroads had right-of-way through the Royal Gorge. The gorge was a savage beauty that had been cut by the roaring Arkansas River. Her sheer cliffs were a wonder of colors in pinks, oranges, reds, and rust, but the passage was a tiny one.

This meant that the gorge would permit only the niceties of one railroad to traverse the expanse. Canon City at the mouth of the mighty gorge was the most direct route to Leadville and her millions of pounds of silver that were being extracted before the boom town went bust. While the court system raged, a more sinister undertone developed. If the court system failed to address the hotly contested issue that each railroad felt it had, then both railroads were more willing to settle things the old-fashioned way—by way of the gun.

Meanwhile, the Union Pacific Railroad in Kansas waited patiently for the outcome in Colorado. Hungrily gobbling its rivals, the UPRR had as its intention some sort of merger between itself and Santa Fe or Denver and Rio Grande. The Denver-South Park, on the other hand, was building track through Leadville as fast as it could.

Facing the Denver and Rio Grande and the Santa Fe Railroads was the staggering logistical problem of how to lay the rails. Both railroads knew they had to be first across the Gorge to win. To tilt the odds in their favor, recruiters from both railroads hired mercenaries to intimidate and harass work crews of the other railroad, while hired thugs were used to protect their own rights. Murder was not out of the question.

As time passed, the Denver and Rio Grande began to suffer a serious weakness in its cash flow. Building across the Gorge was proving more expensive than first thought. To make matters worse, the direct legal and blood feud with the Santa Fe was sinking the Denver and Rio Grande even further in debt.

But there were some things going Denver and Rio Grande's way; a strategic location in the gorge allowed them to hold off the Santa Fe Railroad. If push came to shove, Denver and Rio Grande felt that they had a right to the Gorge.

As time wore on, the situation deteriorated with murders on both sides, attacks on work crews, and continuing financial drain. Finally, it came to a head in Pueblo, Colorado. As an offensive position, the Santa Fe Railroad took up as its base of operation, the Santa Fe roundhouse in Pueblo. Used for storage, maintenance, and servicing of locomotives, the large circular roundhouse was considered an excellent defensive position for the Santa Fe Railroad.

Bat Masterson was considered head of the group with Wyatt Earp and Doc to back him. Doc was very proud of his duties for the Santa Fe and a believer in the railroad. In June, he went with Wyatt and Bat to Pueblo, Colorado. The Roundhouse Battle had begun. All of Denver and Rio Grande's and Santa Fe's rail rights, exhaustive court battles, and open violence were focused on this one pivotal spot. To defend it, there were many able-bodied gunmen hired. There were replacements and others in the event that someone became ill. The Santa Fe team had a Gatling gun.

"We're only going to use this gun in the most dire of circumstances," Bat told the group of Santa Fe railroaders.

"Let's wipe 'em all out."

"Can't do that. I'm sworn to uphold the law. And uphold the law, I will."

Bat was a U.S. deputy marshal, a position that the Denver and Rio Grande felt was unfair and prejudicial. To them, Masterson's deputy marshalship had to have been purchased in blood by the Santa Fe.

Before shots could be fired or blood spilled, the Rio Grande faction approached the Roundhouse. As Bat walked out to confront the opposing side, he turned to the rifleman who covered his back. "I want you to hold your fire. But if you see me go down, go ahead and shoot."

Doc waited with everyone else to see what would happen. The Roundhouse was ringed with Rio Granders. The Santa Fe group inside was ready to fire the big gun. The minutes ticked by. Finally, Bat reappeared. He entered the Roundhouse. In his hand was a large satchel and on his face was an equally large grin.

"Look," Bat said as he opened the satchel. "Ten thousand dollars, gentlemen, to be divided amongst us."

Doc was disappointed. After all the trouble the two groups had gone to, they could have at least fired some shots over each other's heads. There were some, the scuttlebutt said, who thought that Bat had received payoff money from the other side.

By early 1880 a court decision cleared the way for the quagmire both railroads had dug themselves into. For Santa Fe, there was a settlement of $1,400,000 for all rail that had already been laid through the gorge. Also, the railroad had to promise that it would not go through Leadville or Denver. For the Rio Granders, there must be no rail lines through El Paso.

Trinidad, south of Pueblo, was the place that Bat's now defunct army traveled for much needed rest and libation. Doc, in sore need of rest, went with them. The railroad war had taken much out of him. He'd caught a cold from the damp canyons and much cooler climate. With a cough that was troublesome and worrying him more than he cared to admit, he left things as they were in Kansas.

From Trinidad, Doc traveled to Las Vegas, New Mexico via a newly completed rail line. As the train drew closer to its destination, a panorama of beauty in the way of crystal blue skies and water met his hungry eyes. It was an encouraging sign and, according to reports, there were almost three hundred days of sunshine a year. He hoped here to bake the cold from his chest.

Nestled within the granite mountains was Hermit Peak, which formed the north side of Gallinas Canyon. From out of its mouth flowed Rio Gallinas winding across the valley to flow into the Pecos River. Within Gallinas Canyon were forty or so hot springs. Doc had heard of these springs while in Colorado and listened attentively to the stories about their miraculous healing powers. He wanted to believe the stories since his worst fears were being realized. He couldn't lie to himself and say that his lungs were healing, because they were breaking down at a faster rate. He yearned to stay permanently in one place. He yearned every day for things to work out professionally and personally. He desperately wanted to be rid of Kate and her hold over him. As he stepped off the train in Las Vegas, a sudden breeze scented by pine and flowers and warmth ruffled his hair. Life looked promising.

The town was divided into Old Town and New Town. Making up the plaza in Old Town was the Exchange Hotel managed by the Kitchen brothers. The Exchange had a saloon, ballroom, and for those not interested in poker, someplace to lie down. Wyatt had spoken fondly of this hotel and how the cattle moguls came for gambling games that could last three or four days. At Sky's-The-Limit Poker, food and drinks were hand delivered to the tables so no one would have to leave.

Las Vegas felt comfortable and Doc proceeded to open a practice. Sharing the same building with him was a jeweler by the name of William Leonard. He and Doc shared many of the same tastes and outlook on life. They got to be friends. Because of the logistical layout of the town, Doc's dental practice was opened in Old Town, considered to be the respectable part.

Doc didn't think much about location either way. Teeth had always been teeth to him. Everybody had them and everybody lost them. He again held forth his belief that children should come first. If some of the parents were short on funds, he was agreeable.

One barefooted child came regularly for a while. No one ever accompanied her and though Doc asked around town, no one knew where she came from. He gave her quarters and trinkets. She never spoke or giggled. She took the quarters that he gave to her, sticking them in the same half-torn pocket of the calico dress that she always wore. She broke his heart. Her dirty face was the same sweet heart-shaped face as his Mary. It was a face that he would wash carefully before working on her teeth.

Then one day, she stopped coming. Doc frantically asked for information but was only told, "Them squatters moved on."

The other side of town housed what was considered the rougher element, such as saloons and gaming halls. Doc, however, found the right place to open his own saloon. Having been around the best, he knew what he wanted and how to run it. The saloon was on Centre Street.

It was Doc's intention to make his dental profession his primary means of livelihood, but each ugly second of consumption was robbing him of that dream. The problems were the same: coughing that took all of his air and hands that operated with smooth efficiency at the poker tables would fall quivering to his sides if he worked over a patient's mouth for too long.

He remembered his mother's needle falling to her lap. He remembered her hands crashing on the piano keys for no reason. Finally, one day, she put her sewing down.

"My fingers are too heavy," she told him.

Captain John Joshua Webb, a recent émigré of the railroad war, bought into the saloon partnership with Doc. Citing health reasons, Doc's name was never listed as the primary owner on any venture.

"Either way," he told Webb, "the consumption or a bullet will finish me. My bet's on the bullet."

"In other words, Doc, you want an honorable end."

"Something like that," he said.

The Las Vegas trouble began over cards. Bat Masterson had his share as had Wyatt and many professional gamblers. Until the late 1870s, gambling had no stigma attached. Being a professional gambler was highly acceptable. As 1879 drew to a close, there were rumblings that professional gambling was on the way out. Certainly, it was becoming the rule back East. But not so in the West, not yet.

Doc had been quietly adjusting his own schedule for personal reasons. The consumption had progressed so that he could no longer maintain a full-time dental practice. In the mornings he would attend to what dental patients he had the strength for, and in the afternoon he would go to his saloon. He enjoyed both professions, but the disease made the choice for him. It did not, however, make the choice in his gambling. He was having a very good run of luck.

Las Vegas grew rough in a way that surpassed even Dodge City. Daily the trains arrived with prostitutes, murderers, and confidence men. The millions of buffalo that had once thundered black and streaming through the prairie grass were no more. And the Plains Indians, with no buffalo to hunt or feed their families, were being forced to move to reservations.

Of all the fair cyprians that arrived in town that summer, none were more flamboyant or thoroughly outrageous than Kate Elder. She arrived with the likes of Poker Alice, Madame Mustache, and Belle the Blue. Kate's Hungarian nose had not grown any larger since Doc had seen her last, but he was driven to savagery by her appearance. For the rest of his stay in town, she hounded his footsteps, his life, and screeched more vile names at him than he had ever called her.

"You and your Southern ways. It isn't enough that you shamed me with your rutting . . ."

"Rutting? Rutting, my dear?" Doc said in tones that dripped honey and arsenic. "You rutted with most of Dodge City in front of me and laughed. I, at least, had the courtesy to rut, as you call it, behind closed doors with women that, if not beautiful and talented, were quiet!"

In the middle of her vitriolic explosion, Kate stopped, coming to a realization. There was quite a crowd of onlookers gathered and Kate smiled her most engaging smile.

"Doc, where am I going to stay?"

"Where you usually do, darlin'," he replied. Her smile grew larger. "In hell until it freezes over." Doc stalked away in the direction of his saloon.

Kate became an everyday occurrence, much as his morning ritual of clearing his chest. Doc wrote to tell Mattie where he was staying and was pleased when she wrote back. At some point, he feared that she would be so sickened of him and the life he led that she would turn against him forever. This had not happened. And it had been Mattie herself who was so depressed. Doc could date that to his search for Mary. Mattie had never recovered her spirits. Nevertheless, she wrote.

My Dearest John,

You don't know how much pleasure I take in your constant companionship. Would that we could be together. My parents have been at me again to marry, but you know how I feel on the subject. Your father and Rachel are fine. Rachel sends her love. Tell me of the new place and how you are. Again, do what you must to stay alive.

My Deepest Love Always,
Mattie

There were some of her letters that Doc saved for the things that she said or sent. Once she had sent him a dried bit of the Spanish moss that he loved. He had taken that wisp of green and smelled it for weeks until the wonderful musty odor was gone, then put it in the bureau of his boardinghouse room. It would travel with him until it fell apart.

As the rail lines reached deeper into new territory, a steady influx of trouble followed, which included Dave Rudabaugh and the old enmity from Ft. Griffin. Dave wasn't ready to have it out with Doc in the middle of the street, but he was seen having a long conversation with Kate. This Doc was apprised of after he came into his saloon for an evening of poker.

The bartender said, "Bodes no good. Well, Dave's been okay to me, Doc. But she means nothin' but trouble. Unfortunately, together them two is mischief."

"Do tell," Doc drawled. "What else?"

"That there Mike Gordon got off the train today. He's been hangin' on Liddie's skirt something fierce. I don't like the looks of him. Liddie ain't talkin', but then she never does. She's a good girl, Doc. I don't want anything to happen to her."

"I don't either. She is a good girl. Let's take care of that."

Doc went about his business, but he kept his ears and eyes open. Mike Gordon could be seen to lurk from table to table, his stares all for Liddie while she worked. Poor Liddie had come into town on the same day as Kate. She had a kind of desperate beauty about her, as if she was trying to make a go of life and not succeeding. Doc kept a fatherly eye out for all his "girls," and it was well known that he didn't tolerate rough or lewd behavior in his saloon.

Mike was drinking himself up in a calculating manner as the bartender could well testify to given the number of rotgut drinks he was asked to pour.

"Think maybe he's drinkin' courage, Doc."

"Think you're right. Why don't you spell me for a while and I'll talk to him."

When Gordon saw Doc walk up to him, he turned white around the mouth, but he wouldn't relinquish the table.

"Tell ya, Doc, it's true, I've sucked down a bunch. And I tell you what, ain't no J. H. Holliday gonna run me off."

"Well, Mike, you have drunk quite a bit."

It was hot on that New Mexican summer day, but Doc looked cool in his favorite gray suit with an aquamarine blue shirt, black cravat, and blue stone and gray vest. Mike looked like he'd ridden hundreds of miles in the sun, wind, and rain. And the rain hadn't washed him clean.

"I kin look like that," Mike pointed a finger at Doc. He wasn't drunk enough to jab him.

"Well, Mike, why don't we go on over to the Exchange and get a room? You can clean up a bit. Some coffee might help."

"Are you callin' me drunk, Doc?"

"I think you've had too much to drink. Why do you want to go and bother Liddie for?"

"I came back to git her. We had ourselves a nice little arrangement, and I wants it back."

"What did Liddie say?"

"She don't want me. But you know women. Hell, I hear you gots one."

Doc made a sour face. "Yes, I 'gots' one. It seems that if she doesn't want the arrangement, then you wouldn't want her."

"Ah, she don't know what she wants. I do. I tell her what she wants."

"Really?" Doc's baritone dropped two decibels into ice. "I want you to leave now."

"Not without Liddie."

Doc turned and saw Liddie with a tear glistening on her cheek.

"Without Liddie. Leave now and I won't have to do somethin' about it."

"I'll shoot the place up, Doc."

"Tell you what. You kill me, then you can shoot the place up."

Gordon took a step back. Doc might be a good deal shorter, but it didn't seem that way. The famous Holliday stare from his dead blue eyes fixed on Gordon.

"Let's go at it," Doc said and started towards the door.

"Damn you," Gordon hollered and stumbled through the saloon doors to the street.

He whirled in the street and fired two rounds towards Doc and the building, but the next thing he knew he was lying in the street and looking up at the sky. His midsection was ablaze with a curious weight like a hot brick grinding its way towards the marrow of his bones.

Someone yelled for the doctor and the sheriff. A blanket was rushed out and thrown over the wounded man.

"I didn't hear no shots. How'd he do that? I didn't hear no shots," Gordon gabbled as he was carried away.

Doc reentered the now quiet saloon. The faro play had stopped, as had the piano. Walking up to Liddie, Doc reached into his pocket for a roll of greenbacks to put into her hand.

"Use this and get the hell out of here, hear me? This is no place for you. You got family trouble, go patch it up, but I don't want to find you in this hell again. And I'll be lookin'.'"

She swallowed hard. "Thanks, Doc. Won't you be in trouble?"

"Honey, I've been in trouble since the day I was born."

Kate wasn't up early the next morning, but Doc had already boarded the train towards Prescott. According to Wyatt, the gaming tables in Prescott were flush. Knowing of Doc's worsening health he said, "We've got to push on to Tombstone, but I think you'll like Prescott."

For Doc, out a great deal of money from the Las Vegas venture, the stop in Prescott was a necessity. He never cared to travel to a new town without sufficient funds. The flight from

Georgia had been his first and last foray on thin dimes in thinner pockets. Prescott might be a nice place to winter. It was a nice watering hole. There were gamblers who headed towards the sun forsaking the chill in their bones and who lit out for the cool climate in summertime. To those such as Doc with an affliction in the lungs, a warm climate was cherished. In that 1879 autumn, Doc found that he missed the Dodge days with Bat and the Earps. Doc didn't miss Kate.

≈ *Chapter* ≈

FOURTEEN

Winter approached in the dusty blue and purple shadows that rolled across the red canyons early in the afternoon. By six o'clock, the sky was cool with stars. Doc became contemplative as Christmas approached. His bankroll was growing with the speed of a desert thunderstorm, but he readily admitted that there was a pall in the gaiety. The glamour was a false one, and he knew that his life wasn't living.

The winter of 1880 brightened considerably with Wyatt's arrival. He came full of good cheer, loads of Christmas presents, whiskey, and a tale of Texas. Doc's good spirits, however, dampened at the sight of Kate as she sashayed off the train with the other prostitutes.

"I'm sorry," she said with real tears to show for the occasion. She cried them on Doc's neck in the middle of the town square. "I won't throw them cowboys in your face."

"That's good," Doc told her. "I'd only have to kill 'em—or you."

"I won't bring shame or dishonor on you. I understand how sensitive you are."

Doc choked on a cough that wasn't his consumption. He patted her back awkwardly.

"It was just your friendship with Wyatt that made me so crazy. I just had to make you jealous."

"You'd think I was having an affair with Wyatt," he replied.

Kate raised her tear-swollen face. Small, black tangles of curls stuck to her forehead and her teary lashes stuck together as well. Her makeup streamed down her cheeks in black streaks. In her black traveling dress, she looked reasonably sorrowful.

With his arm around her, he looked into the distance towards the mountains of silver and the baked landscape and back at her. She was looking down at the buttons on his shirt as new tears dropped on the fabric. He exhaled regretfully, and it emptied his whole body.

"Well, I'm sorry, too," he told her. "Let's get your things rounded up. You can stay with me." He didn't add "where I can keep an eye on you." Instead he asked, "Have you had dinner?"

Kate shook her head, vainly trying to wipe the tears off his suit.

"I haven't either. I know traveling makes you hungry. There are some good restaurants here."

Kate was contrite through the meal and civil to Wyatt when he joined them. It helped that Wyatt gave her a lovely necklace wrapped in a box with silver tissue paper and a gilded ribbon. She kissed the astonished Wyatt on the cheek before asking him to put it on her please.

"I have to go show it off."

"That was a stroke of luck, Wyatt."

"Well, I figured. She likes baubles. She can gad about, and I can tell you what happened in Texas."

"Besides a shitload of trouble I presume," Doc offered.

"You know Mysterious Dave Mather and me got caught. Dave was so sure that it would work. We had it all set up. Damn, but Dave can pass for you. Never seen the like. He puts a little gold somethin' on his hair and gets all Southerned up and away he goes."

Doc's lips twitched. "And?"

"We got run out of town by the deputy sheriff."

"Well damn, Wyatt."

"And somewhere in Texas we lost the brick. I guess it's somewhere in the Texas dust."

"May I ask why you wanted to do this?"

"Sure," Wyatt grinned. "To see if we could. Mysterious Dave was disappointed, especially since he and Soapy Smith had such a success back in '77. Are you comin' on with us to Tombstone?"

"I don't know. I was thinking of wintering here. It's kind of an unwritten rule about leaving in the middle of a hot streak. Kind of like givin' ol' Lady Luck a swat in the bustle when she's not lookin'. It would be disastrous."

"I've got the family with me and Virge and Morg. Virge thinks we're a bad influence on each other."

"Well hell, Wyatt, nothin' ever happens round us. Old Virge should rest easy. Dull as a tick we are."

"If you change your mind, you know where to find us. Think about it. You could still catch up."

By the time Kate returned to the saloon, Wyatt was gone. "Everybody's goin' to Tombstone," she said tugging at his arm and batting her lashes at him once more. She'd fixed her makeup and changed her dress.

"And we will, too," he said. "After a bit."

"Hours?" she wheedled.

"Days, a week, a month. I'm not comfortable traveling in winter."

Kate blushed. "I know. I was just . . . " she struggled, "fishing."

"Well, fishing's okay, darlin'. And you do look mighty fetching in that frock. Suppose you help me out this afternoon. We might leave for Tombstone sooner than you think."

Tombstone had begun like many other Western towns given over to sudden wealth. In its early days, it was a scrub patch of prairie land. But in 1877, Ed Schieffelin and a number of other men were recruited for service at the newly formed Camp Huachuca. Looking northward from the army camp lay the Huachuca Mountain Range and the Hualipi Nation. Schieffelin looked upon the new opportunity as a challenge and learned all that he could about the barren land.

Schieffelin had always been a scout at heart. Even as a boy he was always looking for new adventures and new sights. With the Arizona air filling his nostrils, he heard a voice that he had never heard before. It whispered to him as he lay on his cot back in camp. It ruffled his hair as he set out across the prairie on his pack mule. It drew him ever further from the camp. One day after riding to the bottom of an unfamiliar arroyo, he saw something glisten in the sunlight.

Wiping the dust from his eyes, Schieffelin looked quickly around to see if anyone was following him. He knew that the Hualipi kept a jealous eye on the white man and were always on the lookout for a man riding alone. With no one in sight, he rode closer to see that the glitter was not an illusion of the shimmering heat. Dismounting, Ed scraped some of the dust into a pocket and remounted his mule. Once back in camp, Schieffelin's compatriots looked upon his new endeavor with scorn.

"All you'll find out there is yer tombstone."

But Schieffelin was not dissuaded by the disparaging remarks. While everyone else flocked to the Black Hills for gold, Ed continued to scrape at the parsimonious Arizona ground. Always he envisioned a roaring river of silver under the earth. As he swung his pick, he found more silver, and then again more silver. The discovery did not go unnoticed. Soon drovers, bankers, outlaws, and pioneers flocked by the thousands to dig for the precious ore. Tents sprung up by the hundreds, and the new town became known as Tombstone.

Tombstone boasted a town marshal and a county sheriff. Virgil had arrived with a ready appointment as a deputy U.S. marshal. On January 6, 1880, Fred White was elected as Tombstone's marshal. Sheriff Charles Shibell represented Pima County and appointed John Behan as his deputy. Both men had headquarters in Tombstone. Strict guidelines kept town matters separate from county law.

By the time Doc arrived in February 1880, a town seething at the seams lay stretched out before him. It struck him like a thunderclap. There were schools, stores, saloons, and gambling twenty-four hours a day. There were hardy frontier folk and newly arrived easterners all awestruck by the promise of silver. Unlike many of the town's populace, the inhabitants of the tent cities wanted quick wealth and fast getaways. It was no holds barred.

It injected Doc with a frenzy he had not felt in a long time. After a long winter, it offered life at a fevered pitch. Primitive urges could be satisfied with money. Tombstone was Denver, Dallas, Cheyenne, and Dodge City at the peak of their prosperity. It throbbed with the impatience of roulette wheels, tinny pianos, clinking faro chips, and boisterous singing.

Transfixed, Doc stood immobile in the middle of the street while humanity surged from one end of town to the other. He decided that he better move or become part of the dust underneath this churning mill.

Methodically, Doc sorted through innuendo, politics, and religious factions and how they made each man tick. Never did he take anyone's rumor as truth.

Silver drove the frenzy. It invoked stage and train robberies and the curious element called the Cowboys. Doc learned that not all cowboys were necessarily rustlers, thieves, or killers. There were those who worked for ranches and tended cattle. They spent their time on the range in legitimate purposes. But the outlaw element gave claim to another kind of cowboy.

Their enemies declared the Cowboys as hard-bitten a bunch to come from the desert floor as any one of the snakes slithering through town. As Doc was told, "Rattlesnakes always lie together. That way, they don't have anything to fear."

Memories were hazy about where Newton "Old Man" Clanton had originated, but he was not a native to Arizona. The Cowboys' network operated from Southern Arizona and Northern Mexico. They had their admirers and hangers-on, including some county sheriffs. Billy, Ike, and Phineas were Old Man Clanton's boys. Ike and Billy did most of the errand running for him.

With the Clanton clan came the McLaurys: Robert Franklin and Thomas. One of the Clanton gang leaders was called Curly Bill Brocius. Running with Curly Bill was John Ringo, Curly Bill's lieutenant.

Northern Mexico was a cattle-rustling heaven for the Clanton gang. The rustlers had their headquarters in the town of Galeyville that was located across the eastern side of the Chiricahua Mountains not far from San Simon Valley. Although the Mexicans tried to stringently enforce lawfulness, the area in question was too vast to effectively police.

Flaunting Mexican authority, the Cowboys used easy entry points such as El Paso to make their way into Northern Mexico where they drove the cattle through the Guadeloupe and Skeleton Canyons to San Simon Valley. Once in Galeyville, the cattle herds were divided into smaller groups for fattening up. In that part of the country, every drop of water was precious to the cattle, especially since the drive from Mexico was so exhausting. To this end, the Cowboys had to secure all the water rights. And secure them they did. Once the cattle were rested and fed, they were sold.

"First come. First served," was Curly Bill's motto echoed by his gang members. "The first Mex to cross our path is the first one to be shot."

The Clantons zealously looked after their holdings on the San Pedro River. The McLaurys tended their operation near Sulphur Spring Valley. Aligned with the cattle rustlers was the faction of stage and train robbers that considered all transportation as fair a game as the cattle. Like all brothers, they guarded each other jealously.

As the Earps settled into their new life, Tombstone fractured along political lines. For instance, *The Tombstone Epitaph* with John Clum as editor heralded the Republican platform, which the Earps supported. *The Nugget* lauded the Democratic viewpoint and was inclined to favor the working class citizens, which included the Clantons and McLaurys. Friend and foe kept a close eye on the whereabouts of the other. The town never slept. It was wary, violent, and silver-hungry.

At the time of Doc's arrival, there was no active dislike on the part of the Clanton-McLaury faction for the newly arrived Earps or Doc.

"I'm intensely uneasy though, suh," Doc told Wyatt one late Thursday evening. "They ask a lot of questions, and they watch. But I don't think they'll make any move until they see which way our hats fall."

Nowhere in Doc's travels had such elegant and dangerous poker or faro games existed than in Tombstone. In June, Doc made a short trip to Las Vegas, New Mexico. Tombstone was not going to shut down in his absence and neither would Kate. She had made good her tearful plea of several months earlier by undergoing an outward metamorphosis that was ridiculous and touching. However, Kate was not one to let the grass grow under her feet. Gone Doc might be, but Kate would quench her thirst with someone else in his absence.

"I shan't be gone long, darlin'. It is business, you understand."

That she did understand with her bright black eyes, a saucy dimple in her cheek, and a demure tip of her head downward. She dutifully saw him off, but Doc couldn't resist turning to watch her saucy behind flounce in the direction of the nearest saloon.

The purpose of Doc's trip was relatively simple: close out his partnership of the saloon on Centre Street. Webb had been a good business partner and an honest one. There was always money wired to Doc from Las Vegas with the week's tally. Doc intended on selling at a loss, but he wanted to let Webb know how pleased he was. His arrival in Las Vegas was made in the relative comfort of the train. Tombstone had no train. The trip back by stagecoach would mean another buffeting that would shake him to death, while clouds of dust would torture his lungs.

Doc did get a sharp pang on seeing the city. He'd always liked the way the sun shown on Las Vegas' plaza. Shrugging off his melancholia, Doc took a last look at Centre Street and paused in the doorway of the saloon for a quick memory he could add to his mental scrapbook. The poker tables were lively and John Webb was happy to see him.

"Come to sell out to you, John," Doc said holding out his hand. "Liddie didn't come back, did she?"

"No. I put her on the train to Omaha myself. Told me she would give her family another go," Webb said.

"That's good."

"I hear you're doing well in Tombstone."

"Here's to Tombstone, Doc," one of the players at another table yelled.

Doc grinned and touched his hat in response. "Tombstone is not to be believed, John."

"That a fact? I might have to swing over there myself and try it out."

The two shook hands. Doc signed the deed to Webb. Webb paid him.

"Be careful in town, Doc. Charley White's here across the way. He's no good. Got it for you bad. I wouldn't put it past the yellow-bellied guttersnipe to go after you in the back."

"You know I've always preferred the frontal approach. Think I'll go and see the man."

Charley White's accusations dated back to Dodge City. He was a braggart and had intimated that he knew Doc to be a cheat, liar, and murderer.

Doc had proved White to be running a confidence game, a thing Bat Masterson loathed. Under a cloud of disgrace, White had left Dodge and taken residence where he thought himself safe from the verbal barbs and bullets of other disgruntled gamblers. He barked foul in a diatribe that was his trademark, never thinking his bluff would be called.

Doc didn't want to kill White, but he very much wanted a retraction of the cheat, liar, and murderer statements. It was a clear insult to Doc's sensibilities. White hadn't changed much since Dodge City. He had the same greasy hair, crisp white shirt and apron that on another man might look elegant. On White, it just made him look sleazy. His hands were clean, though the ragged, dirty nails gave him away. Doc bided his time, knowing that a good entrance was most effective. He liked his height for that reason. It meant that he could slide into a room undetected.

White poured drinks without looking up until he got to Doc.

"Come to finish our business, Charley," Doc told him pleasantly. The bottle that White was pouring from jerked and the liquid splashed across the bar.

"Howdy, uh, Doc. Get you a drink?"

"Want to find out what you're doing spreading filth about me to the folks in this town."

"Well, you know," Charley began to sweat, "I was just sayin' to John Webb over at your place how dull this town is without you. We all wish you was back."

"How utterly and deliciously a bald-faced liar you are. Count your proceeds carefully, suh," Doc called to the owner of the saloon. "You may find you are a bit light in the till."

White's face went pasty and the grease in his hair trickled down the back of his neck. "Damn you, Holliday."

By this time, Doc's eyes were burning blue coals. "Guess it's finally time we brought this little scenario to flower," Doc said as he stepped back.

Predictably, Charlie's hand was filled with a gun underneath the bar. He knew Doc was good, but he felt certain that Doc couldn't see through wood.

White fired a quick volley that broke glasses and sprayed customers, who turned over the tables and hit the floor. Wood chips flew everywhere. The faro table was upended. Doc put in two rounds. One went over Charlie's head, the other creased his skull. Like a wounded water buffalo, White sank beneath the surface of the bar. He wasn't dead as his lamentations soon confirmed.

A grizzled veteran known as Old Timer quipped, "You want to play a couple of hands with us Doc for old time's sake? Would surely like that pleasure."

Doc consulted his watch. "I'd like to Old Timer, but I've done my woeful deed for the day. Tombstone beckons. Come on over to Tombstone."

Charlie's groan, louder than the one before, made both men lean over the bar.

"Kinda likes the drama, don't he?" Old Timer asked.

"He was that way in Dodge. We rode him out on the rail. He likes to collect part of the house take for himself. Has a bag in his apron that he slips the money in."

"That a fact? We might hafta go to his room and check his belongings for extra jingle."

Doc left the saloon and then went to catch the stage. It seemed like he had too much time to think. Folks always talked about leaving things undone. Doc never was one for that. His life was going to be too short anyway. He didn't want to feel bad about leaving Las Vegas. He didn't want to feel nostalgic. He didn't want to feel.

His dental instruments had to be sold. Doc wasn't sure how much they would fetch since most dentists had their own equipment. He'd never meant for his dental artistry to fall victim to the predator. Here he was two months shy of his twenty-ninth birthday and an old man. Recently, he'd detected a gray strand of hair mixed in with gold. He'd plucked it out.

Doc reread Mattie's last letter. His little girl, Mary, would be a long-legged filly by now. She would be eight this December. She would be good in school and run barefoot in the grass. He got out his book of Poe, finished that, and removed the dog-eared copy of *Rime of the Ancient Mariner* from his valise. The stagecoach lurched forward.

♣ ♥ ♠ ♦

In Tombstone, three enterprising gambling sportsmen named Lou Rickabaugh, Dick Clark, and Bill Harris arrived to operate the gambling portion of the Oriental Saloon. With July 4th fast approaching, they wanted to get the lease approved for the official opening. It was sure to be a lavish affair with high rollers from every corner of the West in attendance.

Doc had seen plenty of elegance in his time, but the luxurious candle sconces and the bar outdid any grandeur he had ever seen. If it was possible, the gilt that illuminated the top of the bar outshone the great chandelier. The sideboards were resplendent displays of glass and wood. Upon the crisp linen were placed steaming and sumptuous delicacies. From the outset, both Doc and Wyatt vied to be dealers.

"They won't hire you, Wyatt, because your cravat is crooked."

"No it's not," he looked down. By the time he figured it out, Doc was already at the gaming table.

"I know you gentlemen need a Southerner to grease the wheels of Lady Luck."

Alongside the familiar sporting fraternity, the Cowboys, too, began to congregate in the Oriental. Separately, they were quarrelsome. As a group, they were murderous.

"We're just hardworking men," Ike Clanton told Buckskin Frank Leslie while he was tending bar one night in the Oriental. Leslie, although affable, could when pushed display a temper that far surpassed anything that the Cowboys might hand out.

Frank's scowl reached his crotch. "That drink'll be two bits."

"Two bits? Hell, two bits is two bits too much."

"You want to make somethin' of that?" There was an audible click of a gun much larger than a revolver under the counter at the bar.

Ike's rabbit-shaped nose quivered in alarm. "No, no, Frank, really. I was just kiddin'. You know me, always a laugh."

"Two bits," Frank said as he slammed a shot glass on the bar in front of Ike.

"Hey, Frank, good business today?" Doc asked as he walked up to the bar next to Ike.

"Middlin' good, Doc. Middlin' good. Your usual fare? Thought you'd like to know that I got some real Cuban cigars in a shipment this morning. These are real ones, not the fake. I'll give you one for free."

Leslie handed the cigar to Doc and deftly poured his drink.

"Much obliged, Frank." Doc clipped the end and lit up. "Mmm. Nothing like this." The two men toasted each other. "How are you Ike?" Doc asked pleasantly.

"Leave it to you to speak to Frank first before you talk to me."

"What's wrong with you now?"

"Well I just think it's interestin' that you saunter in here all prettied up and speakin' to Old Buckskin here before you say anythin' ta me. Not only that, you get a free cigar. Them damn Cuban things cost fifteen cent."

Leslie leaned far over the top of the bar and into Ike's face. His rage-filled eyes made Ike's Adam's apple quail. "You listen to me, you've been spittin' all over my nice clean floor. It'll take at least a dollar to clean it up. How abouts I make you clean it up yourself?"

Humiliated, Ike tossed his drink back and then slammed the shot glass back on the bar. Stomping towards the door, he allowed a last hate-filled glance to include both men. As long as he lived, Ike thought, he would never get over his hatred for Doc Holliday. Part of his hatred stemmed from the clothes, like the three-piece dark brown suit that Holliday was wearing. The long jacket cut from expensive cloth was open in the front revealing an equally expensive vest of dark gold brocade. There was a cravat and a diamond stickpin. It was a real diamond, too. Ike hated those clean hands more than he hated Doc. It was those same clean hands that had robbed him of hundreds of dollars in poker winnings. As he walked on down the street, he contented himself with the thought of one day drilling Holliday in the back.

As tensions mounted between the groups, the Earps and Doc were beginning to stick to one side of the bar with the Clantons on the other. The Cowboys had just come back from another murdering and rustling spree and were heady with their success. They had begun whispering amongst themselves and then shooting sly glances at the Earps.

"Do you think they slaughtered them Mexs down there, Wyatt? They are laughin' and talkin' about it," Morgan said.

Doc paused to stare at Morgan and leaned forward so no one could hear him. "Drunk or sober?" Reaching into a newly opened box of Cuban cigars, he removed the band and clipped the end with a cigar cutter.

"They are sober."

"Then they did it," Wyatt replied to no one.

"I'll go nose around for a bit," Virgil chimed in. "Ike talks a lot. Drunk or sober."

"Not to put too dark of a light on our festivities, but I think our days of bein' bridegrooms are over. There's some serious scuttlebutt about the stage robberies. A group of them specialize in Wells Fargo shipments. Hell, they can always spot 'em by the extra lookouts. It's a dead giveaway."

"I was afraid of that. We'll have to keep a closer eye."

"Brocius has been stickin' his face in. He smiles a lot. I don't trust a man with such a smile. It's one of the features that don't reach his eyes," Doc replied with a sweeping glance.

"A lot doesn't reach his eyes. How a man can carry on like that and never have a warrant sworn, I'll never know."

"What we need," Doc leaned forward, "is a county that Tombstone can call her own. Pima County doesn't do us much good with its county seat in Tucson."

"A lot of things around here don't do us much good, includin' them. Hi, boys. How are you tonight?"

Ike and Billy Clanton waved back.

By March, Kate was back to being Kate Elder.

"Just as obstreperous and cantankerous as God ever made womankind," Wyatt remarked.

"You don't have to live with her, Wyatt."

"Actually, Doc, you don't either."

Doc's head snapped up. "Actually, you're right."

For Kate, this was one more reason to hate Wyatt Earp. He took her man away. If Wyatt protected a stage, Doc backed him up. If Doc was dealing faro or even if he wasn't, Wyatt was there. If Wyatt had a party, Doc was invited and went.

"Dammit," she yelled at him on the night of his birthday, "why can't we just be alone? Your name might as well be Earp."

"It is my birthday and my friends are having a party in my honor, to which you received an invitation. In previous years, you have managed to consume vast amounts of food and drinks—especially the drinks—and act like a horse's ass and a bitch's whore rolled into one."

"If I'd asked for your opinion, I would have asked for your opinion."

"Kate, darlin', you are drunk."

"Damn straight and I'm going home."

"You'll be going alone. I'm not through here yet."

"Damn you."

"Do yourself and me a big favor. Go get some sleep. I'll bring you some cake."

"You can take the cake and shove it."

She flounced out pushing past Morgan and Virgil.

"She's got that down anyway," Morgan observed.

⚜ *Chapter* ⚜
FIFTEEN

If there was one thing that Wyatt missed, it was the stability of a normal life with his family. He balked at becoming a sheriff again, but so many things pulled him in that direction. His brothers echoed the same sentiment. It was hard to turn a blind eye and deaf ear to the injustices going on in Tombstone. So many people were in need, and they needed the Earps' help. Peacekeeping, Wyatt knew, was something he did well.

Doc continued to keep his eye on the Clantons, although they remained unfailingly polite to him. Most of the time, Doc dealt with Ike and Billy as Old Man Clanton left much of the errand running to them.

By September, the talk of forming a new county was in high gear. The shifting political landscape of forming a separate county for Tombstone threw the Clanton gang into turmoil. Property lines and water rights would have to be redefined. And a Republican sheriff might well be elected who would cramp a hard-working man's pocket. Long before the county reorganization could be realized, the Earps knew that trouble was coming. The Cowboy faction was upset that the Earps were thwarting their operations of cattle rustling, stage coach robberies, and train robberies. Morgan Earp was riding shotgun on the stage, Wyatt was riding the rails for security, and Virgil was keeping the peace in Tombstone. This didn't suit the Cowboys and since there were many more Cowboys than Earps, the time was drawing near for volatile results.

"We're sitting targets," Virgil told his brothers and Doc.

Luke Short, hearing that remark, left his poker game and came over. Bat Masterson closely followed. From across the room, they all looked at the Clantons huddled in a corner.

"Damn, they look like a den of rattlers," Bat said.

Virgil lowered his voice, "There have been some strange things goin' on. Lots of meetings in that back alley behind the Oriental."

"I caught Barnes tailing old Fred White the other day," Morgan added

Bat chewed on his cigar. "We can't take anything for granted. They slaughter Mexicans and steal cattle. They'll do the same to us. It's all the same to them."

"They've even been pumping Frank Leslie for information."

"Old Buckskin Frank will just take 'em out with that scatter-gun he keeps under the counter. He doesn't like 'em either."

"But what are we gonna do?" Morgan asked.

No one had an answer for him. Luke Short returned to his card game. Bat, chewing hard on his cigar, slapped Wyatt and Doc on the back. "Let's go to dinner."

♣ ♥ ♠ ♦

It happened on a late October evening in 1880 when the last of the working gentry relinquished their gambling activities in the Oriental Saloon for home. The streets were quiet and deserted. While the moon was not yet full, its light was eerie as it slid in and out of cloud cover. To dispel the gloom, the piano player dusted off some lively tunes. Curly Bill had been in earlier, but he had left the saloon after about an hour.

When the first shot was fired, Billy Clanton snapped himself out of a seemingly drunken stupor and bolted for the street. Doc, seated behind Wyatt at the faro table, started for his gun but stilled the impulse. Since Doc hadn't drawn his gun, Wyatt continued the play in a most pleasant voice. Curly Bill's voice, however, cut the night silence like a knife. It filled the Tombstone street.

Several more shots punctuated his "Yeahhoooy." Then the shooting started in earnest.

There was a whispered aside between Behan and White. The latter shrugged and moved towards the door. At this point, Wyatt excused himself and Doc stood up, both moving out of the Oriental at the same time. Upon seeing the Earps' interest, Billy and Ike bolted towards the alley behind the main section of Allen Street.

White ordered Curly Bill to stop firing and hand over his weapon. To Doc, Bill's movements were not those of a drunken man, although Bill was acting very drunk. Doc himself had pretended drunkenness for the benefit of Billy Clanton. Billy firmly believed, as Doc knew that he would, that the Earps were gullible and would suspect nothing about what the gunplay was really about. The Earps and Doc never tipped their hands—neither at poker, nor in life.

Staggering and weaving with a silly smile, Curly Bill playfully pretended to hand over his weapon, each time jerking it back as Fred's hand started forward.

"The trigger's real light, Fred. Here, I'll just hand it over so it won't go off by accident."

Bill moved close to White and thrust the butt towards the man's outstretched hand. The look in Brocius' eye warned Doc. That offering was a fatal trick that Doc had seen practiced before. Keeping an unseen finger on the trigger, the hand could hold the gun and then twist it so that when handed over, the muzzle would be in the correct placement to go off.

Virgil came up behind Bill with his own gun cocked. There were hoofbeats in the back alley and shouts. The moon sank into deep cover. Bill's gun barked fire that exploded from the barrel onto Fred's shirt. Surprised, Fred looked at the fire-lit hole in his chest and then fell backward. Doc caught him as he fell. Fred opened his mouth, but no words came out.

Still holding Fred, Doc went for his gun. Curly Bill by this time had lost his silly grin, though he managed to continue weaving. His gaze locked with Doc's.

"Try me, Bill," Doc said after laying Fred into the arms of the man squatted next to him. "You can try me. We can do it right here in the moonlight in front of the whole town. What say?" He cocked the hammer of his gun.

"I was funnin'," Bill replied. "Just funnin'. I told him the trigger was real light. You remember I did."

Virgil snapped from behind Bill, "You're damned right we'll remember."

"You're not stupid, Brocius," Doc said.

Though taller and heavier, Bill took a step back and ran into Virgil's gun. Bill scanned the crowd, but all he could see were other townsfolk.

"Barnes has already left, Brocius. I heard him ride away," Wyatt said as he covered Ike Clanton who was beginning to inch towards the group.

"I was—" Bill began to whine with a gunmetal smile that matched the weapon in his hand.

"Funnin'?" Doc enunciated so clearly that Bill momentarily looked like a butterfly stuck on a pin. As Wyatt shifted away from Ike, the latter shifted, too.

"No," Morgan replied through clenched teeth and lowered his scattergun towards Ike's midsection.

"No, no. I don't got no gun," Ike burbled and opened his coat to show his innocence.

Wyatt noted that Bill had become remarkably sober by the time he reached the jail cell. In the pasty light of the sheriff's office, he fingered his bandanna and gazed at his two captors with undeniable hatred.

"I'm rememberin' your faces," he said, "so's I'll know 'em in any light."

Doc's eyes glittered back. "Any time you want me, Brocius, you'll know where to find me," he replied with arsenic in his voice.

None of the Clanton gang attended Fred White's funeral, but the rest of the townsfolk paid homage to the man who had given selfless service. In the meantime, Curly Bill continued to proclaim his innocence from his jail cell while waiting for Judge Spicer and the trial. To the delight of the Clantons, there was not enough evidence to convict Brocius of murder, so he was acquitted.

Though the case was closed, Judge Spicer issued a warning: "This matter is far from over. You boys are on notice."

In January of 1881, Cochise County's charter was approved in Prescott, Arizona. A charter spelled out the dimensions of the new county, but rail access so desperately needed would still not go through Tombstone. Law enforcement was the next matter on the agenda. It was assumed that Republican Governor John C. Fremont would nominate another Republican for county sheriff.

To everyone's surprise, including Wyatt's, Fremont picked John Behan. Equally unpleasant was Virgil's loss of the city marshal slot to Ben Sippy. Faring much better, John Clum, editor of *The Tombstone Epitaph*, was elected as mayor. Wyatt tried to put on a good face to cover his disappointment. To his way of thinking, he had much better qualifications to become mayor than Clum and better qualifications by far than Jon Behan for county sheriff. Only in the company of his brothers did he express his displeasure. However the election went, Wyatt offered Clum his continued support and citizen sympathy was high.

The Clanton faction gloated although many things had not been settled. Of vital interest were the Wells Fargo money shipments and the water rights. Many of the towns on the frontier, including Tombstone, had no rail service. Instead, the towns had to rely on the goodwill and guarantee of security companies such as Wells Fargo. Of equal importance were the rights to water for the grazing cattle. The Clantons wanted the rights as badly as they wanted access to money shipments.

Mining companies, banks, gambling halls, railroads, and saloons were clearinghouses for hundreds of thousands of dollars that had to be counted and moved to other locations. Frequently, Wells Fargo posted undercover agents to guard their shipments. Some were stationed in trains as baggage handlers, rail passengers, or in saloons as faro dealers.

Wyatt's rail experience had made him a valuable asset to Wells Fargo in the past. In addition, Morgan was brought in to back Wyatt and guard the stage lines coming in and going out of Tombstone. Although the Clantons knew that the Earps and Doc were on to their setup, a ready cadre of their soldiers seemed willing to take the Clanton's place in the outlaw gang.

The downside of Fred White's killing was the big price tag for the Clantons. It maligned the townspeople as never before. Being placed in such a bad light had never been so damning to the Clantons and the Cowboy gang. Curly Bill was heard to voice his dismay at the number of miners who had witnessed the shooting of White. "I don't want no more accidents, but the Earps can't be everywhere at once."

"That's jes great," Ike Clanton said. "But it's real hard to tell since all three of them brothers look alike."

The drunken brawls increased, however, the Cowboys didn't carry their activities everywhere. They avoided, for example, causing trouble in the Oriental where Buckskin Frank Leslie tended the bar. They knew he was not to be trifled with knowing he had a vicious scattergun under the bar and no compunction about using it. The Cowboys were also careful of Doc Holliday. They knew he rode with the Earps and dared any one of the Cowboys to take him on. They were certain that he had dropped Mike Gordon with one shot.

The Clantons continued to boast. "We got here first. Ain't nobody gonna take that away. Cochise County is ours."

But the Earps, Doc Holliday, and Buckskin Frank Leslie did not scare.

Although the winter of 1880 was not officially over, there were signs that the '81 spring might be a hot one. Doc had entered the Alhambra Saloon for an afternoon's card game. To his dismay, the air felt more cloying in the saloon than it felt outside. Within the saloon, the wood furniture and costly trappings had absorbed the heat, making a casual conversation or a game of poker laborious. Even the liquor had the same annoying taste as the murky air. There was no wind.

Doc held his whiskey glass up to the light and swirled the contents. "Is it just me or does this taste like the Brazos River? Look, I think I see a gnat floating in the bottom."

"You holding up okay?"

"Me? I always hold up fine. It's the rest of me that doesn't." Doc's face was shiny with sweat.

Wyatt looked at him over a cup of coffee. "I ducked in here to get away from 'em. The weather must bring them out. Don't you think the Clantons are like these pesky gnats? If I were a horse, I'd stomp them into the dirt. Ike is an especially smarmy weasel. They're planning something. You ever notice how they smile right before something happens?"

"You mean like a rattlesnake shakes its tail before it strikes?"

"Just like that. How come I haven't seen Kate recently?"

"Me and Kate are on the outs again. Dead or alive, she keeps the payin' customer."

"And you're not a payin' customer?" Morgan asked.

"Guess I do fit that category. Oh hell, Morg," Doc caught the glint in the younger Earp's eye, "I keep hopin' somebody will take her off my hands, but everybody knows her . . . literally."

Morgan laughed. "So what do you think we should do?"

Doc took a swallow of whiskey. "Do what we always do. Sit tight."

Several days later, Morgan caught the last part of a Clanton argument.

Brocius kept his voice low, but every once in a while it carried across the room. "You know I'm worried. We got Luke Short and Bat Masterson, them damn Earps, and Holliday. Sooner or later I think they'll all get involved in our affairs. Masterson rallied all those men in Colorado during the railroad war. How do we know that he ain't gonna do it here?"

Barnes shot a glance over his shoulder. "What about Dodge City? Masterson can get reinforcements from there, too."

"Do you think Leslie would help us?" Brocius asked.

Ike turned very red. "Leslie hates everybody."

"Don't forget Fred White. Them Earps and Holliday was all over us. They brought out that lynchin' party."

"Holliday was waitin' with blood on his hands and liquor in his eye."

Morgan, who remained hunched over at the end of the bar, managed to make his way out of the Oriental before the Clantons saw him.

Later that evening, Morgan told Wyatt and Doc what the Clantons had said. "From the way they talked, Fred White's death wasn't accidental. And you know that murder in Galeyville? I think they were in on that one, too."

Wyatt shook his head. "What makes you think so?"

"He was a respected businessman and he didn't like what they were doing. The Clantons think they run that town."

"I'm afraid that once the bloodshed starts it won't end."

Wyatt's words were prophetic. On March 15, 1881, gunmen held up a routine Tombstone-Benson stagecoach. In the driver's seat was Bud Philpot. Next to him riding shotgun was Bob Paul, protecting Wells Fargo's interests. At a bend in the road, several gunmen rushed the stage. At the first volley of shots, Philpot was killed and slipped towards the wheels of the stage. Feeling the reins go slack, the horses bolted. Paul grabbed at the reins, but only managed to get one set of them. Maddened by the bullets and the smell of blood, the horses continued to career along the bumpy road until Paul at last was able to bring the team under control. By the time Paul stopped the horses, the gunmen rode alongside and demanded all the money. There were too many guns to argue with and Paul relinquished the money.

The rumor mill in town was quick to implicate Doc in the killing and robbery. Many of Doc's detractors were convinced he robbed stages. He didn't, but his enemies fabricated lies. By this time, the Earps began to have a very real worry about the safety of their families. Barnes made no bones about the fact that he thought that Wyatt and Morgan Earp were the real felons of the stage robbery. John Behan smiled broadly and coaxed Kate Elder to have a drink with him.

"Miss Elder," Behan touched his hat, "I have been an admirer of yours for such a long time, but have not dared to speak of my feelings. I must admit to being in fear of your gallant amore."

Behan had been looking in her direction for a long time, although Kate had never given him the time of day. But she was feeling blue so she thought that a new male interest might stir warm feelings from Doc.

In the morning, after a night of merrymaking with Behan, Kate paid special attention to her toilette, extra kohl for her eyes, and more perfume to mask the scent of whiskey. Kate felt she looked quite comely.

In the morning, she was cool again to Behan. There was no sense in upsetting Doc. She couldn't remember what she had said or the order in which she had said it. Behan smiled at her in spite of her coolness and showed her the paper that she had signed the night before.

"You," John Behan said, "swore to me that Doc Holliday killed Philpot and robbed the Tombstone-Benson stage. This document proves that. See, this is your signature."

Kate's dark complexion turned sallow. She goggled at the piece of paper as if it was a pile of horse dung in which she had sunk up to her ankles. "He didn't do that."

"Miss Elder, you told me that he did. You signed this paper."

A coarse oath fell from her lips. Tiny beads of sweat dotted her forehead. "No, you made this up. I never did no such thing."

The next morning Doc was waiting for her in the room that they shared. His lips were white and the pulse in his neck was beating rapidly. Worse, she could see that his hands were clenching and unclenching. "You lying whore. I've been told you sold me out—that you signed a paper saying I robbed a stage and worse, that I killed that nice man Bud Philpot.

She evaded his eyes. "I don't remember doin' it. I really don't."

"Do you honestly think I could have killed Bud Philpot? Do you think I, of all people, would rob someone or something?"

"No. That's what's making this thing so silly. I know you're not like that. I know you, Doc. You know that I would never sell you out."

"You signed a document saying that I was the scurrilous jack-anapes who killed Bud Philpot and robbed the stage." Without warning he slapped her.

Dropping to the bed, Kate rubbed her throbbing cheek. "You shouldna done that," she said as she looked up with hate-filled eyes. "I'll make you sorry."

"You already have." His eyes were colorless in the light.

The slap was not forgotten nor was the signed piece of paper. In the days that followed there was another contention that had to be dealt with, that of Mother Nature. Cinders on the breeze of a strong prairie wind, whether caused by a lightning strike or the dropping of a careless cigar could sweep through a town and burn it to the ground. It was a dread that everyone lived with. In June of 1881, Tombstone realized its worst fear. In a matter of moments, fire consumed residential and commercial buildings as well as the land office containing the deeds to more than half the town's lots.

"Do you think it was an accident?" Wyatt asked Virgil.

Virgil's eyes narrowed as he turned to look at his brother. "No."

The fire came at the worst possible time. Strained from maintaining law and order, town justice now had to contend with claim jumping. Individuals previously not owning lots staked their claim on the newly burned land. Area courts were consumed with questions. Lawyers argued that if someone owned a lot before the fire, then he or she should have the claim afterwards.

Tombstone was not the restful place that Wyatt and his family envisioned. If that was not enough, Wyatt found himself in the middle of a romantic triangle.

Doc was sympathetic to Wyatt. It was rumored that Wyatt's common-law wife, Mattie, had been a prostitute in Kansas where Wyatt met her. Whether or not this was true, Wyatt didn't say. While Wyatt was genuinely fond of Mattie and let her use his last name for protection, it was not love. Since her arrival in Tombstone, Mattie had become increasingly dependent on laudanum. As the narcotic ate away at the affection that Wyatt and Mattie shared, Josephine Sarah Marcus arrived on the Tombstone stagecoach. Immediately, John Behan let the town know that the beautiful Josie had come to marry him. Wyatt was smitten at once.

Doc, seeing Josie through Wyatt's eyes, was completely taken with her as well. She was a real lady. She was regal and beautiful, and Doc knew that Wyatt would sell his soul to have her.

Mattie's intake of laudanum compelled her public confrontations of Wyatt. If she hoped to regain Wyatt's affections by this method, it failed. Wyatt had no idea how to tell Mattie that he wanted to break off the relationship. Shame silenced his words since it was his suggestion that Mattie leave Dodge City to come with him to Tombstone. He couldn't blame Mattie for her illness, but he felt trapped. For Wyatt, loving Josie was as essential as breathing. On the other hand, John Behan vowed vengeance.

The Clantons had been holding their breath over the continued presence of Bat Masterson and Luke Short. When the two gamblers departed for richer playing fields, the Clantons gave a great sigh of relief. Two burrs under their saddlecloth were now out of the way. They reveled about the paper that Kate had signed and were even more gleeful when Doc was arrested for the murder of Bud Philpot and the stage robbery. Fired by liquor and whispered words in her ear from Behan, Kate went on a shooting spree against Doc and the Earps.

"She's liquored to the gills," Virgil said. "I threw her in a cell to sober up. I hate to do this, Doc, but until we get this matter settled, I'm going to have to arrest you, too. I know you didn't kill Bud or rob the stage. Hell, if I had my druthers, I'd shoot Behan for causin' all the trouble."

Wyatt and others put together a $5,000 pot to release Doc. As the hours wore on, a slowly sobering Kate couldn't remember what she'd said or signed or whom she'd shot at.

"Stay out of trouble," Virgil told the sullen Doc. "And get rid of that infernal woman."

For her trouble, Kate was fined $12.50. Her outrage over the fine lasted longer than her regret of having set up Doc.

"I'm sure," Doc told her several nights later, in no mood to be mollified, "all you have to do is lie down and spread your legs. You'll have the money in no time."

Virgil said, "We're offering a reward to catch the robbers of the Benson stage. The ones that go for it are probably the ones who did it."

Ike Clanton was the first one to step forward. "I knowed all about that stage robbery on the coach where Bud Philpot was killed. Doc Holliday did it."

Wyatt paid him the reward under instructions from Wells Fargo to do so.

"I can't say that these troubles are the birthing pains of a new county," Wyatt told Morgan, "but this web seems to get more complicated with every turn of the roulette wheel."

"Wyatt, it's only gonna end in one way."

"Maybe we can stop it before it does."

Behan in the meantime had plenty to infuriate him. Not only was Doc Holliday seeming to pay court to Josie, but Behan's sworn enemy, Wyatt Earp, seemed amused by the whole affair. To make matters worse, Josie was having a good time. Behan seethed while Doc escorted Josie to the best restaurants in town. For one of these occasions, he wore an expensive gray suit with a blue silk shirt and silver vest. A ring with a large blue stone flashed on one of his manicured hands.

Josie was resplendent in a gray silk dress with gloves and a veiled hat. Doc kissed her hand and escorted her to the Occidental, one of the most exclusive eateries in town. There he was seen to pore over her hand with every manner of Southern courtesy.

Behan's fury reached epic proportions. He vowed to do all in his power to bring down Holliday. From the sidelines, Doc laughed at him. If that weren't bad enough, it was reported that Doc took Josie out for a morning's stroll a few days later, and the two walked arm-in-arm over what appeared to be quite an intimate conversation. At their parting, Doc winked at her and touched his hat brim before moving on. Josie blushed and flipped open her fan.

In the Clanton camp, Ike privately worried that his loose tongue, fueled by all of his liquor, would estrange him from his compatriots. Certainly Curly Bill had been belligerent to him. The fact of the matter was, he had taken the money from the Earps for information about the robbery. Sometimes Ike would accuse members of his own gang if it personally got him off the hook, and it looked like this was one of those times. Barnes was a Clanton gang member and he might discover that Ike had given him away. To cast suspicion from himself, Ike publicly ranted that Doc had known of the robbery and set him up. Not only that, but that Doc had robbed the stage himself. Infuriated, Doc denied that he ever knew the plan.

"If I'd known, and I didn't, I wouldn't have shot my mouth off like Ike's in the habit of doing," Doc said after the incident.

To Doc, there was only one cause of the disrupting events in Tombstone: the Clantons.

"It was a decent town," he told Morgan, "before it was taken over by such a ubiquitous den of thieves, murderers, and scum that have ever been spit out of the earth."

Doc hated Behan with all the strength that he was capable of coughing up, and he hated the chaos that continually surrounded the Earps. He tried hard not to distress Wyatt, whose face looked more like old saddle leather every day. Virgil and Morgan, too, were surrounded by the same troubles. It was inevitable that a fight was brewing. It would be a good thing if the Earps could choose the time and place for a confrontation, but he doubted that Curly Bill, the group's new leader, would let that happen.

"It appears," Doc told Josie, "that Old Man Clanton met his death on a cattle raid. The Mexs have been pretty upset by the loss of all their cattle."

Curly Bill, never one to shirk a public display, now strutted through town with his new status. Ike and Billy had walked around in a state of shock for a while over the death of their father and the whole group had worn black armbands, but Curly Bill wasted no time taking over the reins of leadership.

The summer heat continued to sap Doc's strength and fuel his outrage. Mattie's letters were cooling water for his ire.

My Dearest John,

These men are the lowest of the low. Do not, I beg you, put yourself into such a terrible jeopardy by mixing in their horrible vendetta, without the hope or wherewithal of extracting yourself. I can exist here in Georgia, only if I know you are safe, but these men are not such as us. I believe wholeheartedly that they would shoot you in the back without a moment's notice or regret. Promise me, my dearest, if you do fight, use all your skills to stay alive.

Mattie placed him in a terrible bind. This fight she spoke of he hoped would finish him. True and blue, Mattie wished him to live. For her, he would lay aside the gauntlet and walk away, though it would take all of his strength to do so. He thought of mentioning this briefly to Wyatt, but Wyatt was so beset with problems of his own that Doc hesitated. He sorely missed their late night talks that had defused his rage and made his loneliness easier to bear.

Morgan, however, had become a fast comrade. Unburdened by women and political problems as Wyatt, Morgan had become the little brother that Doc never had. He loved the Bird Cage Theater, had a ready repertoire of ribald jokes, could be more outrageous than Doc, and was worth his weight in tigers if there was a fight. Doc adored Louisa, Morgan's wife, who babied and scolded him as much as she did her husband. Louisa was much like Mattie.

It frightened Doc that his image of Mattie was beginning to dim in the same way as that of his mother. Louisa put this superstitious fear of Mattie's impending death to rest one evening at dinner. Morgan was always bringing Doc over for dinner. Lou kept an extra plate on hand at all times. Doc brought her flowers and trinkets and a blue cameo necklace, because Mattie had cherished the one that he had given her. Lou put it on right away and kissed him on the cheek.

Later, when she caught him staring morosely towards the dark street, she made him confess what was bothering him.

"You men never think of the logical thing."

"Excuse me, darlin'?"

"Ask for her to send you a picture. You can put it in your watch and then she'll be there every time you check the time."

Allie Earp, Virgil's wife, was cooler in manner towards Doc, but not from dislike. Doc knew she was afraid of what would happen to Virge when the shooting started. In Doc, she could see a recklessness that might get Virgil killed in defending him, Virgil being the most protective of the three brothers. He worried about the widowed women in town and the prostitutes. He was diffident in bailing Doc and his brothers out of trouble. Doc had a working relationship with Virgil. They played cards together. They drank together and told jokes, but they were not friends.

Towards Kate, Doc had finally shed his addiction. He had, after being released from jail, packed his things and moved out of the room that he shared with her. The Alhambra Saloon had been a temporary Kate-free haven. From his own bankroll he took $1,000 to give to her. When Wyatt heard what he was about, he kicked in $1,000 himself and made sure that Morgan and Virgil anted up.

"I'm sure if Bat were here, he'd do the same thing," Wyatt told Doc.

As a group, they paid a call on Kate, who was plying her ample skills on one of Behan's cohorts. Seeing the four heading in his direction, the man pushed Kate off his lap and ran. Kate noticed the lack of color in Doc's complexion. His cheekbones stood out in gaunt relief. His thin shoulders were very straight, and there was no emotion in his eyes.

In a flat tone he said, "It is in my best interests that our relationship come to an end."

If Kate had been some other woman, she would have fallen to the floor in a faint. Doc, she knew, only used this particular voice and speech pattern when he was getting ready to shoot.

"I don't have a gun," Kate said, sucking in a quick bit of air. Her fan had slipped to the floor.

"You don't need one." Doc thrust the bankroll at her. "Don't cross my doorstep again, under any circumstance."

In vain, she searched for a shred of feeling. "You don't want me to come back?"

"That sums it up, doesn't it?" Virgil asked. His face was still.

"Well, I, uh, have to get packed."

"We've done that for you. Your things are waiting for the next stage out," Wyatt added.

Genuine tears pricked her eyes. "Don't you have anything you want to say to me?"

"No," Doc whispered.

♣ ♥ ♠ ♦

September was hotter than August. The blue sky crackled with thunderheads that cast shadows on the buttes, but no moisture fell. The Mexican cattle herds were on the move in the merciless shale and granite canyons, though there was still gramma grass and small water pools to quench them. By the end of September, those would be gone, too.

Stage holdups sometimes occurred on the day of major cattle drives. Since Curly Bill and crew weren't in Tombstone, the rumor was born that they were the ones orchestrating the holdup. The stage driver reported the incident and a posse consisting of Wyatt and Morgan Earp, plus Marshal Williams, who represented Wells Fargo, were quickly dispatched on the trail heading towards Bisbee. Along the way, Sheriff Neagle as well as Billy Breakenridge joined the group. David Neagle was a very close associate of John Behan and a town marshal. Billy Breakenridge was a deputy who was sometimes called upon to ride with different posses.

Eventually, the group caught up to the stage robbers: Clanton associates, Pete Spence and Frank Stilwell. Morgan Earp drew the lot to escort Stilwell.

"I'm tellin' ya now. No good's gonna come of this. You hear me? No good. I'll remember. You'll be sorry," Stilwell said.

Morgan looked at Stilwell. "If I had money for every remark made by you and your scummy friends, I would lay those dollars end-to-end and fly to the moon."

"You wait and see."

Doc took the conversation more seriously when it was relayed to him.

"He wasn't kidding, Morg."

"Oh, come on, Doc, they threaten so much."

"A rattler shakes its tail before it strikes, too. Watch your back."

♣ ♥ ♠ ♦

Doc, pouring a drink for himself in Hafford's Saloon after a faro-dealing shift, watched Ike Clanton stomp towards the bar, grab a bottle, and swill away.

"Ike," Doc called pleasantly, "if you crook your little finger, the whiskey will go down faster."

Behind the bar, Colonel Hafford momentarily turned away. The rest of the customers laughed into their drinks. Ike's very red eyes looked in Doc's direction. Ike looked at his hand, crooked his little finger, and swallowed.

Colonel Hafford immediately quit the bar. "I'm sick," he was heard to mumble as he headed out the door. His shoulders were shaking.

"Hey, Doc, really," Ike said. "Yeah, you're right. Thanks."

Later when Doc was back in the Oriental, Colonel Hafford approached him. "Has Wyatt told you?"

"Morgan and I returned after a pleasant sporting event in Tucson. I went straight to my faro shift, so I haven't seen Wyatt. What's up?"

Hafford scanned the room before looking at Doc once more, "Clanton's been all over town, Doc. Ike doesn't check his drinkin' like the pappy did. Not that Old Man Clanton was a teetotaler."

"Let me guess. The boys like to mix it up, but they don't mean no harm," Doc told him.

"They mixed it up a little too much. Virgil buffaloed them and threw them in jail. Ike's out and sore. Stilwell and Spence are still nursin' that grudge over the Bisbee robbery."

Doc looked Hafford in the eye. "I am getting testy and irritable myself. Wish this was over. Waiting makes it worse. Thanks for the advice. Sit down for a bit and have a drink. They'll make something of it if you leave too quickly."

"Much obliged," the Colonel said.

After a leisurely drink, Doc and Colonel Hafford parted company. Hafford walked towards his saloon and Doc sauntered slowly down the street. When he was certain that no one was watching, he headed towards the sheriff's office.

"And stay in there," Virgil barked as he slammed the cell door shut. "Doc, I'm glad to see you." Disgustedly, he flung the cell keys onto the desk. "Damn Cowboys, they're all over tonight. Pissin' their money in the wind."

"Along with words, I hear."

"Those, too. Listen, I think I better deputize you."

Doc gazed at the older man. "So it's come to that? Well, I'm not surprised."

"It could be now. It could be next month. Ike Clanton's been all over town. He's still mouthin' and drinkin'. To get the guts to shoot us, I think."

"Anything else?"

"No, that's pretty much it."

"Thanks, Doc."

"For what? Wyatt's my friend. You all are my family."

Once on the street, Doc looked sharply around. Horses were tied everywhere. He recognized the scarred chestnut that Ike rode. All the gambling houses and saloons were operating at a fever pitch. Someone was bound to see him coming from the sheriff's office to make a report to someone else. Under Tombstone's hills, silver was flowing. In the streets of Tombstone, blood would be spilling. The war was coming.

Chapter

SIXTEEN

In the plum-colored twilight, Doc watched the shadows move beyond Tombstone to the desert. The dark fingers had already covered the hills and mountains and more tendrils, like ominous roots, had spread in all directions.

A deep cough brought blood and tissue into his handkerchief. "Come get me, you sons-of-bitches."

Doc's keen hearing took in the sounds emanating from the saloons. In search of a good meal and companionship, he made his way to one of the restaurants that was a favorite of Wyatt and Morgan. The two brothers, he could see from the street, were already seated. Things seemed quiet until Ike burst through the doors.

"Oh, hell," Morgan said as he jumped up.

"I don't care," Ike yelled. "You tell Holliday to come and get me. That yellow-belly cur can kiss my dick. See if I don't make that yellow-belly—" He paused to gulp another shot of whiskey. "This un's empty. Gimme another."

The bartender made no move to satisfy the order. "You're drunk, Ike. Go home."

"I am home. Tombstone's my home and I'm not gonna run from no lunger-weasel Earp-whore like Holliday or you Earp pimps either. You three with yer fancy gold badges—bashin' a guy over the head for having a good time. It ain't fair. I work hard, come into town for a card game, lose all my hard-earned money, and git bashed over the head. I'm a Clanton, by God. Not one of you can stand up to me." Ike turned to look at the patrons in the restaurant and pointed at Morgan and Wyatt. "You," he began and reached for the almost empty whiskey tumbler. "I told you I want another."

Noise at the front drew everyone's attention. Doc burst through the doors behind Ike, spun him around and, after smartly slapping his face, threw back his coat.

"Listen to me, you little prick, you want a fight then commence. Ante up and commence." With each step, Doc pressed Ike against the bar behind him.

"I ain't heeled, Doc, God a mercy, I ain't heeled," Ike gibbered fumbling with his hat and dropping it. He looked desperately around for sympathy and saw none. With a smooth move of his hand, Doc went for his gun just as Morgan jumped between the two.

"Not here, not now," Morgan said as he pushed Doc's arm down. "And you, Clanton, you miserable cur, if you don't get outta here, I swear to God, it will be my pleasure."

"I'll be back. I'll be back. You're gonna be sorry."

Coming up behind him, Wyatt hit him over the head, and Ike sank to the floor like a sack of rotted tomatoes.

"Don't go home tonight, Doc. Sleep someplace else," Morgan warned. "We'll call you if we need you."

"You'll need me, Morgan. I'll bet on that."

Doc took a room at the Cosmopolitan, forgoing another restless night in his boarding room. The Cosmopolitan Hotel was a grand place and the owner made a hot bath available along with a home-cooked meal. Doc stayed away from the windows. Too keyed up, he took out *Rime of the Ancient Mariner*, but it seemed that seafarer was trapped in the room with him.

It was a large, richly appointed room. The four poster cherry-wood bed had fat pillows with lace coverings. He had never understood why rugs and coverlets had to have those red roses on them. White or yellow would have been just as nice. On the side-board were several bottles of whiskey and a hot dinner. Doc left the lamp by the bedside burning and slowly ate his dinner.

He paced the room and glanced out the window without getting too close. He could clearly see the street. Doc could well imagine his demise. Brocius would relish blowing his head off.

He read until the words blurred like the red roses on the white coverlet.

After kicking off his boots, Doc fell asleep across the top of the bed. Restless, he awoke every few moments to grasp his gun, which lay close at hand. After a moment's pause listening to the night sounds, he would go back to sleep. A hard rap on the door sent him bolt upright. Pressing himself against the wall by the door, Doc cocked the hammer on his gun. "Who's there?"

"Doc, the McLaurys and Clantons are in town now. They're knee-deep in blood, spit, and hangovers."

"Are they drunk or sober?"

"Well," the man stammered. "Well, uh, I mean, I don't know. Wyatt don't drink nuthin' but coffee."

It was an odd response. He'd recognized the voice as belonging to a Clanton gang member. They would love for him to stick his head out unawares so they could blow it off. He'd wait, he decided, for a friend to tell him what was happening. After a while, there was silence outside the door again. Doc quietly walked to the door, unlocked it, and opened it.

The hotel proprietor's wife had left him a tray of food and drink. By the time he had finished the meal, his watch read one o'clock in the afternoon. It was October 26. Normally, he would be asleep after a night of gambling and dealing faro. In another hour, he would leave behind the room with the roses. He remembered that his mother had embroidered such a pattern of red roses and gold filigree on her tea cozies.

There was another rap on the door.

"Doc, you gotta come." Doc recognized it as the voice of Colonel Hafford.

"Is Clanton out of jail?"

"God, yes. Virgil couldn't keep him that long."

"Have you seen him?"

"He's drinkin'."

Doc took the last bite of what food remained, shaved in the clean water provided for him, and deliberately sipped on some coffee. For his cough, which had been wicked during the night, he poured a dash of whiskey. In the middle of a swallow of coffee, the room grew fuzzy, tilted, and straightened once more.

"Damn disease."

The disease, unlike some people, never let him down. Slowly, he pulled himself upright, and checked the chambers on both of his guns. He would wear the longer coat. He looked at his watch for the umpteenth time, noted the picture of Mattie that Lou had advised him to get, and left the room. His cane steadied him on his way down the stairs. Of late, the cane had become mandatory when his fever was up. It was a fine walking stick of durable polished oak. Sometimes he would remember his father's cane.

Once outside, the Arizona air and Doc's fever collided. By the time he crossed the street, he was soaked with sweat and the color in his cheeks had shriveled to ash. Seeing the Earp brothers gathered, Doc lengthened his stride. Men noted his passing. If anyone spoke his name, Doc ignored it.

"I have," he told the brothers, "had at least three people coming to my room telling me that the Clantons want to kill me."

Wyatt looked at him, his face a mask.

Morg said, "We're going down there, aren't we? This time we have to go."

"It won't end with this, Morg. It just won't end. They're armed."

"They've got guns," Virgil said. "None of you have to go. I'm going to go disarm them alone. I want all of you to stay here."

Wyatt's jaw dropped. "Alone? You're crazy."

"Maybe, but they can't go around threatening us. We've got to take a stand sometime."

"Here, here," Doc replied.

"I won't let you go alone," Wyatt said to Virgil and looked at Doc with sadness, regret, and friendship. He held out his hand for Doc to shake.

"I guess that's it then. Where are they now?" Morgan asked.

"That vacant lot on Fremont Street across from the Bourland Shop."

They looked at each other. Though it was chilly for the desert, sweat trickled from Doc's brow. There was a scent of rain on the wind.

"Doc?" Wyatt asked.

The dentist shook his head. "Fever."

Virgil held out his hand. "I'll trade you the shotgun for the cane. You won't be able to get to your revolvers so fast. One less thing for me to worry about. I want to disarm them—not shoot them."

As a group, they turned and walked abreast down the street, their footfalls making a sticking sound in the moist sand. Raucous music filtered from the saloons to drift about on the air, but never had it seemed more incongruous. Gradually, the music became muffled and then it stopped altogether. A hush fell on the bustling street. Townsmen had stopped, but no one spoke. From the corner of his eye, Doc could see Morgan keeping pace on his left. Virgil, Doc knew, was on Morgan's left, and Wyatt was on the outside. The long coat was a hot and heavy weight, threatening to drag him down. Doc longed to shrug it off. The air seared his throat. His lungs burned.

Behan approached with a grim smile affixed to his chiseled face, his lips stretched tight. His teeth looked like porcelain bullet casings.

"No need, gentlemen. There's no need for violence," he said so smoothly that Doc longed to execute him on the spot. "There's no need. I've disarmed them already."

"I'll bet," Wyatt replied and kept on walking.

They left Behan mouthing words behind them. Doc felt rather than saw Virgil switch the cane to his right hand, and he tightened his grip on the shotgun.

"We'll have to kill them all," Morgan whispered.

"Yep," Doc whispered back. Virgil and Wyatt were about two paces ahead in front. Concerned that no one was covering their backs, Doc and Morgan hung to the rear. All the parties froze. There was Ike Clanton, Tom and Frank McLaury, and Billy Clanton. Curly Bill and John Ringo were not present. Frank McLaury, standing directly in front of Doc, was holding the reins of a fidgeting horse. Next to Frank and facing Morgan was Tom McLaury, also holding a nervous horse. At his extreme left was Wyatt, whom he could no longer see.

"You've wanted a fight, now you've got one."

Doc was too intent on his opponent, Frank McLaury, to worry about what was said. The fidgeting horse made it impossible to see as Frank kept it moving around him. Doc was perhaps four feet from Frank, but that was all.

"We've come to disarm you. Throw up your hands."

Racked with a fever, all Doc could hear Virgil say was "disarm" and "hands," but he waited for the show of hands that did not come. Frank McLaury's coat kept blowing in the way as the horse brushed by. He snarled something at Doc and half-crouched, reaching into his coat.

Doc opened fire. To Doc's left, Morgan fired on Billy Clanton, but the crazed horse Tom McLaury was holding made it difficult to see. Intent on not being trampled, Doc sensed Ike Clanton behind him. Wyatt yelled. Ike had been wrestling with Wyatt and yelling his brother's name while pleading that he had no gun. Doc in the midst of bullets, melee, and fever heard only "no gun."

Frank McLaury's squealing horse had begun to kick. There was rolling dust from the two horses. In Doc, the bloodlust that had lay dormant during Sherman's March burst forth. Called on to see in three directions at once, Doc kept shaking his head to clear his vision. It did clear long enough for him to get a shot at Ike Clanton, and then the world went fuzzy again.

Turning back, Doc barely dodged the second horse Tom McLaury held, but suddenly he was face to face with Tom. Instinctively, Doc brought the shotgun into play and let go with both barrels. Sweat ran in his eyes. Because he couldn't tell what he had hit, he savagely flung the gun away. The remaining horse reared, snapping its reins, and fled. From the ground, Morgan took aim at Frank McLaury, who was standing and sighting Doc in the crosshairs.

A blaze of pain exploded along Doc's left thigh, but he didn't fall. To his left came the retort of Morgan's gun. Mortally wounded, Frank McLaury fell. Only after the bullets stopped could Doc see who was standing and who had fallen. Virgil was bleeding from a wound in his left leg. Morgan's shoulder looked shattered, although Doc didn't know for certain. The pain along Doc's thigh halted him, and he carefully tested his leg to see if he could move it.

In the span of a minute or less the smell of blood and death prevailed. Wyatt was unscathed. Ike had gotten away, but both the McLaurys and Billy Clanton had cashed in. Doc's cough that had been suspended during the fight erupted with such force that it bent him double before stopping. Wiping his mouth, Doc straightened and looked around.

A blast of cool air made Doc shiver. There was silence from the crowd, even when John Behan tripped out of Fly's Photography Studio and confronted the battered survivors.

Wyatt looked Behan in the eye. He slowly let his gaze flick up and down. "You said you disarmed them. Well nobody, including you, is going to put me away today."

While chaos raged like a wildfire, Doc limped to Virgil's house where Morgan had also been taken. A guard was posted for protection. The next day, the four were arrested.

The newspapers cried foul echoing the bitter divisions in the town. *The Nugget* denounced the Earps and Holliday as murderers. "Killed on the Streets of Tombstone" ran the headline. The paper made no mention that an armed Wyatt Earp and Doc Holliday did not shoot an unarmed Ike Clanton. Instead, it spoke of the other boys cut down in the prime of their youth. Conspicuously unmentioned was Ike Clanton's drunken rampage of the day previous, as he announced how the Cowboys were going to wipe out the Earps and Holliday.

At the onset of the trial, two dozen witnesses swelled to over two hundred, making actual depositions difficult. The trial lasted a month. As it proceeded, the initial defense made by the Cowboys began to collapse. Sheriff Behan had been caught in a colossal lie. If he had indeed disarmed the McLaurys and Billy Clanton, then how were they able to fire their weapons? And if Wyatt Earp wanted to kill as much as some were claiming, then why did he spare an unarmed Ike Clanton? Tom Fitch, the lawyer for Wyatt and Doc, used those facts as part of the defense.

As *The Nugget* lost ground with its bias, *The Epitaph*'s viewpoint became more credible. Ike Clanton was alive to admit that Wyatt Earp hadn't killed him and had actually pushed him aside. And though Virgil and Morgan Earp and Doc Holliday were wounded, they obviously hadn't shot themselves. Judge Spicer's final ruling was of justifiable intent on the part of the Earp Brothers and John H. Holliday. They would be set free. In the Cowboy camp, there was no cheering.

The brothers all agreed with Doc when he said, "Only a fool would accept this as final."

After Judge Spicer's pronouncement, Tombstone became an armed camp between the Clantons and the Earps. In this no man's land, friends could become enemies on the strength of which side they took.

Virgil was mending slowly. Although Doc's thigh sported a deep bruise from the bullet that had glanced across his scabbard, he was otherwise unscathed. Thanks to Louisa, Morgan's shoulder was also on the mend. There were ominous signs, however, that all was not right. Mayor Clum was marked for assassination. Virgil knew he was the target of Curly Bill. Doc had never been endeared to any of the Clantons, especially Ike, whom he referred to in unflattering Latin terms.

Wyatt spoke of leaving several times. The Earp women applauded that, eager to put Tombstone behind them. Virgil urged all of them to stand their ground.

"If we leave now, they've won. They'll pick us off one at a time. Clum almost bought his the other night," Virgil remarked as he looked down the street from the sheriff's office.

Morgan bent over to spit a stream of tobacco juice. "We're not cowards. I'm staying."

"So if you two stay, then I'm supposed to leave? Like I can just do that."

In the end, Wyatt remained also.

The waiting game began. Doc slept with a gun under his pillow, and he made certain there was a wall to his back at poker or faro.

For Doc, staying meant facing a frigid Arizona winter. The cold in his lungs had descended earlier, but he'd finally shaken the fever plaguing him. The consumption aside, he could have left Tombstone as well. But his family was in trouble. Family didn't walk out on family.

Ringo offered an end to it all if Doc would come out on the street and spar bullets with him. Ringo was capable of a lot of fancy gunplay, but it didn't pan out in actual combat. Both men hated each other for what the other represented.

♣ ♥ ♠ ♦

In December of 1881, the Bird Cage Variety Theater opened. It was a merry time, enjoyed by Doc, the Earps, and the Cowboys. In the Bird Cage, there was a truce, but elsewhere in the streets, alleyways, or buildings that wasn't the case. Doc knew that he was watched. For safety's sake, he varied his routine. If he felt threatened, he would swear off his boardinghouse room and take residence in the Cosmopolitan Hotel.

Doc's services in dealing faro or poker were highly sought at any of the high-class gambling establishments in town. As in previous years, he played poker in his off-hours. There were young women who fancied him, but aside from a dalliance or two, he was reluctant to part with his newfound independence from Kate.

She did write him from the mining camps to the north. She was very regretful. She wanted to come back. In a courtly fashion, he answered her.

*No. I am not of a mind to make this dance again. From your let-
ter, it is my understanding that you are lacking in funds. I sincerely
hope by the time you read this letter, you will have rectified the matter by your usual industrious ways.*

Christmas Day was spent in the home of Morgan and Louisa.
Wyatt and Josie came by themselves since Mattie refused to be
caught dead in the same room with Josie. Doc never mentioned
Mattie to Wyatt, there being some things that friends didn't speak
of. There was a continued restlessness in the Cowboys that boded
no good. That was also not spoken of in front of the women. Allie
Earp, since Virgil's injury in the October bloodletting, had
become very closed-mouthed towards Doc. Doc understood.

At half past eleven on the night of December 28, Doc was
involved in a high-stakes, closed poker game at Colonel
Hafford's. The night was cold, and the high wind made it colder. It reminded Doc of those Ft. Griffin winters when sleet and
snow pounded the prairie. Several of the Cowboys entered, but
not together. In the course of about an hour, Frank Stilwell and
John Behan trooped in and took a look at him.

"This is a closed game, gents," Hafford reminded them.

"Yeah, sorry. Just taking a look."

John Behan smiled at Doc, and Behan never smiled unless he
was lying, wanted something, or was about to do something. In
this case, Doc had a strong hunch that something was about to
happen. Behan was armed, which was not unusual since he had
a badge, but Doc knew that Pony Deal and Frank Stilwell were
heavily armed. Not only were there telltale bulges in their coat
pockets, but their hands kept slipping down to pat them. Deal,
being one of the Cowboys, lent himself to a lot of their dirty
work and relished it. Ike Clanton was nowhere about, but Ike
gave him a wide berth these days. Surreptitiously, Doc checked
his watch.

The poker game itself had begun in the Crystal Palace and migrated to Hafford's. The men playing Doc were very much in earnest. There was $8,000 on the table with the stakes going higher. Virgil asked to be dealt in, but excused himself after forty minutes.

"It's a little too rich for my blood."

"Behan's been in," Doc told him in a low voice.

"Yeah, I think he's been all over town tonight."

"And Pony Deal. And Stilwell."

"I'm gonna stop and see Wyatt at the Oriental. See you later."

The ante was raised, and Doc removed the diamond tack on his cravat, placing it atop the pile of chips, jewelry, mining deeds, and gold watches. To minimize the crowd, the closed sign was hung on the door.

It had been said that Doc was parsimonious in his gambling. On the contrary, he would return various trinkets, watches, and rings he'd won. Doc liked to think that it showed his sensitivity. He once refused to take a young man's horse and saddle as payment of a debt.

"Son," he had called out to the youth not long off the range. Boggled, the young man had dropped all the money and belongings he owned in the first saloon he had come to. He had caused a pang in Doc who remembered that lost blush of youth when the world was so green, blue, and warm. Doc had taken a little money, but he refused the horse and saddle. "Son, you came up from Texas, and you're going back to Texas. How the hell are you going to do that without a horse and saddle?"

"Oh," the stripling youth had replied, and then blushed. "Damn."

At the end of his shift, Doc treated the young man to dinner.

"It's a fact you don't have much and you better save what you've got."

He showed the young man some of the gaming tricks pulled on greenhorns. "You're wearing a big sign, boy."

"I'm not a boy."

"No, but these gentlemen—I use the word with much looseness—will not see you otherwise."

Doc shook his head to clear the memories. On the table in front of him was now $8,500. He would not be returning this pot. The gamblers, high-stakes players themselves, were disappointed that Doc won, but not daunted.

"We'll do this again, Holliday."

"Gentlemen, I look forward to that."

Colonel Hafford was helping Doc gather in his take when a messenger ran in from outside. He was breathless and dressed in a black slicker coat that was covered with rain. His hands shook so much that he could scarcely get his fingers to hand over the ink and rain-stained note. It read: "Doc, wherever you are, stay put. They're gunning for all of us."

"Where did you come from?" Doc asked.

"I wasn't supposed to say," the boy stammered. "Oh, God, you're just like they say."

Doc lowered his voice. "Take a deep breath. I only bite on occasion." He pulled a twenty-dollar piece from his winnings and gave it to the boy. "Where did you come from?"

"Well, oh God, well, I, uh, I came from Virgil Earp's place."

"What happened? Was the marshal shot?"

"Real bad."

Doc exchanged glances with Colonel Hafford. The Colonel didn't hesitate. He pulled a shotgun from under the bar. "Frank Leslie's gun. He didn't come back for it. If you're going anyway, three guns are better than one," he told Doc.

"Son, no matter what you think, you did the right thing telling me."

"We'll see you home, son," said Hafford. In an aside to Doc, he exclaimed, "It's them damn Cowboys. Behan came in three times with that silly-assed grin. He's the one who did it."

They walked quickly through the rain.

"God, Doc, I forgot, your consumption. We're walkin' fast."

The night mirrored Doc's expression. "The consumption, suh, never stops me. Where do you live, son?"

"I live across the street a couple of doors down from all the construction."

Colonel Hafford patted the boy on the shoulder. "I wish they'd finish the damn construction. It looks like a bare-boned skeleton."

Doc said, "It's probably where they ambushed Virgil. Too many places for a yellow-bellied cur prick to hide. Sorry, son."

"Oh, that's okay, sir. I've heard worse."

"Is that your house over there? The one with the woman lookin' out the window?"

"That's my mom."

"You tell her that I think her son did a right good thing. Okay?"

"Thanks, Dr. Holliday."

"Looks like Allie's got the window covered, Doc."

Crossing the street, they went to the door. "Allie, it's us, Colonel Hafford and Doc. Let us in." Hafford rapped on the door until he heard a noise on the other side. Doc, with his back to the door, watched for anyone coming down the street after them. A sliver of light appeared at the window and then the door was opened no more than a crack.

"Allie, darlin', we're getting cold," Doc said.

She looked at him and wiped her eyes. "Well, I guess I'm not sorry you're here."

"That's something," Doc replied softly.

"Dr. Goodfellow's here."

"Where do you have him?"

"In the parlor."

She was trying to be brave, but fresh tears were rolling down her face. Doc put his arm around her. Instead of shrugging it off, Allie left it in place.

"I'm sorry, Doc," she whispered.

Wyatt barreled out of the parlor. His sleeves had been pushed back, and there was blood on his arms and shirt. The look on Doc's face brought him up short.

"I'm glad you're here, too," he said as he fought for words.

"What happened?"

"Morg and me were at the Oriental. Virgil stopped in, said that he'd seen you, and that he was going home. They were waitin' for him. The bullets tore the bone out of his left arm. If he'd been standing further over, they'd a gotten him in the back. Pony Deal came in the Oriental. Looked around and left. I should have known. I just should have known."

"Behan came in my place three times," Hafford said.

"Do you think he pulled the trigger, Wyatt?"

"Yeah, I do. Goodfellow said that he won't use the arm much anymore. Said that it would probably have to be amputated."

Wyatt looked towards the parlor. "Allie's all done in. We had to hold Virge down while Doc Goodfellow dug the bullet out. I don't want you to leave. The night's bad. You risked your lives to come here. Doc is family and you're a good friend, Colonel. I can't promise much, but maybe I can rustle us up something in the kitchen."

By morning light, Doc learned that Pony Deal and Behan had been in town with Ike Clanton, Frank Stilwell, and John Ringo. They were all guilty as far as he was concerned. Barely healed from October's fiasco, Virgil had little in the way of strength reserved for the new injury and loss of blood.

♣ ♥ ♠ ♦

The Cowboys were hardly sated by the December shooting of Virgil Earp. For them, honor was not yet satisfied. The Earps and Holliday were still in Tombstone.

As Virgil recuperated from his near fatal wound, the New Year boded ill. The mechanics of law enforcement continued. With matters scarcely under control, Dave Neagle got the nod of approval for city marshal on January 3, 1882, but there seemed little that Neagle could do.

"I don't envy you your job. You've got a bloody set of reins to take up," Wyatt told him.

Mayor John Clum was not reelected, and John Behan was entrenched more firmly than before. The newspapers continued their political play, and the Cowboy faction clamored for revenge. Stages continued to be robbed, cattle were rustled, and silver flowed like water.

"It will be okay. I'll make certain that you brothers and Doc come to no harm," Behan promised.

This statement prompted Doc to rejoin, "Behan, have you ever uttered one word in your life that was straight? You've always dealt from a crooked deck."

Outwardly, Doc's shuttered eyes gave nothing away. Earp supporters were many, but they no longer had the weight of city government behind them. As the threats continued, Virgil and Allie moved to the Cosmopolitan Hotel, Doc's home away from home.

Wyatt gambled, but his heart wasn't in the task.

"You know, Wyatt, you're getting quieter than I am. I can't stand that."

Wyatt allowed his taut features to relax a shade. "Well, what do you suggest?"

"You're not of a body to get all pie-eyed drunk, so the old doctor can't suggest that."

"Well, Doc, I have been thinkin' about takin' up the sport of drinking."

"Do tell. And what, may I ask, brought forth this metamorphosis?"

"I can't do anything about this. I have to wait."

"This is the first spontaneous thing I've heard you utter in ages. Just when I thought you were settling down."

"We are sitting targets."

"We've been targets since coming here. The very things you and I do make us targets."

"Virge is pretty bad."

"I've had a different friendship with you than with Virgil. You might say that the only thing keeping him from locking me up is you because you consider me family. Virgil has a real core of steel down under all of that. He's taken a beating, but he'll come out of it. So will you."

"So what are you suggesting?"

"For old times sake, the two of us have dinner and then you go square things with Josie or Mattie. But not both."

"I'm not seeing Mattie anymore. She won't quit the laudanum. I'm not proud of how I feel, but that's what it is."

Doc swirled the whiskey in his glass before drinking it. "The doctors have been at me to take laudanum for the pain. I'm not sure if that's for the ones around me or myself. And you know what I told them."

"You been back to any of them?"

"The doctors? No. I know what they'll say. It will be this year. It will be next year. Hell, they don't know. They hand out medicine and platitudes like bullets. I'll take the bullets. That's an easy enough drink when you think about it."

Wyatt looked at the floor for a moment. "Don't do anything stupid to prove your point. You're the only sane one around here."

"Much obliged." Doc's whiskey glass was clinked against Wyatt's coffee cup.

March blew in blustery and snowy, and it howled across Skeleton Canyon. The days were no longer as overcast and the nights weren't as long. The winds shifted signaling spring's approach. Desert flowers hadn't popped in view, but the ground was beginning to thaw.

If there was any news to be heard, it was in the proximity of the Wells Fargo office next to Campbell and Hatch's Billiard Parlor. While not directly involved in the city's administration, Wyatt was able to hear of events firsthand before rumor or innuendo altered them. He learned of the stage robberies and cattle rustlings, and Wells Fargo provided a source of steady income. This fact was kept quiet, but Doc and the other Earp brothers knew.

Morgan grew to love pool so much that everyone suggested the young man would make a right good hustler once his law days were over. Morgan constantly badgered those around him to play. Doc didn't care for the game only because the large, plate glass window exposed anyone at the table for too long a time. There was an alley in back and at night the shadows were deep.

Wyatt met Morgan in Hatch's most nights and would play a game of pool with his brother before Morg retired to hearth and home. Louisa was indulgent of her husband's hobby. As she told Doc, "At least I know where he is."

Through February and two weeks into March, Doc had been indisposed with a consumptive fever and pain brought on by the winter. Plagued by a cough worse than usual, he retired quite early for him, went to bed with hot towels, a fifth of whiskey, and a hot meal compliments of Louisa. She had begged him to stay with her and Morgan. With his vision blurring and a hard cough, Doc declined.

"At least, stay somewhere besides that room over Fly's, okay?" Louisa asked.

She harangued him so much in her ladylike way that Doc acquiesced and checked into the Cosmopolitan. Frank Leslie had a co-partnership there, and Doc figured that he and Frank could play cards if either of them got bored.

"There's one good thing, Doc," Frank said as Doc checked in, "about ownin' your own place. If you don't like somebody's face, you kin tell 'em to git. Oh, don't forget to mark the date. It's March 18. We got that big poker tournament comin' up."

There were plenty of people who saw Doc go into the hotel because of the early hour. Doc never stayed in the same room twice, and he knew that the desk clerk, this time Buckskin Frank, was not one to take a bribe. For this reason, the Cosmopolitan was a haven.

It was about eleven o'clock that evening when the action in the saloons began to accelerate. Raucous music filled the streets. The best saloons often had entertainment that was hired from places like Kansas City, San Francisco, or Dallas. Lively music and food made the customers stay put since a hungry man might go to eat someplace else and take his money with him.

Doc lay in bed, almost unable to move. He'd eaten all of the food that Louisa had fixed him and, though he wanted to gag on it, had drunk her herbal tea. Doc mixed some whiskey, sugar, and lemon with it as Lou had told him and knocked it back. It almost laid him out.

Morgan, as usual, began his pool game while Wyatt sat on the sidelines and mulled over the current information from Wells Fargo about the latest train robberies and stage holdups. The Cowboys peered in but refused to enter. As the action heated up in other saloons along Allen Street, the street itself grew emptier and darker. Morgan had just bent forward for a shot when there was a flash of fire from the outside and the sound of an explosion. Two shots rang close together. One whizzed over Wyatt's head. The other entered Morgan's back, toppling him forward onto the table. Wyatt caught his brother and eased him as best as he could. Blood spurted over the green pool table cover. Virgil, Allie, Louisa, and the doctors were sent for, but Dr. Goodfellow could do nothing.

"His spine is smashed. I can't get the bullet out. There is nothing that I can do. Let's see if we can make him more comfortable."

Morgan was gently rolled onto his side and lowered to a sofa that was hurriedly brought in.

Fuzzily awakened from his deep sleep by the shots, Doc lay still thinking there was gunplay in the street. His heart pounded and his forehead was slick with sweat. There was an unaccustomed queasiness in his gut. As the sleep gave way to the adrenaline rush, he stood up and buckled on his gun belt making sure the chambers were full. A frantic pounding on the door stopped him before he opened it. Instinctively, he drew both weapons.

"Doc, they want you to come quick. Morgan's been shot."

No sooner had the words left the speaker's mouth than Doc barreled through the door, almost knocking the man off his feet and into the opposite wall.

"Where?"

"Hatch's. He—"

The Cosmopolitan was four doors away from Hatch's Saloon. Doc ran. The billiard hall's closed sign was out, but Doc pounded on the door until someone appeared.

"Open the goddamn door," he barked. "Where?"

"In the back."

Entering the room, all Doc could see was Morgan on the sofa. Blood was everywhere. Wyatt was covered with it, and Lou was hysterical. Doc knew he was too late. A red pounding in his head momentarily dulled his hearing. Tears ran unchecked down Wyatt's face, and Virgil's head was bent.

Walking up to Lou, he touched her shoulder. She flung herself into his arms. He broke down as she tucked her head into the hollow of his neck. Her sobs came swift and hard. After Doc had dried her eyes and his own, he looked at Wyatt who was as forlorn as he had ever seen him.

Without relinquishing Lou, Doc said in a low, clear voice, "If we stay here, we will all die. They will pick us off one by one. That other bullet was meant for you."

Wyatt roused himself from the sofa where he'd been sitting beside Morgan. He continued to pat his brother's hand. "What do you think?"

"Your parents live in California. This heinous hand cannot reach them there. Virgil is still recovering. Why not send everyone to safety? You send for your brother Warren and together we can take such men as we need and solve this problem. The law will not help us."

"It's true, Wyatt," Virgil replied. "I can't ride with you, but I can look after Allie and Lou and Mattie if she'll go, but we can't stay here. They'll burn us down one at a time just like Doc said."

It was decided to send Virgil and the women on to California with Morgan's body. Warren arrived as fast as was possible. Wyatt and Doc met him at the rail station.

"They're watching the trains," he told Wyatt as he grasped his brother's hand. "They didn't pay much attention to me. Pretty sure they don't know me on sight." A tear rolled down his cheek. "The folks are looking forward to seeing everybody."

"I know," Wyatt said. "We don't have much time. They're like a pack of damn locusts. Virgil, Allie, Lou, Mattie—they're all packed and ready. And as for them watchin' the trains," his voice became hard, "we'll have to take steps. I've been given to understand that Frank Stilwell is in Tucson. I think that's where they'll try it."

"You think Stilwell did it, Doc?" Warren asked in a voice so like Morgan's that Doc's eyes blurred with tears.

"Without a doubt."

"Did you mail your letter, Doc?" Wyatt asked.

"I did. Don't think we'll be back this way again."

My Dearest Mattie,

It was an evil night. It was ruin and destruction. It was too terrible to be borne, but borne it must be. There was no reason and no end to the pain. No way to bring back the laughter whose lifeblood had spilled so black and richly across cheap fabric, so cheap was the life considered in the taking.

Dire consequences require the direst of considerations necessary. Blood spilled on the wind cannot be cleansed by rain, nor earth, or wiped away by time. Souls perish and cast down into perdition are the perpetrators. Nothing can ever be made right over that which was taken.

Your Loving John

Dressed in black, his eyes reddened with grief and outrage, Doc saw Wyatt to the outskirts of town. "If you have enough men, I'll give you a head start, but it won't be a long one. I know you want to do it this way."

"I want the Cowboys to think you're remaining. We've got an escort. As soon as we're gone, they'll ride out."

"As will I."

The women huddled in the buckboard. No one spoke. Lou clung to Doc's hand as long as she could.

"Okay, Doc," Wyatt whispered.

"I'll meet you in Tucson. I have my own escort committee such as Texas Jack, Turkey Creek Jack Johnson, and other friendly acquaintances and fellow sportsmen and gamblers to guard the rear. You won't lack. We'll be at your back the whole time. If I see

Behan at all, he's dead, along with Ringo. I'm through waiting, Wyatt. The Cowboys know you're coming. Hell, the wires have been full of it."

"Once we get clear of those damn rail yards, Doc."

Doc grasped his arm. "We've been in tough spots before. We'll make this one out, too. I won't be more than five minutes behind you. I want to see who leaves town first. They're the first ones I'll kill."

Wyatt took a deep breath, "See to it if I miss."

Doc gave Wyatt a five-minute head start and then rode out linking up with the others at Tucson. By necessity, the Earp party kept together, except for the scouts that the Cowboys might not recognize on sight. Pete Spence and Frank Stilwell had arrived already, but Wells Fargo had no accurate information on their whereabouts. The long layover made their position dangerous. For protection, Wyatt posted several sharpshooters on top of some of the cars. The yards, however, were full of trains and the shadows were deep.

Inside the passenger car, Virgil and the rest of the Earp women waited. While they ate, armed guards posted around the station stood watch. Doc carried a shotgun as well as his two revolvers. Wyatt, also armed, was bearing up well, but had become alarmed at Doc's skin color.

"It's gonna be a long time for you and me. I want you to go inside and get a hot meal. You can take a little time."

Doc ate but was too nervous to touch more than a mouthful and too restless to sit still while death lurked outside. The whistles from the trains echoed mournfully across the plain. Oddly enough, the sound was the most muffled between the trains where the shadows were the deepest. Noting that, Doc picked his way towards the Earps' rail car. He didn't want to be seen returning the way he had come. Every instinct in his body listened for unusual noises.

A stone crackled. Instantly, Doc slid one of his guns from the holster and crept in the direction of the sound, at most twenty-five feet to his left behind another rail car. He came upon Wyatt, just as the latter lowered his shotgun towards the object in front of him. Doc looked at the man's face. It was Frank Stilwell who was staring in terror at the sight of Wyatt.

"Morg?" Stilwell muttered. "I killed you."

Reaching forward, Stilwell took the barrel of the shotgun and tried to push it away. Wyatt's gun retorted at the same time as Doc's. Stilwell dropped. Grimacing, Wyatt opened fire with his revolver until the contents of his weapon had emptied. Doc bent down, ripped the pocket watch off of Stilwell's prone frame and then flung it away as far as possible.

"Time's up."

About half an hour later, the Earps' train prepared to get under way.

"You write, Doc," Louisa said as she kissed his cheek. Her small hands were cold and limp. "You write. Morg'll know."

Doc didn't trust himself to speak. He embraced the rest of the women and shook hands with Virgil.

"You," Virgil said, "I entrust you to look after his hide."

Wyatt's party watched while the train pulled away.

"I imagine they will know by the time we get back, so we might as well finish this thing."

"They'll know all right."

John Behan greeted Doc and Wyatt with a reception committee and warrants. He had been busy in their absence recruiting the Cowboys and deputizing them. But their most prominent members, Curly Bill and Ringo, weren't present.

With Morgan's assassination, Wyatt's rage knew no bounds. Frank Stilwell was dead. Ringo and Brocius were combing the countryside looking for Wyatt's group. At this point in time,

Wyatt cared little about the warrants, and with the look in his eye, Behan was afraid to arrest him.

Doc glanced at Wyatt. "Funny thing about life. I don't have much in the way of worldly goods. What I don't want, the buzzards can pick over. And they will."

Buckskin Frank met Doc at the door of the Cosmopolitan Hotel. "I packed your things as soon as I heard. You wire me. I'll send 'em." The two men shook hands and Frank graced Doc with one of his tight smiles. "I'm glad you got the son-of-a-bitch. He deserved the killin' most of all."

Wyatt looked at Doc. "All things squared away?" Doc nodded. Wyatt took one last look at the town. "I never want to see this place again."

Both men set spur to their horses.

Chapter
SEVENTEEN

Doc admired Wyatt's tenacity and said nothing about the missed meals or the pounding ride through arroyos that the sun had baked to a fine, pink chalk. Doc's lungs seared in the heat, but two things he committed to memory: Morgan's blood spilling black on the pool table and Ike Clanton wearing a badge. In the morning light, Doc's dying flesh renewed and he took up the ride once more.

"You know, I've been thinking," Wyatt said during a mid-afternoon break. The horses had been unsaddled and were feasting on a rare treat of sweet grass. "If we stay here in Arizona, I'm afraid they'll pick us off one at a time. Behan is determined he'll get our hides. What do you think of Colorado?"

Doc looked uncomfortable, not at the talk of Colorado, but from a deeper distress. Wyatt and Doc had lived out of each other's pockets for so long that Doc's mortality, though sometimes discussed, had never seemed so poignant or urgent. Suddenly afraid for his friend, Wyatt didn't know what to do.

The hollow at the base of Doc's neck was caved in. His eyes and hands were steady, but the bones in his arms looked like they were held together by hickory bark and will power. He coughed in his sleep and, when he went to sleep, he slept as if dead already. It haunted Wyatt each night after the campfire burned out. Doc understood Wyatt's concern, but there was nothing he could say to make him feel any better. The consumption was inexorably running its course.

On the trail, morning cleansing of his lungs had to be performed by streams or trees instead of the sanctity of a hotel or boardinghouse room. No one, he swore, must ever see him bent double with coughing until the blood flowed or how clots of lung tissue were expelled with the blood. For a while after this exercise, Doc had no strength to rise from the ground. When he got up, he was so weak that he collapsed against a tree trunk and sat panting. For a moment, Doc put his face in his hands and Wyatt, who had crept to stand ten feet behind him, died a thousand deaths.

By the time Doc got back to the campsite, Wyatt was putting coffee on in the battered pot that had seen campsites and boomtowns from Deadwood to Ft. Griffin.

"You'd think," Doc told him hoarsely, "that we could retire that particular piece of hardware."

Wyatt grinned, trying to let on that he hadn't seen. "I know. But don't you think it has a bit of charm about it?"

"Charm?" the doctor drawled. "Charm it has, but Wyatt, it's plumb worn out."

Wyatt froze for a moment. "Did we decide on Colorado?"

Doc's voice came sharper. "Did we? I suppose."

"I thought maybe we should stick together. I don't know about you, but our best bet is in numbers. We separate and they can pick us off."

Doc's emaciated face flushed. "I think not. Our best bet is to separate."

Wyatt wanted to joke, but he couldn't. In fact, he thought if he broke down in front of Doc, his friend would never forgive him.

"Wyatt, let's make it easy." Doc's extremely blue eyes flashed. Those same eyes that had terrified others were now the warmest shade of sapphire Wyatt had ever seen.

"Easy it is. Where are you heading?"

"Denver I think. I'll see if Ed Chase or possibly some of my acquaintances will hire me. I come with good references."

"Sure. Flip you for the coffee pot."

"You keep it, Wyatt." Doc drank the remainder of his coffee, packed his things, and Wyatt stood up.

"Look, we're just out of Silver City. There's just the two of us. We can unload these horses and then catch the train to Pueblo. Look, goddamn it, do you think you can just ride out without so much as a fare-thee-well, you stubborn-assed, addlepated, miserable-minded, mule-headed Southerner? And that I, goddamn jackass that I am, would let you go?"

"Wyatt, you silver-tongued devil, you have a most uniquely self-righteous way with words, more than any stubborn bastard that I know."

"Thank you."

"And yes, I would be honored to go with you to Pueblo."

Wyatt continued to mutter imprecations and curses the likes of which Doc had never before heard from him. Morgan had possessed a good repertoire, but Wyatt had never so much as used a swear word. The muttering lasted as far as the trail to Silver City.

Wyatt wasn't going to let him ride into the sunset any easier than Doc planned on going. He had seen the one thing that Wyatt had tried so desperately to hide: the tear that had rolled down Wyatt's cheek. At Pueblo's rail station, they shook hands as they'd always done. It was an acknowledgment of a lifetime of friendship.

"It's not done, Wyatt," Doc said as he smiled with a little half-twist to his lips. "Life's funny, isn't it?" And he disappeared into the crowd.

"No, it's not done, you miserable, stubborn s.o.b. I'm gonna only be a three or four day's ride behind you at the most." Wyatt slammed his hat down on his head so hard that it hurt.

♣ ♥ ♠ ♦

Pueblo came as a shock to Doc. There was a change in the air. He could see it in all the development going on around him. Instead of sprawling prairie with waving grasses and plentiful game fowl, there was development. Houses, churches, and schools had displaced saloons, tinny music, and mining shafts. Doc could see men in three-piece suits, but they didn't look like gamblers. His favorite restaurant remained, but it was being crowded from either side by a large bank and a new dry goods store. In the old days, the restaurant would have been complete-ly crowded at such an early hour. Now at one o'clock, there were only a few people. The proprietor was the only one he recog-nized.

"John Holliday, I'll be damned."

"Doin' good, doin' good. And yourself?"

"I still have that bean soup. How about a steak?"

"Mashed potatoes with lots of gravy. Who in hell's name are the suits? They don't look like gamblers and they're scowling."

"They're developers."

"Any gambling?"

"Not much anymore. I'll tell you where you can still get some good action though. Seeing as how it's you, you should do right well."

The food was delicious as always, but the land development left him uneasy. Doc shrugged off his unease and sent a telegram to Bat Masterson in Trinidad. While the two were not friends, it was a courteous gesture, and it was something Wyatt would have done, especially to tell Bat about Morgan

Surprisingly, not long after, Bat took the train to Pueblo and suggested that he and Doc spend dinner catching up. The restaurant they chose happened to be a favorite of both. Over beefsteaks and coffee, Bat was diffident. They had never been friends or even enjoyed a working relationship such as the one that Doc shared with Virgil.

"Wyatt mentioned that he might be going to Gunnison if and when he left Arizona. So, you're headed for Denver?"

"After here. I thought I'd kick about for a while. See the sights."

Bat had been studying Doc quite intently for a while when Doc looked up and correctly interpreted the gaze. Bat had grown older, too. His brown hair had gray. The full cheekbones were less full, and his hands, unlike Doc's nervous fingers, were quiet by his coffee cup.

"I was so sorry about Morgan. I wish I'd been there. God, it was a sad state of affairs. You remember my brother, Ed? You just never get over it. I keep seeing his face. Was Stilwell dead when you came on him?"

Doc said quietly, "All along Stilwell kept saying he was going to get Morg after that Bisbee holdup. Morg was the one who brought him in. You know we all watched them for months. When it came down to it at the rail yard, Wyatt had already emptied his shotgun and revolver. Stilwell kept muttering 'Morg' until he ran out of air. My God, Bat, Morg was shot in the back in cold blood."

"It never makes any sense, Doc. Ed never saw the bullet that got him either. The back— I . . . " Bat shook his head.

"He lived an hour afterwards."

"Dear God. What about Virgil?"

"That shotgun blast in December destroyed his left arm. He had to make Wyatt promise that the doctor wouldn't cut it off."

Bat poured a dash of whiskey in his coffee. "Damn. That night Morg cashed in, was Wyatt shot at?"

"Bullet went over his head. Behan had been goin' around town with that dumb-assed grin of his. After the shooting, he deputized Ike Clanton."

"Clanton? Oh that's great. That makes one black-hearted rattler deputizing another."

The men stopped talking as a man approached their table.

"Mr. Holliday?"

"Dr. Holliday, actually. And you are?"

"Perry Mallen, sir. Perry Mallen. Mind if I sit down?"

Doc and Bat exchanged glances.

"Please be seated," Doc told him. "What can we do for you?" Doc's expression said that he had no clue who this gentleman might be. Neither did Masterson, who looked askance at the newcomer.

Mallen shared a hateful smile between them. "Well, sir, you shot me. It's made me a cripple with the women. I can't get it up no more."

Doc pulled his cloak around himself and looked Mallen in the eye. "I would know if I had shot your privates, and I would know if I had killed you, too. But you're not killed and you're still walking. Either way, I don't recognize you."

Mallen welled up like a toad. "Here, let me show you." Before Doc or Bat could react, Mallen dropped his trousers. "See here. See this. You shot me. I'm done for with women."

Bat raised an eyebrow. "Looks like pox to me. Kind of like syphilis pox, if you understand my meaning."

Mallen blushed to the roots of his furry red hair. He was an ungainly creature with a face like a bloodhound's, red-rimmed eyes, and a short neck. His ears protruded from the sides of his head and the lobes hung low towards his jowls. In comparison to Doc and Bat, Mallen was a dachshund between two golden retrievers.

"You listen, here," Mallen pointed at Doc, "I wanted to tell you, you sorry son-of-a-bitch, that you shot my privates. They're all done blowed away."

"Don't worry, Doc. If he goes for his gun, I'll shoot him myself. And please, please do it." Bat stood up, putting his hand on the outside of his black coat.

Mallen jumped away as if stung. "You'll be real sorry. You'll be sorry you said I had pox."

"Obviously," Doc told him, "if I had killed you. From where I sit your ass looks pretty sorry—not worthy of a bullet."

Bat began to laugh. Mallen gave the two a baleful look, shook his fist at Doc, and walked away.

"Be careful when you get to Denver. No telling if he's drunk or high. If he were in my territory, I'd kick his fat little ass until the cows came home. Since there aren't a lot of cattle in Trinidad, I'd be kicking a long time."

"If that don't beat all. Damn, I thought the bugger was gonna strip right here."

"I mean it, Doc. Watch yourself."

"I have to ask this, Masterson. Did Wyatt send you here?"

Bat smiled. Doc had seen that same smile over cards. He'd been accused of wearing that particular expression himself. The smile had no answers, but it said a lot.

Bat stood up and held out his hand. "I'll see you later, Holliday. As I said, watch out for him."

The incident with Mallen was so strange that Doc was vigilant all the way to Denver. He was careful on the train going up, but he didn't see anyone on the platform that looked like Mallen. When he arrived at the mile-high city, he checked in with the local constabulary. That accomplished, Doc went about the business of setting himself up. Denver was still an exciting frontier town, though leaning a bit on the stuffy side, just as Pueblo.

The altitude was hard to adjust to. He tried to convince himself that it was the altitude and not his consumption. The Mallen incident had been disturbing, but Doc didn't worry, though he had heeded Bat's warning. Just when he'd convinced himself that he'd never see Mallen again, three revolvers were shoved into his face.

"Goddamn you. You're under arrest. Throw up yer hands, you yellow-livered cur."

Mildly, Doc raised his hands and stared into the face of Perry Mallen. "As you can see, suh, I am not armed." Mallen had revoltingly begun to search his person.

"I got the sheriff here from Arapaho County and he don't like curs like you."

"There is no need to speak to me in this manner. I am not resisting arrest. I am peaceable, am I not?"

"You're—" But whatever it was that Mallen might have said or done, the Arapaho County deputies gave him a dirty look. "So you better come along," Mallen snarled, poking Doc very hard with the muzzle of his pistol.

"Mallen," one of the deputies replied, "keep that gun to yourself and in your holster. You're in Colorado and we have laws in Colorado. I'm sorry, Dr. Holliday. We'll have to incarcerate you until such time as we can figure this thing out."

"Well, I think you oughta cuff him," offered Mallen.

"I've listened to your mouth run long enough. Shut the hell up and let the wheels of justice decide."

The jail cell, in Doc's eyes, looked marvelous compared to the things Mallen suggested. It occurred to Doc that John Behan might have engineered the incident. However, the sheriff seemed to be as indifferent to turning Doc over to Mallen as Mallen was anxious to have him.

"How long is it gonna take? Hell, I've got warrants."

"You have warrants, but they look bogus. We don't have extradition papers. This is not some matter where you can bully us and tell us how to run our business. Got it? If Arizona wants him extradited, Arizona's governor is going to have to send us a writ."

"This is outrageous."

There was so much rhetoric that, for safety's sake, Doc was transferred to the county jail. Doc didn't have to wait long for Bat Masterson's involvement either. Bat had a few choice things to say about Perry Mallen and he unloaded quite a bit, judging from the arresting sheriff's sudden change of attitude.

"You have $5,000 for the capture of this man. Are you offering me, a duly appointed official of the court, a bribe for his incarceration?"

"No, no. It's just that I have been so severely tasked by the terrible forces about this villain that I feign to make myself heard above the uproar of humanity."

"Bullshit," Spangler said. "You'll have to wait while we sort this out."

Although Bat figured that John Behan would have them all on trial if he could, he understood that Doc wasn't the only one wanted. Behan's blunder at the trial had been the admission of "disarming" the Cowboys. Now Behan wanted to cover his tracks. Wyatt Earp had made him look like a fool by stealing Josie, ruining his business, and laughing in his face.

The worst, as far as Doc was concerned, was the stealing of Josie's affections. Wyatt, according to Behan, had stolen everything else, but the woman was his pride, whether he really wanted her or not. John Behan knew how Wyatt felt about Doc

Holliday. By hurting Doc, Behan could get back at Wyatt and intended to do so.

"If they get me back to Arizona," Doc said, "well, I know I'll never make it back there."

It didn't matter how good the intentions of Sheriff Bob Paul were. Paul was the same man who had stopped the runaway horses on the night Bud Philpot was murdered. Paul knew Doc. Paul's response to Mallen was the same. "Shut up and wait."

Paul also realized that he wouldn't be able to protect Doc against a concerted effort that would rise against him in Arizona. Doc wouldn't merely be killed, instead he would be tortured and maimed, or as much as his frail body could withstand before being killed.

"This is misbegotten justice," Bat indicated in a telegram to Bob Paul and Sheriff Spangler.

To keep Doc from being extradited required planning. A phony felony charge was designed with Colorado taking precedence over Arizona.

Bat, in the meantime, had gotten word to Wyatt, whose response was, "I'm going to Denver and straighten this damned mess out myself."

Wyatt, however, under contract to Wells Fargo could not surface without creating a real problem, since Mallen would ostensibly try to capture him, too.

A fierce legal battle of money, words, and authority ensued. Doc was hardly languishing in jail. Mallen was showing his true colors as a con. Bat Masterson, in particular, wanted to get his hands on Mallen and said as much to Spangler. In due time, extradition papers from Arizona were sent to Colorado's Governor Pitkin, who looked them over and took his time in doing so.

Some clever sleuthing on the part of Bat Masterson, Doc's attorney, and several of the newspapers determined that Perry

Mallen had never been a lawman anywhere. He had, however, swindled money and did so ingenuously having a ready story with credentials to fit every occasion. The letter sent from Governor Pitkin to the governor of Arizona concisely stated that there would be no extradition of John Henry Holliday. Doc imagined the fury that John Behan must now be consumed with on finding his plans thwarted. As for Mallen, he was now the accused. He had, it was said, left the territory and was the subject of a manhunt.

The Rocky Mountain News, unhappy with the verdict and its own embarrassment, wrote a final column about the ludicrous felony charge that Bat Masterson had fabricated. According to their account, Doc was treated like royalty while in jail. The newspaper had part of the story correct in that Doc's friends came to visit him. This included Wyatt Earp, which the newspaper knew nothing about.

Wyatt showed up for Doc's release. In spite of Wyatt's disguise, Doc recognized him. Wyatt cut quite a figure with black hair, a broad black hat, and black clothes with small white curlicues on the lapel of his shirt.

"What the hell?" Doc asked.

"You like this?"

"What the hell?" Bat asked.

Wyatt held out his hand. "Say no more. Name is Tom McKey."

Bat almost bit his cigar in half. "Tell you what, Tom, if you came to me in Trinidad, I'd have to arrest you for impersonating a peace officer."

"Do tell," Wyatt replied.

Doc choked back a small cough. "I am quite pleased upon seeing you again. Either yourself or Tom will do."

Bat poked Wyatt, "Check out this hair."

"Check out Gunnison," Wyatt said. "I don't know where you two are headed, but you know where to find me."

Doc pondered that remark about Gunnison, but Leadville sounded better. He'd seen jail cells up and down the state of Colorado since May and he'd seen enough to crave a blue sky, vistas, and mountain valleys. If there was money to be made in any of Leadville's saloons, that was all the better.

But Leadville was difficult too. Barely had Doc set foot in Leadville before he was descended upon as a fresh carcass. He was a celebrity, which was not at all to his liking. Rather, he wanted to live the rest of his life, such as it was, in the bosom of good friends and comrades. Since Wyatt had hinted that he had a hankering to visit with Doc in Gunnison, then Gunnison would be Doc's next destination.

Denver's newspapers circulated wild reports that John Holliday was seen as far away as California, Dallas, or even Deadwood, South Dakota. But the truth was that Doc was too exhausted to go anywhere. His body hurt twenty-four hours a day from the hard riding. The unplanned stay in the Denver jail had seriously depleted his remaining strength.

Gunnison sounded good and Doc was pleased to find Wyatt waiting for him on his arrival. Wyatt ran a faro bank at a saloon owned by Ernest Bieble. Doc liked to gamble, but he was not inclined to become the focal point of gossip or encounter another jail visit.

Wyatt could see how tired he was. "You know, the high country is beautiful this time of year and I like to mountain fish the streams."

"Hell, Wyatt, the last time I fished was when I was a boy."

"Then what say?"

"I say we do it."

Gunnison was a boomtown in minerals, cattle, and coal. Times were cold in the winter and coal meant heat. The burning of wood for heat was not possible in an area that had little wood. Doc laughed at the rumors that he was in Deadwood.

"I wintered one time there, Wyatt, and couldn't wait to light out once spring hit. It was miserable. Damn, we used to think the wind howled at Ft. Griffin. If there was one banshee in Griffin, there had to be at least fifty in Deadwood. It got so my teeth rattled harder than the wind blew."

Wyatt looked at him steadily until Doc cleared his throat. "Okay, I recognize that stare. It's the one you leveled at Ike Clanton."

"There's a pretty good physician in town."

"I can't deny that I have been feeling poorly, but I'm hardly ready for a permanent earthen residence."

"Lou's been at me. Does he eat? What he does eat? Is he sleeping okay? You know Lou."

"I miss them both so much, Wyatt, so very much."

"Me, too." Wyatt raised his glass, "To Morg."

"Morg."

"What do you want to do?"

"Thought I'd travel a bit while the weather's warm. Settle here for the winter. I know you still do jobs for Wells Fargo."

"Yep. Just finished a particular assignment before you arrived. What did you think of Leadville?"

"Hasn't changed since the last time I saw it. The people are wonderful. They most love you to death. They did me. So much so I had to leave."

"Do you ever think about going back to Georgia?"

Doc sighed, "Every hour of every day. I got a nice long letter from Mattie. She's been pretty low. I can hear her just assuredly as I'm talkin' to you now. Mary'll be ten this year. I keep seeing her, all eyes and teeth. Guess she'll always be four to me."

"Have you heard anything from your father?"

Doc roused himself from the torpor that he had sunken into and his eyes flashed. "Well, I tried a couple of times. Maybe he never got my letters. Guess I'm the black sheep of the Holliday clan. They probably won't speak to me or of me for another hundred years, if that. Bat's changed a peck."

"Yeah, he's been pretty contented in Trinidad."

Doc coughed and Wyatt averted his head. It had a death knell sound to it, no longer dry, but terribly deep. Doc's thin frame shook. After the paroxysm stopped, his face was white except for the vivid spots of color high on his cheekbones.

"If you want, let's try out some of those mountain streams tomorrow."

"Sounds like a plan."

It was an odd change after so long a time on the road. Doc had seen rivers and streams all over the country. They ran wide and sluggish in Georgia, a pale green-blue to match the blue sky and tangle of green by the water's edge. In Texas, the waterways poured swift and deadly through the broken arroyos before disappearing into briny soil. Water gurgled in Kansas and moved quietly with only a pause to seep from the cracks of rocks and boulders. Colorado's water tumbled white with life and foam, making it clear enough to see where he'd been yesterday and where he might go tomorrow.

The clean smell of the summer meadows washed some of the blood and dust from Doc's soul. He was tired in a way that sucked the very marrow of his bones out through his fingertips. Nights before had been so much his enemy that he could never remember a time when he had not fought valiantly to keep them at bay. Wyatt had never seen Doc in such a state.

While Wyatt ran his faro bank on Virginia Avenue, Doc tended the bar. The winter was hard, but not hard like it would have been in Deadwood or Cheyenne. He knew he had become an anachronism. There were so many stories about him now in the dime novels. How Doc Holliday had done this or how he had "shot the filling out of that thar fella's teeth."

Doc knew what he was and scoffed at the tales of how he arrived in town to shoot his way into a saloon. Luke Short had told him long ago that he was too tall to swagger and too short to be a dandy. And Mysterious Dave Mather had closed up shop and gone who knows where, probably taking Soapy Smith and that fake gold brick with him.

Things always fell apart in the winter. *Rime of the Ancient Mariner* got wet. Doc forgot what happened to the old copy after it disappeared. At Christmas, there was a new copy bound in leather. Wyatt had written an inscription and dated it on the inside sleeve.

May of 1883 saw Doc getting restless again. He traveled with Wyatt to Silverton and met up with Bat.

"Well, Holliday, you're not lookin' too bad."

"Neither are you, Masterson."

He stuck around Silverton long enough to get the lay of the land and find out what was going on in the rest of the world since he hadn't read a newspaper for several months. He'd regained some color and his complexion no longer looked like ivory shoe leather. The old buzz was starting to tingle in his blood, along with a yearning for another town, for a spin of the roulette wheel and a throw of the dice.

"Well, gentlemen," Doc told Bat and Wyatt with an acknowledging tip of his hat. "I feel the tug o' Leadville. Thought I might try the gambling circuit and head up there. I hear it's far from dull." The professional gamblers traveled through all the towns going to the saloons that were ripe with silver and gold and then moving on to another city. "Leadsville had thousands of pounds of silver. But I'm not so sure now. Things are changing."

"That's a fact," Bat said. "Listen, I'm gonna get a drink. I'll be back in a minute."

"Where are you headed?"

"Me?" Wyatt asked. "Thought I'd try the circuit, too."

"Really? You takin' Tom McKey on the road?"

"No. I don't know. I'll cut a swath around the circuit for a while, then I'll figure it out."

Doc held out his hand. "It's not done yet, Wyatt."

Wyatt shook his friend's hand. "Life's funny, isn't it?"

"That's a fact."

When Bat returned Doc had gone. "So I guess he's off to Leadville."

"You know, Bat, I guess I won't really worry until he tells me that it's done."

"What are you talkin' about?"

"Nothin'. Nothin' at all."

The Denver Rio Grande Railroad was now weaving a rail service web to all the mining towns. Doc took the Silverton Branch as far as Durango, Colorado, climbed on the Pueblo and San Juan Division to South Pueblo, then was carried the final leg of the Eagle River Branch to Leadville.

No matter where he went, Doc could see that the once pulse-pounding glamour of the mining towns was giving way to staid civilization. The fresh bloom of silver in some of the smaller boomtowns, however, made up for the lack elsewhere. Doc traded in his diamond cravat pin for a larger one. His amazing aptitude with cards gave him enough of a bankroll so by the time he arrived in Leadville in the fall of 1883, he felt pretty good.

Doc took a job in the Monarch Saloon as a faro dealer. Cy Allen, the owner, seemed a pleasant enough sort, and Doc enjoyed his job. Leadville felt like home. On Harrison Avenue, the saloons played music and racked up cash and steady customers twenty-four hours a day. The Tabor Opera House was a place to repair when the day's work was done. Doc's address at 106 E. Second Street was a good place to go home to.

A fine view of the mountains could be seen from Leadville proper. Westwards from Harrison Avenue were Mt. Elbert and its companion, Mt. Massive. When he wasn't dealing faro, he would ride up to Turquoise Lake to fish. In the early morning hours during the short summer, fish would leap out of the depths of the sparkling blue water. But Doc's intuition failed him in one thing. Leadville's two-mile height made him feel that he was breathing through a straw and it was getting cold in a way that he did not remember.

Doc tried to kid himself that it didn't make any difference and that he'd lived in cold before, but nothing prepared him for the winter of 1884. Rail travel into the passes had to be suspended once the snow started falling in mid-November. Bone-wrenching, gut-destroying cold ate through his flesh no matter how many layers of clothing he wore. By January of 1884, he felt like his teeth had been worn down from chattering.

A small measure of comfort came from the warmth of the Monarch Saloon. But the comfort was soon forgotten when Johnny Tyler came into town. The Earps and Doc had both known Tyler in Tombstone. Wyatt's utter humiliation of Tyler in Tombstone had been so devastating that the man had had to run for cover, and Wyatt had said to him, "Still running, Johnny?" having plagued him all over the frontier. From the day of his departure from Tombstone, Johnny's single most burning desire was to vanquish John Holliday or Wyatt Earp, which ever came first.

The Monarch Saloon became Tyler's favorite haunt. And, as he like to taunt Doc, "Still running, Doc?" became Tyler's favorite phrase. It made him feel good that he could say that to Doc. Doc would know how the humiliation felt.

Various cronies of Tyler began plaguing Doc like swarming locusts.

"Cy, you don't want to have this man here. He's a cheat. He's cowardly."

Doc's bankroll began to dwindle. Not alarmingly at first, because a professional gambler had to be wise to the fact that Lady Luck could be a fickle woman. There had been dry spells before and he had recovered. What he was not prepared for was the dry spell that continued and the trouble that came with it.

Tyler dogged Doc's footsteps to every part of the city, either to work or while on his way home. If it wasn't Tyler, it was a Tyler cohort. They never said anything to him or made any move to harm him physically. Doc had put away his weapons, but now he was seriously considering rearming himself.

Doc was grayer since Tombstone, the blonde of his hair having been replaced with silver. There were streaks in his mustache and his eyes burned a deep blue in their sunken sockets. His full mouth had lines as well. He was glad of his facial hair, because it hid what was the most disturbing part of the disease that was overwhelming him, since by this time the disease was appearing on his skin. The snow burned his flesh from without and the consumption burned his lungs from within.

Doc continued to write letters, knowing if he didn't that Wyatt would soon come over the pass and demand to know, "What in hell's name is going on?" That fact kept him going.

As time wore on, Tyler became more officious, and it was harder for Doc to keep up at his job. He lost his comfortable living quarters when he could no longer pay for the rent. He was told, when the rent was suddenly quadrupled, and the landlord refused to speak with him on the matter, "You're a troublemaker. You attract the wrong crowd. I want you and your trash out of here by the end of the day."

Doc burned with a humiliation that he had not thought possible. Even if he hadn't sold his guns already, the money wouldn't be enough to pay for lodging in a town where even cheap lodging was unavailable. Doc found himself living in a dingy hovel that taxed his meager strength and pride past their limits.

In February, the cough changed to a ragged bark that brought blood with every wheeze. He was frozen through and through. The final straw came when Cy Allen fired him.

"Excuse me?" Doc finally asked, too stunned to believe what was happening to him.

"I'm sorry. I thought you would be an asset, but you're nothing but a damned headache. I want you out of here now."

"It's the middle of my shift."

"I know, but you're taking up space for valuable customers, and I don't have time for the headaches you cause. It plagues you like dying locusts."

Doc had to walk by Johnny Tyler's smirking face on the way out the door.

"Now you know, Holliday, how it feels to be run out of every decent place in the territory, and I ain't done yet." Tyler spat on him.

The spittle hung on his cheek, but he refused to wipe it away. Saying nothing, Doc looked long and hard at Tyler until Tyler looked away.

EIGHTEEN

The snow stopped for a while, but the wind was raging. Sheltered by the warmth in the Monarch Saloon, Doc's blood soon began to freeze once he reached the outside. Staggering forward with each step, he peered through the blizzard. His eyelids felt frozen with ice, and he could no longer feel his feet and hands. Unless he found refuge soon, he knew he would die. Feeling his way along, he suddenly came upon a door and leaned against it. It opened, spilling him to the floor. The face of Mannie Hyman loomed above him.

"Here, Doc, you drink this up. Damn, you're near froze. Hey, one of you fellas help me get him by the stove."

He felt himself hefted to his feet and dragged to a spot by the pot-bellied stove. A steaming bowl of soup was placed in front him along with a cup of coffee. Mechanically, Doc spooned the soup into his mouth and coughed blood into his handkerchief.

After he'd eaten the soup, Doc stuck his hand in his pocket and scrounged for a bit or two that could be given to Mannie.

"I have a room overhead. Why don't you stay here? I've been tryin' to get some class play in here. You're good for business, so it don't matter what them bums think. You said you did some barkeepin' in Gunnison? Pretty country, Gunnison. I can't be here twenty-four hours a day. Figured you kin help me out a spot and I kin help you."

Doc croaked, "I say that sounds most like a deal."

"Come on up. I'll show you the room. It ain't much."

By the time Doc made it to the top of the stairs, he was breathless. A fat stove sat in the corner overlooking the stairs. He held his chilled hands over the heat.

"Give me a moment," he wheezed.

From the rat-infested hellhole of his previous lodging, the sitting room was a clean wash of simple color and the smell of onions and bacon. In the middle was a long table for the serving of food, with enough chairs to accommodate nine rooms of people. On the side closest to the table was a sideboard. There were several bookcases. Doc looked hungrily at the books.

"For light, we've got oil lamps. I keep lots o' whale oil. Gits dark up here after the sun goes down. And the floor creaks."

"Mannie, all good saloons and boardinghouses have creaking floors. The tale is when you hear the creak, it's Lady Luck walkin' by."

"I didn't know that. Guess my wife didn't either. She's back East. Don't think she'll be coming out here. Let me show you where you'll be stayin'."

There were rugs on the floor of red, blue, yellow, and green rags that had been woven for a splash of color to dress the plain wood. The iron bedstead was simple, but big enough. There was a washstand with a pitcher and a washbowl. It was a cozy room, but cold with the westward window that afforded a frigid if bucolic view of Mt. Massive and the Silver Dollar Saloon across the street. Doc tried to imagine the room in the summer and failed. A deep cough rolled up from the pit of his stomach and Mannie saw the blood.

"We gotta doctor in town. I think you need one."

"I can't afford a doctor. I have one change of clothes and nobody's gonna purchase me."

"Well, yer not gonna last the winter in this shape. I'll get the doc. He's pretty good. Together, we'll figure out somethin'."

The something was pneumonia.

"That's it," Doc said. "I'm done for."

The doctor put his stethoscope down. "It's not good." He looked at Doc's caved in chest. "But you must be made of pretty stern stuff, not like one of these hothouse flowers who come out here and wither in the cold. It saw fit not to carry you off when it could have. Somehow we've got to shut this cough off."

"I've been coughing for thirteen years."

"Yes, but you're bringing up raw tissue with it now. Every time you cut loose, you tear out any clot that is forming. I'm going to prescribe laudanum."

"Oh, God."

"You've got to sleep, you've got to eat, and you've got to stop coughing."

"Hell, I'm dyin' anyway."

"It'll make you comfortable."

"Mannie, I've got to get my trunk."

"It's been taken care of. I'll have one of my boys go to the druggist and get the laudanum, and the housekeeper can fix you some hot food. She and her daughter board here."

"There's a little girl here?"

"She's out playing with the cat. I have a grubby tomcat that hangs around. She's not supposed to feed it, but Tom, he keeps the rats and mice out. So I figure he's entitled. He sleeps downstairs where it's warm. Sometimes she brings him up here."

"Thanks, Mannie."

Tottering back to the stove, Doc pulled up a chair and sat close. His head had stopped pounding, but another cough erupted sending him sprawling to the floor. Dazed, Doc looked at the high ceiling and the grain in the wood floor. He coughed again unable to rise. The floor was warm. His vision blurred, cleared, and blurred again. Without the strength to get up, he lay coughing and choking on his blood while the ceiling whirled madly and the faraway music crashed in his ears. No one would hear him if he called out, recognizing the croak as a sound no human could make. "Then it's done, Wyatt," he whispered.

The arms that lifted him off the floor hurt his bones. He tried to cry out, but the sound didn't come through his lips. Someone carried him. He couldn't make out any features.

"Okay, Doc, you've got to drink this up."

"Ohhhh, no more."

"Come on. Don't be a baby."

"It tastes like horse shit," he moaned, and then he peered out from one eye.

He wasn't alone. He'd guessed that much right. Female hands patted a cloth on his forehead and more fiery liquid trickled down his throat. But it didn't make him cough. He looked at her. She was kind. Would the sky ever stop spinning long enough for him to see her face?

"Who are you?"

"Lucille."

"Don't know any Lucilles," Doc mumbled and passed out.

The smell of food and music tickled his senses. When the music became louder, he was back in Georgia listening to his mother play the piano. Then he was sitting on his bed and Mattie was sitting there, too. They were holding hands. He was brushing Tom, and Tom was purring. Outside the moon blossomed on the outstretched fields as the fireflies danced. Tom disappeared. Atlanta burned. He was a young man, not yet a dentist. Mattie was with him in Savannah, and Mike Gordon was hurling insults. Doc stepped into the street and there was a blast from a gun.

His eyes snapped open. The woman was wringing out another cloth. She had a stained apron with an odor of onions and bacon. A wet light glimmered about the window and the shadows danced.

"You said your name was Lucille."

"I've been told your name is John."

"Only in emergencies."

"What should I call you then?"

"Doc."

"Okay, Doc."

"Not more of that stuff," he mumbled.

"Open wide."

"What is it?"

"It will make you feel better."

"I feel better now."

"You are a very stubborn man."

"Everybody says that," but he drank the liquid.

Most of the time he couldn't remember seeing her. He couldn't remember a lot of things. Words hurt as they rang in his ears, but his chest didn't hurt anymore. He floated in and out and wondered bitterly why it was that his body refused to give up. Sometimes Lucille sponged him off. Doc kept his eyes closed, not because it felt good, but for the humiliation that had rendered him in such a state. He thought if his eyes were open, she would be able to see that in them.

One afternoon, he woke to find a little girl staring at him only inches from his face. She had, he guessed, crept close and stared at him while he slept, then tweaked his mustache ever so slightly.

"What are you doing?" Doc asked.

Like a frightened rabbit, the child jumped halfway across the room and stood watching him with her large eyes. She held a dolly in one arm.

"What were you doing?"

She bobbed her head and shuffled her feet. Her hair was brown, and she wore a homespun brown dress. Her eyes blinked. Doc stayed very still and closed his eyes, pretending to be asleep to draw her near. Her breath blew softly across his cheek. She smelled of new soap. That light touch on his mustache came again. When he opened his eyes, she jumped back.

"Sarah Elizabeth, what are you doing?"

"Sorry, Mama. I'm sorry."

"Doc, did she hurt you?"

He chuckled. "No, she didn't mean any harm. She was feeling my mustache."

"Honestly, child, what will I do with you?"

"I'm sorry. But it's pretty. It's soft like Tom's fur. That's why I wanted to touch it."

"You, young lady, run along now and don't bother Doc here."

"No, it's okay. She didn't harm me."

He felt the touch of Lucille's hand on his forehead. "I think your temperature is down. How does your chest feel?"

"Better. I can breathe again. I don't remember coughing."

"You did, but you get fluid out now instead of blood. So the hemorrhaging seems to be under control."

"You've been taking care of me all this time?"

"Yes. Oh no, don't try to sit up yet."

"Is it still snowing?"

"Flurries. The sun's out. Want to look?"

"I'll take your word for it."

Lucille was not a young woman. Her full-figured body spoke of a hard life, one in which she had raised a child by herself. Her face was like a crinkled apple. She had black currant eyes that had enough kindness in them not to yell at a little girl for feeling a man's mustache or for lugging a cat around.

Sarah Elizabeth carried Tom upside down like she carried her dollies. Tom allowed it as he allowed many indignities. If the cat had a mustache, Doc guessed that the child would have tweaked that, too.

Lucille kept her away from the boarders, some of whom didn't like children. Left to her own designs, the child played quietly in the corner by her mother's room. She tried hard to be as unobtrusive as possible.

All through the winter, Doc was confined to his bed. He could hear the lively chatter of the Silver Dollar Saloon across the street. He could feel the cool cards between his fingertips and the easy camaraderie of Wyatt or Luke Short. The room reminded him of everything that was lost to him. The floor creaked enough to remind him that it was not Lady Luck walking by.

On good days, Doc huddled by the gray stove and watched the activity going on around him. On bad days, he was confined to his bed while Lucille brought him hot soup and coffee laced with laudanum. Not knowing what they were supposed to do, the boardinghouse guests genially came forward to welcome him.

After the illness, he wrote Mattie once more. He hadn't written her for eight months. He was at a loss to explain to her what had happened and terribly ashamed as if he'd let her down.

My Dearest John,

If only I had been there for you, you wouldn't have lacked for care. As you have written to me about the changes in your life, I must write you about the changes in mine. Mother was so insistent that I get married that I could not cope any longer. But perhaps I was fooling myself as you have often thought that you were fooling yourself. I have my dearest, dearest, and most loving John, taken holy orders from the Sisters of Charity. Please do not be angry at my choice. I am not strong like you. I don't want anyone but you and nothing has changed because I will and shall always love you as the first, best, and only one for me. There are those who are so bereft of hope and life that I believe that I might be able to do some good. We shall correspond as before. Nothing will change that. I shall keep you in my heart as before. I shall always remain yours.

Your Loving Mattie

The contents of the letter hit Doc so hard that he cried by the metal colored stove, the letter still clutched in his hand. It was all the tears that he'd kept inside for Mattie and for all that could have been and wasn't. She, who was so wonderful with children and who loved to teach, should have had children of her own and a husband. He heard her words so clearly. "I don't want anyone but you . . . you are the first, best, and only."

He lost track of how long he sat there, but suddenly there was a feathery body nestling in his lap. Opening his eyes, he found himself looking at Sarah Elizabeth. Her eyes were so soft and brown, his heart felt as if it might explode.

"I'm sorry you're so sad. Do you want me to get my kitty? He always feels so soft and purry when I'm sad?"

Before Doc could say anything, Sarah jumped off his lap and ran out of the room. When she returned, she was carrying her cat.

"Here's my kitty. He really likes to be petted. I call him Tom."

"I had a tomcat once." Doc's hand caressed the soft, heavy cat's body.

He grew stronger in the warmer weather. The consumptive cough started once more, but it wasn't the ragged croup that tore his insides to shreds. The odd jobs that he was able to perform, such as providing spelling and math lessons for Sarah and taking care of the books, helped repay Mannie Hyman for his kindness.

Sarah had a quick mind and an odd knack of giggling at inopportune times. Lucille was glad of the diversions for her daughter, and of the companionship, since Sarah had so few playmates.

"The one thing I won't do is allow you to put a bonnet on my head like you do the cat's."

Sarah giggled.

The spring of 1884 came with a rush of melted snow. Miners took to their picks and shovels, and the trains rolled once more.

In the meantime, Lucille had developed a real feeling for Doc, as he had for her. The two uncomfortably stumbled over each other without knowing what to say. He saw her every day as he saw Sarah. While it was a pleasant and unexpected feeling, it was not welcomed. Doc said a few words under his breath, and Lucille echoed the sentiment. She knew that Doc was going to leave, if not today, then tomorrow, while she remained in Leadville with her child.

When Doc was well enough, he began to deal faro for Mannie Hyman. On the days that he couldn't, he tended the bar. The best thing about both occupations was the stories, which made the liquor taste all the better. Either way, it felt good to be employed once more, although the physical toll on his body was a tremendous one.

Doc's hair was almost completely silver now, the only touch of gold remaining in his mustache. There were other signs of aging. His once keen eyesight now had a decided dullness, and his gait, once lithe, had lost its finesse. But the old fire began to burn with the coming summer and his mind was as sharp as it ever had been. Tyler was once more on the streets and, though Johnny might chide him unmercifully, the warning in Doc's eye was plain.

As the snow melted and ran down into the valleys, the trains got rolling. Doc's stay in Leadville had been longer than he had bargained for. Now that he was on the road to wellness, the events of the past months were catching up to him. There remained a sore spot in his heart that Mattie had joined the convent.

Then there was Tyler, who had almost succeeded in making Leadville Doc's last stop. It hadn't been enough to be fired or the appalling lack of food and warmth, but to be spat upon in front of everyone in the saloon was the worst insult of all. In the West of his day, a professional gambler was respected. Doc's humiliation coursed so fiercely that it seemed hotter still than the disease that was consuming him.

Billy Allen was a bartender at the Monarch Saloon where Doc had dealt faro. He had been a friendly sort and had lent Doc five dollars. Doc, eking out a bare subsistence, had not been able to get the five dollars together to return to him. Under pressure from Tyler, Allen decided to call in the note. He gave Doc a deadline by which time he wanted his money: August 18, four days after Doc's thirty-third birthday. Doc knew that he would not have the money. Too often these people had goaded him when he was down. But he was not so far down that he couldn't get mad, which he did. As Allen went from street to street flapping about the news, Mannie and Doc decided on their course of action.

In Hyman's Saloon, there was a glass-enclosed cigar case filled with various pipes and smokes. The till, often as not, was not far from that. Doc could stand behind the case and keep an eye on the money. He supposed that he could have borrowed the money from Hyman, because Mannie offered more than once.

"Thanks, but no thanks. I take the money from you to give to him and then I owe you. It never stops. I owe you enough as it is. He's not going to make me run, Mannie. I faced Ike Clanton and the McLaurys in Tombstone, and there isn't half the shit going on here as there was in Arizona. If Allen comes through the room at me, I'll know how to handle myself."

"Look," Mannie said. "Why don't we have someone oversee what will happen? Like a neutral observer? There's this reporter who wants to write about it. Let him be the one to see the event through objective eyes. We can make sure Allen doesn't bring a gun."

"Good idea. How about a fair reporter like Cowen? I know that he'll see what's going on and stay neutral."

"Let's ask him," Mannie said.

Doc stopped for a moment. Mannie had sounded so much like Wyatt in those three words, especially the "let's." This reminded him that if he didn't write Wyatt quite soon, Wyatt would storm Leadville. Actually, Wyatt had not left the state of Colorado, and Doc had noticed an interesting trend. Wyatt stayed away because he knew Doc didn't want to see him while he was dying. Wyatt never told him how far away he was or made any promise to keep a certain distance. The more violently ill Doc became, the closer Wyatt's camps seemed to take him to Doc's proximity. It was an interesting but true observation borne out from postmarks on the letters Doc received. While Doc was in Leadville, Wyatt clung to Denver only a three or four days ride on the rails from Leadville. With Doc so desperately ill in the winter of the previous year, the letter had been postmarked from Aspen, very close to Leadville. Now that Doc was more or less recovered, Wyatt's addresses, while further away, were within shouting distance. He didn't want Wyatt to see him now. Better to remember his old friend from the Dodge City and Tombstone days than this gray ghost of his former self.

Being a keen observer, E.D. Cowen was not intimidated by Billy Allen. With his reporter's expertise, Cowen uncovered the fact that Allen was a close pal of Johnny Tyler. As the whole town waited for the final showdown, Doc's anger swelled to a righteous fury. How dare this man make his life a mockery for five dollars?

334 ♥ The Last Gamble of Doc Holliday

He had given his word that he would return the money and Dr. J.H. Holliday's word was worth its weight in gold.

The day dawned, and the town rose with the expectations that this was to be a day of a killing. Many of the locals were uneasy as they knew Doc and liked him. But Billy Allen had shouted his tale to the rafters throughout Leadville, and everyone wanted to know the outcome.

Billy swaggered like Ike Clanton.

Hyman loaned Doc a Colt firearm, Doc's gun of choice. The gun was kept under the cigar case next to Doc's hand to use against Billy Allen if he stormed through the door, as everyone knew he would. There was a large crowd of Tyler's supporters eager to see John Holliday gunned down. Doc, seething as the morning wore on, stood behind the cigar case, his blue eyes firmly pinned to the front door.

Using his reporter's knack for detail, Cowen described what Doc was wearing. "Ladies and gentlemen, he cut quite a figure in his gray suit with his silver hair and strong hands. And his eyes look like burning blue coals. In spite of his most dire of circumstances, the man remains a gentleman among men. He has in his very straight frame a resolute dignity that neither time nor disease can conquer."

When Billy blustered through the door, Doc was ready for him. Doc's first shot lodged in the doorframe. It was not a miss; Doc wanted to scare Allen. But Billy didn't know that. What he did know was that Doc actually shot at him. Doc's second shot got Billy in his gun arm. Billy dropped his weapon in terror. Any fun that he might have had at Doc's expense was lodged in the doorframe with the first bullet. On the third shot, Doc was restrained by Cowen.

Billy screamed like a scalded cat. "He done shot me. He done shot me."

Doc looked at Mannie, who was relieved that the gunplay was over. "What did he think? That this was some kind of joke? I gave my word. I didn't want to kill the bugger."

Before Allen left, Doc said in his best arsenic and honey Southern drawl, "Know this, I haven't taken this matter lightly. You'll see me again." Allen bolted down the street.

By the end of the day, Doc was arrested and escorted to jail.

"You know, suh, that there are those who want to see me die."

"Yeah, I know, Doc. That reporter Cowen's already told me what happened, including all those threats against your life. I think that Allen and his cronies are going to have to distance themselves from this. They're none too clean."

Doc had many friends in Leadville. They had come to care about this wry stranger with the soft accent and modest manners. They demonstrated their affection by pooling the $8,000 necessary for his bail. This represented a large sum of money to folks who didn't have much, but Doc was one of their own.

Lucille was justly proud to have Doc again under her care. She had come to love him, and she realized his love for her. When she heard his footsteps on the stairs, she rushed forward and flung her arms around him. It was the first time she had offered to do so. Doc stood for a long time in her embrace, his anger draining away in her arms.

"It's not over, is it?"

"No. Sometimes it's never over," he whispered back. For a moment, he laid his head and his cares on her shoulder before straightening.

"You could have left your head there."

Doc raised her face. "I might never have raised it again. I might have just left it there."

"Would that have been so bad, John?"

"It would be unfair to you. Unfair to Sarah."

"Sshh."

He couldn't stop her from kissing him. He guessed he could have flung her away if he'd been a man of intemperate behavior or a saint. He was neither, and he hadn't received a kiss in a long time that had not been bestowed for money or pleasure. Hers was an embrace of passion and comfort. It raised the dreams once more of him practicing dentistry, of a home for Lucille and her not having to remain a housekeeper to people who ate her food and took her strength while she cooked and cleaned for them. It meant a garden for Sarah to play in with a tabby cat at her heels.

Surfacing from the kiss, he stepped back. "It's a nice dream. But it won't work."

"Sshh."

"No, Lucy, I am dying. I can't saddle you with me. I watched my mother die of it. I can't have you nurse me. I can't die and have your face as the last thing I see when I fade away."

"Why?"

"Well, hell, Lucy, I don't know." When he looked down, she was chuckling in a very feminine way. "You weren't supposed to respond that way."

"You're used to pushing too many women around."

"Excuse me?"

"It's okay. You make me dream, too. Do you suppose we could kiss again?"

A smile broke free across his mouth. "We shouldn't."

Lucy's smile was bigger. "Maybe that's why we should."

It was so tempting to stay in Leadville. He liked it. The people were accepting. He wasn't the black sheep of a fine, old Southern family anymore. He was himself and that was okay. But Lucy deserved so much better than cooking and cleaning. Would he come to hate her because she was healthy and he was not? Would he become one more mouth for her to cook and clean for and one more drain on her energy when she needed someone to feed energy back to her? He couldn't do it to Mattie.

He couldn't do it to Lucille. The kissing made it worse. Once done, the embrace wanted doing all over again. He'd be a damned fool and liar if he said he wanted it to stop.

In a short span of time, Doc was a celebrity once more and able to run a faro bank or be a dealer if he preferred. The Monarch Saloon wanted him back. He was good for business. Men slapped him on the back. Women kissed him. Doc, however, was not one to be gulled by pretty words or embraces that meant nothing. When the hullabaloo died away, life would return to normal.

There were diversions, however. This time it was the completion of a rail section of the Denver, South Park, and Pacific Railroad to Breckenridge on September 1884. To celebrate the auspicious occasion before the winter snows, there was an event planned to outdo all others. On October 26, 1884, passengers would board the trains in Leadville and travel to Breckenridge, where they would be met with food and drink aplenty as well as entertainment.

Lucille heard about the picnic from the other boarders, but she didn't say anything to Doc about it. It all sounded so grand, but it was meant for the richer folk and not her.

"I want you to come with me to Breckenridge's gala."

"What?" Lucille asked, almost dropping her pan of onions on Doc's head.

"I said," he told her smiling, "I want you to come with me to Breckenridge."

"But what about Sarah?"

"That's all been taken care of."

"I don't have a nice dress or anything."

"It's all been taken care of."

And it had all been taken care of. One of the women Doc knew lent Lucille a pink lace dress with matching gloves. There were also pink shoes with buckles and a hat with pink velvet bows guaranteed to turn the head of any man in town.

Overwhelmed, she stammered, "You're the best time I've ever had."

The excursion started early, but Lucille hardly minded. For the first time in her life, she was treated like a queen. The vista offered snow-swept peaks, tumbling waters, and dark trees. No one noticed the gathering clouds. Lucille comfortably held Doc's hand in hers, listened to the stories told gently for the ears of the ladies present, and sampled all the food that tasted delicious because she didn't have to cook it. It was a wonderful day even if it had to be abbreviated by the advent of inclement weather.

By November, snow was falling. Doc's teeth told him about it early, as they started chattering and didn't stop. He was testy in cold weather, he told Lucille. She reminded him that she'd already spent one winter with him.

"That didn't count, darlin'. I was mostly comatose."

His room, cozy in the summer months, was frigid in the winter. The rag rugs afforded no warmth, and the western window radiated the cold. Chilled to the bone, Doc huddled like a half-frozen animal. He cursed the cold, the consumption, Leadville in general, and his own stupidity for staying. At sunrise, the curses and imprecations would fall away, and Lucille would greet him. Life was hard but bearable. And the next day, the process would repeat. Sometimes his strength would not allow him to get up at all. Trapped, he would snarl in his frozen lair that served as a room. Lucille longed to have him in her bed where at least he could take ease and be warm, but she dared not risk his pride. In loving him, it was hard to see him so cold and wounded. It was harder to watch him fight the monster that was devouring him from within.

He suffered in his room. Bleary-eyed, he would stagger to the stove and stand close, holding his hands to the warmth as his teeth chattered. On the worst of nights, one in which he did not come out for two days, the cold became arctic. One morning, after drinking more than he liked and having taken laudanum as well, he rocked back and forth by the stove, praying to die.

Lucille came out of the room she shared with Sarah, grasped his shriveled body, and yanked him towards the open door. Doc balked. "Just a damn minute now."

"I'm not watching you freeze to death. My room is warmer than your room. I don't care what you say, you're in no condition to stop me." She yanked him forward again.

Doc grumbled and coughed all the way to bed until he began to warm. With his head on her breast, his arm grew increasingly heavy as it lay draped over her. Around him, the room was warm like a thick blanket.

"Oh God," he whispered.

He slept so hard the next morning that Lucille was able to detach herself and slide out of bed without waking him. Breakfast had to be made. Somehow leaving Doc and Sarah alone didn't seem like the wrong thing either. Sarah didn't stay down for long in the mornings and liked buzzing about the table with her mother. Doc wandered out around noon. He looked more refreshed than he had in days and in a much better mood.

"We shouldn't make this a habit, Lucy. In the end, it will be too hard and painful. I can't trap you into the kind of life I have. We've been over this so many times."

"The bottom line is that you won't let yourself go."

"Dear Lucille, if I let myself go, ruin will come upon us all."

"Will you remember that there is a warm place for you when the weather is so very chill?" she asked in so gentle a way that it twisted his heart.

"I will."

As the winter wore on, the frenzy over Billy Allen's shooting started anew. This time it was the same problem with a different face. Constable Kelly still nursed a grudge. Unable to wait for another continuance, though cautioned strongly to do so, Kelly was infuriated by the judge's decision. Constable Kelly was part of the Billy Allen problem. He was self-righteous about the five dollars and felt that Doc deserved much more than a slap on the hand; in other words—a showdown.

"He walks the street. He walks the damn street."

"What are you going to do? Shoot him in cold blood? Then you get locked up."

"As a matter of fact, yes. That's exactly it."

"Keep talking about it and I'll run you in right now."

So malicious was Kelly's intent that word finally reached Doc's ears by way of the sheriff's office. Kelly's superior—in this case, the judge—tried to rein Constable Kelly in to no avail. Kelly was reprimanded again and again, but it made little difference.

Hyman said, "Doc, I can put the closed sign out."

"Mannie, if not Kelly, it'll be someone else."

Constable Kelly made good his threat with an intensity that Billy Allen had lacked. Doc read the tells from the beginning. Kelly was a man with a mission.

Doc met him, stepping out from behind the cigar stand. In a clear voice, he asked, "Suh, I hear that you have come to do me bodily harm. Are you heeled?"

Kelly went for his gun and Doc shot him. Surprised by the stain of red over his chest and the sudden weakness in his legs, Kelly dropped like a stone. He succumbed the next day. Doc's arrest for the shooting was deemed self-defense, and the matter never came to trial. In the shooting of Billy Allen, Doc was told that he would have to stand trial on March 28, 1885.

The night before Doc's trial, he told Lucille, "I don't know what's going to happen or how the chips will fall."

The trial lasted two days. On March 30, 1885, the judge acquitted Doc of the crime of shooting Billy Allen.

"You have until evening to get your affairs in order. The damnable thing is that I don't hold you responsible for what goes on in this town. There is a wrongful element that lives in this city and has never seen fit to leave. This element preys on the good, decent folk of this city," the judge told him. "Basically, if the truth be told, you shouldn't have to leave here at all. If you stay you'll be gunned down. You don't carry a gun on your person anymore."

Lucille wanted to leave with Doc. She said none of this, but it showed in her eyes.

She watched him take the diamond cravat pin off of his tie. "I want you to have this. It's something for you and Sarah."

"Oh Doc, I can't take your jewelry. I can't."

"I want to make sure you're okay. It's not right you working here year after year."

"You're sweet, but I can't. It's my pride I guess, so I just won't. But you can write me. Please? And when you come back, I'll be waiting."

"No. Someone else already did that for me. You take this."

"No. I know what I want."

R. Smith, a druggist when Doc had been in need and a friend when he wasn't, mixed bottles of laudanum for him to take on his journey.

"It's gonna be dull without you here. I'll miss talking to you about medical discoveries, science, and cures. Kept me on my mettle. I mixed up your brew triple strength."

"I don't know when I'll be back, but I have an account to square with Billy Allen and he knows it."

"Wish you could stay."

"Me, too."

Doc tried not to look at the disappearing platform that evening, but he faltered and turned. Lucille was standing on the platform. She didn't wave or make a big scene, but she was there.

The first place Doc visited after his arrival in Denver was the Metropolitan Hotel. Travel of any kind was becoming difficult. It wouldn't be long, a year from now or sooner, when travel would no longer be possible. One thing he did concede to was a visit from Wyatt. In spite of Wyatt's disguise as Tom McKey, Doc recognized his old friend.

At least Doc was still able to hold his own in a poker game. He'd been on the circuit for so many years that he had an intuitive knack for the right scores at the right time. And he was so well known that he was readily accepted. It was more than a sense about cards. With his blue eyes flicking a go-for-the-throat glance at each of the players, Doc forced the rest at the table to play up to par. In Denver, he got a chance to play for some real money. He was able to send money to Mannie and Lucille.

Doc never told Mattie about Lucille. In his heart-of-hearts, Doc felt that Mattie would understand, but he was confused enough about his feelings for Lucille to know that he would not be able to explain them to Mattie. Wyatt understood how that could be. Wyatt's hair was just barely turning gray, but outdoor living had put a burnish to his skin giving him the kind of lived-in look that Virgil had. For a brief moment, Morgan stared back at Doc through Wyatt's eyes and smiled. Wyatt was thoroughly shocked by Doc's appearance, although he had tried to prepare himself. Doc's bone crunching handshake remained steady, but there was a hollow look in his blue eyes.

Wyatt remembered what his mother had said, "Folks are like candles. There are those that burn low, steady-like, and they go on for years. Some have just a flicker of a flame that never gets started and dies out. Others have a flame so very bright that the wick is consumed in a flash." Doc was like that last candle.

Wyatt could see that Doc was taking laudanum now, and there was nothing he could do to make the situation any better.

"So, how are the folks?"

"Well, Virgil is talkin' about becoming a sheriff again. If he hasn't already."

"One arm? Damn, and he called me a bit o' the devil. And Lou?"

"Lou's doin' okay. I don't know that she's ever gonna get over Morg. I guess none of us will. Sometimes I think it's harder on women, Doc."

"I'll drink to that."

"Leadville, how was it?"

An enigmatic smile floated across Doc's mouth. "Parts, Wyatt, were just fine. You through with Gunnison?"

"I don't think I'm ever gonna settle. I know that the West is drying up, and I don't know what to do about it. Seems I've spent my whole life roaming and now I can't stop."

"Don't I know that? Funny you should say that about the West. But, you're right. Rail service connects almost all of the towns. The ones that don't, they're workin' like crazy to get there.

Ft. Griffin is gone, like it never existed. Dodge is all dried up. The silver in Tombstone's going that way, too."

"Denver is holding it's own though."

Doc's eyes twinkled a bit. "Yeah, it certainly is. I got enough to get my jewelry outta soak. Are you gamblin'?"

"Hell, I'm driftin'."

"To driftin'," Doc raised his glass to Wyatt's coffee cup.

"Seems that I needed to check in," Wyatt shrugged.

"With me?"

"Yeah."

"You worried about embarrassing me?"

"Nope."

Doc threw back his head and laughed. "That's a fact. What's old Bat up to?"

"Bat's got woman trouble."

"Damn."

Wyatt nodded. "Yep. Seems he's got some filly with a lariat all ready for him."

"Well, damn. What about you and Josie?"

"Um, I don't know."

"Say," a demonic smile started at Doc's mouth and traveled all the way to his ears, "I understand you were real close to Leadville that winter of 1884. Right over the hill so to speak."

"Really? I was driftin' around. Railroad job. Takes me all over."

"Uh huh."

"You're full of shit, Holliday. D'you know that?"

They parted after dinner and a round of poker. Doc shook his hand and said, "It's not done, Wyatt." Wyatt breathed easier for a moment.

The cough was getting around the laudanum now and he had to take more just to sleep. There was a surfeit of health spas that touted miraculous cures. Doc knew that he wouldn't be one of the cures. He was fading as fast as the West. It was eerie to see civilization gobbling up the vast expanse of prairie. The developers and the railroads came. The black sod was turned over and another chunk of sweet prairie grass was sundered. However impervious the purple granite mountains looked, Doc knew that it was only be a matter of time before dynamite gouged ugly furrows into the slopes. He knew he didn't want to see it.

"Discovery is always good, Doc."

"I believe it is."

"How's Denver?"

"Tight."

"Denver's always tight. It's got pretensions now, but that's mostly for show. Bunch o' hypocrites."

Going back to Leadsville one last time wasn't pretentious. It was easy to watch the blue sky crawl by at a snail's pace rather like Georgia's waters that bubbled true and deep. Doc made a point to see Lucille, to save the best for the last and it was the hardest. She would hug him, give him the special kiss reserved only for him and look at him anxiously, because she could see his body winding down. Fixing him food was her way of saying that she loved him. She knew that sometime before the nightfall, he would slip away. He couldn't bear to spend the night.

Some of the toughs that had hung around Leadville were still there, but they kept out of sight. Doc kept track of Wyatt knowing that Wyatt shadowed him never more than two or three days by horse or rail at the most. Doc always knew where to reach him. Wyatt always knew how to get in touch. It was a game they played.

These days, the gambling circuit was the only way to make decent money. Unfortunately, Doc couldn't stay in any one place for too long a time, as the local law enforcement officials would arrest him for loitering, or worse, running confidence games. Jackpots had to be made on the quiet. With the myriad of rail lines, the *Travelers' Official Railway Guide* had become an important part of his profession whether he made a small fortune in Aspen, lost it in Silverton, or won it back in Pueblo.

The newspapers made it difficult for Doc to come into town unannounced. Reporters dogged his footsteps. No matter how circumspect he was, there was always a sheriff or deputy on the platform to greet him with handcuffs. He found it interesting to be arrested for loitering when he'd just stepped off a train. The charges were flimsy, but none of them could be proven. By early 1887, Doc was living in Pueblo once more. Denver had become too mean to go back.

There were no earth shattering portents in January of 1887 that made it different than any other year. Doc wintered fairly well in Pueblo, but left town before spring. That April, he noticed a spot on his chest. It was quite sore and eventually erupted, followed by other sores of the same type. Doc wasn't alarmed at first, but then he got queasy.

His mother, before her death, had experienced those same outbreaks. Doc remembered boiling leaves for poultices. Telling himself that it was nothing, he stopped by Leadville. Although the silver was dried up, he wanted to see old friends. If his worst fears were true, he'd have scant time before the world found out. Leadville would protect him in a way that Denver wouldn't.

Stripped down, Doc could see how wrecked his body was.

Doc waited for the pronouncement. He knew what it was going to be. The older man paused, removed his stethoscope, and put his hand on Doc's shoulder. "You might try Glenwood Springs. But I don't know if it will help."

"I'm a sportin' man. I'll take the gamble."

Meticulously, Doc made preparations for his journey. He went to his good friend, Smith, who always mixed him the magic elixir free of charge.

"No payment."

"I can afford—"

"No."

There were people that Doc wanted to see one last time. There were some accounts to be squared with several people, but Doc couldn't square with Lucille. It was better that she remember him as the silver-haired gentleman that she had cared for. Mannie Hyman met Doc at the corner of Harrison, not in sight of his saloon where Lucille might see him.

Doc looked at him very steadily and reached into his pocket. There was a roll of bills. "I want you to make sure that Lucy gets this."

Diffidently, he shook hands with Mannie, tipped the brim of his hat, and hailed a horse-drawn taxi to take him to Leadville's stage line. The rails hadn't been laid all the way to Glenwood Springs, so it was necessary to take a stage to Buena Vista that would carry him over Cottonwood Pass. His valise had shrunk to a meager twenty inches long, one-foot wide, and about a foot deep. Doc figured he wouldn't need much in Glenwood Springs. He had a curious lack of physical sensation on the stage journey. The bumping and jouncing had always left him bruised in the past, but now his shriveled flesh felt nothing.

It was May in Glenwood Canyon. In his opinion, this was the best part of the Rockies. Here dynamite and hacksaw hadn't destroyed the slopes with their foaming water or the bright pinks, purples, and yellows of the wildflowers. Doc took his last look around and checked in at the Hotel Glenwood. He was met courteously and was taken to the back part of the hotel that housed the other tuberculosis patients.

It was a fine hotel, having been built in 1886. The appointments were lavish, from the hot and cold running water in the bathrooms to the exquisite cuisine of pheasant under glass, smoked oysters, and rich chocolate desserts in the dining room.

Glenwood Springs was a mountain valley town, squeezed in amongst the craggy Rockies. The jagged cliffs protruded upward, while the waters of the Colorado and the Roaring Fork joined together into whitewater foam. The sky was breathtakingly blue as only Colorado could boast.

People were obsessed with health, and there were a variety of places to choose from. The Hotel Colorado boasted mineral water baths. With the steaming water rising around him, Doc tried to imagine health and the healing of his lungs. There were also the Vapor Caves where miracles were said to happen. Doc was given a linen sack to make his body sweat, because the air had to draw out the poisonous chemicals from his body. But the caves made his lungs feel like they were on fire.

If he wasn't taking the mineral bath cures, he was in his room at the Glenwood, enjoying the luxury of a hot bath any time he chose. A special treat was a hot bath with a bottle of whiskey in a fine glass. Remembering those cold Leadville winters made him draw the bath water much hotter than normal.

By the end of June, he knew he was cashing in. Lady Luck had departed. Doc wrote letters as cheerfully as before, and he figured those family and friends like Wyatt would know. Wyatt, it seemed, had developed a fondness for Aspen again, but would not come unless invited by Doc, who had no intention of letting Wyatt see him.

His hair, once thick silver, was thinning. Soaking wet, he weighed one hundred pounds. He couldn't deny that his chest was caved in.

"There's just no more lung tissue, son. I'm sorry."

He began to spend days in his room. The staff was kind and provided a hotel delivery boy to bring him whiskey and cheer. Mattie sent him a Bible. Of the rest of his possessions, Doc wrote Ham Bell, still in Dodge. Doc had met Ham in Old Granada. Ham Bell became sheriff in Dodge, and Doc felt a kinship to him. All of the West was rolling away like chaff on the prairie.

Many of the Westerners were faced with the same problem. The U.S. had become civilized, and their way of life was over.

Dear Ham,

You keep this for me. I'm not dead, but I know what's going to happen. The carcass isn't cold, but the vultures are circling. You keep the gun; maybe it'll bring you fame and fortune. Maybe somebody else will want it if you don't. I took Mike Gordon in Las Vegas with this gun.

Ham replied:

Dear Doc,

I'll cherish the gun. Seems we have to stick together, us "old-timers." Can you imagine that? I'm not fifty and I'm an old-timer. These punks don't know what roughin' it was like. Dodge City and Ft. Griffin separated the men from the boys.

Before he knew it, he was writing Mattie that he was taking instruction from the Holy Church in Rome. Father Feeney was an Irishman who made regular rounds to all in need.

Dear Mattie,

It doesn't matter if one isn't Catholic or even agnostic. Father Feeney ministers to all. I've seen him go into the bedrooms of the sickest patients and offer them solace.

He studied Christianity for his mother's sake. As always there were scoffers.

Before Doc's pen dropped forever, he wrote Mattie one last time.

My Dearest Mattie,

I think it is quite ironic now that I am dying, finally it seems, from the bullet that has been killing me from within since 1872.

Mary will be fifteen this year. I was fifteen when my mother died. She will be fifteen after I die. Pray for us both.

Mattie, now Sister Melanie, did.

By July, Doc began to have trouble staying awake, his eyelids becoming more and more heavy. As his sight shut down, other senses picked up the slack. Doc had a strong sense that Wyatt was now in Glenwood Springs. Wyatt would be dressed appropriately in his Tom McKey undercover garb, which he seemed to favor. Sure enough, one afternoon when Doc opened his eyes, he saw old Tom McKey sitting by his bed. Tom smiled.

At ten o'clock in the morning on the eighth day of November in 1887, Doc's eyes snapped open. There was a group of people around his bedside, Tom McKey being one of them. He had always introduced himself as Tom McKey, so no one would know that he was really Wyatt Earp. It was nobody's business.

There were so many images behind his eyelids that it was hard to make out one from the other. There was Tombstone. There was Georgia. There was his mother. There was Tom.

In due course, Sister Melanie of the Sisters of Mercy received notification of her first cousin's death. In a place within her heart she remained Mattie to him. In that silent place, because Doc's words and laughter were stilled, he was husband, though no formal ceremony had ever joined them. She sent notices to Henry, but she could not, no matter how hard she tried, offer much solace to the man who had driven his son away. Henry, on being told of John's death, never shed a tear.

She received Doc's letters telling of his instruction from the Church of Rome and of his Christian faith, having been baptized before his soul departed. Mattie read the words written in the silence of her room at night. Nearby, the Virgin Mary's eyes were awake and made no accusations against her for that reading or the prayers that were spoken in a hush afterwards. Her dearest John would remain her dearest John. He had had to live hard upon the earth.

She wrote to Wyatt and said simply to him: "It's not how you go through life that matters. It's whom you travel with. John taught me that."

When he answered her letter he wrote, "I went the last mile with him. If ever you need me, let me know. I think he'd want to be buried in Georgia."

She had agreed, "Dear Wyatt, I think so, too. Can you arrange for this?"

Wyatt did.

Mattie tried to save all that she could of their correspondence, but other members of the Holliday family burned whatever they found. They were against John Holliday as they ever had been, even in death. Mattie mourned long and hard. She could not even travel to his graveside to put down flowers.

Wyatt replied, "When I get him to Georgia, there will be enough flowers for everyone to place."

Mattie, now alone, bore the memory and grief of her only child, John's only child. She treasured the mental picture that John had painted for her and the wonderful letter that had been sent detailing the hour spent with Mary. John had had such a wonderful gift with words and language. Mattie had reveled in how the little girl had adored the horse ride. John had given his beloved crucifix so that their daughter might have some inkling of the people who had loved her so dearly and not been allowed by circumstance to keep her.

Mattie held a silent celebration for her daughter until her own death on April 19, 1939.

♣ ♥ ♠ ♦

Mary Kelly flourished. She had no memory of the stranger who had placed her on the back of his horse so many years before. Her mother told the story so many times that Mary came to believe that it was real.

"What did he look like?"

Mrs. Kelly's words failed her. She cleared her throat. "Oh, honey, it wasn't real. Just make-believe."

But Mary had doubts. When she got older, she realized that something was being withheld. As Mrs. Kelly lay dying, shortly after Mary's eighteenth birthday, she tried once more to speak of it, but death robbed her of the words.

Mary remained alone on the farm. Well meaning relatives told her to not sell it, but her wanderlust after her mother's death grew stronger every day. When the first grief had passed, she thought about becoming a teacher, but it didn't seem like the right fit. There were still veterans of the Civil War and their families and it was to these people that she felt an unmeasured kinship. She thought about becoming a nurse.

"Why would you want to leave this area and nurse a bunch of stiff-necked strangers?"

"They're not strangers. Mayhap, he was my—" and she stopped unable to put words to a mental image that exploded so brightly through her mind, and now was the wind whispering about a fallen leaf. "Life is kinda funny."

Mary Kelly had seen the survivors of war, poverty, reconstruction, and hunger. Some settled in and around Kansas City to farm. Mary saw many with tuberculosis and decided that she could help. Not that she could make a cure, but a difference was what she was looking to make whether it was a kind word or a pat on the hand. These things could not be found in books or newspapers and could not be found in the halls of learning. It was incredible that academia had no idea how to stop the scourge, though many had been struggling to do so.

Mary loved learning and science, often toiling at books while her classmates played. Sometimes she put up with their teasing, other times she suddenly erupted in anger. Her eyes were corn-flower-blue in warmth and hot, jagged lightning-blue when she was aroused. With all that blonde hair, she was pretty as a picture and prickly as a thorn, the boys thought. For them, there was never any warning when the change might take place. Mary could fight with the best of them and ride a horse with the best of them. She could easily cry over a pricked finger, but never a black eye.

She was not tall, but she was very straight in her frame so that it seemed she towered above her male counterparts. She stood at five feet, seven inches in her bare feet, and she had quick, nervous hands that could scrub a floor or pound out an awkward melody on a piano. She loved music, but she was tone deaf.

Mary's chin was finely boned, as were her cheeks, her fore-head coming to a slight widow's peak. Her lips were full. With her light coloring and high spirit, she thought of herself as hav-ing sprung from Irish or Scotch ancestors, not knowing if that was true. She loved life and wanted to live a long time. If only life would leave her alone, she thought, then laughed at her own pomposity. By the age of ten, she knew the names of diseases and how they killed people.

"This learning can come to no good," her father said. "It's unnatural for a girl-child to know and want to know."

Mary's mother disagreed. "Let the child be. I think she'll make a fine scientist or scholar, but she will never have the wherewithal to just stay put. Never."

And Mary Kelly's mother stared to that far off place of six years previous. She never told her husband about the stranger with the hair and eyes the same color as Mary's, who had put the child on the back of his horse. How the same stranger had led the horse around in a circle. How the child had laughed and snatched at the horse's hair. How the stranger had gently lifted the child down to the safety of her mother and said that he was never coming back.

After her mother's death, Mary found a box of clippings in the cellar. Yellowed and brittle from moisture, she unfolded them carefully. The clippings were about a gambler by the name of John Holliday. She had no idea what possessed her mother to keep this treasure trove that had been taken from the newspapers of the day. The clippings had been placed in order according to date, with the final clipping detailing the death of J.H. Holliday three years earlier. Mary fingered the crucifix that had been given to her by her dying mother and puzzled over the mystery that was attached to it. She had kept it because it was a part of her mother's past. Or maybe it was a part of her past. There was an answer out there. She would find it.

References

Angelo, F. Michael. 1999. Independence Seaport Museum Archives. "Maritime Register lists of Wyoming and Charles W. Lord from 1870-1872." Also, "Abbreviations of specifications for ships of the time and types of sailing vessels, etc."

Athearn, Robert. 1962. *Denver and Rio Grande Western Railroad*. Yale University. First Bison Printing.

Ball, Kimberly. Reference Archivist, Georgia Historical Society. 1999. *Central of Georgia Railway and Connecting Lines.* Includes directory of city of Savannah, 1870, various hotel advertisements, excerpt from *Savannah Morning News Index, "1872."*

Brown Robert L. 1978. *Saloons of the West.* Sundance Publications Ltd.

Burns, Walter. 1929. *Tombstone.* Grossett and Dunlap.

Callon, Milton. 1962. "Las Vegas, New Mexico: The Town That Wouldn't Gamble." *Las Vegas Daily Optic.* Las Vegas Publishing Co.

Cash, W. J. 1941. *The Mind of the South.* Alfred Knopf (Vantage Books. Div. of Random House).

Cavanaugh, Barbara. 1998. School of Dental Medicine, including copy of *Fourth International Dental Congress Volume III, 1904,* edited by Kirk, Edward C., Litch, Wilbur F., Endelman, Julio. Press of the "Dental Cosmos" The S.S. White Dental Mfg. Co.

Cincinnati Daily Commercial. February 24. in toto. 1862.

Cincinnati Daily Commercial. August 5. in toto. 1863.

Dammon, Dr. Gordon. 1983. *Pictorial Encyclopedia of Civil War Medical Instruments Vol I.* Pictorial Histories Publishing Co.

Dammon, Dr. Gordon. 1988. *Pictorial Encyclopedia of Civil War Medical Instruments Vol II.* Pictorial Histories Publishing Co.

Dammon, Dr. Gordon. 1997. *Pictorial Encyclopedia of Civil War Medical Instruments Vol III.* Pictorial Histories Publishing Co.

Davis, Maj. George B. (U.S. Army), Perry, Leslie Jr. (Civilian Expert), Kirkley, Joseph W. (Civilian Expert). 1983. *Official Military Atlas of the Civil War.* Arno Press and Crown Publishers.

DeArment, Robert K. 1979. *Bat Masterson.* University of Oklahoma Press.

DeArment, Robert K. 1982. *Knights of the Green Cloth.* University of Oklahoma Press.

Dodge, Fred. 1969. *Undercover for Wells Fargo.* Houghton Mifflin.

Drago, Harry Sinclair. 1965. *Great American Cattle Trails.* Cornwall Press, Inc.

Dykstra, Robert R. 1968. *The Cattle Towns.* Athenum.

Eberhart, Perry. 1969. *Guide to Colorado Ghost Towns and Mining Camps.* Swallow Press/Ohio University Press.

Faust, Drew Gilpin. 1996. *The Mothers of Invention.* University of North Carolina Press.

Fishberg M.D, Maurice. 1922. *Pulmonary Tuberculosis.* Maurice Fishberg, M.D. Philadelphia.

Foster-Harris. 1955. *The Look of the West.* Viking Press.

Frazier, Robert W. 1972. *Forts of the West.* University of Oklahoma Press.

Gard, Wayne. 1960. *Great Buffalo Hunt.* Alfred Knopf.

Gard, Wayne. 1976. *The Chisholm Trail.* University of Oklahoma Press.

Glennar D.D.S., Richard, Davis Ph.D., Audrey, Burns M.D., Stanley B. 1994. *American Dentist.* Pictorial Histories Publishing Co.

Heitman, Francis B. 1986. *Historical Register and Dictionary of the U.S. Army, Vol I.* Reprinted Olde Soldiers Books, Inc.

Heitman, Francis B. 1988. *Historical Register and Dictionary of the U.S. Army, Vol II.*

Historic Griffin. 1958. "History of Newspapers." Flint River Regional Library.

Jackson, General James. Chapter D.A.R. 1995. *History of Lowndes Co. Georgia (1825–1941).* Valdosta, Georgia.

Lake, Stuart. 1956. *Life and Times of Wyatt Earp.* John McCormack. Riverside Press.

Larsh, Ed B. and Nichols, Robert. 1993. *Leadville, USA.* Johnson Publishing Co.

Livingston, Evelyn L. 1984. *The Tabor Opera House.* National Writers' Press.

Masterson, V. V. 1978. *The KATY Railroad and The Great Frontier.* University of Missouri Press.

McCuteson, Marc. 1993. *The Writer's Guide to Everyday Life in the 1800s.* Writers' Digest Books.

The Medical Record: A Weekly Journal of Medicine and Surgery. New York. August 28. in toto. 1886.

Mott, Frank Luther. 1860–1872. Excerpt from "Journalism in War and Reconstruction." *American Journalism History: 1690–1960.* MacMillan.

O'Neal, Bill. 1979. *Encyclopedia of Western Gunfighters.* University of Oklahoma Press.

Osterwald, Doris B. 1991. *Highline to Leadville.* Western Guideways Limited.

Pendleton, Albert S., Jr., Thomas, Susan McKey. 1973. *In Search of the Hollidays.* Little River Press.

Rister, Carl Coke. 1956. *Fort Griffin on the Texas Frontier.* University of Oklahoma Press.

Robertson, William H. P. 1964. *History of Thoroughbred Racing in America.* William Robertson Publishing.

Sandoz, Mari. 1955. *Buffalo Hunters.* Hastings House.

Scarne, John. 1949. *Scarne on Cards.* Revised 1965 by Signet.

Settle, R. W. 1939. *Western Scrapbook, Vol V.* "Lamar Daily Sparks," pp. 27–28. William Jewell College.

Sprague, Marshall. 1987. *Life and Good Times of Colorado Springs Newport in the Rockies.* Swallow Press/Ohio University Press.

Stanley, F. 1961. *Dave Rudabaugh: Border Ruffian.* World Press, Inc.

Stanwood, Christopher, 1998. College of Physicians of Philadelphia "Information on the Sixteenth Annual Session of the Pennsylvania College of Dental Surgery, 1871-1872, plus matriculants and graduates of the same session."

Thacker, Emily. 1995. *Home Remedies from the Old South.* Tresco Publishers.

Thomas, Susan McKey. 1994. Picture postcard of Holliday residence in Griffin.

Thomas, Susan McKey. 1994. Personal letter from Susie.

Travelers' Official Railway Guide of the United States and Canada. June 1868. National Railway Publication Co.

Travelers' Official Railway Guide of the United States and Canada. October 1871. National Railway Publication Co.

Travelers' Official Railway Guide of the United States and Canada. June 1874. National Railway Publication Co.

Travelers' Official Railway Guide of the United States and Canada. November 1875. National Railway Publication Co.

Travelers' Official Railway Guide of the United States and Canada. December 1876. National Railway Publication Co.

Travelers' Official Railway Guide of the United States and Canada. November 1878. National Railway Publication Co.

Travelers' Official Railway Guide of the United States and Canada. November 1879. National Railway Publication Co.

Travelers' Official Railway Guide of the United States and Canada. November 1881. National Railway Publication Co.

Travelers' Official Railway Guide of the United States and Canada. February 1883. National Railway Publication Co.

Travelers' Official Railway Guide of the United States and Canada. March 1886. National Railway Publication Co.

Urquhart, Lena M. 1970. *Glenwood Springs: Spa in the Mountains.* Frontier Historical Society.

Vestal, Stanley (Campbell, Walter Stanley). 1952. *Queen of Cowtowns: Dodge City.* Harper and Brothers.

Volck, Dr. Thomas D.D.S. 1999. Lengthy interview on chemicals used in dentistry.

Wellikoff, Alan. 1996. *Civil War Supply Catalogue.* Crown Publishers.

Wooster, Robert. 1987. *Soldiers, Sutlers, and Settlers.* Texas A&M University Press.

Wright, Robert M. 1913. *Dodge City: The Cowboy Capital of the Great Southwest.* Ayer Company Publishers.